FIC
Sidebotto
Warrior of art 1,
Fire in the st
c2008.
D0978756

Warrior of Rome: I

Fire in the East

Warrior of Rome

PART I

Fire in the East

DR HARRY SIDEBOTTOM

MICHAEL JOSEPH
an imprint of
PENGUIN BOOKS

MICHAEL JOSEPH

Published by the Penguin Group
Penguin Books Ltd, 80 Strand, London WC2R 0RL, England
Penguin Group (USA) Inc., 375 Hudson Street, New York, New York 10014, USA
Penguin Group (Canada), 90 Eglinton Avenue East, Suite 700, Toronto, Ontario, Canada M4P 2Y3
(a division of Pearson Penguin Canada Inc.)
Penguin Ireland, 25 St Stephen's Green, Dublin 2, Ireland
(a division of Penguin Books Ltd)
Penguin Group (Australia), 250 Camberwell Road, Camberwell, Victoria 3124, Australia
(a division of Pearson Australia Group Pty Ltd)
Penguin Books India Pvt Ltd, 11 Community Centre, Panchsheel Park, New Delhi – 110 017, India
Penguin Group (NZ), 67 Apollo Drive, Rosedale, North Shore 0632, New Zealand
(a division of Pearson New Zealand Ltd)
Penguin Books (South Africa) (Pty) Ltd, 24 Sturdee Avenue, Rosebank, Johannesburg 2196, South Africa

Penguin Books Ltd, Registered Offices: 80 Strand, London WC2R 0RL, England

www.penguin.com

First published in 2008
1

Copyright © Dr Harry Sidebottom, 2008

The moral right of the author has been asserted

All rights reserved
Without limiting the rights under copyright
reserved above, no part of this publication may be
reproduced, stored in or introduced into a retrieval system,
or transmitted, in any form or by any means (electronic, mechanical,
photocopying, recording or otherwise), without the prior
written permission of both the copyright owner and
the above publisher of this book

Set in 12/14.75 pt Monotype Dante
Typeset by Rowland Phototypesetting Ltd, Bury St Edmunds, Suffolk
Printed in Great Britain by Clays Ltd, St Ives plc

A CIP catalogue record for this book is available from the British Library

HARDBACK ISBN: 978–0–718–15329–8
OM PAPERBACK ISBN: 978–0–718–15428–8

www.greenpenguin.co.uk

Penguin Books is committed to a sustainable future for our business, our readers and our planet. The book in your hands is made from paper certified by the Forest Stewardship Council.

To Frances, Lisa, Tom and Jack Sidebottom

Contents

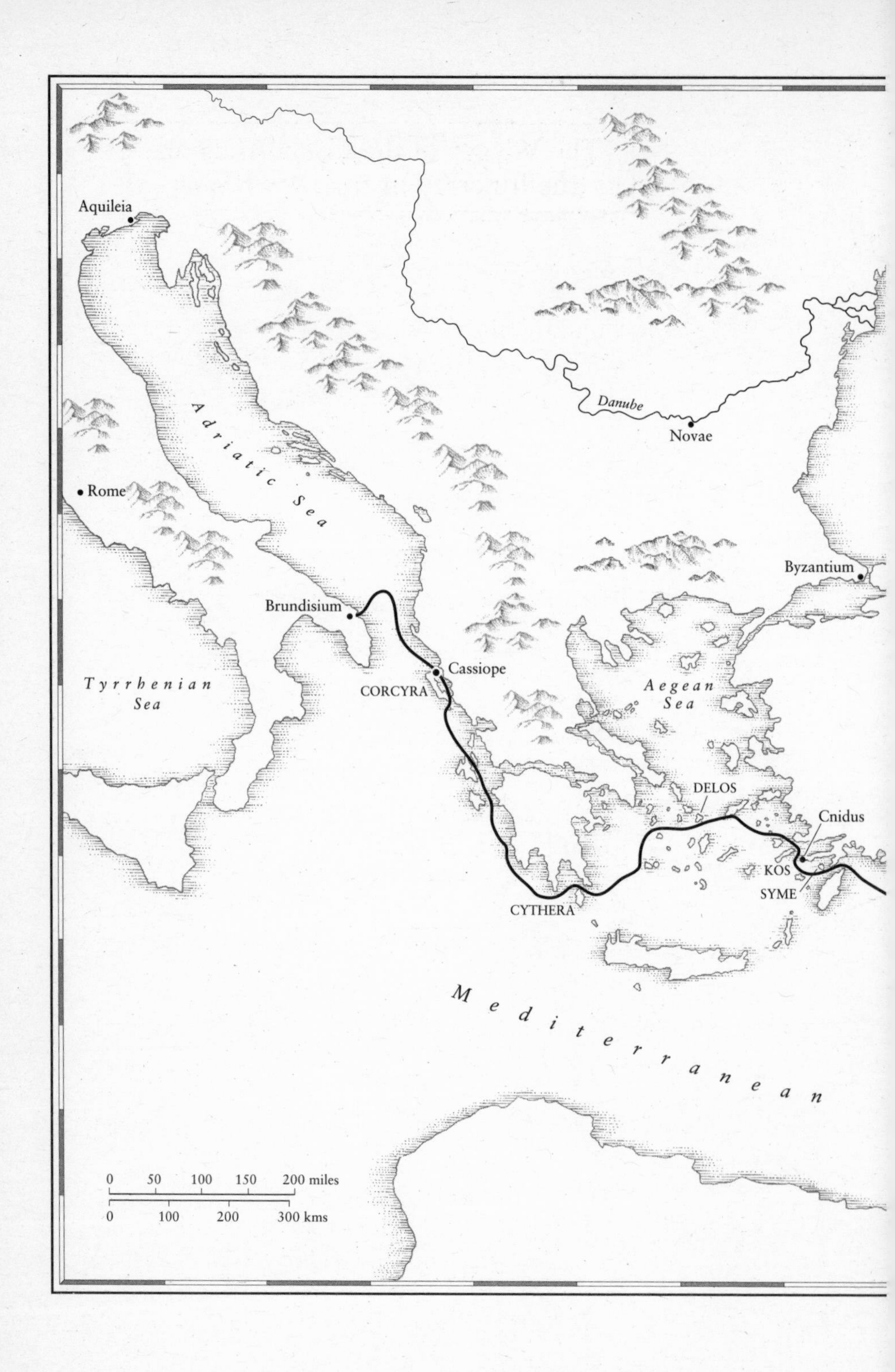
Aquileia
Adriatic Sea
Rome
Tyrrhenian Sea
Brundisium
Cassiope
CORCYRA
Danube
Novae
Byzantium
Aegean Sea
DELOS
Cnidus
KOS
SYME
CYTHERA
Mediterranean
0 50 100 150 200 miles
0 100 200 300 kms

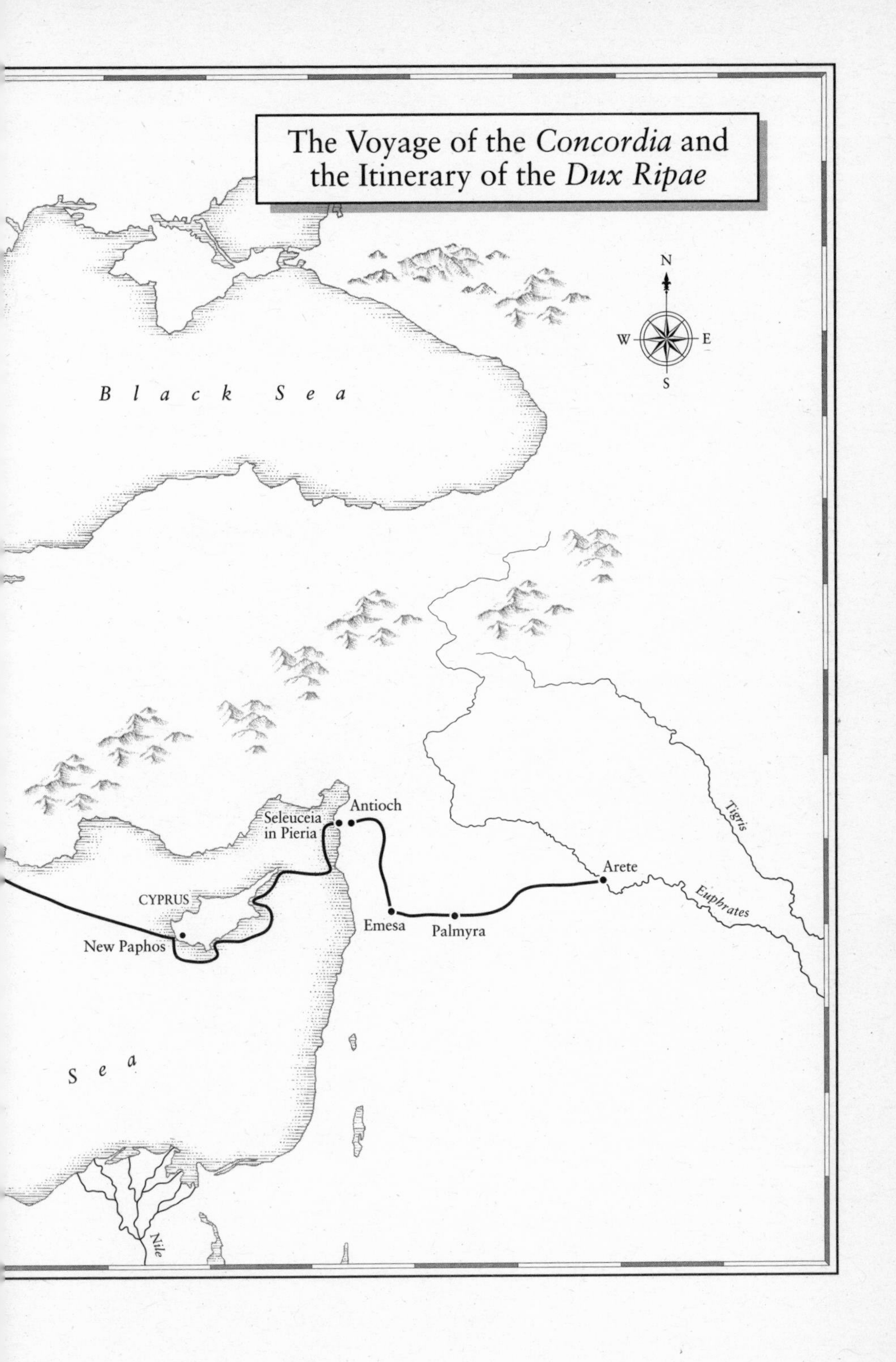
The Voyage of the *Concordia* and the Itinerary of the *Dux Ripae*
N
W
E
S
B l a c k S e a
Antioch
Seleuceia in Pieria
Tigris
Arete
CYPRUS
Euphrates
Emesa
Palmyra
New Paphos
S e a
Nile

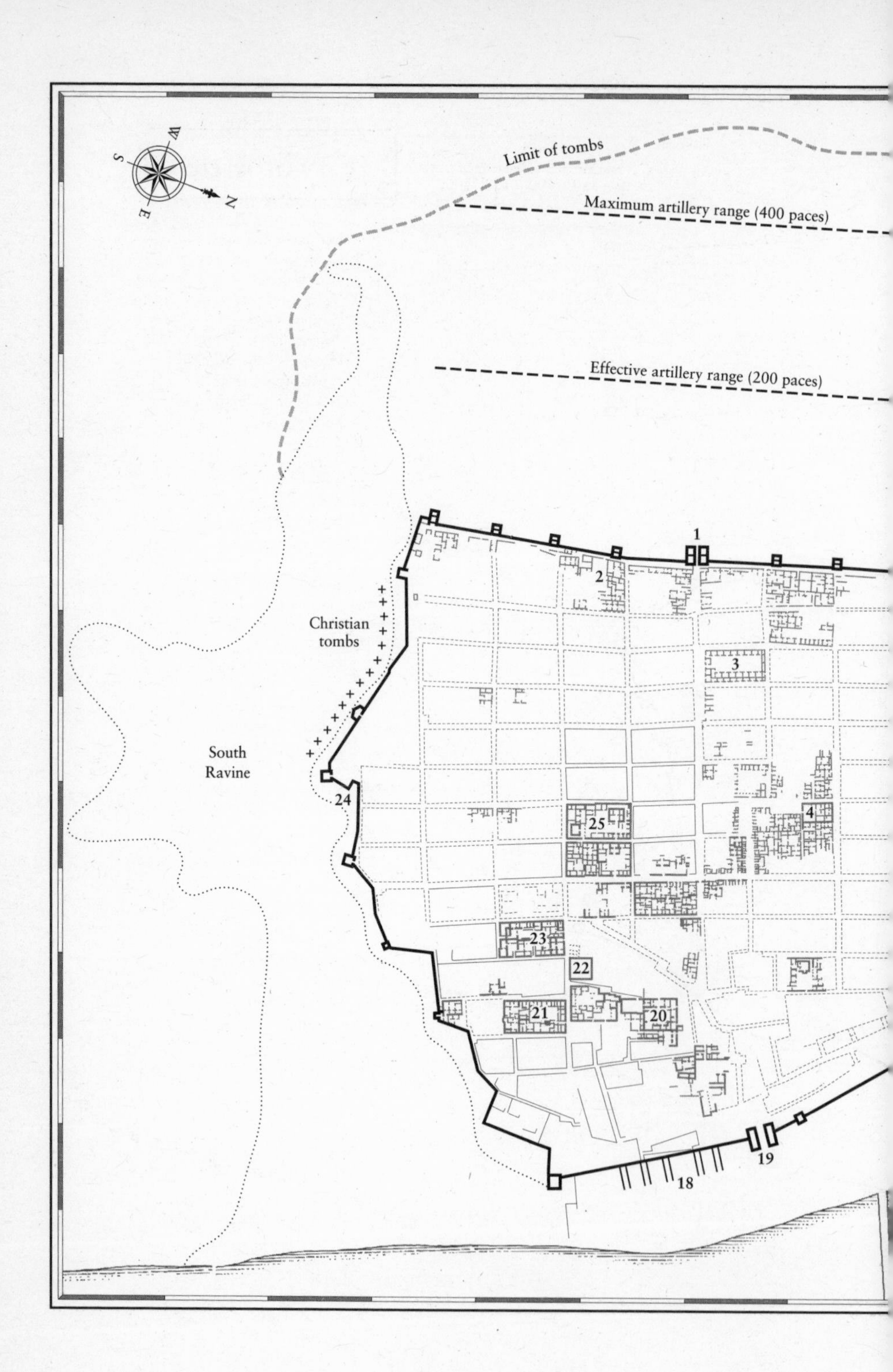
W
S
E
N
Limit of tombs
Maximum artillery range (400 paces)
Effective artillery range (200 paces)
Christian tombs
South Ravine
1
2
3
4
18
19
20
21
22
23
24
25

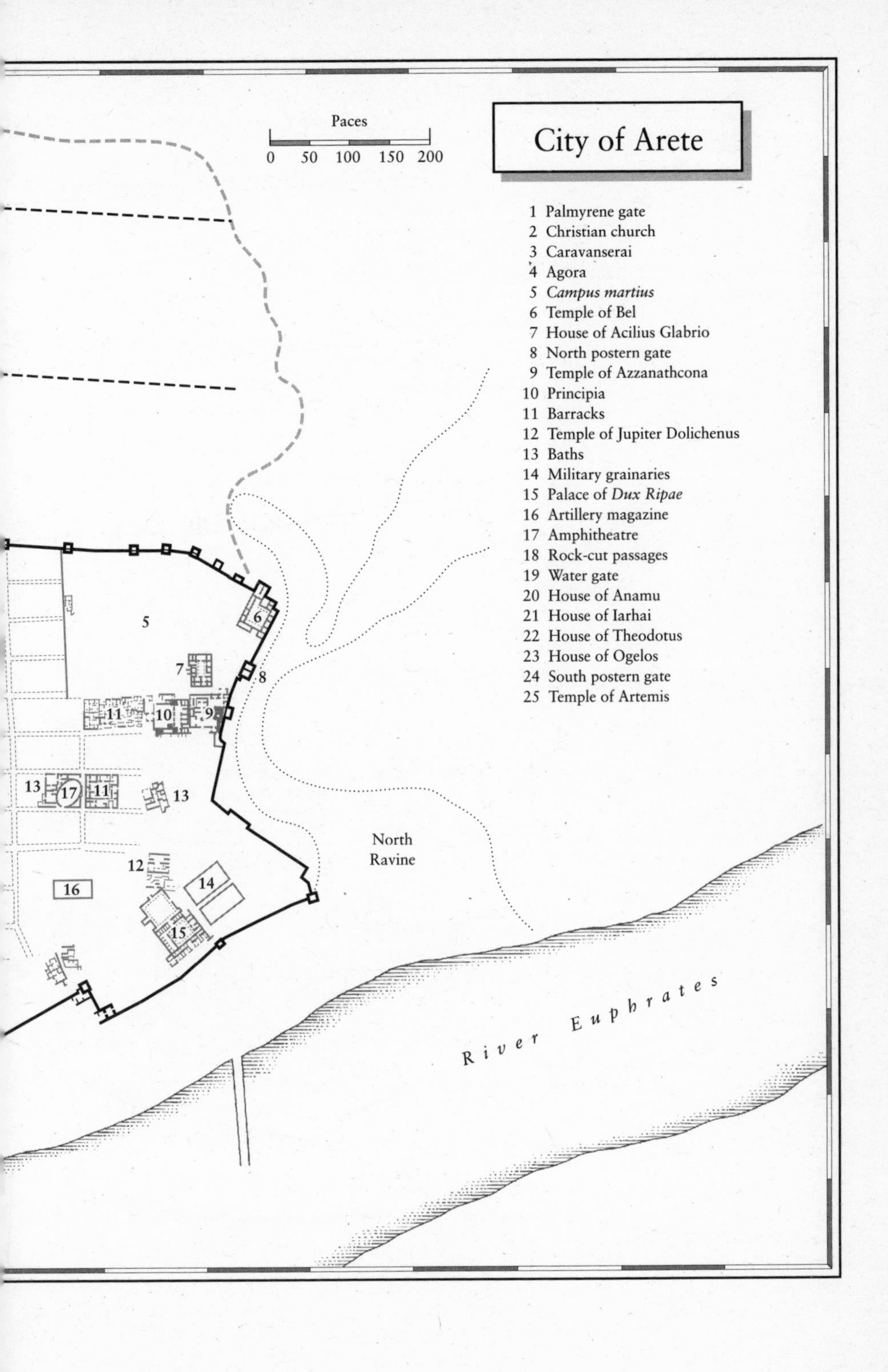
Paces
0 50 100 150 200
City of Arete
1 Palmyrene gate
2 Christian church
3 Caravanserai
4 Agora
5 Campus martius
6 Temple of Bel
7 House of Acilius Glabrio
8 North postern gate
9 Temple of Azzanathcona
10 Principia
11 Barracks
12 Temple of Jupiter Dolichenus
13 Baths
14 Military grainaries
15 Palace of Dux Ripae
16 Artillery magazine
17 Amphitheatre
18 Rock-cut passages
19 Water gate
20 House of Anamu
21 House of Iarhai
22 House of Theodotus
23 House of Ogelos
24 South postern gate
25 Temple of Artemis
North Ravine
River Euphrates

'And let them, when besieging a fortress, strive to win over whomsoever possible of those inside the fortress and the city, in order to attain through them two things: one – the drawing out of their secrets, and the other – intimidating and frightening them through themselves. And [let] a man be sent by underhand means who should unsettle their minds, and deprive them of any hope for succour, and who should tell them, that their sly secret is unravelled, and that tales are told about their fortress, and that fingers are pointed at their fortified and weak places and at the places against which battering-rams will be directed, and at the places where mines will be conducted, and at the places where ladders will be placed, and at the places where the walls will be ascended, and at the places where fire will be set – in order that all these should fill them with terror . . .'

– Fragment from the Sassanid *Book of Ayin*;
translation James [2004], 31

Prologue (Summer AD238)

War is hell. Civil war is worse. This civil war was not going well. Nothing was going to plan. The invasion of Italy had ground to a halt.

The troops had suffered crossing the Alps before the spring sunshine had melted the snows in the passes. They had expected to be welcomed as liberators. They had been told that they only need set foot in Italy for everyone to come running, holding out olive branches, pushing forward their children, begging for mercy, falling at their feet.

It had not happened as they had hoped. They had come down from the mountains into an empty landscape. The inhabitants had fled, taking with them everything that they could move. Even the doors of their houses and temples were gone. The normally bustling plains were deserted. As the soldiers passed through the city of Emona the only living thing they found was a pack of wolves.

Now the army had been camped for over a month outside the walls of the north Italian city of Aquileia. The legions and auxiliaries were hungry, thirsty and tired. The hastily improvised supply chain had broken down. There was nothing to be had locally. What the citizens had not gathered within the walls, the soldiers themselves had wasted when they first arrived. There was no shelter. All the buildings in the suburbs had been torn down to provide materials for siege works. The river was polluted with the corpses of both sides.

The siege was making no progress. The walls could not be breached; there were not enough siege engines, the defenders were too effective. Each attempt to storm the walls with siege ladders and mobile towers ended in bloody failure.

Yet you could not fault the big man's courage. Every day the Emperor Maximinus Thrax would ride around the town, well within bowshot range of the enemy, calling out encouragement to his men in the siege lines. As he passed through the ranks he promised them the town and everyone in it to do with as they pleased. While his courage had never been in doubt, his judgement had always been suspect. Now with every new reverse he became more savage. Like a wounded animal or, as many said, like the half-barbarian peasant he would always remain, he struck out at those around him. The officers who led the doomed attempts to scale the wall were executed in ever more inventive ways. Especial ingenuity was reserved for those from the nobility.

Ballista was even more hungry, thirsty and dirty than most. He was a tall youth, only sixteen winters and over six foot, and still growing. No one felt the lack of food more keenly than he did. His long blond hair hung lank down his back. A residual squeamishness held him back from washing on the riverbank. Since yesterday, a smell of burning, a reek of charred flesh, had joined the other odours which hung about him.

Despite both his youth and his status as a diplomatic hostage for his tribe, it had been considered by everyone the right thing that one of his birth, one of the Woden-born, should lead one of the units of German irregulars. The Romans had calculated the height of the wall, they had issued ladders of the correct length and, with Ballista at the front, the five hundred or so expendable barbarians had been sent off. The men had advanced at a jog, bent forward into the storm of missiles. The large bodies of the Germans and their lack of armour had made them good targets. Again and again there was a sickening sound as a missile struck home. They had fallen in droves. The survivors had pushed on in brave style. Soon the smooth walls had towered above them. More had fallen as they put aside their shields to raise the ladders.

Ballista had been one of the first to mount. He had started to climb one-handed, his shield held above him, his sword still in its scabbard. A falling stone had hit the shield, almost knocking him off the ladder. The noise was indescribable. He saw a long pole appear over the wall and push out over the next ladder along. At the end of the pole was a large amphora. Slowly the pole was turned, the amphora tipped, and a flaming mixture of pitch and oil, sulphur and bitumen poured like rain on to the men on the ladder. Men screamed, their clothes burning and shrinking, clinging to them, their flesh roasting. One after another they fell from the ladder. The incendiary liquid splashed out over those at its foot. They beat at the flames with their hands, rolled themselves on the ground. There was no way to put out the flames.

When Ballista looked up there was another amphora above his head, its pole beginning to turn. With no hesitation Ballista threw himself from the ladder. He landed hard. For a moment he thought that his ankle was broken or turned and that he would be burnt alive. But self-preservation had overcome the pain and, yelling for his men to follow him, he ran away.

Ballista had been thinking for some time that a conspiracy was inevitable. Impressed as he was by Roman discipline, no body of fighting men would put up with this siege for long. And after the disaster that day, he had not been surprised when he was approached.

Now, as he waited to play his part, he realized the depth of his fear. He had no wish to play the hero. Yet he had no real choice. If he did nothing, either Maximinus Thrax would execute him or the conspirators murder him.

The conspirators had been right. There were very few guards around the imperial tent. Many of those present were asleep. It was the drowsy time just after midday. The time when the siege paused. The time when the emperor and his son rested.

A nod from one of the conspirators, and Ballista set off towards the huge purple tent with the standards outside. Suddenly he was very aware of what a beautiful day it was; a perfect Italian early June day, hot with a light breeze. A honey bee buzzed across his path. Swallows were wheeling high above.

A praetorian guardsman blocked Ballista's way with his spear. 'Where do you think you are going, barbarian?'

'I need to talk to the emperor.' Ballista spoke reasonable if heavily accented Latin.

'Who does not?' The praetorian was uninterested. 'Now fuck off, boy.'

'I have information of a conspiracy against him.' Ballista dropped his voice. 'Some of the officers, the nobles, are plotting to kill him.' He watched the guardsman's evident indecision. The potential danger of not passing on to a suspicious and vengeful emperor news of a possible conspiracy eventually overcame the natural fear of waking an increasingly short-tempered and violent man for whom things were not going well.

'Wait here.' The praetorian summoned a fellow soldier to watch the barbarian and disappeared into the tent.

He reappeared in short order and told the other praetorian to disarm and search the barbarian youth. Having given up his sword and dagger, Ballista was ushered into the tent; first into an antechamber, then into the inner sanctum.

At first, Ballista could see little. The purple gloom in the depths of the tent was profound after the bright sunlight outside. As his eyes adjusted he made out the sacred fire that is always carried before the reigning emperor burning low on its portable altar. Then he could see a large campbed. From it rose the huge pale face of the Emperor Caius Julius Verus Maximinus, commonly known as Maximinus Thrax, Maximinus the Thracian. Around his neck glittered the famous golden torque which he had won for his valour as a private soldier from the Emperor Septimius Severus.

From the far corner of the tent a voice snapped, 'Perform adoration, *proskynesis*.' As Ballista was pushed forward on to his knees by the praetorian, he saw Maximinus Thrax's handsome son walk out of the darkness. Ballista reluctantly prostrated himself on the ground, then, as Maximinus Thrax held out his hand, kissed a heavy gold ring set with a gemstone cut with an image of an eagle.

Maximinus Thrax sat on the edge of the campbed. He was wearing just a simple white tunic. His son stood by his side, wearing his customary, elaborately ornamented, breastplate and ornamental silver sword, its handle in the shape of the head of an eagle. Ballista remained on his knees.

'Gods, he stinks,' said the son, putting a perfumed cloth to his nose. His father waved a hand to silence him.

'You know of a plot on my life.' Maximinus Thrax's great grey eyes looked into Ballista's face. 'Who are the traitors?'

'The officers, most of the tribunes and a few of the centurions, of Legio II Parthica, *Dominus*.'

'Name them.'

Ballista looked reluctant.

'Do not keep my father waiting. Name them,' said the son.

'They are powerful men. They have many friends, much influence. If they hear that I have denounced them, they will do me harm.'

The big man laughed, a horrible grating sound. 'If what you say is true, they will be in no position to harm you or anyone else. If what you say is not true, what they might want to do to you will be the least of your concerns.'

Ballista slowly named a string of names. 'Flavius Vopiscus, Julius Capitolinus, Aelius Lampridius.' There were twelve names in all. That they were the real names of the men in the conspiracy hardly mattered at this stage.

'How do you know these men want to kill me? What proof do you have?'

'They asked me to join them.' Ballista spoke loudly, hoping to distract attention from the growing noise outside. 'I asked them for written instructions. I have them here.'

'What is that row?' Maximinus Thrax bellowed, his face twitching with habitual irritation. 'Praetorian, tell them to be quiet.' He held out a huge hand for the documents that Ballista proffered.

'As you can see –' Ballista continued.

'Silence,' ordered the emperor.

Rather than abating, the noise outside the tent grew. Maximinus Thrax, his face now contorted with rage, turned to his son. 'Get out there and tell them to shut the fuck up.'

Maximinus Thrax read on. Then a surge of noise made him lift his pale face. On it Ballista read the first glimmer of suspicion.

Ballista leapt to his feet. He grabbed the portable altar bearing the sacred fire and swung it at the emperor's head. Maximinus Thrax caught Ballista's wrist with an unbelievably strong grip. With his free hand he punched him in the face. The youth's head snapped back. The big man hit him in the stomach. Ballista collapsed in a heap. With one hand the emperor pulled Ballista back to his feet. He brought his face, a face like a rock, close to Ballista's. His breath stank of garlic.

'You will die slowly, you little fucker.'

Maximinus Thrax threw Ballista away almost casually. The youth crashed through some chairs and overturned a camp table.

As the emperor picked up his sword and headed towards the door, Ballista desperately tried to get some breath in his lungs and struggle to his feet. He looked around for a weapon. Seeing none, he picked up a stylus from a writing desk and stumbled after the emperor.

From the antechamber, the whole scene outside was framed and brightly lit as if it were a painting in a temple or portico. In the distance, most of the praetorians were running. But some had joined the legionaries of Legio II and were pulling the imperial portraits down from the standards. Nearer, there was a thrashing tumult of bodies. Just beyond the threshold was the mighty back of Maximinus Thrax. Sword in hand, his huge head turned this way and that.

The tumult stopped, and above the crowd rose the severed head of Maximinus Thrax's son, stuck on a spear. Even smeared by dirt and blood it was still beautiful.

The noise the emperor made was not human. Before the big man could move, Ballista launched himself unsteadily at his back. Like a beast hunter in the arena trying to despatch a bull, Ballista stabbed the stylus down into Maximinus Thrax's neck. With one mighty sweep of his arm, the big man smashed Ballista back across the antechamber. The emperor turned, pulled out the stylus and hurled it, bloodied, at Ballista. His sword raised, he advanced.

The youth scrabbled to his feet, grabbed a chair, held it in front of him as a makeshift shield and backed away.

'You treacherous little fucker, you gave me your oath – you took the military oath, the *sacramentum*.' Blood was flowing freely down the emperor's neck, but it did not seem to be slowing him down. With two strokes of the sword he smashed the chair to pieces.

Ballista twisted to avoid the blow but felt searing agony as the sword thrust scraped down his ribs. On the floor now, holding his arms to the wound, Ballista tried to shuffle backwards. Maximinus Thrax stood over him, readying himself to deliver the killing blow.

The thrown spear punched into the emperor's unprotected back. He staggered an involuntary step forward. Another spear slammed into his back. He took another step, then tipped over, landing on Ballista. His enormous weight was crushing the youth. His breath, hot and rank, was on Ballista's cheek. His fingers came up to gouge the boy's eyes.

Somehow, the stylus was back in Ballista's right hand. With a strength born of desperation the youth drove it into the emperor's throat. Blood sprayed out. The emperor's fingers jerked back. Blood stung Ballista's eyes.

'I will see you again.' The big man uttered his final threat with a hideous grin, blood gurgling and foaming from his twisted mouth.

Ballista watched as they pulled the body outside. There they fell on it like a pack of hounds breaking up its quarry. His head was hacked off and, like that of his son, hoisted on a spear. The huge body was left for anyone to trample on and desecrate, for the birds and dogs to tear to pieces.

Much later, the heads of Maximinus Thrax and his son were sent to Rome to be publicly exhibited. What was left of their bodies was thrown in the river to deny them burial, to deny rest to their spirits.

Navigatio

(Autumn AD 255)

I

By the time the warship had cleared the harbour breakwater of Brundisium, the spies had found each other. They sat on the deck, inconspicuous among the men of the *Dux Ripae*. From their position near the prow they looked back down the narrow hull of the galley to where, over one hundred feet away, stood the object of their professional attention.

'Sodding barbarian. All three of us just to watch one sodding barbarian. Ridiculous.' The *frumentarius* spoke quietly, lips barely moving.

The speaker's accent pointed to the slums of the Subura in the teeming valley between two of the seven hills of eternal Rome. His origins may have been low but, as a *frumentarius*, he and his two colleagues were among the most feared men in the Roman Empire, the *imperium*. As *frumentarii* their title should have implied that they had something to do with grain distribution or army rations. No one fell for that. It was like calling the wild Black Sea 'the hospitable sea', or the daemons of retribution 'the kindly ones'. From the most patrician consular in Rome to the lowliest slave in a far-flung province like one of the Britannias, the *frumentarii* were known and hated for what they really were – the emperor's secret police: his spies, his assassins, his knife men – at least, they were known collectively. They were a special army unit, its members transferred out of other units, its camp on the Caelian Hill. Individually, the *frumentarii* were seldom known at all. It was said that, if you recognized a *frumentarius*, it was because he wanted you to, and then it was too late.

'I don't know,' said one of the others. 'It might be a good idea. Barbarians are naturally untrustworthy, and often as cunning as you can imagine.' His voice summoned up the sun-drenched mountains and plains of the far west; the provinces of Further Spain or even Lusitania, where the Atlantic broke against the shore.

'Bollocks,' said the third. 'OK, they are all untrustworthy bashtards. They have been lying since they could crawl. But the northern ones, like this bashtard, are thick, slow as you like. Your northerners are big, ferocious and stupid, while your easteners are small, sly and shit shcared of anything.' The intermittent slurring showed that his first language was not Latin but Punic, from North Africa; the tongue spoken almost half a millennium ago by Hannibal, the great enemy of Rome.

All the men on deck and the crew below fell silent as Marcus Clodius Ballista, *Vir Egregius*, Knight of Rome, and *Dux Ripae*, Commander of the Riverbanks, raised his arms to the heavens to begin the usual ritual at the start of a voyage. The water was calm here at the threshold of the sea, where the sheltered waters of Brundisium harbour met the Adriatic. With its outstretched oars at rest, the galley lay like a huge insect on the surface of the waters. In good Latin, which nevertheless had a twang of the forests and marshes of the far north, Ballista began to intone the traditional words:

'Jupiter, king of the gods, hold your hands over this ship and all who sail in her. Neptune, god of the sea, hold your hands over this ship and all who sail in her. *Tyche*, spirit of the ship, hold your hands over us.' He took a large, finely worked golden bowl from an attendant and, slowly, with due ceremony, poured three libations of wine into the sea, emptying it.

Someone sneezed. Ballista held his outstretched pose. The sneeze had been unmistakable, undeniable. No one moved or spoke. Everyone knew that the worst omen for a sea journey, the clearest possible indication of the displeasure of the gods, was if someone sneezed during the rituals which marked the departure. Still Ballista held his pose. The ceremony should be over. An air of expectation and tension spread through the ship. Then, with a powerful flick of the wrist, Ballista sent the bowl flying through the air. There was a collective sigh as it splashed into the water. It glittered for a moment below the surface, and then was gone for ever.

'Typical fucking barbarian,' said the *frumentarius* from the Subura. 'Always the big, stupid gesture. It cannot take away the omen, nothing can.'

'That bowl would have bought a nice bit of land back home,' said the North African.

'He probably stole the thing in the first place,' replied the Spaniard, reverting to their previous topic. 'Sure, northern barbarians might be stupid, but treason comes as naturally to them as to any easterner.'

Treason was the reason the *frumentarii* existed. The old saying of the emperor Domitian, that no one believed a plot against the emperor was real until he was assassinated, most certainly did not apply to them. Their thoughts were suffused with treason, plot and counter-plot; their ruthless combination of secrecy, efficiency and obsession guaranteed that they were hated.

The captain of the warship, having asked Ballista's permission, called for silence prior to getting underway, and the three *frumentarii* were left to their own thoughts. They each had much to think about. Which one of them had been set the task of reporting on the others? Or was there a fourth *frumentarius* among the men of the *Dux Ripae*, so deep undercover they had not spotted him?

Demetrius sat at the feet of Ballista, whom in his native Greek he called *kyrios*, 'master'. Yet again he thanked his own daemon for guiding his recent path. It would be hard to imagine a better *kyrios*. 'A slave should not wait for his master's hand,' ran the old saying. Ballista had not raised his hand in the four years since the *kyrios's* wife had purchased Demetrius as his new secretary, one among many wedding presents. Demetrius's previous owners had had no such compunction about using their fists, or doing far worse.

The *kyrios* had looked magnificent just now as he made his vows and threw the heavy golden bowl into the sea. It had been a gesture worthy of the Greek boy's hero, Alexander the Great himself. It had been an impulsive gesture of generosity, piety and contempt for material wealth. He had given his own wealth to the gods for the good of them all, to avert the omen of the sneeze.

Demetrius considered that there was much of Alexander about Ballista: the cleanshaven face; the golden hair pulled back, standing up like a lion's mane and falling in curls on either side of the wide brow; the broad shoulders and straight, clean limbs. Of course Ballista was taller; Alexander had been famously short. And then there were the eyes. Alexander's had been disconcertingly of different colours; Ballista's were a deep, dark blue.

Demetrius balled his fist, thumb between index and forefinger, to avert the evil eye, as the thought struck him that Ballista must be about thirty-two, the age at which Alexander had died.

He watched uncomprehendingly as the ship got underway. Officers bellowed orders, a piper blew shrill notes, sailors pulled on mystifying patterns of ropes and from below came the grunts of the rowers, the splash of the oars and the sound of the hull gathering pace through the water. Nothing in the great historians of the immortal Greek past – Herodotus, Thucydides and Xenophon – had prepared the bookish young slave for the deafening noise of a galley.

Demetrius looked up at his *kyrios*. Ballista's hands were unmoving, seemingly clenched around the ends of the ivory arms of the folding *curule* chair, a Roman symbol of his high office. His face was still; he stared straight ahead, as if part of a painting. Demetrius half wondered if the *kyrios* was a bad sailor. Did he get seasick? Had he ever sailed further than the short crossing from the toe of Italy to Sicily? After a moment's reflection, Demetrius dismissed such ideas of human frailty from his mind. He knew what oppressed his *kyrios*. It was none other than Aphrodite, the goddess of love, and her mischievous son Eros: Ballista was missing his wife.

The marriage of Ballista and the *kyria*, Julia, had not started as a love match. It was an arrangement, like all of those of the elite. A family of senators at the top of the social pyramid yet short of money and influence gave their daughter to a rising military officer. Admittedly, he was of barbarian origins. But he was a Roman citizen, a member of the equestrian order, the rank just below the senators themselves. He had distinguished himself in campaigns on the Danube, among the islands in the distant Ocean and in North Africa, where he had won the Mural Crown for being the first man on to the walls of an enemy town. More importantly, he had been educated at the imperial court and was a favourite of the then emperor, Gallus. If he was a barbarian, at least he was the son of a king, who had come to Rome as a diplomatic hostage.

With the marriage, Julia's family gained present influence at court and, with luck, future wealth. Ballista gained respectability. From such a conventional opening, Demetrius had watched love grow. So deeply had the arrows of Eros struck the *kyrios* that he did not have sex with any of the maidservants, even when his wife was confined bearing their son; a thing often remarked in the servants' quarters, especially given his barbarian origins, with all they implied about lust and lack of self-control.

Demetrius would try and provide the companionship his *kyrios* so greatly needed, he would be at his side throughout the mission – a mission the very thought of which turned his stomach. How far would they have to travel towards the rising sun, across stormy seas and wild lands? And what horrors would await them at the edge of the known world? The young slave thanked his Greek god Zeus he was under the protection of a soldier of Rome like Ballista.

What a pantomime, thought Ballista. An absolute bloody pantomime. So someone had sneezed. It was hardly surprising that, among the three hundred men on the ship, one would have a cold. If the gods had wanted to send an omen, there had to be a clearer way.

Ballista very much doubted that those Greek philosophers he had heard about could be right that all the different gods known to all the different races of man were really all the same just with different names. Jupiter, the Roman king of the gods, seemed very different to Woden, the king of the gods of his childhood and youth among his own people, the Angles. Of course, there were similarities. They both liked dressing up in disguise. They both enjoyed screwing mortal girls. They were both nasty if you crossed them. But there were big differences. Jupiter liked screwing mortal boys, and that sort of thing did not go down at all well with Woden. Jupiter seemed rather less malevolent than Woden. The Romans believed that, if approached in the right way, with the right offerings, Jupiter might actually come and help you. It was highly unlikely that Woden would do the same. Even if you were one of his descendants – Woden-born, as Ballista himself was – probably the best you could hope from the Allfather was that he would leave you alone until your final battle. Then, if you fought like a hero, he might send forth his shield maidens to carry you to Valhallah. All of which left Ballista wondering why he had dedicated that golden bowl. With a heavy sigh, he decided to think about something else. Theology was not for him.

He turned his thoughts to his mission. It was reasonably straightforward. By the standards of the Roman imperial bureaucracy, it was *very* straightforward. He had been appointed the new *Dux Ripae*, commander of all the Roman forces on the banks of the rivers Euphrates and Tigris and all the land in between. The title was rather grander on paper than in reality. Three years ago, the Sassanid Persians, the new and aggressive empire to the east, had attacked Rome's eastern territories. Burning with religious fervour, hordes of their horsemen had swept up the riverbanks through Mesopotamia and on into Syria. Before returning laden with plundered treasures, driving their captives before them, they had watered their horses by the Mediterranean sea. Thus, now there were next to no Roman forces for the new *Dux Ripae* to command.

The specifics of Ballista's instructions, his *mandata*, perforce revealed the feeble state of Roman power in the east. He was commanded to proceed to the city of Arete, in the Province of 'Hollow Syria' (Coele Syria), at the easternmost reaches of the *imperium*. There he was to ready the city to withstand siege by the Sassanids, a siege which was expected to fall the following year. There were only two units of regular Roman troops at his command, a detachment, a *vexillatio*, of legionary heavy infantry from Legio IIII Scythica of about one thousand men, and an auxiliary *cohors* of both mounted and foot bowmen, again of about a thousand men. He had been instructed to raise what local levies he could in Arete and to ask the client kings of the nearby cities of Emesa and Palmyra for troops, although, of course, not to the detriment of their own defence. He was to hold Arete until he was relieved by an imperial field army commanded by the emperor Valerian himself. To facilitate the arrival of the field army, he had been further instructed to look to the defence of the main port of Syria, Seleuceia in Pieria, and the provincial capital, Antioch. In the absence of the governor of Coele Syria, the *Dux Ripae* was to have the full powers of a governor. When the governor was present, the *Dux* was bound to defer to him.

Ballista found himself grimly smiling at the absurdities of his instructions, absurdities typical of military missions planned by politicians. The potential for confusion between himself and the governor of Coele Syria was immense. And how could he, with the completely inadequate forces allotted him and whatever local peasants he could conscript, while under siege by a huge Persian army in Arete, also defend at least two other cities?

He had been honoured to be summoned to the presence of the emperors Valerian and Gallienus. The imperial father and son had spoken most kindly to him. He admired both men. Valerian had signed Ballista's *mandata* and invested him with the office of *Dux Ripae* with his own hand. But it could not be said that the mission was anything other than ill conceived and under resourced: too little time, and too few men in too vast an area. In more emotive terms, it looked much like a death sentence.

In the last, rushed three weeks before leaving Italy, Ballista had found out what he could about the distant city of Arete. It was on the western bank of the Euphrates, some fifty miles below the confluence of the Euphrates and the Chaboras. It was said that its walls were well founded and that, on three sides, sheer cliffs made it impregnable. Apart from a couple of insignificant watch towers, it was the last outpost of the *imperium Romanum*. Arete was the first place a Sassanid Persian army advancing up the Euphrates would reach. It would bear the full force of an attack.

Such history of the city as Ballista had been able to discover did not inspire much confidence. Originally founded by one of the successors of Alexander the Great, it had fallen first to the Parthians, then to the Romans then, only two years ago, to the Sassanid Persians, who had overthrown the Parthians. As soon as the main Persian army had withdrawn to their heartlands in the south-east, the locals, with help from some Roman units, had risen up and massacred the garrison the Sassanids had left behind. Its walls and cliffs notwithstanding, clearly the city had its weaknesses. Ballista could find what they were when he was on the ground, when he reached Syria. The commander of the auxiliary *cohors* stationed at Arete had instructions to meet him at the port of Seleuceia in Pieria.

Nothing was ever quite as it seemed with the Romans. Certain questions ran through Ballista's mind. How did the emperors know that the Sassanids would invade the following spring? And that they would take the Euphrates route rather than one of those to the north? If the military intelligence was sound, why was there no sign that an imperial field army was being mobilized? Closer to home, why had Ballista been chosen as *Dux Ripae*? He did have a certain reputation as a siege commander – five years ago he had been with Gallus in the north at the successful defence of the city of Novae against the Goths; before that he had taken various native settlements both in the far west and in the Atlas mountains – but he had never been to the east. Why had the emperors not sent either of their most experienced siege engineers? Both Bonitus and Celsus knew the east well.

If only he had been allowed to bring Julia with him. As she had been born into an old senatorial family, the labyrinth of politics at the Roman imperial court, so impenetrable to Ballista, were second nature to her. She could have cut to the heart of the ever-shifting patterns of patronage and intrigue, could have blown away the fog of unknowing that surrounded her husband.

Thinking of Julia brought a pang of longing, acute and physical – her tumbling ebony hair, eyes so dark as to appear black, the swell of her breasts, the flare of her hips. Ballista felt alone. He would miss her physically. But, more, he would miss her companionship, that and the heart-melting prattle of their infant son.

Ballista had asked permission for them to accompany him. Refusing the request, Valerian had pointed to the manifest dangers of the mission. But all knew there was another reason for the refusal: the emperors' need to hold hostages to ensure the good behaviour of their military commanders. Too many generals of the last generation had gone into revolt.

Ballista knew that he would feel lonely, despite being surrounded by people. He had a staff of fifteen men: four scribes, six messengers, two heralds, two *haruspices*, to read the omens, and Mamurra, his *praefectus fabrum*, chief engineer. In accordance with Roman law, he had chosen them from central lists of officially approved members of these professions, but he knew none of them, not even Mamurra, personally. It was in the natural course of things that some of these men would be *frumentarii*.

As well as his official staff, he had some of his own household with him – Calgacus, his body servant, Maximus, his bodyguard, and Demetrius, his secretary. That he had appointed the young Greek youth who now sat at his feet to run his headquarters, to be his *accensus*, would be resented by all the official staff, but he needed someone he felt he could trust. In Roman terms, they were part of his *familia* but, to Ballista, they seemed a poor substitute for his real family.

Something unusual about the motion of the ship caught Ballista's attention. Its familiar smells – pine from the pitch used to seal the hull, mutton fat from the tallow used to waterproof the leather oar sockets, and stale and fresh human sweat – reminded him of his youth on the wild northern ocean. This *trireme Concordia*, with its 180 rowers on three levels, its two masts, its two huge steering oars, 20 deck crew and some 70 marines, was an altogether more sophisticated vessel than any longboat from his youth. It was a racehorse to their pack animal. Yet, like a racehorse, it was bred for one thing, and that was speed and manœuvrability in smooth seas. If the sea turned rough, Ballista knew he would be safer in a primitive northern longboat.

The wind had backed in a southerly direction and was picking up. Already the sea was rising into ugly, choppy cross-waves which were catching the beam of the *trireme*, making it difficult for the rowers to clear their oars and giving the vessel the beginnings of an uncomfortable lurch. On the horizon to the south, dark stormclouds were building. Ballista now realized that the captain and helmsman had been deep in conversation for some time. As he looked at them, they came to a decision. They exchanged a final few words, both nodded, and the captain walked the few feet back to Ballista.

'The weather is turning, *Dominus*.'

'What do you recommend?' replied Ballista.

'As our course was to sail due east to rise Cape Acroceraunia and then coast south to Corcyra, as the gods would have it we are roughly midway between Italy and Greece. As we cannot hope to run for shelter, if the storm comes, we must run before it.'

'Take what actions you think fit.'

'Yes, *Dominus*. Could I ask that you order your staff to move away from the masts?'

As Demetrius scrabbled across the deck to pass the order, the captain again briefly conferred with the helmsman, then issued a volley of commands. The deckhands and marines, having herded the staff to the side rails, efficiently lowered the mainyard by some four or five feet on the mast. Ballista approved. The ship would need to catch enough wind to give her steerage way, but too much would make her hard to control.

The *trireme* was now lurching violently, and the captain gave the order to bring her round to run to the north. The helmsman called to the rowing master and the bow officer and then, at his signal, all three called to the rowers, the piper squeaked and the helmsman pulled on the steering oars. Tilting alarmingly, the galley came round to her new heading. On a further volley of orders the mainsail was set, tightly brailed up to show only a small area of canvas, and the oars on the lower two levels were drawn inboard.

Now the vessel's motion was a more manageable fore and aft lift. The carpenter appeared up the ladder and made his report to the captain.

'Three oars on the starboard broken. Quite a bit of water came inboard as the dry wood on the starboard went underwater, but the pumps are working, and the planks should swell and cut off the flow on their own.'

'Get plenty of replacement oars to hand. This might be a bit bumpy.' The carpenter sketched a salute and disappeared below.

It was the last hour of the day when the full force of the storm hit. The sky became as dark as Hades, blue-black with an unearthly yellow tinge, the wind screamed, the air was full of flying water, and the ship pitched savagely forward, her stern clear of the sea. Ballista saw two of his staff sliding across the deck. One was caught by the arm of a sailor. The other slammed into the rail. Above the howl of the elements, he could hear a man screaming in agony. He saw two main dangers. A wave could break clean over the ship, the pumps would fail, the vessel would become waterlogged, unresponsive to the helm, and then, sooner or later, turn broadside on to the storm and roll over. Or she might pitch pole, a wave lift her stern so high and drive her prow so deep that she would be upended or forced down beneath the waves. At least the latter would be quicker. Ballista wished he could stand, holding on firmly and letting his body try to move with the motion of the ship. But, just as in battle, an example had to be set, and he had to remain in his chair of office. He saw now why they had bolted it so securely to the deck. He looked down and realized that the boy Demetrius was clinging to his legs in the classic pose of a suppliant. He squeezed the boy's shoulder.

The captain dragged himself aft. Holding fast to the sternpost, he bawled the ritual words: 'Alexander lives and reigns.' As if in rejection, a jagged bolt of lightning flashed into the sea to port and a thunderclap boomed. Timing the fall of the deck, the captain half ran half slid to Ballista. All deference to rank gone, he grabbed the *curule* throne and Ballista's arm. 'Got to keep just enough way to steer. The real danger is if a steering oar breaks. Unless the storm gets worse. We should pray to our gods.'

Ballista thought of Ran, the grim sea goddess of the north, with her drowning net, and decided that things were bad enough already.

'Are there any islands to the north that we might get in the lee of?' he shouted.

'If the storm drives us far enough north, and we are not yet with Neptune, there are the islands of Diomedes. But . . . in the circumstances . . . it may be best for us not to go there.'

Demetrius started to yell. His dark eyes were bright with terror, his words barely audible.

'. . . Stupid stories. A Greek . . . blown into the deep sea . . . islands no one has seen, full of satyrs, horses' tails growing out of their arses, huge pricks . . . threw them a slave girl . . . raped her all over . . . their only way to escape . . . swore it was true.'

'Who knows what is true . . .' shouted the captain, and disappeared forward.

At dawn, three days after the storm first hit and two days overdue, the imperial *trireme* the *Concordia* rounded the headland and pulled into the tiny semicircular harbour of Cassiope on the island of Corcyra. The sea reflected the perfect blue of a Mediterranean sky. The merest hint of the dying night's offshore breeze blew into their faces.

'Not a good start to your voyage, *Dominus*,' said the captain.

'It would have been a great deal worse without your seamanship and that of your crew,' replied Ballista.

The captain nodded acknowledgement of the compliment. Barbarian he might be, but this *Dux* had good manners. He was no coward either. He had not put a foot wrong during the storm. At times he had almost seemed to be enjoying it, grinning like a madman.

'The ship is much knocked about. I am afraid that it will be at least four days before we can put back to sea.'

'It cannot be helped,' said Ballista. 'When she is repaired, how long will it take us to get to Syria?'

'Down the west coast of Greece, across the Aegean by way of Delos, across open sea from Rhodes to Cyprus, then open sea again from Cyprus to Syria . . .' The captain frowned in thought. '. . . At this time of year . . .' His face cleared. 'If the weather is perfect, nothing breaks on the ship, the men stay healthy, and we never stay ashore in any place for more than one night, I will have you in Syria in just twenty days, mid-October.'

'How often does a voyage go that well?' Ballista asked.

'I have rounded Cape Tainaron more than fifty times, and so far, never . . .'

Ballista laughed and turned to Mamurra, '*Praefectus*, get the staff together, and get them quartered in the posting-house of the *cursus publicus*. It's up on that hill to the left somewhere. You will need the *diplomata*, the official passes. Take my body servant with you.'

'Yes, *Dominus*.'

'Demetrius, come with me.'

Without being ordered, his bodyguard, Maximus, also fell in behind Ballista. They said nothing but exchanged a rueful grin. 'First, we will visit the injured.'

Thankfully, no one had been killed or lost overboard. The eight injured men were lying on the deck towards the prow: five rowers, two deckhands and one of Ballista's staff, a messenger. All had broken bones. A doctor had already been sent for. Ballista's was a courtesy call. A word or two with each, a few low-denomination coins, and it was over. It was necessary; Ballista had to travel to Syria with this crew.

Ballista stretched and yawned. No one had got much sleep since the night of the storm. He looked around, squinting in the bright early morning sunshine. Every detail of the bleak, ochre mountains of Epirus could be made out a couple of miles away, across the Ionian Straits. He ran his hand over four days' growth of beard and through his hair, which stood up stiff from his head, full of sea salt. He knew he must look like everyone's memory of every statue of a northern barbarian they had ever seen – although, in the vast majority of statues, the northern barbarian was either in chains or dying. But before he could shave and bathe, there was one more duty to perform.

'That must be the temple of Zeus, just up there.'

*

The priests of Zeus were waiting on the steps of the temple. They had seen the battered *trireme* pull into harbour. They could not have been more welcoming. Ballista produced some high-denomination coins, and the priests produced the necessary incense and a sacrificial sheep to fulfil the vows for safe landfall which Ballista had very publicly made at the height of the storm. One of the priests inspected the sheep's liver and pronounced it auspicious. The gods would enjoy dining off the smoke from the burnt bones wrapped in fat while the priests enjoyed a more substantial roast meal later. That Ballista generously waived his rights to a portion was generally thought pleasing to man and gods.

As they left the temple, one of those small, silly problems that come with travel occurred. The three of them were alone, and none of them knew precisely where the posting-house was.

'I have no intention of spending all morning wandering over those hills,' said Ballista. 'Maximus, would you walk down to the *Concordia* and get some directions?'

Once the bodyguard was out of earshot, Ballista turned to Demetrius. 'I thought I would wait until we were alone. What was all that stuff you were ranting during the storm about myths and islands full of rapists?'

'I . . . do not remember, *Kyrios*.' The youth's dark eyes avoided Ballista's gaze. Ballista remained silent and then, suddenly, the boy started talking hurriedly, the words tumbling out. 'I was scared, talking nonsense, just because I was frightened – the noise, the water. I thought we were going to die.'

Ballista looked steadily at him. 'The captain was talking about the islands of Diomedes when you started. What was he saying?'

'I do not know, *Kyrios*.'

'Demetrius, the last time I checked, you were my slave, my property. Did not one of your beloved ancient writers describe a slave as "a tool with a voice"? Tell me what the captain and you were talking about.'

'He was going to tell you the myth of the island of Diomedes. I wanted to stop him. So I interrupted him and told the story of the island of satyrs. It is in *The Description of Greece* by Pausanias.

I meant to show that, seductive as they are – even men as educated as the writer Pausanias have fallen for them – all such stories are unlikely to be true.' The boy stopped, embarrassed.

'So what is the myth of the islands of Diomedes?'

The boy's cheeks flushed. 'It is just a silly story.'

'Tell me,' commanded Ballista.

'Some say that after the Trojan War the Greek hero Diomedes did not go home but settled on two remote islands in the Adriatic. There is a sanctuary there dedicated to him. All round it sit large birds with big, sharp beaks. The legend has it that, when a Greek lands, the birds remain calm. But if a barbarian should try to land, they fly out and dive through the air trying to kill him. It is said they are the companions of Diomedes, who were transformed into birds.'

'And you wanted to spare my feelings?' Ballista threw his head back and laughed. 'Obviously, no one has told you. In my barbarian tribe, we do not really go in for feelings – or only when very drunk.'

The gods had been kind since Cassiope. The unexpected fury of Notus, the south wind, had given way to Boreas, the north wind, in gentle, kindly mood. With the tumbling mountains of Epirus, Acarnania and the Pelopponese off to the left, the *Concordia* had proceeded mainly under sail down the western flank of Greece. The *trireme* had rounded Cape Tainaron, made the passage between Malea and Cythera and then, under oars, headed north-east into the Aegean, pointing her wicked ram at the Cyclades: Melos, Seriphos, Syros. Now, after seven days and with only the island of Rheneia to round, they would reach Delos in a couple of hours.

A tiny, almost barren rock at the centre of the circle of the Cyclades, Delos had always been different. At first it had wandered on the face of the waters. When Leto, seduced by Zeus, the king of the gods, and hounded by his wife, Hera, had been rejected by every other place on earth, Delos took her in, and there she gave birth to the god Apollo and his sister Artemis. As a reward Delos was fixed in place for ever. The sick and women near to childbirth were ferried across to Rheneia; no one should be born or die on Delos. For long ages the island and its shrines had flourished, unwalled, held in the hands of the gods. In the golden age of Greece, Delos had been chosen as the headquarters of the league created by the Athenians to take the fight for freedom to the Persians.

The coming of Rome, the cloud in the west, had changed

everything. The Romans had declared Delos a free port; not out of piety but from sordid commerce. Their wealth and greed had turned the island into the largest slave market in the world. It was said that, at its height, more than ten thousand wretched men, women and children were sold each day on Delos. Yet the Romans had failed to protect Delos. Twice in twenty years the sacred island had been sacked. With a bitter irony, those who had made their living from slavery had been carried off by pirates into slavery. Now, its sanctuaries and its favourable position as a stopping place between Europe and Asia Minor continued to pull some sailors, merchants and pilgrims, but the island was a shadow of its former self.

Demetrius continued to gaze at Delos. Away to his right was the grey, humped outline of Mount Cynthus. On its summit was the sanctuary of Zeus and Athena. Below clustered other sanctuaries to other gods, Egyptian and Syrian, as well as Greek. Below them, tumbling down to the sea, was the old town, a jumble of white-washed walls and red-tiled roofs shimmering in the sunshine. The colossal statue of Apollo caught Demetrius's eye. Its head with its long braided hair, sculpted countless generations ago, was turned away. It smiled its fixed smile away to the left, towards the sacred lake. And there, next to the sacred lake, was the sight Demetrius had dreaded ever since he had heard where the *Concordia* was bound.

He had seen it only once, and that had been five years ago, but he would never forget the *Agora* of the Italians. He had been stripped and bathed – the goods had to look their best – then led to the block. There he had been the model of a docile slave, the threat of a beating or worse in his ears. He could smell crowded humanity under a pitiless Mediterranean sun. The auctioneer had done his spiel – 'well educated . . . would make a good secretary or accountant'. Fragments of the coarse comments of rough men floated up – 'Educated arsehole, I would say' . . . 'Well used if Turpilius has owned him.' A brisk bidding, and the deal was done. Remembering, Demetrius felt his face burn and his eyes prickle with unshed tears of rage.

Demetrius tried never to think of the *Agora* of the Italians. For him, it was a low point in three years of darkness after the soft spring light of the previous time. He did not talk about either; he let it be understood that he had been born into slavery.

The theatre quarter of the old town of Delos was a jumble of narrow winding lanes overhung by the leaning walls of shabby houses. Sunlight had difficulty getting in here at the best of times. Now, with the sun setting over the island of Rheneia, it was nearly pitch dark. The *frumentarii* had not thought to bring a torch or hire a torch-bearer.

'Shit,' said the Spaniard.

'What is it?'

'Shit. I have just stepped in a great pile of shit.' Now that he mentioned it, the other two noticed how the alley stank.

'There. A sign to guide the shailor to port,' said the North African. Sculpted at eye level was a large phallus. Its bell-end sported a smiling face. The spies set off in the direction it indicated, the Spaniard stopping now and then to scrape his sandal.

After a short walk in the gathering darkness they came to a door flanked by two carved phalluses. A large brute of a doorman admitted them, then they were led to a bench at a table by an unimaginably hideous crone. She asked for money upfront before she brought them their drink: two parts of wine to five water. The only other customers were two elderly locals deep in conversation.

'Perfect. Absolutely fucking perfect,' said the spy from the Subura. If anything, the smell was worse in here than outside. Stale wine fumes and ancient sweat joined the prevailing odour of damp and decay, piss and shit. 'How come you two get to be well-paid, well-respected scribes on the *Dux*'s staff while a native-born Roman, one of Romulus's own, like me, has to play the role of a mere messenger?'

'Is it our fault you write so badly?' said the Spaniard.

'Bollocks to you, Sertorius.' The nickname came from a famous Roman rebel who had been based in Spain. 'Rome is nothing more than a stepmother to you and Hannibal here.'

'Yesh, it must be wonderful to be born in Romulus's cesspit,' said the North African.

They stopped bickering as they were served by an elderly prostitute wearing a great deal of make-up, a very short tunic and a bracelet with a range of amulets: a phallus, the club of Heracles, an axe, a hammer and an image of three-faced Hecate.

'If she needs that lot to deflect envy, imagine what the others look like.'

They all drank. 'There is another imperial *trireme* in the harbour,' said the Spaniard. 'It is carrying an imperial procurator from the province of Lycia to Rome. Maybe the *Dux* has arranged to meet him here?'

'Except he has not gone to meet him yet,' replied the one so proud of his birth in the city of Rome.

'That might be all the more suspicious.'

'Bollocks. Our barbarian *Dux* came here because he heard there was a consignment of Persian slaves for sale and he wanted to buy a new piece of arse; a Persian with a bottom like a peach to replace that worn-out Greek boy.'

'I was talking to Demetrius, the *accenshush*. He thinks that it is all some type of political statement. Apparently, a very long time ago, the Greeks used this wretched little island as the headquarters for a religious war against the Persians. Where are we going, if not to defend civilization from a new lot of Persians? It seems our barbarian *Dux* wants to see himself as a standard-bearer for civilization.'

The other two nodded at the North African's words, even though they did not believe them.

The door opened, and in walked three more customers. As any member of the staff should, the *frumentarii* got to their feet to greet the *praefectus fabrum*, Mamurra. They also spoke to the bodyguard, Maximus, and the valet, Calgacus. The new arrivals returned the greetings and went and sat at another table. The *frumentarii* flicked each other glances, revelling in their perspicacity. They had chosen the right bar.

The two brothers who owned the bar eyed their latest customers with some trepidation. The ugly old slave with the misshapen head who had been greeted as Calgacus would not cause any trouble – although you could never tell. The *praefectus*, Mamurra, like all soldiers, could be a problem. He wore camp dress – white tunic embroidered with swastikas, dark trousers and boots. He had a *cingulum*, an elaborate military belt, around his waist, to which was buckled an equally ornate baldric, which went over his right shoulder. The *cingulum* had an extravagant swag tucked in to form a loop to the right of the buckle. It hung down and ended in the usual jingling metal ornaments. Both belts proclaimed his length of service and status. They were covered in awards for valour, amulets and mementoes of various units and campaigns. On his left hip lay a *spatha*, a long sword, and on his right a *pugio*, a military dagger. In the good old days, he would have only worn the dagger, but unsettled times changed things. His large square head, like a block of marble, was grizzled; beard, hair and moustache were cut very short. A mouth like a rat trap and serious, almost unblinking, eyes added to the suggestion that he was far from a stranger to violence.

The third man, the talkative one whom the attendants had greeted as Maximus, was worse. He was dressed in similar fashion to the officer, but he was no soldier. He wore an old-fashioned *gladius*, a Spanish short sword, an ornate dagger and a mass of cheap gilt ornaments. His black hair was longer than the other man's and he had a short but full beard. The scar where the tip of his nose had been showed white against the deep tan of his bird-like face. The barmen thought it looked like a cat's arse. They had no intention of telling the man. His whole appearance pointed to his time in the arena and his current employment as a hired tough. But what was really worrying were his eyes. Light blue, wide open and slightly blank, they were the eyes of a man who could turn to extreme violence at a moment's notice.

'This one is on me.' Mamurra raised his slab-sided face to catch the eye of one of the owners. The barman nodded and gestured to a girl to take drinks to the three men.

'Jupiter, that barman is one ugly bastard,' said Calgacus in an atrocious northern accent.

'You see, my dear *Praefectus*,' Maximus spoke to Mamurra, 'Calgacus here is something of an expert on beauty. It all comes from his youth. You may find it hard to credit, but when he was young his beauty shone like the sun. Men and boys – even women and girls – they all wanted him. When he was enslaved, kings, princes and satraps showered him with gold hoping for his favours. They say that, in Athens, he caused a riot. You know what dedicated pederasts the Athenians are.'

It was not so much hard to credit as completely impossible to believe. Mamurra regarded Calgacus closely; he had a weak chin, not concealed by a growth of stubble, a sour, thin mouth, a wrinkled forehead, short-cropped receding hair and, the most distinctive feature, a great dome of a skull rising up and out above the ears. It had taken Mamurra a moment or two to realize that Maximus had been joking. Neptune's bollocks, this is going to be hard work, he thought. He was not a man who had an affinity with light, playful irony.

A girl with small breasts and a bony behind arrived with their wine. As she set down the large mixing bowl Maximus ran his hand up her leg under her short tunic and over her arse. She simpered. Both were doing what they thought was expected of them.

In the normal run of things, the *praefectus fabrum*, Mamurra, would not have been drinking with a couple of barbarian slaves, let alone paying for the drinks. But everyone dances when Dionysius demands. In the *imperium* power came from proximity to greater power. The *Dux Ripae* had power because he had a commission direct from the emperors. These two slaves had power because they were close to the *Dux Ripae*. They had been with Ballista for years. It was fourteen years since the *Dux Ripae* had purchased Maximus, and Calgacus had come to the *imperium* with him. If Mamurra's own commission were to be a success, it was vital to find out everything he could about the new *Dux*. Anyway, he accepted that, given his own status, it would be hypocritical to stand on ceremony. It was not even as if Mamurra was the name he had been given at birth.

He studied his two companions. Calgacus was drinking slowly, steadily, determinedly. Like an Archimedes screw pumping out the hold of a ship, he lowered the level of his cup. Maximus was also getting through his share, but he took sips or gulps as and when the waving, chopping hand gestures which illustrated his never-ending chatter allowed. Mamurra awaited his moment.

'Strange that the Greek boy Demetrius turned down a drink. Do you think he is put out that Ballista bought that pretty Persian boy today? One bum boy fearing another bum boy in the house? Nothing is lower in a household than yesterday's favourite.' Mamurra watched Maximus's normally mobile features still, his face become closed.

'The tastes of the *dominus* do not run in that direction. In his tribe such people are killed; just like . . . in the Roman army.' Maximus turned to look Mamurra full in the face.

The *praefectus fabrum* held the bodyguard's gaze for a moment or two then looked away. 'I am sure that is the way it is.' Mamurra noted the barman exchanging a significant look with the man ugly enough to be his brother who was in charge of the door.

Mamurra decided to try another tack. His wine cup was decorated with a scene of a vigorous orgy. It was a crude copy of the ancient style of painted vases which now were so often collected by the rich as antiques, as conversation pieces. Like the whole decoration of the room, including the two ludicrously oversized fake Doric columns which flanked the door to the stairs, the drinking cups were intended to give the poor patrons of the bar an illusory sense of an elite lifestyle. Mamurra knew, because he had often been in the houses of the rich, sometimes even legitimately.

'I think I could do with a fuck,' he said. 'If either of you want a girl, be my guest.'

'That is awful kind of you, my dear *Praefectus*. We have been at sea a long time and, as I am sure an educated man like yourself knows, there is no sex to be had at sea. The sailors say that it brings the worst sort of luck. I wonder if that includes sex with yourself. If so, it's a wonder we made port at all, what with Calgacus here strumming like Priapus in the women's quarters.' Maximus looked around the room. 'There! Over there! A vision! A vision of beauty!'

'What, the fat girl?' Calgacus asked, following the direction of his gaze.

'Warmth in the winter, shade in the summer.' Maximus beamed and went off to strike a deal.

Now let's see if we can get anything out of this miserable old Caledonian bastard, thought Mamurra.

'How do you put up with it?' he asked.

'It's just his way.'

'I have noticed sometimes he even talks that way to the *Dux*. How does he get away with that?'

There was a lengthy pause as Calgacus further lowered the level of his drink. 'On account of saving his life,' he said finally.

'When did Maximus save his life?'

Another long pause. 'No, the *dominus* saved Maximus's life. Creates a bond.'

Beginning to despair, Mamurra refilled Calgacus's cup. 'Why is the *Dux* named after a siege engine?'

'Maybe he got the name Ballista because he has always had an interest in siege engines.'

This is sodding hopeless, thought Mamurra. 'He must be a good *dominus* to serve.'

The old slave drank and seemed to mull this over. 'Maybe.'

'Well, he seems an easy master. No special demands.' Mamurra was nothing if not persistent.

'Boiled eggs,' said Calgacus.

'Sorry?'

'Soft-boiled eggs. Very fussy about them. Have to be just so.'

Ballista sat on some stone steps which ran down to the water from the dock. For the first time since Brundisium he felt happy. He had just written a letter to Julia and included a short note for her to read to their son. He had sent a crapulous-looking Calgacus off to the other imperial *trireme* to ask if the procurator would be kind enough to deliver it. Even if they had already left Rome for the villa in Sicily, which was not likely, it should soon reach them. The autumn sunshine was warm on his face, and it sparkled on the vivid blue sea.

He picked up his copy of *How to Defend a City under Siege* by Aeneas Tacticus and scrolled through the papyrus roll to find his place. 'Announce a monetary reward for anyone denouncing a conspirator against the city . . . the reward offered should be advertised openly in the *agora* or at an altar or shrine.' Ballista had read the script before. Its main thrust was the need to be on constant guard against traitors within. When Aeneas wrote, the Mediterranean had been a mosaic of warring city states, each one well stocked with potential revolutionaries. One should never discount the possibility of treachery, but times had changed. Issues were simpler now; unless there were a civil war, it was the *imperium Romanum* against those outside. The main danger Ballista would face at Arete would be regular Persian siege works – artillery, rams, ramps and mines. This was the sort of practical siege engineering that the big northerner understood.

His bodyguard was approaching, shepherding the newly acquired Persian slave along the dock. Ballista thanked Maximus and gave him leave; under the bodyguard's tan there was an unhealthy pallor, he was sweating much more than the sun merited and his eyes peered out from behind lids almost screwed shut. Maximus gave a slight nod and left. As if by magic, Demetrius appeared, his stylus and writing block ready.

Ballista studied the Persian boy. He was tall, nearly as tall as the northerner himself, with curly black hair and beard. His dark eyes were suspicious, and he had an unmistakable air of hostility. 'Sit,' he said in Greek. 'Bagoas is a slave name?' The Persian boy nodded.

'Show respect! Yes, *Kyrios*!' snapped Demetrius.

'Yes, *Kyrios*,' said the Persian in heavily accented Greek.

'What was your name before you were enslaved?'

There was a pause.

'Hormizd.'

Ballista suspected he was lying. 'Do you want to be called Hormizd again?'

The question wrongfooted the youth. 'Er . . . no . . . *Kyrios*.'

'Why not?'

'It would bring shame on my family.'

'How were you enslaved?'

Again there was a pause while the Persian considered his answer. 'I was captured by . . . some Arab . . . bandits, *Kyrios*.'

Another shifty answer, thought Ballista, his eyes following the flight of a seagull away towards the north.

The boy seemed to relax a little.

'I will tell you why I purchased you.' Instantly, the boy tensed. He feared the worst. He seemed ready to run or even to fight. 'I want you to teach me Persian. I want to learn both the language and the customs of the Persians.'

'Most upper-class Persians speak a little Greek, *Kyrios*,' said the boy, sounding relieved.

Ballista ignored him. 'Carry out your duties well and you will be treated well. Try and run and I will kill you!' He shifted in his seat. 'How did the Persians under the Sassanid house overthrow the Parthians? Why do they so frequently unleash their horsemen on the *imperium Romanum*? How have they so frequently defeated the Romans?'

'The god Mazda willed it' came the instant reply.

If the first stratagem to bring down the walls fails you must try another. Ballista continued. 'Tell me the story of the Sassanid house. I want to know the ancestors of King Shapur and the stories of their deeds.'

'There are many stories of the origins of the house.'

'Tell me those that you believe.' The boy was wary, but Ballista hoped that pride would lead him to start talking.

The boy collected his thoughts. 'Long ago, when the lord Sasan travelled through the lands, he came to the palace of King Papak. Papak was a seer, and he could tell that the descendants of Sasan were destined by Mazda to lead the Persians to greatness. Papak had no daughter or female relative to offer Sasan, so he offered him his wife. He preferred the lasting glory of the Sassanid Persians to his own shame. The son born to Sasan was Ardashir, the King of Kings, who thirty years ago overthrew the Parthians. The son of Ardashir is Shapur, the King of Kings, the King of Aryans and

Non-Aryans, who by the will of Mazda smites the Romans.' The youth glared defiantly at Ballista.

'And Shapur wants back all the lands which were once ruled by the Persians in ancient times before Alexander the Great took their empire? So he would take from the Romans Egypt, Syria, Asia Minor and Greece?'

'No . . . well, yes.'

'Which? No or yes?'

'Yes in the sense that they are ancestral lands that must be reclaimed, but no in the sense that they are not all that he will take from the Romans.' The boy's eyes shone with zeal.

'Then what other lands would he have?' Ballista suspected the worst.

'The King of Kings Shapur in his perfect humility accepts that he is just the instrument of the god Mazda. He understands that it is the destiny of his house to bring the sacred fires of Mazda to the whole world, to make all peoples worship Mazda, to make all the world Aryan!'

So there it was. Ballista's transient feeling of happiness had evaporated. The Persians had no need for temporal niceties such as just cause. There was no hope of compromise, or delay. Seemingly, there was no hope of an end: it was a religious war. For a moment Ballista saw the world as the Persian boy saw it: the armies of the righteous, their numbers those of the stars in the sky, sweeping west to cleanse the world. And all that was standing in their path was Ballista himself and the isolated city of Arete.

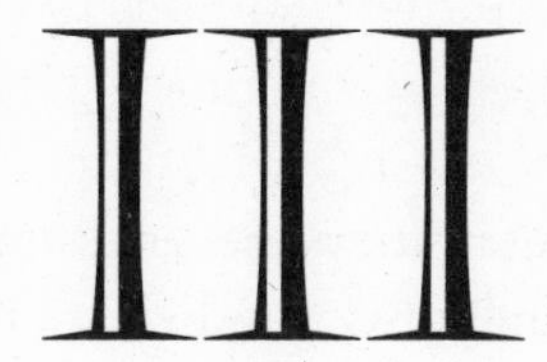

It had taken time for the drink to die out of Maximus. As soon as Ballista had given him leave he had bought bread, cheese, olives, water and a small piece of honeycomb from the main marketplace and gone in search of a quiet place to sit. He found a deserted garden and chose a spot where both possible points of entry were in view. After checking the shrubbery for snakes, of which he had a particular horror, he settled down with the one book he owned: Petronius's novel *The Satyricon*. Maximus had tried other books since Ballista had taught him to read Latin in Africa some years ago, but none spoke to him like this one. It showed the Romans as they really were: lustful, drunken, greedy, duplicitous and violent – men much like himself.

The next day, Maximus felt full of life. Just after dawn the captain had announced that, as he could see the peak of Mount Tenos, the day was well omened for voyaging. Ballista had carried out the correct ritual, and the *Concordia* had slipped her moorings. Maximus was now standing on the *epotis*, or ear timber, just behind the ram of the ship, enjoying a perfect view ahead over the azure sea. What a nice irony: here was he, a slave, enjoying the sun and spray in the best seat on the ship, while behind and below him 180 freemen, technically soldiers of Rome, many of them volunteers, sat on hard benches in the airless semi-dark rowing this great ship. Let the poor bastards get splinters in their arses, he thought.

Slavery sat lightly on Maximus. Others took it hard – young Demetrius for one. The Greek boy had looked down in the mouth ever since it had been announced that they would stop at Delos. Maybe it had to do with how you came to be a slave. Some were born slaves. Some were abandoned on dunghills as babies and taken in by slave dealers. Some were so poor they sold themselves into slavery. Some were enslaved for crimes; others captured by pirates or bandits. Outside the *imperium*, many had been enslaved by the mighty armies of Rome – fewer now that Roman armies seemed to have acquired the habit of losing. And then there were those who had come into the condition like Maximus himself.

Back when he had been a freeman, he had been known by the name Muirtagh. His last memory of freedom was of laughing with some other warriors. They had tied a peasant to a tree, on the off chance that he had perhaps a hidden pot of gold, and were passing a skin of beer from hand to hand. His first memory of servitude was of lying in the back of a cart. His hands were tightly bound behind his back and, with each jolt of the unsprung wagon, the pain in his head grew worse. He had no memory of anything between the two. It was as if someone had taken his papyrus roll of *The Satyricon*, ripped out several sheets and then glued the torn ends together again, or maybe better had torn several pages from one of those new bound books. The story just jumped from one scene to another.

Another warrior whose life had been spared for slavery, Cormac, had been in the cart too. Apparently, they had raided a neighbouring tribe of some cattle and some of its warriors had caught up with them. There was a running battle and Muirtagh had been hit in the head by a slingshot and dropped like a stone. Now they were being taken down to the coast to be sold to Roman slave traders.

Cormac had not been sold. A minor wound to his leg had turned bad, and he had died. Muirtagh had. His first owner thought Maximus was a suitable name for a potential recruit to the arena, so he was called Muirtagh no longer. Maximus was shipped to Gaul and sold to a *lanista*, the trainer of a travelling group of gladiators. At first he had fought with the cruel *caestus*, the metal-spiked glove of a boxer. But there had been an incident: Maximus and a *retiarius*, a net and trident fighter, in the troupe had fallen out over money. To recoup the loss incurred by the crippling of the *retiarius*, Maximus had been sold to another troupe, where he had fought with the oblong shield and short sword of a *murmillo*.

Maximus had been fighting in the great stone amphitheatre of Arelate when Ballista first saw him. The Angle had paid well over the odds for him, and for good reason. Back then, on his way to the far west, Ballista would need two things: someone to watch his back and someone to teach him Celtic.

Maximus was not obsessed with winning his freedom as other slaves were. The Romans were uncommon generous with manumission – but only because freeing lots of slaves was the carrot that worked with the stick of crucifixion to keep them from acts of desperation, from mass flight or revolt. At an individual level, it was a way for the Roman elite to show their largesse. Freeing large numbers of slaves fuelled the demand for new ones. Freedom, for Maximus, was all bound up with expectations and obligations. Maximus was not too fussed about a roof over his head, and certainly not bothered whether the roof was his own. He wanted his belly full, of booze as well as food; he wanted a string of willing girls, although, at times, reluctance had its attractions; and he enjoyed a fight. He was good at violence, and he knew it. If he had stayed at home and had managed to stay alive, he would have gained these things in the retinue of a local Hibernian king. Here, serving as Ballista's bodyguard, he got all of them, with wine as well as beer, and a greater range of women. And then, there was no question of freedom until he had paid off his obligation to Ballista. It often played through his mind: his hobnails slipping on the marble floor (never wear those bastards again), his sword knocked out of reach as he fell (always have a wrist loop of leather on the pommel), the fierce brown face, the sword arm lifted for the killing blow, and the cut with which Ballista had severed that arm.

When he was young and had travelled nowhere, his endless talk had won him the name Muirtagh of the Long Road. Now the name fitted the truth, only Ballista ever called him that, and then only occasionally.

He was happy enough where he was. Sure, he would like to go back home one day, but only once, and then not for long – just long enough to kill the men who had enslaved him, rape their women and burn down their homes.

The cruise of the *Concordia* had run as smoothly as the water out of a clock in court. All was warm early October sunshine and gentle breezes for the two days it took to sail from Delos to Cnidus; first east to the island of Ikaros, then south-east down the Sporades chain between the puritans of the island of Kos and the decadents of the mainland of Asia Minor and, finally, to peninsular Cnidus. Here they had stopped for a day to take on water and to inspect the semen-stained thighs of the statue of Aphrodite of Cnidus.

On the morning they pulled out of Cnidus a sea mist had settled. The captain said that they were not that uncommon in these waters of the southern Aegean; not usually as bad as this, but there was some sort of fret at least half the year. With visibility down to under two miles he set a course along the south coast from Cnidus to Cape Onougnathos, then striking out south-east for the north coast of the island of Syme. An anchored merchantman indicated proximity to Syme. The *Concordia* slid by and shaped to make for Rhodes.

'Two sails. Directly ahead. Pirates. Goths!'

There was pandemonium on the deck of the *Concordia* until the captain bellowed for silence. As the hubbub subsided, he ordered everyone to sit down. Ballista walked with the captain to the prow. There they were, emerging from the sea mist about two miles ahead. There was no mistaking the shape of the vessels, the distinctive double-ended outline, as both fore and aft seemed to sweep up into a prow. One central mast, one steering oar over the starboard quarter, lots of shields hung along the sides. The two Goth craft were each about two-thirds the length of the *Concordia* but, with only one level of rowers, they were considerably lower in the water.

'Judging by the length of them, there should be about fifty of the bastards in each,' said the captain. 'Of course, you would know all about them.'

Ballista ignored the implicit gibe at his barbarian origins. He did know a lot about them. They were Borani, a German people within the loose confederation known as the Goths. All such Gothic pirates in these waters were Borani. In recent years, more and more of them had slipped out of the innumerable harbours and creeks of the Black Sea, run down through the Bosphorus and taken to plundering the coasts and islands of the Aegean. These two ships had taken up a good station on a well-used shipping route between the Diabetai islets and the island of Syme.

'Permission to clear for action, *Dominus*?'

'Carry on. There is no need to run every order through me. You are the captain of this ship. My bodyguard and myself will just add numbers to your marines and put ourselves at the disposal of your *optio*, your second-in-command.'

'Thank you, *Dominus*.' The Captain turned away, then back. 'Would you order as many as possible of your staff to cram themselves in your cabin below deck, and the rest to shelter in the stern awning?'

Demetrius had appeared out of nowhere. As Ballista relayed the instructions, he noticed that the youth looked terrified. 'Demetrius, would you make sure that the staff remain calm?' The boy seemed to rally with the implied trust placed in him.

'Main deck crew, lower the mainyard, then unstep the mast. Lash both down securely. Forward deck crew, do the same with the bowsprit,' yelled the captain. On a warship these would be left ashore during action but the captain was not in a position to jettison good timbers at any possible sighting of pirates.

As Ballista reached the stern, Maximus appeared carrying their war gear, fighting his way against the rush of the staff going below. Ballista slipped his sword belt over his head, unbuckled his military belt and draped them both over his *curule* chair. He sank to his knees and held his arms aloft to make it easier for Maximus to help him into his mail coat. He felt its weight on his shoulders increasing as he got back to his feet. He buckled his *cingulum* tightly, pulling some of the mail shirt up through the belt to take some of the weight from his shoulders, and re-slung his sword belt. He tied the thick scarf in the neck of his mail shirt. As he settled his war helm on his head, his fingers fumbled with the laces under his chin. Ballista was always clumsy before battle, but he knew that his fear would go when the action started. By the time he picked up his shield, the three-foot circle of closely joined planks with leather cover and metal boss heavy as he hoisted the central grip, he saw that Maximus had virtually finished wriggling into his own mail shirt, 'like a salmon swimming upstream', as the Hibernian himself would have said.

'Marines, arm. Break out the axes and boarding pikes!' More orders issued from the captain. 'Engine crews, remove covers, check springs and washers. One test shot.'

Both Ballista and Maximus were now armed. 'Another stage on the long road of Muirtagh,' said Ballista.

'May the gods hold their hands over us.'

At Maximus's words each man grinned and punched the other on the left shoulder. As always, Maximus took up his place on Ballista's right. Without any conscious thought, Ballista went through his own silent pre-battle ritual: right hand to the dagger on his right hip, pull it an inch or so out of its sheath then snap it back; left hand on the scabbard of his sword, right hand pull the blade a couple of inches free then push it back; finally, right hand touch the healing stone tied to the scabbard.

'Oh, shit, here we go again. At least this time it's not my responsibility.'

His words were cut off by the twang, slide and thump of the first bolt-thrower's test shot. The bolt flew far out to the left. It was rapidly followed by three more, two to the right, one to the left. The crew of the starboard rear engine worked feverishly, adjusting the tension of the springs, the twisted bundles of hair that provided its awesome torsion power.

Yet more orders flowed from the captain: 'Spare oars to all levels. Spread sand on the deck. Complete silence. Listen for the commands. Only officers to speak.'

Like the wings of a great bird, the *Concordia*'s three banks of oars brought her towards her prey. The gap was less than half a mile now.

'Why are they just sitting there? Why don't the bastards run?' whispered Maximus.

'Maybe they think that, if they can avoid the ram, about a hundred of them can take our seventy or so marines in a boarding action, despite the *Concordia*'s advantage in height.'

'Then they are fools, and deserve all they are going to get!'

'Forward engines open fire at 150 yards!'

Water hissed down the hull, and the gap closed swiftly. Twang, slide, thump went the starboard bolt-thrower. With staggering speed, the bolt shot away from the *Concordia*. For a second it looked as if it would hit the enemy boat head on but instead it skimmed just above the heads of the Gothic warriors. Already the crew were winching back the slide for the next missile. The near miss had the effect of stirring an anthill. Across the water rolled the *barritus*, the German war cry, a rising roar. One barbarian was frantically waving a bright-red shield above his head.

'Shit! Oh shit!' someone shouted in the prow. Out from behind the low rocky humps of the Diabetai islets rowed two more Goth ships.

'I suppose we know now why they didn't run,' whispered Maximus.

'Prepare for fast turn to left!' There was little over one hundred yards separating the *Concordia* from the first two Gothic vessels. 'On my signal starboard side row on at full pressure, port side back her down hard, helmsman hard over!' There was just the noise of the ship slicing through the water. 'Now!'

The *Concordia* heeled to the right. The lowest level of oar ports were on or even below the surface. A thousand joints of wood screamed in complaint. The mainmast shifted against its restraining ropes. But the ship turned like an eel. She raced broadside on across the prows of the Goths only some twenty yards distant. Then she was levelling out and heading away. She had turned through 180 degrees in less than three times her own length.

A whir, and something slammed into the deck a couple of yards from Ballista.

'Arrows! Shields up!' Cursing his own thoughtlessness, Ballista crouched behind his heavy planks of linden wood. There were more thumps and clangs as arrows found wood or metal. Somewhere, a man screamed as one found exposed flesh. Then, twice in close succession, twang, slide, thump as the rear two bolt-throwers answered the Gothic bowmen. Ballista peeped over his shield, then ducked down. Another flight of arrows was coming. This time, more men screamed. The captain was standing beside Ballista. The northerner felt shamed by the man's coolness.

'We can outrun them no problem. But we might fi–' The arrowhead appeared shockingly out of his throat. There was surprisingly little blood. The captain seemed to look down at it in horror, then toppled forward. As the arrowhead hit the deck the shaft broke deep in his neck, wrenching the wound open, and now blood spurted everywhere.

Keeping his shield raised towards the stern, and with Maximus also trying to shield him, Ballista went over to the helmsman. He moved hunched forward as if walking into heavy rain. The helmsman, although protected by the up-curved stern of the ship and the shields of two marines, looked frantic. His eyes were fixed on the dead body of his captain. If something were not done, the morale of the *Concordia* could collapse like a punctured wineskin. Dozens of bowmen were shooting into the ship, and her only reply was two bolt-throwers.

'I am assuming command,' Ballista said to the helmsman. 'Are you unhurt?'

'Yes, *Dominus*.' The man looked dubious. Ballista knew that he doubted if this northerner had ever commanded a *trireme*. He was right to doubt.

Raising his voice against the noises of the ship and the unequal missile battle, Ballista called out, 'I am in command! *Optio* to me! Rowing master, are you injured? Bow officer, are you?'

Both the ship's officers raised their hands in a stiff-armed salute and called back the standard military response: 'We will do what is ordered, and at every command we will be ready.'

'Where the bloody hell is the *optio*?'

'Among the wounded, *Dominus*,' someone answered.

'Right. Marines, you will take commands from me. Helmsman, take charge of the rowing of the ship. Just get her out of this arrow storm, now! But not too far out. I know that we can outrun them. But they probably won't know that. Northern barbarians cannot imagine what an imperial *trireme* can do in action until they see it. I should know!' He laughed grimly. 'Try and keep her about a hundred to a hundred and fifty yards in front of them. Just at the limit of effective bow shot. Keep them interested. If they don't keep together we can pick them off one by one.' At that instant, Ballista remembered the merchantman anchored off Syme and, with a determined grin, said, 'I have a plan.'

By the time the merchantman came into sight again, the swan stern of the *Concordia* looked like a pin cushion but only a few more men had been hit, and Ballista's hopes were being realized. The largest of the Gothic longboats had pulled seven or eight boat lengths ahead of its original companion. Ballista estimated the crew to be at least a hundred warriors, who rowed with purpose, as if galvanized by the presence of 'red shield', who was obviously their leader. The original two longboats had a sizeable headstart over the other two enemy craft, which had been hiding behind the Diabetai islets. The latter were now tailed off, lagging a good half-mile behind the second boat. Ballista told the helmsman to take the *Concordia* to the right of the merchantman, keeping as close to her side as possible. It was almost time to put his plan into operation.

As the ram neared the prow of the motionless merchantman, Ballista called out a string of orders. 'Prepare for fast turn to left! On my command, port oars bank down hard, starboard oars row hard, helmsman put steering oars hard over!' The high side of the big round ship shot by the *Concordia*.

Allfather, let me get this right, thought Ballista. He could all too easily imagine calling the order too soon and the *Concordia*'s port-side oars breaking on the stern of the merchantman, or too late, and the whole plan failing at the start.

'Turn now!'

Again, the long warship tipped, her starboard lower oar ports dipped to the water line. Again, thousands of pieces of wooden joinery squealed, and the great mainmast strained against its lashings. Two bearded faces looked on in astonishment over the stern rail of the merchantman as the *Concordia* raced past. In a matter of moments, Ballista shouted for the helmsman to straighten her up and for the left-hand rowers to resume their stroke. Now the *Concordia* was racing back the way she had come but down the other side of the merchantman.

Just as Ballista had hoped, when they emerged from the shadow of the merchant there was the following Gothic ship still chasing the *trireme*'s wake, blindly following her original course. The Goth's beam was wide open to the *Concordia*'s ram.

'Helmsman, sheer the enemy oars! Rowers, ramming speed!' In a deft movement the steering oars angled the warship into the longboat. 'Port oars, prepare to come inboard.' Seconds passed. How soon, how bloody soon? worried Ballista. *Now!* 'Oars inboard!'

Not a moment too soon the great sweeps were drawn inboard out of harm's way. The helmsman threw the steering oars to the right, and the iron ram struck the hull of the Gothic ship at a glancing angle. There was a terrible noise of metal into wood as the ram raked down the flank of the enemy longboat. The Goths, taken completely by surprise, had no time to recover their oars. They splintered like kindling. As the *Concordia* passed, some of her marines, without being ordered, hurled darts down from her higher deck into the northern ship. Cries of anguish and pain floated up.

Bugger! I should have thought to tell the marines to do that, thought Ballista as the stern of the *trireme* cleared the enemy. But his stratagem had worked. The Goths had been given no time to react and, now, with half their oars gone, they lay dead in the water.

'Aim for the second longboat, bow to bow ram,' Ballista shouted to the helmsman.

The second crew of Goths was as surprised as the first. Now they tried to turn away. Their rising panic was easy to see in their missed strokes and the longboat's sluggish response.

'Ramming speed!' bellowed the helmsman. The *Concordia* surged ahead. 'Brace for ramming!' With an almighty crash of splintering wood the ram punched into the enemy beam. The impact knocked Ballista to the deck. Maximus hauled him up. Ballista was winded. Bent double, he tried to suck air back into his lungs. He heard the helmsman shout, 'Back water! Back water! Full pressure!'

The *Concordia* seemed stuck fast, her ram embedded deep in the wreckage of the other ship. This crew was quicker-thinking than the other Goths. Already, grappling hooks trailing lines of thick rope were curving through the air towards the *trireme*'s prow.

'Back water! Push, you fuckers! Push!' The helmsman's shouts sounded desperate. 'Marines, use the boarding pikes to fend her off!'

Straightening up, Ballista set off at a painful run to the prow. If they did not get clear, they would be sitting ducks when the other two Goths came up. Grabbing a boarding pike, he moved to the rail. As he got there, a bearded face appeared over the side. From the right, Maximus's shield punched into the Goth's face, sending the man sprawling and bloodied to the deck of his ship. Ramming the pike into the hull of the rapidly settling longboat, Ballista pushed with all his strength. A marine joined him. Maximus held his shield over them. For what seemed an eternity, nothing moved. Out of the corner of his eye Ballista saw a marine leap up on to the rail itself. Somehow, the man balanced there, swinging an axe down on to one of the ropes that now bound the *Concordia* to the Gothic ship. After three cuts an arrow caught the marine in the thigh. With a yell he fell over the side. By the time Ballista had drawn two or three laboured breaths a second marine was on the rail. One powerful swing of his axe, the rope parted, and the marine jumped back down on to the deck.

'One, two, three, PUSH!' Ballista realized that it was he who was shouting, trying to get the words out despite his aching chest, trying to make them heard above the terrible din of battle. 'PUSH!'

At last, with a wrenching sound, the *Concordia* began to move. Slowly at first, then gathering way, she backed away from the Goth. Twang, slide, thump, the crew of the two forward bolt-throwers had the presence of mind to add to the problems of the Gothic crew. A three-foot artillery bolt punched through one Goth's mail shirt and nailed him to the mast.

The barbarian vessel was unlikely to sink to the bottom. Wooden warships tended to become waterlogged, settle in the water and eventually break up. The Goths in the water or clinging to the wreckage could be left to drown of their own accord or, if there were time, used for target practice later. Either way, they were no longer of any account in this battle.

Ballista needed to know what the other Goth ships were up to. Peering from well behind his shield, he saw that the two unengaged vessels were already turning away. They were still almost half a mile away, and the *Concordia* had a tired crew. There was no point in thinking of giving chase. Ballista ran to look over the stern. The Goth ship they had raked had managed to redistribute its remaining oars and was trying to limp from the scene.

'Helmsman, put us about a hundred and fifty yards away from that ship. We will call on them to surrender. But we will be ready to fight them.' As his order was carried out, Ballista, with Maximus at his right shoulder as ever, moved along the deck, talking to the marines and deckhands; words of praise here, sympathy for the wounded there.

The *optio* who had been wounded early on made his report. There were just three dead, including the captain, but ten wounded, including the *optio* himself. All the casualties were marines except one. As he finished, he stood awkwardly, fidgeting with the bandage on his arm. Then Ballista spoke the words the *optio* had been praying for. 'With the captain dead you will assume command of the ship as acting *trierarch* until you return to Ravenna.'

As the *Concordia* manœuvred into position, Ballista reflected that it said a lot about Roman thinking on the respective status of the navy and army that the captain of a *trireme* was equivalent in rank to a centurion in the legions, yet a *trierarch* commanded nearly three hundred enlisted men and a centurion usually not more than eighty.

'Surrender!' Ballista called in German.

'Fuck you!' The Borani accent was strong, but there was no mistaking the words.

'I am Dernhelm, son of Isangrim, Warleader of the Angles. I give you my word as one of the Woden-born that your lives will be spared, that you will not go into the arena.'

'Go to hell! Mercenary. Serf. Slave!'

'Think of your men.'

'They have given me their oath. It is better that we die on our feet now than live a long time on our knees. Like you!'

For two hours the bolt-throwers of the *Concordia* bombarded the Gothic ship. Out of effective bowshot, the Goths could do nothing but wait. For two hours, the awesome force of the bolts pierced the sides of the ship and tore through the leather and metal that failed to protect the soft flesh within. Some bolts ripped through two men at once, grotesquely pinning them together.

When there was no danger of resistance, Ballista ordered the *Concordia* to ram the Goth amidships.

'So many of them. They were brave men. It is a pity they all had to die,' said Ballista as the *trireme* backed away from the wreck.

'Yes,' agreed Maximus, 'they would have fetched a good price.'

Ballista smiled at his bodyguard. 'You really are a heartless bastard, aren't you?'

It was so frustrating. About half a mile to the left, Demetrius could see Cyprus, the island of Aphrodite, the goddess of love, sliding past. All his young life the Greek boy had wanted to visit her shrine there, but now there was no time to lose. It had been like this ever since the encounter with the Goths. It seemed to have energized Ballista. Fighting northern barbarians had stirred his blood in some strange way, made him keener to get at eastern ones. He had fretted away the four days on Syme that it had taken to repair the *Concordia* (the *hypozomata*, whatever that was, had needed tightening). Meanwhile, the dozen captives that had been fished out of the wreckage of the first Gothic boat were sold to slave traders. No promises had been made them; their future was not good. The *Kyrios* had paced the decks on the one-day crossing to Rhodes. His impatience was infectious, and when Cyprus appeared after three days, Maximus, Mamurra and Priscus, the acting *trierarch*, were pacing about as well.

During the crossing from Rhodes to Cyprus, the first time on the voyage when the *Concordia* had been deep out at sea, even the bookish Demetrius had realized that a *trireme* was a terribly crowded place. There was nowhere for the rowers to exercise or wash. They had to sleep at their benches. There was no provision for hot food. The routine whereby, if possible, a *trireme* came to shore twice a day – at midday for the crew to eat lunch, and again at dusk for them to take supper and sleep – now made complete sense.

The twin necessities of practicality and observing social niceties had enforced a two-day stop at New Paphos, the seat of the Roman governor of the island of Cyprus. He outranked Ballista and thus could not be ignored. The proconsul received them in a large house, well sited, towards the end of the headland, to catch any sea breezes. It had been an occasion of some formality, which had taken up much of the first day.

On the second day the travellers had each pursued their own duties or interests. Demetrius walked half a mile or so to the *agora* to buy supplies; the *kyrios*, accompanied by Calgacus, returned for more discussions with the proconsul of doings in the eternal city. Priscus and Mamurra fussed over the *Concordia*. New concerns with something called the *parexeiresia* had joined the ongoing worries about the *hypozomata*. Maximus went to a brothel and came back drunk.

The next day at dawn the *Concordia* pulled up her boarding ladders and left her mooring. The rowers took her out of harbour until a northerly air filled her sail and she stood away south-east from the island. Demetrius leant on the port rail by the stern. They were sailing away from one of the most sacred places in all the Greek world. Here, at the very dawn of time, Cronus had castrated Uranus and thrown his severed genitals into the sea. From the foam Aphrodite had been born. Somewhere just to Demetrius's left was the rock which marked where she had stepped from the scallop shell and, naked, first set foot on land.

A mile or so inland, Demetrius thought that he could see the walls of her sanctuary. This had been Aphrodite's first dwelling. It was so ancient that the cult object was not a statue made by man but a conical black stone. When taken in adultery it was here that Aphrodite had fled. Here, the Graces had bathed, anointed and dressed her, away from the anger of her husband and the laughter of the other gods.

Ballista said something that drew Demetrius's attention back onboard: 'So the great Greek historian Herodotus got it wrong.' How could the *kyrios* sit and listen to this drivel? Zoroaster, who had founded this Persian religion, was often counted as a sage, but the teachings that were peddled now were nothing but superstition and charlatanism.

Ballista continued, 'While he was right to say that a Persian boy's education consists only of being taught to ride, shoot a bow and not lie, he misunderstood the last part. Being taught not to lie does not mean that no Persian is ever economical with the truth, never alters reality just a little. Instead, it is a religious teaching that one should turn away from "the lie", meaning evil and darkness.'

Bagoas's head bobbed up and down fit to bust; Demetrius's heart sank further.

'And "the lie" is the daemon Ahriman, who is locked in perpetual combat with the god Mazda, who is light, and who is represented by your sacred *bahram* fires. And in the final battle Mazda will win and, from then, the lot of mankind will be a happy one . . . But how does all this play out in this life?'

'We must all struggle with all our might against Ahriman.'

'That includes the king Shapur?'

'Shapur above all. The King of Kings knows that it is the will of Mazda that, just as the righteous Mazda fights the daemon Ahriman, so in this world the righteous Shapur must fight all unrighteous, unbelieving rulers.' There was a gleam of certainty and defiance in Bagoas's eyes.

'So warriors are well thought of by Mazda?' Maximus, who had been sitting quietly with his eyes shut, giving every impression of being unconscious with his hangover, took up the questioning.

'Know that the Aryans are one body. The priests are the head, the warriors are the hands, the farmers are the belly, and the artisans the feet. When the unbelievers threaten the *bahram* fires, the warrior who does not do battle and who flees is *margazan*. He who does battle and is killed is blessed.'

'*Margazan*?'

'One who commits a sin for which he deserves death.'

'Blessed?'

'One who goes straight to the first of the heavens.'

*

It was five nights later, the very last night of the cruise, the middle of the night, maybe about the third watch. Ballista lay on his back. He did not move. His heart was beating fast, and he was sweating heavily. There again was the noise by the door. Already knowing what he would see, he forced himself to look. The small clay lamp was slowly going out, but it still shed enough light to illuminate the tiny cabin.

The man was huge, both tall and broad. He was wearing a shabby dark-red *caracallus*. The hood of the cloak was pulled up, and its tip touched the ceiling. He stood at the end of the bed without a word. His face was pale even in the shadow of the hood. His grey eyes shone malevolent and contemptuous.

'Speak,' commanded Ballista, although he knew what would be said.

In Latin, with an accent from the Danube, the man said, 'I will see you again at Aquileia.'

Gathering his courage, as he had many times before, Ballista said, 'I will see you then.'

The man turned and left and, after a long, long time, Ballista fell asleep.

Ballista woke to the rocking motion and the mingled smells of wood, tallow and pitch: he was safe in his small, snug cabin aboard the *Concordia*, about to embark on the final day of crossing the open sea to the *trireme*'s ultimate destination, the port of Seleuceia in Pieria. Without conscious thought he knew that the wind was westerly, on the beam of the *Concordia* as she sailed north up coast of Syria. Surfacing a little from sleep, he wondered if Priscus was keeping the ship far enough out to sea, giving her enough leeway to clear the promontory of Mount Cassios.

Suddenly all comfort left him. The vague disquiets at the back of his mind coalesced into an awful memory. *Fuck. I thought I had seen the last of him.* The sheet under him felt damp, clammy with sweat. He began to pray: 'Allfather, One-Eyed, Worker of Evil, Terrible One, Hooded One, Fulfiller of Desire, Spear-Shaker, Wanderer.' He doubted that it would do much good.

After a while he got up. Still naked, he opened the door, stepped over the sleeping Calgacus, went up on deck, and pissed over the rail. The early morning air was cool on his skin. When he returned to the cabin Calgacus was putting out his breakfast, and Maximus was eating most of it.

There was no point in asking, but he had to. 'Calgacus?' The Caledonian turned. 'Did you see or hear anything last night?' The ill-favoured old man shook his head.

'Maximus?'

The bodyguard, his mouth full of bread and cheese, also shook his head. After washing the food down with a swig of Ballista's watered wine, he said, 'You look terrible. It is not the big fellow back again, is it?'

Ballista nodded. 'Neither of you mention this to anyone. Anyone at all. The staff are jumpy enough ever since that bastard sneezed when we were setting off. Think how they would feel if they knew that their commander, their *barbarian* commander, came complete with his own personal evil daemon?'

The other two nodded solemnly.

'It could be that the staff are jumpy because they know where we are going,' suggested Maximus with a smile. 'You know, the very high probability that we are all going to die.'

'I am unfit,' said Ballista. 'Maximus, get our kit out. We need to practise.'

'Wooden practice swords?'

'No, naked steel.'

Everything was ready. It was the fifth hour of the day, just under an hour from noon. Although it was late October, it was hot. Ballista had chosen late morning for the practice fight with various things in mind. It allowed him to show politeness to the acting *trierarch* by asking his permission to practise on the deck of his warship. The delay let the crew eat breakfast and carry out any essential tasks. Above all, it gave a chance for expectation to grow, maybe even for some bets to be placed.

Ballista laced up his helmet and looked around. All the marines, deckhands and Ballista's own staff, as well as those rowers who could get permission, sat lining the rails of the ship. The audience would be well-informed. Only the marines were trained swordsmen but all aboard were military personnel. Where there were soldiers there were gladiators, and where there were gladiators there were people who thought they knew about sword fighting. Ballista stepped forward into the cleared area. The light seemed much brighter here, the space around him wider, and the deck, which until now had seemed to tilt or move hardly at all, heeled and shifted alarmingly. The sun beat down, and he squinted as he looked around at the circle of expectant faces. A low murmur ran through the crowd.

Ballista carried out his usual ritual, gripping the dagger, the scabbard of his sword and the healing stone tied to it in turn. He wondered why he was fighting. Was it a calculated attempt to impress his men? Or a way of washing away the memory of the man, dead for nearly twenty years, who had visited him last night?

Maximus now stepped into the makeshift enclosure. The Hibernian was wearing the same kit as Ballista – helmet, mail shirt, shield – but the two were carrying different swords. Maximus favoured the *gladius*, the short, primarily thrusting sword, which had long fallen out of favour with the legions but was still used by many a type of gladiator, including the *murmillo*. Ballista used the longer *spatha*, known more as a cutting weapon.

After a few fancy passes with his *gladius* – inside and outside rounds, figures of eight around his head and so on – Maximus went into the low crouch typical of a shorter man armed with a thrusting sword. Ballista found that he was twirling his *spatha* in his hand. He hastily slipped on the leather wrist loop. He got into his ready stance: upright, feet apart, weight evenly distributed, side on, shield held well away from his body, eyes looking over his left shoulder, sword raised behind his right.

Maximus came on at a run. Knowing the Hibernian's impetuosity, Ballista half expected it. Their shields collided. Letting himself be pushed backwards, Ballista stepped away to the right with his rear foot and brought his leading left foot back behind his right, turning his body through 180 degrees. His opponent's own momentum drew him in – a perfectly executed Thessalian feint. As Maximus slid past, Ballista brought his sword over, palm down and taking most of the force out of the blow, stabbed the Hibernian's shoulder. He was rewarded with a loud chink as the point of the *spatha* struck mail shirt. Less agreeably, a moment later he felt and heard the impact of Maximus's *gladius* in his back.

The two men circled and began to spar with more circumspection. Maximus, busily darting, feinting, keeping his feet moving, was doing most of the attacking.

The only other person who knew about the big man was Julia. She had been raised an Epicurean and dismissed dreams and apparitions as tricks of the mind. They came when you were tired, when you were under physical and mental stress. Ballista had not felt good since the encounter with the Borani. The words of their chief had, to some extent, struck home. Half a lifetime in the *imperium Romanum* had changed Ballista, had led him to do things he would rather not have done – and first among them was the killing of the big man. Maybe Julia was right: it was not a daemon, it was just guilt. But still . . .

Ballista jerked his head back out of the way as Maximus's *gladius* went past, far too close for comfort. Bugger, he thought. Concentrate, you fool. Watch the blade. Watch the blade. He fought best when he relied on a mixture of training, practice and instinct, letting the memory in the muscles deal with things as they happened. But his mind needed to be focussed two or three blows ahead in the fight – not on a killing seventeen years earlier.

Ballista moved to take the initiative. He shifted his weight on to his left foot and stepped forward with his right to make a cut to the head. Then, as Maximus brought his shield up to parry, Ballista altered the angle of his blow to aim at the leg. Maximus's reactions were quick. The shield came down just in time.

Maximus punched his shield towards Ballista's face. Giving ground, Ballista dropped to his right knee and swung the *spatha* in at ankle height below his opponent's shield. Again Maximus's reactions got him out of trouble.

Ballista aimed another cut at the side of the head. This time Maximus came forward, stepping inside the blow, and brought his *gladius* down in a chopping motion towards Ballista's forearm. The Angle was not quite quick enough dropping his arm. Maximus had turned the sword, but the blow from the flat of the blade hurt.

Ballista could feel his anger rising. His arm was smarting. He was buggered if he was going to be beaten in front of his own staff, bested by this cocky Hibernian bastard. His fear from the previous night mixed with the pain in his arm to form a hot jet of rage. He could feel himself losing self-control. He launched into a series of savage cuts, at Maximus's head, legs – any body part he thought he might hit. Again and again his blade nearly got through but Maximus either blocked the blow or twisted away. Finally, the opening was there. Ballista launched a vicious back-hand cut at Maximus's head. The Hibernian's face was completely open. Ballista's *spatha* could not miss. The rowing master's pipes, shrill over the noise of laboured breathing and heavy foot-falls, cut into Ballista's consciousness. At the last second he pulled the blow.

'Harbour. Seleuceia in Pieria. Off the starboard bow,' came the bow officer's call.

Ballista and Maximus stepped apart and put their swords down. Ballista physically jumped when the men cheered. It took him a moment to realize that they were cheering not the appearance of the *Concordia*'s final destination but his and Maximus's sword work. He raised a hand in acknowledgement and walked over to his bodyguard.

'Thank you.'

'Sure, it was a pleasure trying to stay alive,' replied Maximus. 'You would have slaughtered a horde of worse-trained men.'

'And in my anger I left myself open again and again to a killing blow from a good swordsman if he wanted me dead. Thank you.'

'Oh, I knew you were not really trying to kill me. I would cost a lot to replace.'

'That was my main thought.'

*

It had been a bad mistake remaining in armour. As each member of his staff appeared on deck in clean clothes, looking scrubbed and cool, Ballista inwardly cursed himself for a fool for not thinking to ask the acting *trierarch* how long it would be before the *Concordia* docked at Seleuceia. He called for some watered wine. Tired and hot from his swordplay, he was sweating profusely under the Syrian sun.

Now, there was this added delay. A big fat-bellied merchantman had made a complete mess of wearing round in the fresh westerly breeze. Somehow she had fallen foul of an imperial warship. Their bowsprits thoroughly entangled, they blocked the mouth of the canal which led to the main harbour.

Standing on the prow, Ballista checked the position of the *Concordia*. To the south off the starboard beam rose the green hump of Mount Cassios. To the south-east off the starboard quarter lay the flat, lush-looking plain of the Orontes river. Directly ahead was Seleuceia, in the foothills of Mount Pieria, which rose in a long reach to port before falling away in a series of switchbacks.

The warship, a little Liburnian galley, freed herself from the roundship, spun round and, with an interesting variety of obscene gestures from the deck, skimmed off north-west towards the Bay of Issos. Possibly chastened, the merchantman plied its sweeps to push its way into the wind until it had enough sea room to make its intended course up or down coast.

Seleuceia, the main port of Syria, had two harbours. One was a wretched thing. Little more than a semicircle open to the prevailing winds, it was widely considered unsafe, fit only for the local longshore fishermen. The other was an altogether grander affair, a huge manmade polygonal basin protected from the westerly winds by a long dog-legged canal.

Ballista was mindful of his imperial *mandata* to look to the safety of Seleuceia, if still unsure how he would carry this out when several hundred miles away in Arete. He studied the approaches to the city. As the canal was only wide enough for two warships abreast, it would be quite easy to rig up a chain or a boom to close it. There was no sign of any such thing.

The harbour was little more encouraging. It was large, and there were several merchant vessels moored, yet the whole had an air of neglect. A jetty had collapsed, and there was a large amount of floating rubbish. Of more concern to Ballista, there were only three warships in the water. The rams of another six pointed out of their ship sheds. This was the home port of the Syrian fleet, and there were just nine warships. Looking at the state of the ship sheds, Ballista doubted that any of the galleys within would be ready for action.

The *Concordia*, ignoring an impudent boy in a skiff who nearly disappeared under her ram, cut a tight circle through the harbour, came to a halt and neatly backed water to the main military dock. From the top of one of the boarding ladders, Ballista could see a well-turned-out welcoming party: sixty soldiers and a couple of officers with a standard-bearer in front. Certainly they had had plenty of time to prepare, both in the long term, as the *Concordia* was several days overdue, and in the short, as she negotiated the canal.

'The officer ordered to meet you is Gaius Scribonius Mucianus. He is the tribune commanding the auxiliary *cohors*.' Demetrius whispered the reminder in Ballista's ear. Some large Roman households would keep a special slave for such moments but in Ballista's small *familia* his secretary had to double as his *a memoria*.

The new *Dux Ripae* began to disembark. He was very aware of all the eyes on him – those of his own staff, the crew of the *trireme* and the ranks of the auxiliary soldiers. It is strangely hard to walk normally when you are conscious of being watched. As Ballista stepped off the ladder, he stumbled. The dock seemed to shift under his boot, then rush up at him. On his knees, he had to think quickly. This was embarrassing. Worse, some could take it as a bad omen. Of course it was just his land legs deserting him after three days at sea, it happened all the time. It had happened to Alexander, to Julius Caesar. They had turned it to their advantage with a few clever words. As he climbed to his feet, trying to dust down his knees in an unconcerned way, he wished he could remember what they had said.

'I have hit Asia hard.' He spread his arms wide. With a grin he turned to the *trireme*.

The crew and his staff laughed. He turned to the auxiliaries. A laugh began to spread through the ranks. It was checked by a harsh look from the officer.

'Marcus Clodius Ballista, *Vir Egregius*, Knight of Rome, *Dux Ripae*, Commander of the Riverbanks.'

It seemed unnaturally quiet after the boom of the herald's voice. Possibly there was a moment's hesitation before the officer of the auxiliaries stepped forward.

'Titus Flavius Turpio, *Pilus Prior*, First Centurion, of Cohors XX Palmyrenorum Milliaria Equitata. We will do what is ordered, and at every command we will be ready.' The man snapped a smart salute.

The silence stretched out. Ballista's hot face turned pale as his anger mounted.

'Where is your commanding officer? Why has the tribune of the *cohors* not come as he was ordered?' In his fury the tribune's name had slipped Ballista's mind.

'I do not know, *Dominus*.' The centurion looked unhappy – but shifty too.

Ballista knew this for a terrible start to his mission in Asia. To hell with the stumble, it was this snub that made it so. This bastard tribune had disobeyed a specific order. Why this deliberate and very public rudeness? Was it because Ballista was only an equestrian, not a senator? Was it – much more likely – his barbarian origins? Flagrant disobedience like this could only undermine the authority of the new *Dux* among the troops. But Ballista knew that the more he made of it the worse it would become. He forced himself to speak in a civil tone to the centurion.

'Let us inspect your men.'

'May I present the *decurion*, commander, of this *turma*, cavalry unit, of the *cohors*?' The centurion gestured to a younger man, who stepped forward.

'Titus Cocceius Malchiana. We will do what is ordered, and at every command we will be ready.'

As the three men walked across the wide dock, the centurion Turpio kept up an anxious stream of talk. 'As I am sure that you know, the Cohors XX Palmyrenorum Milliaria Equitata is a double-strength unit of archers, over one thousand men. It is a mixed unit, 960 infantry and 300 cavalry. What makes us unique in the army is our organization. The *cohors* has only six centuries of infantry and five *turmae* of cavalry, but all are at double strength. So we have 160 men not 80 in a century, and 60 not 30 cavalry in a *turma*. We have twenty men mounted on camels as well; mainly for messages and the like, although they are useful for scaring untrained horses – how horses do hate the smell of a camel, ha, ha.' Ballista wondered at the mixture of obvious pride and extreme nervousness. The rapid flow of the centurion's words stopped as it reached the line of soldiers.

There were indeed sixty men in the *turma* of Cocceius. The troopers were dismounted, horses nowhere to be seen. The men were drawn up in a line thirty across and two deep. Their cavalry helmets and waist-length scale armour were brightly polished. Swords hung in scabbards on left hips. Combined quivers and bowcases poked over left shoulders. Right hands grasped spears and on each left forearm was strapped a small round shield painted with a picture of a warrior god. Above their heads the standard of the *turma*, a rectangular green *signum*, fluttered in the westerly breeze.

Ballista took his time. He walked the lines, looking closely. The troopers were indeed well turned out. But they had had plenty of time to get ready. A parade was one thing, action quite another. He wondered if he detected a sullen, dumb insolence in the men's faces – but possibly his stumble and the non-appearance of Scribonius Mucianus were making him oversensitive.

'Very good, Centurion. Have the men had lunch?' It was the eighth hour of daylight, nearly mid-afternoon. 'No? Then let them be dismissed to their quarters. It is too late in the day to think of setting out to Antioch. We will march tomorrow. If we leave at dawn we should be there with plenty of time before nightfall. Isn't that so?'

Having been assured that his understanding was correct, Ballista announced that he would make his way up to the acropolis of the town to make sacrifice for the safe arrival of the ship.

Assessing the defences of Seleuceia in Pieria under the cloak of honouring the gods was paradoxically depressing. The town was well fortified by nature. It had ravines on three sides and the sea close by on the fourth. It was well fortified by man. It had walls of fine ashlar masonry, with tall semicircular towers well placed at intervals. The great market gate on the road to Antioch was almost a fortress in itself. The only way up to the acropolis was by twisting and turning stairways cut steeply into the rock. It was eminently defendable. And yet, three years earlier, it had fallen to the Sassanids.

The bathhouse attached to the new imperial fortress in Antioch was sumptuously decorated. Turpio thought it typical of the *imperium Romanum* these days that it was fully functioning while the fortress was unfinished. He was waiting in the corridor outside the *apodyterium*, the changing room. Under his feet was a mosaic typical of bathhouses all over the empire: a black attendant, a water vessel in each hand, a wreath of laurel on his head.

Marcus Clodius Ballista, the new *Dux Ripae*, might rejoice in the three names which were the mark of a Roman citizen but he was a complete barbarian. On their ride into Antioch he had stared about him like a bumpkin. Turpio had lead him in by the bridge gate, through the town's colonnaded streets, then over to the island in the Orontes where the new fortress was being built. Trust the present empire to send an imperial favourite – and a barbarian one at that – above a Roman who had worked his way through military service.

Turpio looked again at the mosaic. An enormous penis escaped from under the attendant's tunic. The artist had carefully detailed the bell-end in purple. Turpio laughed, as the artist had intended. Laughter was good here. Bathhouses could be dangerous places and everyone knew that laughter drove away daemons.

At last they stepped out of the *apodyterium*. Like Turpio, they were naked except for the wooden clogs which would protect their feet from the hot floors. All except Ballista carried flasks of oil, *strigils*, towels.

'Fuck me! Calgacus, it must be one of your relatives,' said the one with the nose like a cat's arse, pointing to the mosaic on the floor. 'Look at the terrible size of the thing.'

The Greek boy blushed. Ballista and Calgacus ignored the comment. Turpio, unaccustomed to such bold talk from a slave, followed their example. Ballista in the lead, they went into the *caldarium*, the hot room, the way indicated by the attendant's jutting cock.

'Is it not true, Calgacus dear, that for years you were known in Rome as Buticosus, "the big stuffer"?' The bodyguard was enjoying himself.

Turpio noted that the slave called Calgacus actually did have a large penis. Well, barbarians were notorious for it. Their big cocks were indicative of their lack of self-control in matters of sex, as in all other matters. A small penis had always been the mark of a civilized man.

'They say that only the untimely death of that magnificently perverted emperor Elagabalus prevented the *frumentarii* kidnapping Calgacus here from the public baths so that he could employ that mighty weapon on his imperial majesty.'

It was amazing that this new *Dux* let one of his slaves go on in this way in the company of freemen, of Roman citizens. It was a sign of weakness, of stupidity, a sign of his barbarian nature. All of which was good, very good. It would make it less likely that Ballista would find anything out.

It was cold and foggy. The weather had closed in during the week in Antioch. Ballista pulled his waxed cloak up around his ears. It was just before dawn, and there was no wind at all. He sat on his new grey horse by the side of the road to Beroea. He was warm enough so far, and well fed: Calgacus had somehow produced a hot porridge of oats, with honey and cream. Ballista looked up at the outside of the gate: brick built, two huge projecting square towers. There would be double gates inside, creating a good killing ground, and shuttered ports for artillery among the ornamental brickwork.

Ballista's feeling of relative well-being began to fade as he studied the scorch marks around the artillery port holes. Seven days of buying supplies and organizing a caravan had allowed time to confirm his initial impression that Antioch was a reasonably strong site. To the east, Antioch climbed up the slopes of Mount Silpius to a citadel, while the Orontes river curled round the other three sides, creating a moat. At the northern extent of the city an oxbow lake enclosed a large island. The town walls looked in decent repair. Apart from the citadel and the fortress on the island, there were several large buildings (amphitheatre, theatre, hippodrome) which could serve as improvised strong points. The wide main streets made for good interior lines of communication and reinforcement. There was a fine supply of water from the Orontes and two small streams that ran off the mountain. And, despite all this, it had fallen to the Persians.

It was a typically Greek story of personal betrayal. A member of the aristocracy of Antioch, Mariades, had been caught embezzling funds from one of the chariot teams. Escaping from certain conviction, he had turned outlaw. After a brief but initially successful career as a bandit, he had fled across the Euphrates. When Shapur invaded Syria three years ago, Mariades had acted as his guide. When the Persians encamped a short distance from Antioch, the rich fled the city. The poor, maybe more ready for a change, maybe without means of escape, stayed put. Friends of Mariades opened the gates. If promises had been made to the traitors, it seems they were not kept. The city was looted and large parts of it burnt. Mariades had returned to Persia with Shapur.

For a man ordered to look to its safety, for a siege engineer, Antioch, like Seleuceia, was most depressing. There were two straightforward conclusions to be drawn. First, the Sassanid Persians were good at taking strong, fortified places. Second, the locals were bad at defending them. Ballista wondered how many locals would prove to be like Mariades, how many might decide to go over to the Persians, or would, at least, not fight against them. The more he saw of Syria, the worse his mission looked. He wondered what had happened to Mariades.

His thoughts turned to Turpio. Why was he taking so bloody long to get this *turma* of cavalry in order of march? He and Cocceius, the *decurion*, were riding up and down the column, in and out of the pools of torchlight, shouting.

To Ballista's eyes, individually, the troopers looked the part – horses in good condition, helmets and armour cared for, weaponry complete and ready to hand. They looked tough. They handled their mounts well. But something was wrong. They did not work together as a unit. Men were getting in each other's way. They appeared sullen. There was none of the banter Ballista expected in a happy unit.

At last, Turpio appeared. He was bareheaded, his helmet strapped to his saddle. His short-cropped hair and beard were damp from the fog.

'The column is ready to march.' It always sounded to Ballista as if Turpio were challenging him to question what he said while at the same time dreading just that. He had not called Ballista *Dominus*.

'Very good. Maximus, unfurl my personal banner, and we will inspect the men.'

The bodyguard took the protective covering from the white *draco*. The windsock shaped like a dragon hung limp in the still air when he held it aloft.

Ballista squeezed his horse with his thighs, and the grey set off at a walk. They first passed the rearguard, thirty troopers under Cocceius, then the staff and baggage train under Mamurra and, finally, the advance guard of the other thirty troopers, which would be under the direct command of Turpio. Leaving aside the usual problems with the hired civilians of the baggage train, all seemed serviceable enough.

'Good. I will ride here with you, Centurion. Send out two scouts ahead of the column.'

'There is no need. There are no enemy for hundreds of miles.'

Ballista knew he needed to assert his authority. 'Have them ride about half a mile in front of the column.'

'We are just outside the main gate of the provincial capital. There is not a Persian this side of the Euphrates. No bandit would take on this number of men.'

'We need to get used to being on a war footing. Give the order.'

Turpio gave it, and two troopers clattered off into the thick fog. Ballista then gave the command to begin the march, their long march to the client kingdoms of Emesa and Palmyra, and then to the city of Arete, that isolated outpost of the *imperium Romanum*.

'It was only three years ago that there were a lot of Persians here,' he said.

'Yes, *Dominus*.'

Despite the man's attitude, Ballista decided to tread carefully. 'How long have you been with Cohors XX?'

'Two years.'

'How do you find them?'

'Good men.'

'Was Scribonius Mucianus already in command when you joined?'

'Yes.' Again, at the mention of the absent tribune's name, Turpio took on that aggressive, hunted look.

'How do you find him?'

'He is my commanding officer. It is not my place to discuss him with you. No more than it would be my place to discuss you with the Governor of Syria.' There was no great effort to hide the implicit threat.

'Did you fight the Sassanids?'

'I was at Barbalissos.'

Ballista encouraged Turpio to tell the story of the terrible defeat of the Roman army of Syria, the defeat which had led directly to the sack of Antioch, Seleuceia, and so many other towns, to so much misery in the time of troubles just three years earlier. The attack by swarms of Sassanid horse archers had seen the Romans caught in a cleft stick. If they opened ranks and tried to chase the archers away, they were run down by heavy cavalry, the *clibanarii*, mailed men riding armoured horses. If they stayed in close order to hold off the *clibanarii*, they made an ideal, dense target for the archers. Hours in the ranks under the Syrian sun, tormented by fear with the safety of the walls of Barbalissos visible in one direction, tormented by thirst with the glittering waters of the Euphrates visible in another. Then the inevitable panic, flight and slaughter.

While Ballista heard little about the battle that he had not heard before, he did gain the impression that Turpio was a proficient officer – so why then was this *turma* of Cohors XX so miserable and unhandy?

'What were the Persian numbers?'

Turpio took his time replying. 'Hard to say. A lot of dust, confusion. Probably fewer than most people think. The horse archers keep moving. Makes them look more than they are. Possibly no more than ten to fifteen thousand all told.'

'What about the proportion of horse archers to *clibanarii*?'

Turpio looked over at Ballista. 'Again, hard to be sure. But a lot more light horsemen than heavy. Somewhere between five to one and ten to one. Quite a lot of the *clibanarii* carry bows, which confuses things.'

'They were all cavalry?'

'No. The cavalry are the noblemen, they are the Sassanids' best troops, but they have infantry as well – the mercenary slingers and bowmen are the most effective; the rest are levies of peasant spearmen.'

The fog was lifting. Ballista could see Turpio's face clearly. It had lost some of its defensive look. 'How do they manage sieges?'

'They use all the devices we do: mines, rams, towers, artillery. Some say they learnt from us; maybe when the old king Ardashir took the city of Hatra some fifteen years ago.'

They were riding over one of the foothills of Mount Silpius. Dead black leaves clung to the trees which flanked the road. Wisps of fog wound round the base of the trees, slid up through the branches. As they neared the crest of the ridge, Ballista noticed one of the leaves move. Ahead, the sun was beginning to break through and Ballista realized that it was not a leaf he had seen but a bird – a raven. He peered more closely. The tree was full of ravens. All the trees were full of ravens.

This time, Ballista knew that there was no phrase or gesture that might turn the omen. A sneeze had a human explanation; so did a stumble. But ravens were the birds of Woden. On the Allfather's shoulders sat Huginn, Thought, and Muninn, Memory. He sent them out to observe the world of men. Ballista, Woden-born, carried a raven as the device on his shield, another as the crest of his helm. The eyes of the Allfather were on him. After a battle, the stricken field was thick with ravens. The trees were thick with ravens.

Ballista rode on. Some long-forgotten lines of poetry came to mind:

> The dark raven shall have its say
> And tell the eagle how it fared at the feast
> When, competing with the wolf, it laid bare the bones of corpses.

Off to the left of the road Ballista saw signs that they were within a few miles of the city of Emesa. The pattern of the fields changed abruptly. The broad, rambling, often ill-defined meadows, normal in the valley of the Orontes river, gave way to smaller, rigidly rectangular fields in grids, their boundaries clearly drawn by ditches and marker stones. This system, *centuriation*, was the product of Roman land surveyors, *agrimensores*, imposed originally when Rome settled her veterans in colonies on land taken from her enemies. Later, as here at Emesa, it was adopted by Rome's subjects, either for practical reasons or to indicate their closeness to Rome, their aspirations to become Roman. *Centuriation* had been so widespread within the empire for so long that it now seemed the natural order of things here. But to those born and bred outside the *imperium Romanum*, including Ballista himself, it still looked alien, still carried a freight of connotations of conquest and lost identity.

Ballista pulled his horse to the side of the road and waved the column on, calling out to Turpio that he would catch up in a short while. The men passed at a walk. Nine days on the road had shaken the unit down to some extent. The men seemed a little bit more disciplined and quite a lot happier. Even the civilian baggage train, thirty pack horses and their drivers and the fifteen men of his staff, was no longer the atrocious sight it had been on leaving Antioch.

It had been an easy march, never more than twenty miles in a day, billets in a town or village at almost every stop, only once camping beneath the stars. An easy march, but it had done them some good.

Ballista watched the men as they passed. How strong was their commitment to Rome? The *cohors* was a unit of the regular Roman army, but its men had been recruited from Palmyra, at once a client kingdom and a part of the Roman province of Syria Coele. Their first language was Aramaic; for those that had a second it was Greek. Their Latin was limited to army commands and obscenities. Their helmets, armour, shields and swords were Roman army issue but their combined bowcases and quivers were of an eastern design, and highly personalized. Eastern ornaments swung and clashed on the tack of their horses and their own belts and striped and brightly coloured baggy trousers beneath the Roman armour pointed to the men's eastern origins.

How would this affect his mission in the east? He had always been told that Syrians lacked the courage for a fight, and the fall of the well-fortified cities of Seleuceia and Antioch seemed to bear this out. Yet generations of being told that they were cowards may have had an effect. Possibly the cliché shaped reality rather than reflecting it. And what about the client kings of Emesa and Palmyra? Would they feel Roman enough to give Ballista the troops he had been ordered to ask for?

The looming, uneasy task of asking for troops set Ballista's thoughts back down familiar paths. Why had he not been given Roman troops to bring to the east? Anyone could see that the two units in Arete were hopelessly inadequate for the task ahead. Why had he, who had no experience of the east, been chosen to defend these remote outposts against attack?

From human worries to supernatural was an easy step for one raised in the forests and fens of northern Germania. Why had the daemon of the big man sought him out again? Ballista had been free of him this last couple of years. No matter, he had faced the bastard down many times, once when Maximinus was alive and many times since Ballista had killed him. The omen of the ravens was different. It was much worse. No mortal could win against the Hooded One, the One-Eyed, Woden the Allfather.

To shake such bad thoughts out of his mind, Ballista wheeled his grey gelding and set him to jump the ditch at the left-hand side of the road. The horse cleared it easily. With a rising yell not unlike his native *barritus*, Ballista pushed his mount into a wild gallop across the fields.

'Emesa is my kind of town,' thought Maximus. 'Get through the religion, and then it's time to plough the field.' He was not looking for any old field but a new and exotic one, with any luck, the daughter of one of the local nobles. In any event, a virgin, and a complete stranger.

It was the custom in these parts that every girl had to go up to the temple once before her marriage. There, the majority of the girls, a band of plaited string tied round their head, would sit in the sacred precinct. There, each had to wait until one of the men strolling the marked walkways threw a silver coin in her lap. Then she would go outside with him, no matter who he was, rich or poor, handsome or hideous, and let him take her virginity.

Sure, it must be tough for some of the girls (the really ill-favoured must be out there in all weathers for years) but, overall, it seemed an excellent idea to Maximus. The going outside slightly puzzled him. Surely they were already outside? Did it mean you had to hire a nearby room? Or were you talking about up against a wall in a backstreet? He had never been totally happy with that sort of thing since that unfortunate incident in Massilia.

However, that was not what had really caught his imagination. Although they could not escape the demands of their gods, the daughters of the nobility could not mix with the daughters of swineherds (actually, probably not swineherds, as these people seemed not to eat pork). They might all be forced to have sex with strangers, but certain social barriers had to be maintained. Surrounded by servants, the rich girls were driven to the temple in closed carriages. And, in those, they waited. Maximus savoured the thought.

He was even quite looking forward to the religious ceremonies.

They were said to put on a good show, these Syrians – Phoenicians, Assyrians, whatever they were. If truth be told, it was rather hard to tell what the inhabitants of the city of Emesa were. Anyway, whatever they were, they were known for the elaborate ceremonies in which they worshipped their sun god, Elagabalus.

It took place just before dawn. The audience was stationed according to rank in a semicircle around an altar, each person holding a lit torch. They began to chant, and Sampsigeramus, the King of Emesa and Priest of Elagabalus, came into view. A band of flutes and pipes struck up and Sampsigeramus began to dance around the altar. He wore a floor-length tunic, trousers and slippers, all in purple and decorated with jewels, a tall tiara and a multitude of necklaces and bangles. Others joined him in the dance, twisting and turning, crouching and leaping. The music reached a crescendo and they stopped, each striking an attitude. The audience applauded, Ballista's entourage politely, the majority rather more enthusiastically.

The lowing of cattle indicated the next stage. A large number of bullocks and sheep were driven into the semicircle. The delicate-looking priest-king delegated the killing of the first two animals but inspected the entrails himself, lifting the steaming coils in his hands. They were auspicious; Elagabalus was happy.

The ceremony ended as the first rays of sun appeared over the temple. Splendid, a bit lacking in monkeys, snakes, and severed genitals, but splendid, and now that it's over . . . Maximus's thoughts were interrupted when Ballista motioned for his entourage to follow him into the temple. Inside, there was a large golden eagle, a snake writhing in its beak. But what dominated the scene was the dark, massive bulk of the conical stone that was Elagabalus. In the candlelight, the enigmatic markings on its smooth black surface seemed to move.

The diminutive priest-king Sampsigeramus spoke to Ballista, and the northerner turned to his men.

'The god wishes to favour me with a private audience.' His voice was neutral. 'Demetrius and Calgacus, you had better wait. Mamurra, Turpio, Maximus, you are free to do what you want.' The doors of the temple shut behind him.

Maximus wondered where to start. Presumably, the whole temple complex counted as a sacred precinct. Where were the girls?

With Mamurra following, he started by looking in the street outside the main gate. There were a few carriages, but people of both sexes were getting into them and driving off. Obviously they did not contain waiting virgins. He extended his search to the streets bordering the sacred precinct. Still no luck. Then, Mamurra still in tow, he cross-quartered the grove of conifers. Finally he searched in the courtyard behind the temple.

He marched back to the temple, turning on the Greek boy. 'Demetrius, you little bum boy, you set me up! There is not one fucking carriage, not one piece of fucking string around one head. There is probably not one fucking virgin in the whole city, let alone here.' The young Greek looked apprehensive. 'You told me there were virgins here. Just like you said that there were virgins waiting in the temples at Paphos, and outside Antioch, if we had got there.'

'No, no, not at all,' Demetrius stammered. 'I just read you the famous passage in Herodotus about sacred prostitution in ancient Babylonia and said that it was rumoured that the same had happened at Old Paphos, the grove of Daphne near Antioch, and here.' The secretary's face was an image of innocence. 'And that some people said that it might still go on.'

Maximus glowered at Demetrius, then at Calgacus. 'If I find out . . .' He tailed off, and looked back at the Greek boy. 'Oh well, I suppose that'll stop you moaning about not visiting that old shrine of Aphrodite on Cyprus – there's a bloody great black stone here that's just the same.' He turned to Mamurra. 'Still, no need to waste the whole day. A good huntsman knows where to spread his nets for stags. Come, my dear prefect, we are off to draw the coverts – I will sniff them out. Pity we will have to pay full price.'

He walked away, glad that he had got in that dig at Demetrius. His precious Greek shrines were just the same as those of a bunch of Syrians, or whatever the fuck they were here in Emesa.

Another dawn, another departure. Ballista stood by his pale horse: a four-year-old grey gelding with some dappling to his quarters but otherwise white. He was finer-boned than Ballista was used to but not too delicate. He had a good mixture of spirit and docility; what he lacked in speed he made up for in stamina; and he was supremely sure-footed. Ballista was pleased with him; he would call him Pale Horse.

Man and horse flinched as the gate was thrown open and orange lamplight flooded the palace courtyard. From behind there was a muffled curse and the sound of hooves scraping on flagstones.

Sampsigeramus minced into view, stopping at the top of the stairs. Ballista handed his reins to Maximus and walked up to him.

'Farewell, Marcus Clodius Ballista, *Vir Egregius*, Knight of Rome, *Dux Ripae*, Commander of the Riverbanks. My thanks for the honour that you have shown my home.'

You odious little fucker. I bet your arse is as wide as a cistern, thought Ballista. Out loud he said, 'Farewell, Marcus Julius Sampsigeramus, Priest of Elagabalus, King of Emesa. The honour is all mine.' Ballista leant forward and assumed an expression of wide-eyed sincerity. 'I will not forget the message the god gave me, but will speak of it to no one.'

'Elagabalus, *Sol Invictus*, the Unconquered Sun, is never wrong.'

With a melodramatic swing of his cloak, Ballista turned, bounded down the steps two at a time and threw himself on his horse's back. He wheeled the horse, snapped a salute and rode out of the courtyard.

No troops. The king of Emesa would provide no troops to fight the Persians. An unambiguous refusal, followed by veiled hints about the possibility of troops being available for other purposes. As he and his party clattered off towards the eastern gate, Ballista considered why Emesa had become a hotbed of revolt. For centuries, if it existed at all, it had not troubled history. Now, in just over a generation, it had produced a series of imperial pretenders. First had come the perverted youth who was widely known by his god's name, Elagabalus (he had been despatched, shoved in a sewer in Rome in the year in which Ballista was born). Then, a few years ago, there was Iotapianus (decapitated), and only last year Uranius Antoninus, who had been dragged in chains to the imperial court.

It might be money. The ever-increasing demand of the Romans

for luxury goods had vastly increased trade from the east. Emesa was on the best trade route: India to the Persian Gulf, up the Euphrates to Arete, across the desert via Palmyra to Emesa and on to the west. It might be chance. A woman from the family of the priest-kings had married a senator called Septimius Severus, and he had later, quite unexpectedly, become emperor. Her sons had inherited the throne. Once a town has produced a couple of emperors, it feels it should produce more. It might be Roman failings. When Rome could not protect her from the Persians, the rich, confident, god-loved town of Emesa had to look to her own salvation.

The pretenders were all from different branches of the same family of priest-kings. You could see why the emperors had chosen to elevate this Sampsigeramus to the throne of Emesa. Surely if anyone in this extended family of turbulent priests would cause no trouble it was this ineffectual, mincing little man? But now he seemed to be acting true to his line: in these troubled times Emesa could not spare any men to defend Arete, a town far away and probably already doomed – but the brave men of Emesa would always answer Elagabalus's call in a just cause with a hope of success. There had been vague but not very veiled implications of revolution in the god's message to Ballista – 'the ordered world will become disordered . . . a dark-skinned reptile . . . raging against the Romans . . . a sideways-walking goat' – probably treasonous, although the obscurity of the prophetic language might make that hard to prove.

The reptile was, presumably, the Persian king. Was the goat meant to be Ballista himself? They could have come up with a rather more impressive animal, say a lion or a boar. It mattered little. He would write to the emperors with his suspicions. Despite Sampsigeramus's insinuations, Ballista doubted they would think him already implicated.

Allfather knew what sort of chaos they would find at the Palmyrene Gate. Yesterday, Ballista had agreed to a caravan owned by a merchant from Arete travelling with them. Turpio had strongly urged it. The merchant, Iarhai, was one of the leading men of Arete. It would be unwise to offend him. While it might avoid offence (had that bastard Turpio taken a bribe?), it would almost certainly cause confusion and delay, with camels, horses and civilians wandering all over the road.

The sky was a delicate pink. The few clouds were lit from underneath by the rising sun. Mamurra was standing in the middle of the road, waiting.

'How is it looking, *Praefectus*?'

'Good, *Dominus*. We are ready to march.' Mamurra had the air of wanting to say more. Ballista waited, nothing happened.

'What is it, *Praefectus*?'

'It is the caravan, *Dominus*.' Mamurra appeared troubled. 'They are not merchants. They are soldiers.'

'From what unit?'

'They are not from a unit. They are mercenaries – part of the private army of this man Iarhai.' Mamurra's almost square face looked baffled. 'Turpio . . . he said he would explain.'

Surprisingly, Turpio looked, if anything, slightly less defensive than usual. There was even the hint of a smile. 'It is quite legal,' he said. 'All the governors of Syria have allowed it. The great men of Arete owe their position to protecting caravans across the deserts. They hire mercenaries.' It was unlikely that the man was telling a straightforward lie.

'I have never heard of this, or anything like it,' said Ballista.

'It happens in Palmyra as well. It is part of what makes these two cities so different from anywhere else.' Turpio smiled openly. 'I am sure that Iarhai will explain more eloquently how it all works. He is waiting to meet you at the head of the column. I persuaded Mamurra it would be best if Iarhai's men led the way; they know the desert roads.'

Turpio and Mamurra mounted and fell in on either side of Ballista. With his bodyguard and secretary just behind, he set off at a loose canter. The white *draco* whipped above their heads. Ballista was bloody furious.

As they passed, men from Cohors XX called out the sort of well-omened things that one says before setting out on a journey. Ballista was too angry to do more than force a smile and wave.

The mercenaries were silent. Out of the corner of his eye the northerner inspected them. There were a lot; all mounted, drawn up in columns of twos, probably the best part of a hundred in all. There had been no attempt by authority to impose uniformity on them. Their clothes were of different colours, the colours faded by the sun. Some had helmets, pointed eastern or Roman ones, some none. Practicality had imposed uniformity in some things. They all wore eastern costume suitable for the deep desert: low boots, loose trousers and tunics, voluminous cloaks. They all had a long sword on a baldric, and a bowcase, quiver and spear strapped to their saddle. They looked disciplined. They looked tough. 'Marvellous, bloody marvellous, outnumbered by mercenaries we know nothing about. Bastards who are every bit as well kitted out and organized as we are,' muttered Ballista to himself.

One man waited at the head of the column. There was nothing showy about him or his mount, but it was obvious that he was in charge.

'You are Iarhai?'

'Yes.' He spoke quietly, in a voice that was used to being heard the length of a camel train.

'I was told that you were a merchant.'

'You were misinformed. I am a *synodiarch*, a protector of caravans.' The man's face backed up his words. It was deeply lined, the skin coarse, blasted by the sand. The right cheekbone and nose had been broken. There was a white scar on the left of the forehead.

'Then where is the caravan that your hundred men protect?' Ballista looked round, as much to check that none of the mercenaries was moving as for rhetorical effect.

'This was not a journey to help the merchants. It was to fulfil a vow to the sun god.'

'You have seen Sampsigeramus?'

'I came to see the god.' Iarhai remained expressionless. 'Sampsigeramus is why I needed the hundred men.'

Ballista did not trust Iarhai one inch. But there was something about his manner which was appealing, and mistrusting the prancing priest-king struck Ballista as a good thing.

Iarhai smiled, a not altogether reassuring thing. 'A lot of you westerners find it hard to believe that the empire allows the nobles of Arete and Palmyra to command troops. But let me prove that it is so.'

At a gesture, one of the riders moved forward, holding a leather document case. It took Ballista a moment to realize that it was a girl, a beautiful girl dressed as a man, riding astride. She had very dark eyes. Black hair escaped from under her cap. She hesitated, holding the case out.

They are not sure if a northern barbarian can read, thought Ballista. He pushed aside his irritation (Allfather knew he had practice). It could be useful if they believed he could not. 'My secretary will tell us what they are.'

As she leant across to hand the case to Demetrius, her tunic pulled tight across her breasts. They were bigger than Julia's. She looked more rounded in general, a touch shorter. But fit from riding.

'They are letters thanking Iarhai for guarding caravans, from various governors of Syria and some from emperors – Philip, Decius, others – Iarhai is sometimes referred to as *strategos*, general.'

'I must apologize, *Strategos*. As you say, we westerners do not expect such a thing.' Ballista held out his right hand. Iarhai shook it.

'Do not mention it, *Dominus*.'

It was not just the girl that had made Ballista decide that he would ride with Iarhai in the lead; it was Turpio's discomfort in his presence.

The white *draco* of Ballista and the elaborate flag of Iarhai, a semicircle with streamers, a red scorpion on a white background, flew over the head of the column. The green *signum* was halfway down, where the eighty mercenaries ended and the sixty men of Cohors XX began. Iarhai had sent ten of his men ahead as an advance guard, while another ten had been despatched as flanking guards.

'Tell me about the weather at Arete,' said Ballista.

'Oh, it is delightful. In the spring there are gentle breezes and every little depression in the desert is filled with flowers. One of your western generals said the climate was healthy – apart from dysentery, malaria, typhoid, cholera and plague,' answered Iarhai.

The girl, Bathshiba, smiled. 'My father is teasing you, *Dominus*. He knows that you want to know about the campaigning season.' Her eyes were jet-black, confident and mischievous.

'And my daughter forgets her place. Since her mother died I have let her run wild. She has forgotten how to weave, and now rides like an Amazon.'

Ballista saw that she was not only dressed but also armed like her father's men.

'You want to know when the Persians will come.' It was a statement. Ballista was still looking at her when Iarhai again began to speak.

'The rains come in mid-November. We may be lucky and reach Arete before they fall. They turn the desert into a sea of mud. A small force like ours can get through, if with difficulty. But it would be much more difficult to move a large army. If that army was encamped before a town, it would be impossible to get supplies through to it.'

'For how long will Arete be safe?' Ballista saw little point in denying what they clearly already knew.

'The rains tend to stop in January. If it rains again in February it means a good growing season.' Iarhai turned in his saddle. 'The Sassanids will come in April, when there is grass for their horses and no rain to ruin their bowstrings.'

Then we must survive until November, thought Ballista.

It was the improbability of Palmyra's location that first struck Mamurra. It was a completely unlikely place to find a city. It was as if someone had decided to build a city in the lagoons and marshes of the Seven Seas at the head of the Adriatic.

It had taken six days to get there from Emesa, monotonous days of tough travel. There was a Roman road, and it was in good repair, but the journey had been hard. Two days climbing up to the watershed of the nameless range of mountains, four days coming down. In the first five days they had passed through one hamlet and one small oasis. Otherwise there had been nothing, an endless jumble of dun-coloured rock echoing back the noise of their passage. Now, suddenly, on the afternoon of the sixth day, Palmyra appeared before them.

They were in the Valley of the Tombs. Horses, camels and men were dwarfed by the tall, rectangular tombs which lined the steep sides of the valley. Mamurra found it unsettling. Every town had a necropolis outside it but not of towering, fortress-like tombs like these.

As *Praefectus Fabrum*, he was kept busy sorting out the baggage train, trying to stop it becoming entangled with the seemingly endless traffic heading to town. Most of the traffic was local, from the villages to the north-west, donkeys and camels carrying goatskins of olive oil, animal fat and pine cones. Here and there were traders from further west bringing Italian wool, bronze statues and salt fish. It was some time before he had been free to look at Palmyra.

To the north-east were at least two miles of buildings, row after row of ordered columns. Gardens stretched a similar distance to the far corner of the walls to the south-east. The city was huge, and it was evidently wealthy.

Its walls were mud-brick, low and only about six foot wide. There were no projecting towers. The gates were just that – simple wooden gates. On the heights to the west the walls did not form a continuous barrier. Rather, there were isolated stretches of wall intended to reinforce natural barriers. A wadi ran through the town, and the gardens pointed to a water source within the walls, but the aqueduct that ran from the necropolis would be easy enough to cut. Slowly, and with care, Mamurra came to the conclusion that the defences of the city were not good. He had once been a *speculator*, an army scout, and every abandoned identity left its mark. Mamurra was proud of this insight; the more so as he could not voice it.

There was a great hubbub at the gate but eventually they moved inside. The men and animals were allocated their quarters and

Mamurra went to find Ballista. The *Dux* was standing waiting with Maximus and Demetrius.

'His name is Odenaethus,' the Greek boy was reminding Ballista. 'In Greek or Latin, he is known as the King of Palmyra. In their native dialect of Aramaic, he is the Lord of Tadmor. He speaks perfect Greek. It is thought that he put at least thirty thousand horsemen in the field against the Persians three years ago in the time of troubles.'

Iarhai, together with that wanton-looking daughter of his, approached on horseback. Mamurra and the rest mounted. Ballista requested Iarhai to guide them to the palace of Odenaethus, and they set off, progressing slowly through the busy colonnaded streets lined with shops. They were a riot of colour. The smell was overpowering but not at all unpleasant, exotic spices mixed with the more familiar odours of horse and humanity. They negotiated a fine square, passed an *agora* and a theatre, and arrived at the palace, to be ushered in with courtly grace by a waiting chamberlain.

Apart from stepping forward when presented and then stepping back again, Mamurra had no part to play in the reception of the new *Dux Ripae* by Odenaethus, King of Palmyra, so he was able to focus on the people playing their parts. Odenaethus made a brief formal speech of welcome: great distances had been unable to diminish Ballista's martial reputation . . . all confidence for the future now he was here, etc, etc. Ballista's reply, after an equally fatuous beginning, ended with a polite but unambiguous request for troops. Odenaethus then dwelt at length on the unsettled nature of the east since the Persian invasion – brigands everywhere, the Arabs, tent-dwellers stirring up to a fury of avarice; he was devastated, but all his men were employed holding, and only just holding, the peace in the desert.

It was hard to number the things that Mamurra disliked about Odenaethus, the Lord of Tadmor, and his court. You could start with the king's carefully curled and perfumed hair and beard. Then there was the delicate way he held his wine cup with just thumb and two fingers, the embroidered stripes and swags of his clothes, the soft, plump cushions he sat on, again thick with patterns, reeking of perfume. And, if anything, his court was even worse. The chief minister, Verodes, and the two generals were outfitted as copies of their lord, and the latter had virtually identical ridiculous barbarian names, Zabda and Zabbai. There was a simpering little son who looked like he should be selling his arse on a street corner and, to add insult to injury, both sitting there as bold as could be, were not only a eunuch (probably some sort of secretary if he was not part of the entertainment) but a woman (a sly-looking bitch called Zenobia – Odenaethus's new wife).

'It must be because it is in the middle of nowhere,' Mamurra quietly said to Ballista. The reception was over. They were outside again waiting for their horses.

'What must?'

'This place.' Mamurra waved his hand around. 'Palmyra is as rich as Croesus. Has fuck all in the way of defences, and is held by a bunch of effeminates with fewer balls than their eunuchs or women. Its safety must lie in it being in the middle of nowhere. If you ask me, it is a good thing they are too scared to give us any troops.'

Ballista paused before speaking. 'I think that is exactly the conclusion I would have come to if I had not spent so long talking to Iarhai. Now I am not so sure.'

Mamurra did not reply.

Ballista smiled. 'Cohors XX was originally raised here, and still draws most of its recruits from here. They seem tough enough. Then again, there are Iarhai's mercenaries. Some are recruited from among the tent-dwellers, the nomads of the desert, but the majority come from here or Arete. Both towns have a tradition of mercenary service – for the Romans and for others.'

The horses were led up. As they mounted, Ballista continued, 'You and I expect warriors to look like warriors, a grizzled Roman or a hairy northern barbarian. Maybe in this case appearances are deceptive. Maybe not all easterners are cowards.'

'I am sure that is the way it is.' Mamurra was not sure. But he would not dismiss the idea out of hand. As was his measured way, he would mull it over.

In truth, Ballista's thoughts had been ranging wide when Mamurra's words had pulled him back. Ranging in many, many directions but always circling back to the refusal of the king of Palmyra, and before him the refusal of the king of Emesa, to supply troops. It was not that these Syrians were afraid to fight; they had fought three years before. It was that they did not want to fight. Why? Palmyra and Emesa depended for their wealth on trade passing between Rome and her eastern neighbour. They were poised between Rome and Persia. To refuse Ballista's request was in effect to refuse the request of the Roman emperors. Had they decided to incline to Persia? And then there was the confidence with which they turned him down, almost as if there could be no reprisal by the Roman emperors, nor even any lingering ill will. Had the emperors covertly told them that they could refuse Ballista's request? Did they all expect Ballista to fail?

The three *frumentarii* were in the sort of environment they liked, a backstreet bar. It was dark, dingy and secure. Their cover was in place. To anyone glancing in they looked like two scribes and a messenger having a few drinks, only a few, because their *dominus* had ordered yet another dawn departure. Tomorrow they would set out on the last leg of their long journey to Arete.

The *frumentarius* from the Subura placed three coins on the table. 'What do you think?'

From the three *antoniniani* three not all that dissimilar profiles of men wearing radiate crowns stared fixedly off to their viewers' right.

'I think that the rise in prices is appalling. But, working on the theory that a girl charges about a soldier's daily pay, you should still get a good-looking one for that,' said the Spaniard.

The *frumentarii* all laughed.

'No, Sertorius, you sad fuck, I wanted you to look at the heads on the coins, and think where we have been.' The Roman picked up one of the coins. 'Mariades, a rebel based in Antioch.' Then the other two. 'Iotapianus and Uranius Antoninus, two more rebels, both based in Emesa. And where have we been? Antioch then

Emesa. Our barbarian *Dux* has taken us on a tour of the sites of recent revolutions. He is seeing if there are still embers of revolt.'

They drank in silence for a time.

'Possibly we should go in the other direction. Arete to Palmyra to Emesa gives you the western end of the shilk road,' said the North African.

'So what, Hannibal?' The Roman was as sharp as ever.

'The revenues from taxing the shilk road could fund any sort of uprising.'

'I am still not convinced that there is a silk road,' said the one from Spain.

'Oh, don't start all that again, Sertorius. You really do come up with some ludicrous theories. The next thing you will do is claim that this barbarian is not up to something. And we all know he is, that he is plotting treason because, otherwise, the emperor would not have assigned all three of us to this case.'

Unseen behind the curtain, a fourth *frumentarius* watched and listened. He was pleased with what he heard. His three colleagues were perfect – an object lesson in the dangers of *frumentarii* working as a team: the rivalry, the hothouse atmosphere that forced the growth of ever larger, ever more ludicrous conspiracy theories. To give them credit, perhaps they were all playing a duplicitous game. If one of them came up with a conspiracy plausible enough to convince the emperors, he would not be so stupid as to wish to share the glory of its discovery, let alone the advancement and material benefits that would follow. In any case, they were still perfect in another way: the *Dux Ripae* almost certainly suspected there were *frumentarii* on his staff, and if he searched, he would find these three long before they found him.

Praeparatio
(Winter AD 255–256)

VI

The distance as the crow flies from Palmyra to Arete was a matter of some debate. Turpio thought it only about 120 miles; Iarhai considered it nearer 150. It mattered little. Both accepted that it was far further by road – and what a road. It made the previous journey from Emesa to Palmyra seem like a gentle ride in an ornamental Persian game park, one of those parks the Persians called a *paradise*. The first three days were not too bad, a Roman road running north-east, with a village to stop at every night. On the fourth day they turned due east and, from then on, they followed an unmade caravan track. It took them three days to come down from the mountains. Then they were in the desert.

Despite his years in north Africa, Ballista, like so many northerners, expected a desert to consist of miles of golden sand dunes, something like a larger version of the beaches of his childhood but without the sea. The desert here was nothing like that. There was sand, but the dominant feature was the multitude of rocks, sharp, hard rocks lurking to lame animals, and under the rocks were scorpions and snakes waiting to wound humans.

The caravan crept from well to well. It averaged probably little more than ten miles a day. Every day was the same as the last. In the saddle before sunrise, then man and beast sweating in the heat of the day. Every mile or two a halt would have to be called as an animal went lame or lost its load. The silence was broken only by the footfall of the animals, the creak of leather and the occasional mechanical curse from the men.

The seemingly endless repetition of the days put Demetrius in mind of Sisyphus, punished in the underworld by having to roll a huge stone up a sharp incline every day only to see it bounce back down again. Ballista thought of Skoll the wolf who chases the tail of the sun. Maximus worried a lot about snakes.

On the sixth day a range of steep hills appeared in the distance ahead. They were almost there: Arete could be seen clearly from the crest of the hills. Ballista set off at a fast canter, ahead of the column. Maximus, Demetrius and a newly appointed standard-bearer, a Palmyrene who on joining the Roman army had taken the ludicrously Roman name of Romulus, spurred after him. The *draco* he held snapped and whistled in the air.

Ballista sat on his pale horse on the summit and looked down at the city of Arete. It was about a mile away, and 300 feet below him. From this vantage point he could see into the city and make out its chief features. His first appraisal was quite encouraging.

On the far side, to the east, at the bottom of what appeared a steep cliff, the Euphrates. It justified its reputation as one of the great rivers, one of the *limes imperii*, the limits of the empire. It was enormous, as big as the Rhine or the Danube. Like them, it did not run in just one course. There were several islands in it, a largish one quite near the town. Yet so broad was the Euphrates that there was no realistic chance of the enemy crossing it without amassing a huge number of boats or building a bridge. Either way would take time, could not be hidden and could be opposed.

To the north and south the city was bounded by ravines. The engineer in Ballista imagined the waters from the winter rains gouging them out from the weaknesses in the rock over millennia. The southern ravine was the shorter. It ran close to the walls, rising to the level of the plain some 300 yards beyond the town. There was a bit more of a gap between the walls and the lip of the northern ravine, although of only a few yards. This ravine split in two, one spur curling around the western wall of the town, the other disappearing off towards the hills to the north-west. For the majority of their course both ravines were at least 200 yards across – just within the range of effective artillery fire.

The obvious line of attack was from the west. From the foot of the hills a flat dun-coloured plain ran to the city walls. Apart from scattered rocks, it had no natural features whatsoever.

Ballista studied the scene with a professional eye. From this distance the walls looked fine; tall, and in good condition. He could see five rectangular towers projecting from the southern and eastern walls, three in the northern, and no fewer than fourteen in the western. The walls facing the plain and the Euphrates boasted fortified gates, each with its own flanking towers. A group of men with donkeys was approaching the main gate, probably peasants bringing in produce from the villages to the north-west. Using them as a measure, Ballista estimated that the wall facing the plain was almost a thousand yards long. That meant an average distance between the projecting towers of about sixty-six yards. Although the towers towards the northern end clustered closer together, undermining the average, a careful look indicated that no two towers were as far as a hundred yards apart. This was all good. The projecting towers allowed defenders to aim missiles along as well as away from the walls. Most of the gap between the towers was within effective javelin range; all was within effective bowshot. An attacker approaching the wall would thus face missiles coming from three directions. The builders of the walls of Arete had concentrated their resources (towers took time and cost money) on what appeared to be the right place.

The only obvious problem was the necropolis. Tomb after tomb – at least five hundred of them, he roughly calculated, probably more, stretching out about half a mile from the western wall, halfway to the hills. And they were like the ones at Palmyra: tall, square stone-built towers. Each one provided cover from missiles fired from the walls of the town. Each one was a potential artillery platform for attackers. Together, they were a huge, ready-to-hand source of materials to build siege works. They were going to make his life very difficult, in more ways than one.

Ballista shifted his attention to inside the walls. Beyond the desert gate the main street of Arete ran straight, other streets opening off it at set intervals at exact ninety-degree angles. The arrangement of neat rectangular blocks covered the town, breaking down only in the south-east corner, where there was a jumble of twisting lanes. In the north-west corner Ballista could see an open area, probably the *campus martius*, the army parade ground that Turpio had mentioned.

Ballista scanned the town again, this time for what was *not* there: no theatre, no circus, no obvious *agora* and, above all, no citadel.

His appraisal was mixed. The open area and the neat Hippodamian plan of regular town blocks would facilitate the assembly and movement of defending troops. But if the enemy breached the walls, there was no second line of defence, nor any suitable buildings from which to improvise one, and the regularity of the city's layout would then help the attackers. So many men were going to die in Arete the following spring.

'The *kyrios* is thinking!' Demetrius's furious stage whisper cut into Ballista's thoughts. He turned in the saddle. Maximus and Romulus looked impassively through and beyond their commander. Demetrius had turned his horse across the path.

'Let her through, Demetrius.'

Bathshiba smiled at the Greek boy, who was obviously trying not to glower back. She drew her horse alongside the northerner's.

'So, you are thinking, is it worth it?' she asked.

'In a sense. But I imagine not in whatever sense you mean.'

'Is it worth it for a famous Roman general and northern warrior such as yourself to travel all this way to defend a fly-blown dump like this? That is what I mean. And a fly-blown dump full of luxurious, decadent Syrian effeminates.'

'My people tell a story – obviously in the few moments when we are not painting ourselves blue, getting drunk or killing each other – that one evening a strange man appeared before Asgard, the home of the gods, and offered to build a wall around it if the gods let him have Freyja, the beautiful goddess.'

'I am not sure that my father, or your wife, would appreciate your attempts at paying me compliments.'

Ballista laughed. 'I am sure they would not. And I am sure that you are not here just for my company.'

'No, my father wants your permission to send a messenger ahead so that our people are ready. His messenger can also tell the town councillors, so that they come to meet you at the gate.'

Ballista thought for a moment. 'Of course your father may send a messenger to your own people. But I will send one of my staff to tell the other councillors. Thank your father for his offer.' That is one political upset avoided, thought Ballista.

Bathshiba wheeled her horse. 'And did the stranger get her?'

'No, the gods tricked him. The stories of the north tend not to have happy endings.'

Anamu was waiting for the new *Dux Ripae* at the gate of Arete.

The column of dust was leaving the hills and heading for the town. At least the new barbarian overlord had the good manners, or had been well enough advised, to send a messenger. In fact, almost everything had been ready for some days and, that morning, the scouts that Anamu had posted on the crest of the hills had reported that the new *Dux Ripae* was at hand. Ogelos's men had been there as well.

Anamu looked across the road at Ogelos. As often, Anamu was irritated by the ostentatious simplicity of his dress: the plain tunic to mid-calf belted with a white cord, the nondescript pointed white hat, the bare feet. The image of a simple, otherworldly priest was undercut by Ogelos's ridiculously trimmed and tweaked two-pointed beard (going grey, Anamu noted with satisfaction). Ogelos held a palm branch in one hand, a jug, bowl and two knives in the other. He stood by a tall vase of holy water and a portable altar. A haze of heat wavered above it. The fire had been lit in good time; there was no longer any smoke. Ogelos was organized. Anamu had never underestimated him.

Behind Ogelos was an acolyte in a deliberately contrasting magnificent costume in scarlet and white. He held an incense burner and a rattle. Behind the boy, and clad like Ogelos, were two burly priests waiting with the sacrificial bull.

The other priests were standing back towards the gate. All the religious groups in Arete were represented: the priests of Zeus Megistos, Zeus Kyrios, Zeus Theos, Atargatis, Azzanathcona and Aphlad, of Bel and Adonis, and many more. Even the priests of the groups that denied the gods of the others existed were there – the head of the synagogue, and the leader of the Christians.

Legionaries from the *vexillatio* of Legio IIII Scythica stationed in Arete lined the last hundred yards of the road to the gate. Their presence was both to show respect for the new *Dux* and to keep back the *demos*, the lower classes – not that any trouble was expected. Their commander, Marcus Acilius Glabrio, the only one mounted, sat on a very fine chestnut in the middle of the road blocking the gateway exuding an air of calm superiority.

On Anamu's side of the road stood the majority of the council, bedecked in embroidered togas, bracelets, amethysts and emeralds, and their precious walking sticks, with silver knobs, and golden tops wonderfully carved. There was little division between religion and politics in Arete. Most of the priests were also councillors, and every man was the head of religion in his household. The real divisions were those between the three leading men of the town.

In our fathers' day there must have been thirty caravan protectors in Arete, thought Anamu. Even two years ago there had been a dozen. But it had taken skill to avoid exile, to remain alive when the city first opened its gates to the Persians, then rose up and massacred their garrison. Now there were three. Ogelos had survived, prospered, his treacheries masked by his false piety as priest of Artemis. Iarhai had fled to the Romans, returned and organized the massacre. He had always been like a bull at a gate; sudden changes of heart, a burning certainty that he was right. Anamu had not had strong feelings about either the arrival of the Persians or their violent end. He saw himself as a tamarisk bending with the wind, possibly one of those groves of tamarisks on this side of the Euphrates, one that conceals a wild boar. Anamu played with the image; poetry was very dear to his soul.

The column of dust was high now, its leading point halfway across the plain. Everything was ready. As the year's *archon*, the leading magistrate, it was Anamu's duty to make sure it was. Barley, hay, suckling pigs, full-grown pigs, dates, sheep, oil, fish sauce, salt fish – all had been delivered to the palace of the *Dux Ripae*. He ticked them off in his mind; all were to be paid for by the *Dux*. Profit and poetry sat easily together in Anamu's soul.

Further along the road into the plain the band struck up. The drums and stringed instruments laid down fast, chopping rhythms while the whistles soared above. A children's choir joined in, to herald the *adventus*, the ceremonial arrival of the new *Dux*.

First rode a standard-bearer, with a standard in the shape of a dragon; the wind whistling through it made it writhe and hiss like a real beast. A couple of lengths behind came the new *Dux Ripae*. He cut a dramatic, if barbaric figure.

'You bastard, Iarhai!' Anamu was not sure if he had said it out loud. The music would cover it anyway. *You devious bastard!* Anamu had expected to see Iarhai. He had known for some time that Iarhai was travelling with the *Dux* (he expected that Ogelos knew it as well). But he had not expected to find Iarhai's men leading the column. It looked less like Iarhai was travelling with the new *Dux* than that he was escorting him, protecting him. 'You conniving reptile, you . . .' Anamu stopped at the same time as the band and choir.

The *Dux Ripae* pulled his horse to a halt. He lifted his right hand, palm forward, the ritual gesture of benevolent greeting and power. The townsmen of Arete lifted their right hands in return and began the acclamations.

'May the gods keep you! May the gods keep you! May the gods keep you!'

You camel-fucking bastard! Outwardly, Anamu was waving his palm branch and chanting with the rest. Inwardly, he was raging. You fucking pimp! How could you prostitute your only daughter?

Bathshiba and Iarhai had walked their horses forward. They halted just behind the *Dux*. Iarhai caught Anamu's eye, and his battered face smiled a slight smile.

Anamu had not survived the time of troubles by giving way to his emotions. By the time the chanting was done he was fully in control. He watched as Ogelos dipped the palm branch into the tall vase, flicked the holy water, threw handfuls of incense on to the altar, poured a libation and drew his knife across the throat of the bull. The bull behaved and died in a not inauspicious way.

The sophist Callinicus of Petra stepped forward to make the formal speech of welcome. Ogelos claimed to prefer simple truths simply said, and Iarhai made no secret that display oratory bored him, but Anamu had been looking forward to it. Appreciation of the art of rhetoric was one of the signs of a cultured man.

'With fortunate omens have you come from the emperors, brilliant as a ray of the sun that appears to us on high . . .' The introduction, based on joy as was the tradition, had been solid enough. How would he deal with the main body of the speech, focussing on the subject's actions, his native city or nation and his family? 'You will face up to danger like a good helmsman, to save the ship as the waves rise high . . .' Straight to theoretical virtues, a good move. The orator had wisely avoided mention of the *Dux*'s origins; and they knew nothing as yet of his actions. It continued in the same vein, courage followed by justice, temperance and wisdom, and finally, the epilogue, 'We have come to meet you, all of us, with joy . . . calling you our saviour and fortress, our bright star . . . a happy day dawns out of darkness.' Callinicus ended with a sophist's flourish, breathing heavily and wiping away the sweat to show the effort of *extempore* composition.

Not bad, thought Anamu – although Callinicus's stuff always smelt of the lamp. It would be interesting to see how the barbarian got on with his reply. It was tradition to speak of having long yearned to see the gymnasia, theatres, temples and harbours of the city. This would be difficult enough, even if the *Dux* were not a barbarian, with a city he had almost certainly never heard of before his orders came, and which lacked gymnasia, theatres and, unsurprisingly in the middle of a desert, harbours.

'The *Dux* began:

'In the past I was distressed and grieved. I could not behold the loveliest city on which the sun shines down. Now I see her, I cease from grief, I shake off distress. I see all I longed for, not as in a dream, but the walls themselves, the temples, the colonnades, the whole city a harbour in the desert.'

Impressive the way he cut straight into what would normally be the second section. The whole city as a harbour was clever. Now he was off into a lengthy encomium of the mighty Euphrates – river and god, unsleeping guardian, unwearying road, bringer of food and riches. After nature came nurture: the people of Arete were hospitable, law-abiding, dwelt in harmony and treated strangers as they did each other. All very well – despite the unintentional irony of the last point.

The *Dux* ran through accomplishments and actions and returned in the brief epilogue to the city as a harbour in the sea of the desert.

Anamu felt his uneasiness lift. This barbarian had been worth waiting for. He spoke good Greek. He understood eloquence and speechmaking. Anamu could deal with him.

The civil side of the ceremony of *adventus* had passed off well. Now Ballista issued a volley of commands: he felt it was important to be seen to be in charge from the beginning. First he would sacrifice to the *tyche* of the city and other gods for the safe arrival of the column, then he would go to his official residence, the 'palace'. In two hours' time he would address the council.

Civic affairs may have gone without a hitch at the gate, but the same could most certainly not be said for the military side of things.

A military officer, his horse across the road, had blocked Ballista's entry into the town.

'Marcus Acilius Glabrio, *Tribunus Laticlavius*, commanding the *vexillatio* of Legio IIII Scythica in Arete.' His accent and manner would have shown him to be from an old Roman senatorial family if his title *Laticlavius* had not already done so.

He had not dismounted to meet the new *Dux*. Ballista took one look at the supercilious young man on his elaborately outfitted horse and disliked him instantly.

'We will do what is ordered, and at every command we will be ready.' Ballista had never heard the standard army formula spoken with less respect.

'I will inspect your men tomorrow at the second hour of daylight on the *campus martius*,' said Ballista.

'As you wish.' Glabrio did not add *Dominus*. This was proving something of a habit among the officers in the eastern provinces.

'And then at the fourth hour we will inspect the accounts of your unit in the military headquarters building.'

'I will tell the *exactor* and *librarius*.' Glabrio's tone implied that he left such things to his accountant and secretary.

His attitude promised trouble, but at least, so far, he had not directly disobeyed orders – unlike the commander of Cohors XX. Again, as at Seleuceia, there was no sign of Gaius Scribonius Mucianus. There was no likelihood that Ballista would ever forget the tribune's name now. What was this bastard Scribonius doing? This second deliberate snub was even worse than the first. It was one thing that Scribonius had failed to travel to Antioch to greet his new *Dux*, even though such had been his orders, it was quite another not even to bother to go to the city gate. It could only be a deliberate attempt to undermine the authority of Ballista's new command, to wreck the northerner's mission almost before it had started.

Ballista looked around. There was Turpio, clearly wishing he was somewhere else.

Glaring at him, Ballista said, '*Pilus Prior*, I want Cohors XX on the *campus martius* at the third hour tomorrow. The unit accounts will be inspected at the sixth hour.'

Turpio curtly acknowledged the order. Whatever rapport the long journey had fostered between the two professional soldiers had dropped away as if it had never existed. Turpio's face was closed and hostile.

'Tell your tribune that if he values his future he should attend.'

Ballista was certain that Turpio knew more about Scribonius's absence than he would willingly say. Accepting that he would find out nothing in front of a large audience of troops and half the population of the town, he turned away.

Having made sacrifice, and bathed in his new palace, Ballista walked to the temple of Artemis. There, at the threshold of what passed for a *bouleuterion*, town hall, he stood and waited. He did not feel at all nervous about the speech he had to make now. It was not like his earlier one; this one had a hard edge of reality to it.

The precinct of Artemis took up the whole block. The council used a smallish building in the south-east corner. It said a lot about the political balance between rich and poor in this town that the *bouleuterion* could be removed from the *agora*, that the councillors felt free to meet in seclusion, away from the common people.

'*Dominus*, would you please step this way?' said the *archon*.

Demetrius whispered his name in Ballista's ear. Anamu was a strange-looking man. It was not intentional. His dress was a formal toga with a narrow purple stripe and his full beard and receding hair were conventionally cut. It was his head that was the problem: his face was far too long and his eyes were far too wide, their turned-down corners matching those of his mouth.

Anamu led them into a U-shaped room containing about forty men, the councillors of Arete. 'Marcus Clodius Ballista, *Vir Egregius*, *Dux Ripae*, welcome.' Anamu sat down where his name was inscribed in the first tier. Only Iarhai and Ogelos the priest of Artemis were already seated there. Many of the other names in the front tier had been defaced. Obviously, politics was a deadly business in this town. These three survivors were the men who really mattered. Yet it would not be safe to discount the other councillors. Ballista saw that most of the priests who had met him at the gate sat as councillors, including the hirsute Christian priest.

It was quiet. Motes of dust moved in the sunlight. Ballista began to speak.

'Councillors, you must prepare yourselves for very great sacrifices. The Sassanid Persians are coming. Next spring they will advance up the Euphrates. They will be led by Shapur, the King of Kings himself. As the people of Arete massacred his garrison last year, he will stop at nothing to take the city. If he succeeds, the living will envy the dead.' Ballista paused. 'I have been sent by the emperors Valerian and Gallienus with full powers to ready Arete for defence. We can hold out until the great Valerian brings an imperial field army to our aid. But it will be difficult. I will need your unquestioning help. You can be sure that if we do not all hang together, we will all hang separately on the cross of crucifixion.'

It had been a long, long day. Ballista found it hard to believe that he had seen Arete for the first time that morning. He sat sideways on the low wall of the terrace. The Euphrates was 250 feet below him. There were groves of tamarisk and the occasional date palm on this side; on the other cultivated fields stretched almost as far as he could see. A pair of plovers chased each other over the river. Julia would love it here. Bathshiba would too.

'I will have a drink, thank you.'

Maximus poured the watered wine and put the jug down carefully. He sat on the wall, one knee bent, facing Ballista. Neither felt the need for formality when alone.

'It is not good, your *palace*.' Maximus gave the word a strange emphasis and smiled. 'It is a death trap.' He took a drink. 'The first courtyard is all right, just the one great gate. The second has no security at all. There is a gate in the north wall for the stables, a gate in the south for the kitchens, and doors connecting back to the first courtyard and through here.' He nodded at the private apartments of the *Dux*. 'The doors are not the real problem. The walls are low, easy to climb. There is open ground to the south but buildings come right up to us on the north. In at least three places you could jump from one roof to another.' He took another drink and picked up an olive.

'Demetrius.' Ballista waved the young Greek over from where he had been waiting politely across the terrace. 'Help yourself to a drink, and sit down.'

The boy sat cross-legged on the floor.

'We must get some furniture out here.' As Ballista spoke, Demetrius produced a hinged wooden writing block and, with a stylus, wrote in the wax. 'So how does it look?'

Demetrius produced a piece of scrap papyrus. He studied his neat small writing. 'Overall, fine, *Kyrios*. In fact, we have too many provisions, far too much wine. We do not have enough papyrus but, apart from that, we have no worries about quantity or quality.

The problem lies with the cost. I will make enquiries in the *agora* before we pay out a *denarius* to the *archon*, that man Anamu.'

'That's easterners for you,' said Maximus. 'They know an illiterate northern barbarian eats like a pig and drinks like a fish, and then they cheat him.'

The Greek secretary looked slightly pained. The three drank and ate in silence.

Ballista watched a boat make its crossing from the far bank. The current was very strong and the boat had set out a long way upstream to compensate. The two oarsmen pulled hard, taking the opportunity to rest when they could get into the shelter of one of the islands. They set off again. The angle looked right to bring them to the main jetty at the foot of the steep steps up to the *porta aquaria*, the water gate.

From the doorway came a strangled coughing, the closest thing to a formal introduction Calgacus could manage. Mamurra took it as such, and walked out from the portico.

Ballista got off the wall. '*Praefectus*.'

'*Dominus*.' They shook hands.

'Please give me your report.'

'We will do what is ordered, and at every command we will be ready.' Mamurra stood very straight. 'I have chosen twenty men from Cohors XX to be your *equites singulares*, your horse guard. Ten for the nightwatch, ten for the day. I have posted two at the main gate, one each at the stable and kitchen gates, and another at the door to your apartments. The remaining five on duty are to be in the guardroom opening off the first courtyard. When off duty the men remain billeted and the horses stabled where they were.'

'It is good, *Praefectus*.'

Mamurra stood more at ease. 'All your staff are settled into the servants' quarters in the southern range. They have been fed. It has been a long journey. I gave all except one messenger leave for the night. I hope that is all right.'

Mamurra declined a drink when offered one by Ballista. He left and Ballista asked Calgacus to fetch Bagoas; he could sing some songs from his homeland to pass the evening.

One Moment in Annihilation's Waste
One Moment, of the Well of Life to taste –
The Stars are setting and the Caravan
Starts for the Dawn of Nothing – Oh, make haste!

The words of the Persian boy's song carried out into the immense Euphrates twilight. Even Demetrius and Calgacus, who could not understand a word, enjoyed it. Each was bound to his fate, like a dog to a cart. They were all a long way from home.

Across the moonlit city a man sat in a tightly shuttered room. Often he looked up from what he was doing to check that he was still alone.

If reading was a rare skill, almost entirely confined to the upper classes and a tiny minority of specially educated slaves, how much rarer was the ability to read in silence. Granted, as he followed his moving finger his lips formed the words, and he mumbled now and then, but he was proud of the accomplishment. In any case, his occasional mumblings were largely inaudible – and just as well, given his reading matter.

He knew he should not be so proud of his skill but at least he never boasted about it. Circumstances ruled it out: self-regard could jeopardize his mission.

He tipped the broken pieces of wax into the small metal bowl and placed it on the brazier. He opened the hinged wooden writing tablet. It was empty of wax. The words were written directly on to the bare wood. He re-read them for the third time.

The northern barbarian sent by the emperors has arrived. He brings no troops. He talks of Valerian arriving with an army next year. He does not say when. People do not believe him. He does not expect to be attacked until next spring. The rains are late this year. When they are over, if it were possible to gather the army early and bring it here, it might arrive before the defences are ready. Was it not in February that the King of Kings crushed the Roman aggressors at Meshike, may the town now be known forever as Peros-Shapur, and killed the war-loving emperor Gordian III? In any event, I will unravel their sly secrets, unsettle their minds, and point my fingers at the weak places in their walls.

With an old stylus, he stirred the now molten wax. With a pair of tongs he picked up the bowl and poured the wax into the recess in each of the leaves of the writing tablet. Putting the bowl aside, he smoothed the surface.

He knew that many would call him traitor, many of those close to him, those he loved. Only a few would understand. But what he was doing was not designed to win passing praise from his contemporaries. It was a work to last for all time.

The wax had set. He took a new stylus and began to inscribe the blandest of letters in the smooth, blank surface.

My dear brother, I hope that this finds you as it leaves me. The rains are late this autumn . . .

Demetrius woke up and reached for his writing materials. He was anxious not to forget anything, but at the same time it was important to get things right. He looked at the water clock. It was *conticinium*, the still-time, when the cocks have stopped crowing but men are still asleep. He wrote, 'the fourth watch,' then, more precisely, 'the eleventh hour of the night'. Time mattered in these things. Then, 'vultures . . . agora . . . statue'. These aids to memory fixed, he relaxed a little and lay back on the bed.

He began to reconstruct events from the beginning. He had walked into the *agora*. But which *agora*? There had been a lot of people there, dressed in many different ways – Greek tunics and cloaks, Roman togas, the high, pointed hats of Scythians, the baggy trousers of Persians, the turbans of Indians – so no real help with the location there: large numbers of foreigners travelled to many of the great cities of the *imperium* these days.

What had struck him most was that none of the people had paid any heed to the vultures wheeling above. Dangerously close to sleep again, Demetrius followed his line of thought. The Persians laid out their dead to be eaten by carrion – crows, ravens, vultures. Would that mean that they venerated vultures (they were the instruments of their god's will), or had an overwhelming horror of them?

The vultures had been circling above the statue in the middle of the *agora*. The statue was gold; it glittered in the sun. It was big, possibly larger than life, but then it depicted a big man. He was nude, in the pose of a *doryphoros*, a spear-carrier. The muscles of his left arm were tensed as he held a shield away from his body, those of his right more relaxed as he loosely held a spear close to his side. Most of his weight came down through his right leg, the left being slightly advanced, the knee bent. Nestling below the iliac crest, the ridge which marked the junction of midriff and thighs, the penis and testicles were small and neat enough to speak to a Greek of an admirable, civilized self-control. In several ways the statue veered from the canon laid down by the great sculptor Polykleitos. The figure was more heavily muscled; it stood more solidly on the ground.

Demetrius wrote, 'Gold statue in middle of *agora*, portrait of Ballista, in pose of spear-carrier, not totally Polykleitan.'

Demetrius lay still for a few minutes, turning the dream over in his mind, weighing up the positive and negative omens. But it was best not to prejudge things: so often the interpretations of professional dream-diviners confounded expectation. Not today, but as soon as he could, he would find one in the *agora* of Arete.

'Good morning, *Dux Ripae*,' said Acilius Glabrio. The young patrician's vowels made it sound as if it were a title to be found among one of the remoter tribes of the Hyperboreans.

'Good morning, *Tribunus Laticlavius*.' 'I'm afraid we are a little early.' Ballista and his party had set out early. They had walked slowly through the town but had deliberately arrived at the parade ground ahead of time. 'If your men are not ready . . .'

The young tribune did not falter. Indeed, he smiled. 'We will do what is ordered, and at every command we will be ready.' He waved Ballista and his party towards the reviewing stand with a proprietorial air.

They walked the 150 or so yards in silence. Ballista took his rightful place in the centre at the front on the raised tribunal, Acilius Glabrio and Mamurra theirs, to the right and left respectively. Maximus stood behind Ballista's left shoulder, Demetrius his right.

Ballista had also brought the senior *haruspex*, both heralds, three scribes and four messengers, as well as five of his *equites singulares*, and Romulus, as ever bearing the white *draco*, which stirred in the light breeze.

There were four soldiers in attendance on Acilius Glabrio. While one was sent off to give the men the order to begin their display, Ballista studied the tribune out of the corner of his eye. The young patrician wore his hair long. Swept back from his brow, it was teased into artful curls which fell either side of his ear and down to the nape of his neck. His beard was trimmed short, except for a pronounced ruff at its lowest extremity. Ballista much admired the younger emperor Gallienus – but not those who almost slavishly copied the imperial hairstyle and beard.

A blast of a trumpet, and the two cohorts that made up the Arete detachment of Legio IIII Scythica marched in step on to the parade ground. Each entered separately from the right in a long column 4 men wide and 120 deep. They halted, turned smartly towards the tribunal, saluted and called out as one: 'We will do what is ordered, and at every command we will be ready.'

Ballista's first impression was one of confident and understated proficiency. A quick calculation indicated that the detachment was up to its full strength of 960 men. As far as he could see, all the legionaries were fully equipped: metal helmet or the like, mail body armour, oval shield, heavy wooden practice javelins and swords. All the shields had protective leather covers; no fancy crests bobbed above the helmets. No martinet had tried to impose complete uniformity on the men – helmets differed slightly in style, some favouring a mail coif instead. This was a unit dressed for war not for an imperial palace.

As soon as the new *Dux Ripae* had returned the salute, both cohorts moved into a more open order. The nearer unit turned away and, at a command, the two marched through each other. Then, each cohort pivoting on a centurion, they reconfigured themselves from two lines facing the tribunal into two lines stretching away. It was all most handsomely done.

Acilius Glabrio leant forward on the wooden rail and yelled, 'Are you ready for war!' Almost before he had finished nearly a thousand men roared back: 'Ready!' Three times the call and the response then, nearly without waiting for the signal, the centuries of the left-hand cohort re-formed themselves into *testudo* formation; six close-packed tortoises of eighty men, shields held to front, flanks and rear, and close as roof tiles overhead. The shields slammed together not a moment too soon. The front rank of the right-hand cohort ran forward and hurled a volley of untipped javelins. As their javelins were still arcing through the air, the second rank ran past them to hurl their weapons in another neat volley. Again, and again. There was a deafening rolling noise as volley after volley of javelins thumped into the heavy leather-covered shields. A trumpet blast, and the roles were reversed. Another faultless display.

There was a pause, the two lines facing one another. Then they began the *barritus*. Low at first, shield over mouth for reverberation, the roar built to an unearthly sound. The *barritus*, the war cry of the Germans adopted by the Romans, always brought the sweat to Ballista's palms, made his heart beat faster, always reminded him of the things he had lost with his first home.

As the sound hung in the air, the two cohorts launched into each other. The weapons might be heavy wood, without metal points or edges, but they could still hurt, maim, even kill when wielded with skill and intent.

The signal was given, and the two sides pulled apart. Medical orderlies removed the dozen or so legionaries with cracked ribs, broken limbs or injured heads. Then the cohorts moved smoothly into a close-ordered phalanx sixteen men deep facing the tribunal. One of Ballista's heralds stepped to the rail and shouted at the completely silent ranks: 'Silence! Silence in the ranks for Marcus Clodius Ballista, *Vir Egregius*, *Dux Ripae*.' The legionaries remained silent.

Ballista and the legionaries looked at each other. The legionaries held themselves with a shoulders-back, chest-out swagger. They had done well, and they knew it. But Ballista sensed they were curious. He had seen them in action now, while they knew nothing of him beyond rumour. It was quite likely they shared Acilius Glabrio's prejudice against northern barbarians.

'*Milites*, soldiers' – Ballista had thought of calling them *commilitiones*, fellow soldiers, but he detested officers who shamelessly courted popularity: 'fellow soldier' was a title that had to be earned on both sides – '*Milites*, there are many things against you. There are many excuses for poor drill. It is always difficult for a *vexillatio* detached from its parent legion. It is away from the example and rivalry of the rest of the cohorts. It is not under the experienced eye of the legion's commander.'

If possible, the ranks of the legionaries were even more silent. To give him his due, Acilius Glabrio's patrician calm did not waver.

'In your case, none of these excuses is necessary. You did everything asked of you in exemplary style. The *barritus*, in particular, was outstanding. Many do not know the importance of the battle cry, especially when facing unseasoned troops. How many untrained Persian peasants driven into battle by the whips of their masters will stand against your *barritus*? Well done! I am impressed.

'Raised by that great Roman warrior Mark Antony, Legio IIII Scythica has seen action all over the *imperium Romanum*. From the frozen north to here in the fiery east, Legio IIII has seen off the enemies of Rome. Parthians, Armenians, Thracians, Dacians, Sarmatians and countless hordes of Scythians have fallen to her swords. The long and proud history of Legio IIII Scythica is safe in your hands. We will see off the reptiles that go by the name of Sassanid Persians.'

Ballista concluded: 'All except essential details, to be determined by your commander, will take a day's leave. Enjoy yourselves – you have earned it!'

The legionaries cheered, moved smoothly into one column of fours and, saluting, marched past the tribunal and out of the *campus martius*.

It was now almost the third hour. Ballista had ordered that the tribune Gaius Scribonius Mucianus should lead Cohors XX on to the parade ground at that time. Ballista had been dreading this part of the day; he did not know what he would do if his orders were disobeyed. In an attempt to convey an air of unconcern, he studied the *campus martius*. It was separated from the civilian city behind him by a six-foot wall, more of a barrier to trespassers than a deterrent to an attacker. To his left it was bounded by the inside of the western wall of the city. These were both nice clean lines. The other two were messier. To his right the boundary was a large barracks block, the *principia*, and a temple to a local deity called Azzanathcona which he knew had been taken over to serve as the headquarters of Cohors XX. But in the far-right corner, Acilius Glabrio's residence, a requisitioned large private house, stuck out into the parade ground. It was not the young patrician's fault that it was there, but somehow it was another reason to dislike him. On its final boundary, the *campus martius* petered out before it reached Arete's north wall. Here Ballista could see the large temple to the local god Bel, smoke rising from the eternal fire in the courtyard. To its right was the first of the towers in the northern wall, the one with the postern gate. It was odd that the wall was colonnaded there but nowhere else.

It was now the third hour. For the third time, Gaius Scribonius Mucianus, *Tribunus Cohortis*, commanding officer of Cohors XX, had not turned up. Was he deliberately trying to undermine Ballista by showing ostentatious disrespect?

Whatever was happening with the tribune, Turpio had been given a direct order. If the auxiliary unit was not on the parade ground in the next few moments, the first centurion would be later – in the middle, tied to a stake, his ribs bared by the flogging.

Ballista's rising temper was stemmed when a mounted soldier appeared from behind the barracks block and conveyed the request of the first centurion that Cohors XX be allowed to begin its manœuvres.

The infantrymen of Cohors XX marched on to the *campus martius* in a column of fives. There should have been 960 of them but, to the various experienced military eyes on the tribunal, it was obvious there was nowhere near that number. The column executed a simple series of manœuvres, very shabbily: century collided with century, man bumped into man.

The order was given for the first rank to shoot. Ballista counted several seconds between the first arrow and the last. By the turn of the fifth rank, almost all semblance of shooting by volleys had disappeared. For some seconds after the order to cease, arrows still arced through the air. It was a sign of very poor discipline that a bowman who had taken an arrow from his quiver, notched it and drawn his bow would disobey an order rather than go to the trouble of putting it back. The unit's manœuvring to re-form as a line at the far end of the *campus martius* was, if anything, worse than its earlier efforts.

'Where the fuck are the rest of them, and how come, of those who turned up, only about half have all their kit?' Maximus whispered in Ballista's ear.

Ballista thought the same. The only redeeming feature that he could see was that the individual marksmanship was not too bad; most of the arrows were fairly closely grouped around the man-sized targets of wood inside the western wall.

A trumpet sounded *Pursuit!* and, after an interval, two groups of horsemen – presumably two *turmae* of Cohors XX – galloped on to the *campus martius*. There looked to be about sixty troopers in each. The nearer appeared to be the *turma* of Cocceius which had accompanied Ballista from Seleuceia, but the troopers in both groups were so lacking in order that it was hard to be certain of anything. They approached the fixed targets and, as soon as they were within range, began shooting arrows. At fifty yards each trooper wheeled his mount to the right and attempted to execute the Parthian shot, firing backwards over the horse's quarters as he galloped away. As the *turmae* were not in disciplined columns but rode as two amorphous clumps, this was a manœuvre fraught with the dangers of trooper shooting trooper and horse colliding with horse. In the event it passed off not too badly. One horse bolted, refusing to turn and galloping straight ahead. Its rider threw himself off before he reached the target area where the arrows were falling. Another horse, turning and finding one of its fellows heading straight for it, dug its feet in and refused. Its rider shot over its neck and was deposited on the sand.

While this was going on, the other three *turmae* had entered quietly and taken up a four-deep line to the right of the parade ground, but these seemed barely at half strength, about thirty troopers in each. Ballista could see what Turpio was trying to do: to disguise both that the unit was massively under strength and that its units were in a dreadful state of training. The centurion must have stripped men from three of the five *turmae* to bring just two up to strength, hoping that the antics of these two full-strength *turmae* would draw attention away from the undermanning of the others.

When the two loose horses had been caught and their troopers remounted, the original two *turmae* formed up in front of their companions. An order rang out for them each to perform the Cantabrian Circle, little more than a simple piece of formation riding in which a cavalry unit galloped in a circle, always turning to the right to keep its shielded side to the enemy. As each man came to the point closest to the enemy he shot his weapon at a target. Every mounted unit in the empire practised it but Ballista had never heard of a Roman army actually employing it in battle.

At first all went well. The *campus* was filled with two whirling circles of horsemen, turning in the same direction as the sun. The horses moved at an easy canter. The noise of drumming hooves, the twang of the bows, the whoosh of the arrows tearing through the air, the thump as they hit, bounced back off the walls. Dust rose in the air. More and more arrows flew. Then disaster struck. The only real difficulty with the Cantabrian Circle was if the horsemen lost the line of the circle – cornered too fast, or spun out of the intended path. The latter happened. One horseman strayed from the nearer circle. The frantic efforts of a trooper from the further one to get out of the way merely confused his mount. The collision was sickening. The two horses and men went down in a tangle of limbs and bodies. After a moment one horse struggled to its feet and ran off. Some seconds later, its rider sat up. But the other man lay motionless, and his horse thrashed with awful screams as it tried to rise with a broken leg.

Now there were long delays before the medical orderlies carried off the motionless trooper. Ballista noticed that they used a door instead of a stretcher which showed their complete lack of preparedness but, at the same time, a certain ingenuity. It was also some time before the unit's farrier arrived to put down the injured horse. While three men sat on the doomed animal, the farrier pulled its head back. With an almost unbearable affection he stroked its muzzle, then pulled the glinting knife across its throat. The initial spray of blood shot out several yards; then cane the arterial blood. It spread quickly, relentlessly over the sand. The dying horse's efforts to breath through its severed windpipe added a pink foam to the bright-red pool.

Eventually the *cohors* had clumsily manœuvred itself to stand before the tribunal. Many of the men had a hangdog air. They looked not at their new *Dux* but at the ground or at the back of the man in front of them. An unnerving number, however, looked up at Ballista with dumb insolence, the very set of their shoulders challenging this northern barbarian.

What will I say to them? thought Ballista. Allfather, how am I going to play this?

'Silence! Silence in the ranks for Marcus Clodius Ballista, *Vir Egregius, Dux Ripae*.'

A murmuring continued.

'Silence in the ranks!' bellowed Turpio. This time, there was some response.

'*Milites*,' said Ballista, 'it seems to me that military manœuvres have their own rules. Add too much, and the whole thing becomes an over-complicated pantomime but, equally, take too much away, and you are left with nothing to show the skill of the units.' Ballista paused. The murmuring was stilled.

'You carried out very few manœuvres. The infantry did not adopt skirmish order, did not countermarch. The cavalry tried no complicated manœuvres; neither the *xynema* nor the *touloutegon*.' The murmuring returned. 'Yet you are not to be blamed too savagely. Your depleted numbers and your lack of equipment point to your being neglected by your officers, as do your limited range of manœuvres and your limited success in carrying them out. Your marksmanship, however, points to your own skill.'

The men were silent. More of them looked up at Ballista. Now it was not just those whose demeanour said 'fuck you' who would catch Ballista's eye.

'By tonight you will have a new commander. In two days' time you will begin to train again. By the spring, Cohors XX Palmyrenorum Milliaria Equitata will be at the peak of efficiency, as befits a proud unit, one established under Marcus Aurelius, one which has campaigned under Lucius Verus, Septimius Severus, Caracalla, Valerian and Gallienus.' Again Ballista concluded: 'All except essential details, to be determined by First Centurion Titus Flavius Turpio, will take a day's leave.'

Again the troops cheered and, in no better order than before, the unit made its way off the *campus martius*.

The courier stood by the head of his camel and waited. The *telones*, the customs official, had disappeared into the registry on the ground floor of the southern tower of the Palmyrene Gate. The courier looked up at the northern wall of the courtyard between the two great wooden gates. Above head height the wall was plastered and painted with an offertory scene. Glancing down, the courier noticed a merchant come out of the registry, climb on a donkey and, leading another donkey, ride off. The courier returned to studying the wall. Below head height the wall was plain brick, but covered in graffiti, most scratched or painted in Greek or Aramaic, some in Latin. Some just consisted of a man's name and that of his father. For the most part, these two words were preceded by 'I thank you, *Tyche* of Arete.' Without having to look, the courier knew the southern wall was much the same.

'Ah, it is you again,' said the *telones*. 'Business is good.'

'No, business is bad,' replied the courier.

'Where are you going?'

'Downriver. To Charax. To Persia.'

'Men of business need their letters to get through no matter what politics says. What do you have to declare?' The customs officer began to open the near-side pannier on the camel.

'Nothing. There is nothing in there except my spare clothes and bedding.'

'I had a philosopher come through here not long ago,' said the customs officer, rummaging in a desultory way. 'He looked the complete part – naked except for a rough cloak, big bushy beard, hair down to his arse. Dirty. Absolutely fucking filthy. But he was no poor Cynic. Had a pretty-boy attendant, a shorthand writer and a calligrapher to write down his wisdom.'

The courier watched the *boukolos*, the controller of herds, on the other side of the road counting a herd of goats a tent-dweller wanted to bring into town to sell. He wondered how soon it would rain.

'So, I say to the philosopher, "What are you taking out of the town?" and he says, "Temperance, Justice, Discipline" . . . and a couple more I forget.' The customs official moved round the camel, and started to open the other pannier.

'There is nothing in there except the three sealed writing blocks that I have to deliver.'

'So then I say, "Well, it does not matter what fancy names you have given them, you will have to pay export duty on these whores!" And he says something like, "You cannot tax virtue!"' The customs official laughed. The courier smiled politely.

The *telones* did up the pannier, the writing tablets undisturbed inside. The courier passed some coins into his hand. 'Talk about not getting a joke. Silly fucker is standing just where you are, in the middle of the road, with his pretty boy, shorthand writer and calligrapher. Not a girl in sight! Silly fucker!'

The courier climbed into his saddle, flicked his whip and the camel got to its feet.

'Safe journey.'

And so it was that the traitor's letter left Arete.

Big dark clouds were piling up in the north-west. Now and then a rumble of thunder was just audible. Ballista had a nagging headache. It would get better when the storm reached Arete.

Several hours had passed since the manœuvres on the *campus martius*. What had promised to be a long day had become even longer. As ordered, prompt at the fourth hour, Acilius Glabrio, his accountant, and his secretary had presented themselves at the *principia*. The *exactor* and the *librarius* had explained all the relevant paperwork in minute detail to the new *Dux Ripae*, his *praefectus fabrum* and his *accensus*. Ballista, Mamurra and Demetrius had concentrated hard. Acilius Glabrio had sat in a chair examining his highly ornate sword belt. Absolutely everything with the *vexillatio* of Legio IIII Scythica was in good order. The unit was virtually at full strength; very few men were missing, in hospital or in jail. Pay and provisions were up to date. Not only were the men fully equipped but there was quite some number of weapons, shields and armour in reserve. After nearly two hours Ballista had turned to Acilius Glabrio, who was now reading a book of poetry, Ovid's *The Art of Love*, and congratulated him on the state of his unit. The young patrician took it as no more than his due. If anything, he seemed somewhat put out to find himself in a position where he could be commended by the likes of Ballista.

The sixth hour, of course, was lunchtime. Yet that was when Ballista had ordered Turpio to present the accounts of Cohors XX. Hunger never improved Ballista's temper. When the first centurion had arrived, with the unit's *exactor* and *librarius* in tow but without its commanding officer, the northerner had made a conscious effort to rein in his anger. Not even asking about Gaius Scribonius Mucianus, he ordered all the paperwork they had with them to be handed over. Next, he announced that they would go next door to the headquarters of the *cohors*. Military clerks had scattered like chickens as the party, headed by Ballista, swept into the converted Temple of Azzanathcona. In the record office Ballista had demanded the two general registers previous to the current one, and the register of soldiers' money on deposit 'with the standards' in the unit's bank. Deciding to enlist hunger on his side, Ballista commanded that Turpio, the accountant and librarian should attend him at the palace at the tenth hour, dinner-time (and if by some miracle he appears before then, you can bring your *tribunus* with you – under arrest). He said heavily that this would allow time for he and his staff to study the documents closely, very closely indeed.

Back at the palace, Calgacus had produced a late lunch: cold roast partridge, black olives, the local round unleavened bread, figs, nuts and dried damsons. This was spread at one end of a long table in the dining room. At the other were the accounts of Cohors XX.

After they had eaten they had got down to work. Mamurra had gone through the current general register reading out the name of each soldier and the annotation that indicated his posting. A straight line meant that the soldier was with the unit and available for duty; *ad frum(entum)* that he had gone to secure supplies of wheat; *ad hord(eum)* that he was getting barley for the horses; *ad leones* that he was hunting lions; and so on. Finally, there were the unlucky ones against whose name was just the Greek letter *theta*, the army shorthand for dead. Other annotations indicated where detachments of the *cohors* were stationed – Appadana, Becchufrayn, Barbalissus, Birtha, Castellum Arabum, Chafer Avira and Magdala.

At last they had finished. But the pattern had emerged almost from the start: on paper the unit was at full strength – but there were far too few straight lines and far too many soldiers off hunting lions or stationed in places with strange names. There were just two *thetas*.

The next stage was to cross-reference the information in the general register with the list of deposits 'with the standards' to find those who did and did not have savings in each type of posting.

It was approaching the ninth hour, and they were about two-thirds of the way through. Again a pattern had emerged: almost all those with just a line against their name had savings. Next to none of those on detached duty had a *denarius* to their name.

The thunder was closer now. Flashes of lightning lit the interior of the line of black clouds. There was a yellow tinge to the rest of the sky. Ballista's headache was no better. He had ordered food, and issued instructions that, when they arrived, the accountant and librarian were to be put in a room off the first courtyard. Calgacus was to make sure that Turpio heard them being offered food and drink. Turpio himself was to wait in the main reception hall off the second courtyard. He was not to be offered even a chair and Maximus was to keep an eye on him – or hang about in such a way that Turpio thought he was keeping an eye on him.

Calgacus coughed. 'They are here.'

'Good, let him sweat a bit.'

Ballista walked up and down the terrace for a while. On the other side of the Euphrates a man on a donkey was heading for the river. Ballista wondered if he would get there before the rain came. He turned to Mamurra and Demetrius. 'Bring him in. We might as well get on with it.'

'First Centurion.'

'*Dominus*.' Turpio looked at the end of his tether. His shoulders were rounded and his head stuck forward. There were blue-black pouches under his eyes.

Ballista leant on his fingertips on the table. He looked down at the papers for some time, then suddenly looked up. 'How long have you and Gaius Scribonius Mucianus been defrauding the military treasury?'

Turpio did not flinch. 'I have no idea what you mean, *Dominus*.'

'It is the oldest trick in the book.' Ballista tried to suppress the jet of anger that rose in him. 'The first centurion and the unit commander conspire together.' Turpio looked away. Ballista continued remorselessly. 'When a man dies or is transferred he is kept on the books. When recruits are called for, invented names are entered. The imaginary recruits and the dead are sent on "detached duty". Their pay is still drawn. It is kept by the commander and the first centurion.' Ballista paused. 'You would have me believe that this unit has eighty-five men hunting lions. Several of the places you would have me believe large detachments of this unit are stationed – Castellum Arabum, Chafer Avira, Magdala – do not exist in the official itineraries of this area.' At the first name Turpio looked up, then looked down again. 'It worked well for a time. Now it is over. Gaius Scribonius Mucianus and you were quite thorough, but not thorough enough. You failed to create savings for the imaginary soldiers.' Ballista leant further towards Turpio.

'It is over. Scribonius has run away. He is leaving you to shoulder the blame. If you remain silent, the best you can hope for is being broken to the ranks. If you tell me everything, things might go better for you. Was it Scribonius's idea?'

Turpio set his shoulders. 'He is my commanding officer. I will not inform against him.'

'Your loyalty does you some credit. But he deserves no loyalty. Like a coward, he has run.' Ballista paused again. His headache was making him nauseous. 'You will tell me everything. One way or another.' The last words needed no emphasis. 'If you tell me everything you have a chance of redemption, a chance of regaining your self-respect and the respect of your men. I will leave you to think.'

Ballista turned and, followed by everyone except Turpio and Maximus, walked back through to the terrace. He went to lean on the rail. His head was splitting. The man on the donkey had disappeared.

The first fat drops of rain landed. By the time they had got back under the portico the air was full of water. Turpio hadn't needed long to think.

'Gaius Scribonius Mucianus told me what we were going to do last year after the fighting to expel the Persians from Arete,' Turpio said as soon as Ballista entered. 'The *cohors* had taken casualties. He said it was a good moment to start the scheme.' The centurion stopped to think. 'It is as you say. Most of the men registered as on detached duty do not exist. Magdala and Chafer Avira do not exist. Or not any more. Becchufrayn is miles down the Euphrates. It is in Sassanid hands. There has not been a Roman soldier there for years. Castellum Arabum is real. Perhaps it is too new to feature on the official itineraries.' He stopped.

'What percentage did you take?'

'Ten,' Turpio answered promptly. 'I deposited it, all of it, with a man in the town. I have not spent any of it. I can pay it all back.'

Thunder crashed overhead. They were silent in the room.

At last Ballista spoke. 'What did he have over you that you had to join him?'

Turpio did not speak.

'Was it gambling debts? A woman? A boy?'

'Does it matter?' A flash of lightning lit the room. Turpio's face looked whiter than ever.

'Yes, if it could happen again.'

'It cannot happen again,' said Turpio.

'I should have you beheaded in the middle of the *campus martius*.' Ballista let his words hang in the air for a long time. 'Instead, I appoint you acting commander of the *cohors*.' Turpio looked stunned. 'Now you must prove that you are a good officer. It is too late to get new recruits but, by next spring, I want you to have that *cohors* ready to fight. I want you to train them until they drop. Oh, and you can pay the money back to Demetrius. It can go towards replacement equipment.'

Turpio began to thank Ballista, who cut him short. 'This conversation need go no further than these walls. Just do not betray my trust.'

They could hear the rain beating on the flat roof. Ballista's headache had almost gone.

It had rained all night, then all day. Demetrius was beginning to wonder if it would ever stop. The previously unnoticed gutters on the terrace of the palace threw strong jets of water away from the side of the cliff. By late afternoon, in the bed of the northern ravine, there was a torrent capable of moving small rocks. At the mouth of the ravine the waters of the Euphrates had turned a muddy dun colour.

The primeval flood must have started like this. Zeus, disgusted by the crimes of mankind, had sent a flood to put a stop to the killings, the human sacrifices and cannibalism. One man, Deucalion, warned by his immortal father the Titan Prometheus, had built an ark. Nine days later, guided by a dove, the ark had deposited Deucalion and his wife, Pyrrha, on Mount Parnassus – or, as others said, Mounts Aetna, Athos or Othrys. Others escaped to high ground, warned by the screaming of cranes or the howling of wolves. Sometimes Demetrius was unsure if Zeus had been right to relent.

As soon as Iarhai's invitation to dinner had arrived, Demetrius knew that it spelt trouble. Ballista had accepted instantly despite knowing that his acceptance was impolitic: it would further alienate Ogelos and Anamu. Demetrius was sure it was Bathshiba that made Ballista ignore such considerations.

It was almost dark when the ten-strong party set out. The guests,

Ballista and Mamurra, were accompanied by Demetrius, Bagoas, Maximus and five troopers of the *equites singulares*. The torches went out straight away in the torrential rain and within moments Demetrius knew that he was lost. He envied Ballista and Maximus their ability always to find their way.

A porter ushered the party inside in response to their knock and Demetrius and Bagoas were swept along as Ballista and Mamurra were led deeper into the house.

The dining room was a mixture of east and west. Underfoot was a typical Greek or Roman mosaic depicting the remains of a meal: fish and animal bones, nut shells, olive stones, discarded cherries. Persian rugs hung from the walls. Elaborate metal lamps cast a soft light. Braziers warmed and perfumed the room with cinnamon, balsam, myrrh.

There was just one *sigma* couch, a semicircle with settings for seven, with one table in the middle. Four men stood drinking *conditum*, warm, spiced wine. One was the host, two Demetrius did not recognize, and one was Acilius Glabrio.

'Welcome to my house, Ballista and Mamurra.' Iarhai held out his hand.

'Thank you for inviting us.' They smiled and shook his hand.

Ballista turned to Acilius Glabrio. '*Tribunus Laticlavius*.'

'*Dux*.' Neither smiled.

Iarhai offered the new arrivals a drink, which both accepted, and introduced the other two men. Demetrius marked them down as *umbrae*, shadows, clients of the host. 'My daughter said that we were not to wait for her, that she would join us soon.'

Both Ballista and Acilius Glabrio brightened visibly. Demetrius's spirits sank.

'Tell me, *Dux*, how do you find our weather?' Iarhai smiled.

'Wonderful. I am surprised that the *eupatrid* senators of Rome do not all abandon the Bay of Naples and begin to build their shamefully extravagant holiday villas here.' As he said the words Ballista regretted them. Acilius Glabrio would not take kindly to a barbarian laughing at the patrician classes. He turned what he hoped was an inoffensive, open smile on the tribune. He was met by a face like a blank wall. It seemed that every time they met they disliked each other more. Would Acilius Glabrio's attitude extend to disobeying orders? Surely he wouldn't desert or turn traitor like Scribonius Mucianus?

'Salted almonds?' Iarhai stepped between the two men. 'Some fool once told me that if you eat enough almonds before drinking you never get drunk.'

Mamurra joined in. 'I once heard that if you wear a certain gem you also never get drunk – an amethyst possibly?' The uncomfortable moment passed.

'Let us go to the table.' Iarhai took the highest place on the far left and indicated where the others should recline, Ballista next to him, an empty place reserved for Bathshiba, Acilius Glabrio then Mamurra. The two *umbrae* occupied the places of least honour.

The first course was brought in. By the standards of the rich of the *imperium*, and there could be no doubt that the host was one of their number, the food was unostentatious. Salted anchovies hid under slices of hard-boiled eggs, there were snails cooked in white wine, garlic and parsley, and a salad of lettuce and rocket – nicely balanced: rocket was thought to be lubricious, lettuce antaphrodisiac.

The diners ate. Demetrius noted that, while the others were being quite abstemious, Ballista and Iarhai were drinking hard.

> Arrive late, when the lamps are lit;
> Make a graceful entrance – Delay enhances charm

As he recited the fragment of Latin poetry, Acilius Glabrio rose gracefully to his feet.

Bathshiba stood, backlit in the doorway. Even Demetrius had to admit that she was stunning. She was wearing a thin robe of white silk which clung to and emphasized her full breasts and hips. Demetrius knew she would be almost irresistible to Ballista. The other men scrambled to their feet, none with the grace of Acilius Glabrio.

Bathshiba gave the young patrician a dazzling smile, her teeth very white against the dark olive of her skin. As she walked to the couch her breasts swayed, heavy yet firm, obviously unfettered under the robe. She graciously allowed Acilius Glabrio to give her his hand as she took her place, smiling a smaller smile at Ballista to her side.

The main course was, again, almost aggressive in its simplicity: wild boar, lamb meatballs, cabbage dressed with oil, marrow with a pepper sauce and local flat bread. Two musicians, one with a lyre, the other a flute, began to play softly. Both looked vaguely familiar to Demetrius.

For a time, Bathshiba's arrival made the conversation falter slightly. Her generous cleavage and olive skin obviously attracted both Ballista and Acilius Glabrio, yet the northerner seemed to be finding it hard to think of much to say. After only a short while, he resumed his conversation with Iarhai about the relative endurance levels of the camel and the horse. Acilius Glabrio, on the other hand, was thoroughly enjoying himself. Attentive, light-hearted and witty, he clearly thought himself any girl's ideal dinner companion. Although the conversation was in Greek, he could not resist the occasional sally into Latin verse:

Wine rouses the heart, inclines to passion:
Heavy drinking dilutes and banishes care
In a sea of laughter, gives the poor man self-confidence,
Smoothes out wrinkles, puts paid
To pain and sorrow. Then our age's rarest endowment,
Simplicity, opens all hearts, as the god
Dissipates guile. Men's minds have often been enchanted
By girls at such times: ah, Venus in the wine
Is fire within fire!

The final course showed the same almost flamboyant restraint that had marked the previous two: dried fruits, Damascene prunes, local figs and dates, pistachios and almonds, a smoked cheese, and some poached pears and fresh apples. The wine was changed to a sweet dark Lesbian.

Demetrius did not like the way things looked. If anything, Ballista and Iarhai were drinking even faster now. There was an awkward glint in the eye of his *kyrios* and a mulish set to his shoulders. Clearly he was annoyed by Acilius Glabrio's ease with Bathshiba. The young patrician was liable at any moment to bring out the worst in the northerner. In all honesty, the gathering frequency of the tribune's recitation of Latin poetry was beginning to irritate Demetrius too. After each display the young patrician sat back with a smile which suggested that he was enjoying a private joke. He carefully avoided naming the poet. His audience was either too polite or too reluctant to show its ignorance to ask. Like the majority of educated Greeks, Demetrius claimed ignorance of Latin literature in public while privately knowing a great deal about it. He knew the poetry, but for the moment could not quite place it.

An exaggerated run on the lyre ended a tune and drew Demetrius's attention to the musicians. He suddenly realized who they were: they were not slave musicians at all, they were two of Iarhai's mercenaries. He had heard them play at the campfire. With mounting apprehension, the young Greek looked round the room. Iarhai's four slaves were all older, capable-looking men. And they weren't slaves – they were mercenaries too. Although he could not be sure, the two *umbrae* relaxing at the table could well be two officers of the mercenary troop. *Gods, he could kill us all in a moment.* A scene in Plutarch came to mind: Mark Antony and Octavian are dining on Sextus Pompey's flagship, and the pirate Menas whispers in the admiral's ear, 'Shall I cut the cables and make you master of the whole world?'

'Demetrius!' Ballista was waving his empty cup impatiently and the Greek boy snapped back to the present. Iarhai and Ballista were happily drinking together. Why would the protector of caravans want the northerner dead? Even Sextus Pompey had rejected the offer: 'Menas, would that you had acted, not spoken about it beforehand.'

> . . . don't waste precious time –
> Have fun while you can, in your salad days; the years glide
> Past like a moving stream,
> And the water that's gone can never be recovered,
> The lost hour never returns.

Acilius Glabrio leant back, a half-smile playing on his lips, his hand fleetingly brushing Bathshiba's arm.

Ovid. Demetrius had it. And the poem was 'The Art of Love'. The pretentious swine. Acilius Glabrio had been reading it only yesterday – so much for his scholarship. So much for his smug little smiles. Demetrius remembered how the passage continued:

You who today lock out your lovers will lie
Old and cold and alone in bed, your door never broken
Open at brawling midnight, never at dawn
Scattered roses bright on your threshold! Too soon – ah, horror! –
Flesh goes slack and wrinkled, the clear
Complexion is lost, those white streaks you swear date back to
Your schooldays suddenly spread,
You're grey-haired.

The passages Acilius Glabrio had recited had been a series of snide jokes at the expense of the other diners, whom he undoubtedly thought far too ill-educated to detect him.

How did that passage about arriving late go on?

Plain you may be, but at night you'll look fine to the tipsy:
Soft lights and shadows will mask your faults.

Demetrius could not say anything to anyone at the moment. Indeed, if he did tell a drunk Ballista the results might well be catastrophic. But at least he had unravelled the smug Roman patrician's sly little secret.

Iarhai made a signal, and wreathes of fresh roses and bowls of perfume appeared, symbols that the time for eating was over and the time for serious drinking and toasting about to start. Demetrius placed a wreath on Ballista's head and put his bowl of perfume by his right hand. After anointing himself, Ballista gestured the young Greek to stand closer. The northerner took the spare wreath which Iarhai had provided for just this reason and placed it on Demetrius's head. He then anointed the boy.

'Long life, Demetrius.'

'Long life, *Kyrios*.'

'A toast' – Acilius Glabrio had not thought enough of his slave to anoint or wreath him – 'a toast to our host the *synodiarch*, the caravan protector, the *strategos*, the general. The warrior whose sword never sleeps. To the man who waded ankle-deep in Persian blood to free this city. To Iarhai!'

Before the company could drink, Iarhai turned and glared at the young Roman. The *synodiarch*'s battered face was twisted with barely suppressed anger. A muscle twitched in the broken right cheekbone.

'No! No one shall drink to that in my house.' Iarhai looked at Ballista. 'Yes, I helped end the Sassanid occupation of this city.' His lip curled in disgust. 'You are probably still too young to understand,' he said to the northerner, 'that one probably never will understand' – he jerked his head at Acilius Glabrio and paused. His eyes were on Ballista but he had withdrawn into himself. 'Many of the Persian garrison had their family with them. Yes, I waded ankle-deep through blood – the blood of women, children, babes in arms. Our brave fellow citizens rose up and massacred them, raped, tortured, then killed them – all of them. They boasted they were "cleansing" the city of the "reptiles".'

Iarhai's gaze came back into focus. He looked at Bathshiba then at Ballista. 'All my life I have killed. It is what a *synodiarch* does. You protect the caravans. You talk to the nomads, the tent-dwellers. You lie, cheat, bribe, compromise. And when they all fail, you kill.

'I have dreams. Bad dreams.' A facial muscle twitched. 'Such dreams I would not wish even on Anamu and Ogelos . . . Do you believe in an afterlife, a punishment in an afterlife?' Again his gaze became unfocussed. 'Sometimes I dream that I have died. I stand in the grove of black poplars by the ocean stream. I pay the ferryman. I cross the hateful river. Rhadamanthys judges me. I have to take the road to the punishment fields of Tartarus. And they are waiting for me, the "kindly ones", the demons of retribution and, behind them, the others: all those I have killed, their wounds still fresh. There is no need to hurry. We have eternity.' Iarhai sighed a great sigh then smiled a self-deprecating smile. 'But perhaps I have no monopoly on inner daemons . . .'

The patrician drawl of Acilius Glabrio broke the silence. 'Discussing the immortality of the soul. This is a true symposium, a veritable Socratic dialogue. Not that I ever suspected for a moment that after-dinner conversation in this esteemed house would resemble that at the dinner of Trimalchio in Petronius's *Satyricon.*' Everything about his manner suggested that was just what he thought. 'You know, all those dreadful jumped-up, ill-educated freedmen talking nonsense about werewolves and the like.'

Ballista swung round heavily. His face was flushed, his eyes unnaturally bright. 'My father's name is Isangrim. It means "Grey-Mask". When Woden calls, Isangrim lays down his spear, offers the Allfather his sword. He dances and howls before the shield wall. He wears the wolfskin coat.'

There was a stunned silence. Demetrius could hear the oil hissing in one of the lamps.

'Gods below, are you saying that your father is a werewolf?' Acilius Glabrio exclaimed.

Before the northerner could answer, Bathshiba began to recite in Greek:

> Hungry as wolves that rend and bolt raw flesh,
> Hearts filled with battle-frenzy that never dies –
> Off on the cliffs, ripping apart some big-antlered stag
> They gorge on the kill till their jaws drip red with blood
> . . . But the fury, never shaken,
> Builds inside their chests.

No one in the *imperium* could fail to recognize the poetry of Homer.

Bathshiba smiled. 'You see, the father of the *Dux Ripae* could not be in better company when he prepares to fight like a wolf. He is in the company of Achilleus and his Myrmidons.'

She glanced at her father. He took the hint and gently indicated that it was time for his guests to depart.

*

The rains confounded local knowledge. The first rains of the winter always lasted three days; everyone said so. This year, the rains lasted five. By mid-morning on the sixth day the blustery north-east wind had blown away the big black clouds. The washed-out blue sky brought the inhabitants of Arete into the muddy streets and quite a large number found their way to the palace gates. They all arrived claiming it was vital that they saw the *Dux*. They brought reports, complaints, requests for justice or help. A section of the cliff in the northern ravine at the far end from the postern gate had tumbled down. A row of three houses near the *agora* had collapsed. Two men who had been foolish enough to try to row across to Mesopotamia were lost, presumed drowned. A soldier of Cohors XX had been accused of raping his landlord's daughter. A woman had given birth to a monkey.

Ballista dealt with the flood of petitioners, at least to the extent of ordering the arrest of the soldier and, sending a messenger ahead, at midday he set out to meet Acilius Glabrio at the north-west tower, by the Temple of Bel, to begin a tour of inspection of both the artillery and the walls of Arete. He was accompanied by Mamurra, Demetrius, Maximus, the standard-bearer Romulus, the senior *haruspex*, two scribes, two messengers and two local architects. Five troopers of the *equites singulares* had been sent on horseback to clear the area outside the walls.

Ballista was not looking forward to this meeting. If only he had kept quiet at Iarhai's dinner party. What had made him admit that his father, Isangrim, was a warrior dedicated to Woden, a warrior who at times felt the battle madness of wolves? Of course, he had been drunk. Possibly he had been affected by the confession of Iarhai. Certainly he had been angered by the supercilious attitude of Acilius Glabrio. But these were excuses.

It could have been worse. It was not a secret like the visits of the ghost of Maximinus Thrax. If he blurted that out, people would either think that he should be shunned because he was haunted by a powerful daemon or that he was completely insane. Further admitting to emperor-killing, even if the emperor you killed had been universally hated, was frowned on by reigning emperors. It might test the tolerance of even so mild and well disposed a pair of rulers as Valerian and Gallienus.

Ballista climbed the stairs and walked out on to the fighting platform at the top of the tower.

'*Dux Ripae.*' There was a barely suppressed smirk on Acilius Glabrio's face, but Ballista's attention was on something else. There, in the middle of the windswept platform, its covers off, stood a huge artillery piece, a *ballista*. It was a lifelong fascination with such weapons that had won the northerner his name.

Ballista knew that Arete possessed thirty-five pieces of artillery. One was stationed on top of each of her twenty-seven towers. The Palmyrene Gate and the Porta Aquaria each boasted four; two on the roof and two shooting through portholes on the first floor. Twenty-five of the weapons shot a two and a half foot bolt. These were anti-personnel weapons. Ten shot stones. These were primarily intended to destroy enemy siege engines but could also be used to kill men. All were crewed by legionaries of Legio IIII.

The northerner had chosen to begin his tour here because this tower housed one of the biggest *ballistae*. A rectangular frame of iron-reinforced hardwood some ten feet wide held near each end a torsion spring of twisted sinew, each as high as a very tall man. Inserted into these springs were the bow arms. The stock, some twenty feet long, projected back from the frame. A slider dovetailed on to it at the rear of which were catches which caught the bowstring. Two powerful winches pulled back the slider and bowstring, forcing back the bow arms. The missile was placed in the slider. A ratchet held the slider in place, and a universal joint allowed it to traverse easily from side to side, and up and down. The soldier took aim, and a trigger unleashed the awesome torsion power of the springs.

Ballista happily let his eyes run over the dark polished wood, the dull gleam of the metal. All *ballistae* worked on the same principles but this was a particularly fine example. A beautiful and deadly piece of engineering, this enormous weapon hurled a carefully rounded stone ball weighing no less than twenty pounds. Arete had three other such massive engines; two on the roof of the Palmyrene Gate and one on the fourth tower north of there. Arete's six other stone-throwers threw six-pound missiles. All except one covered the western wall, the wall which faced the plain – for it was across the plain that any enemy siege engines must approach.

Acilius Glabrio introduced Ballista to the crew – the one trained artilleryman, the *ballistarius* in charge of the piece, and his unskilled helpers: four winch men and two loaders. They seemed delighted when Ballista requested a demonstration shot. He pointed out a rock some 400 yards away, towards the limit of the machine's range. It was all Ballista could do not to take over as they spanned and lay the weapon.

Twang, slide, thump went the artillery piece, and the missile shot away. The stone shone white in the eight or nine seconds it was airborne. A fountain of mud showed where it landed; some thirty yards short and at least twenty to the right.

'What rate of shooting can you maintain?'

The artilleryman did not attempt to answer Ballista's question but looked rather helplessly at Acilius Glabrio. The latter for once looked vaguely embarrassed.

'I cannot say. The previous *Dux Ripae* did not encourage – actually, he specifically forbade – practice shooting. He said that it was a waste of expensive ammunition, a danger to passers-by and would damage the tombs out on the plain. My men have never been allowed to shoot before.'

'How many trained *ballistarii* are there?'

'Two in each century, just twenty-four,' replied Acilius Glabrio, making a brave show of things.

Ballista grinned. 'All that is going to change.'

The party, now augmented by Acilius Glabrio, set off south on their tour of inspection. They halted to consider the walls, the two architects to the fore. Built directly on to the bedrock, the walls were about thirty-five feet high, with crenellations on top. They were broad, with wall walks of about five paces across. The towers reached up some ten feet above them and extended out both front and back. The crenellations of the towers extended to the sides, interdicting easy movement along the wall walk by any enemy who had managed to scale the walls.

The local architects were as one in assuring their audience that the walls were in good repair; probably there were no finer walls in the *imperium*, none behind which one could rest more secure.

Ballista thanked them. A century of Cohors XX marching out to drill on the *campus martius* caught his eye. Turpio was taking his orders seriously. Ballista returned his attention to the walls.

'The walls are good,' continued Ballista, 'but they are not enough on their own. We must dig a ditch in front of the western wall to prevent rams or siege towers having an easy run up.' He glanced at Demetrius, who was already making notes. 'The spoil from the ditch can form part of the glacis, the earth bank we need to cushion the walls from both rams and artillery.' He paused to consider how he would phrase the next bit. 'If there is a glacis, there has to be a counter-glacis on the reverse of the wall. Otherwise, the pressure of the earth bank on the outside will collapse the wall.' He looked at the architects, who both nodded.

One of the architects gazed over the wall, imagining the ditch and glacis. 'The ditch would have to be superhumanly deep to provide enough material for a glacis on one side, let alone both,' he ventured. 'And where else can the material come from?'

'Do not worry about that.' Ballista smiled enigmatically. 'I have a plan.'

By mid-afternoon of the second day Ballista had finished off his inspection with a lengthy tour of the artillery magazine, a large complex in the open ground south of the palace where new machines were built, old ones repaired, spare parts kept and missiles created – stones chipped to the right weight and near-perfect roundness, the evil iron points of the bolts forged and fitted to their wooden shafts.

It was only then that Demetrius found time finally to pursue his guilty secret passion: *oneiromanteia*, divining the future through dreams. He slipped out of the servants' door and into the streets. The grid plan of the town and broad daylight should have made things easy, but the young Greek still managed to get lost on the four-block walk to the *agora*.

It was surprisingly small for a town of this size and it was easy for Demetrius to find what he wanted: an *oneiroskopos*, a dream-scout. He was sitting in the far corner, by the entrance to the alley where the prostitutes stood. Despite the chill in the wind he was clad in just a ragged cloak and a loincloth. His milky eyes gazed unseeingly upwards. His neck was emaciated, the veins standing up, pulsing through the almost translucent skin. He could be nothing but.

At Demetrius's footfall the unnerving white eyes moved in his direction.

'You have a dream that may reveal the future,' the old man said in Greek, his voice a hoarse croak. The dream-diviner asked for three *antoniniani* to unveil its meaning, and settled for one. 'First I need to know you. What is your name, the name of your father, your home town?'

'Dio, son of Pasicrates of Prusa,' Demetrius lied. His fluency came from always using the same name.

The aged head tipped to one side, as if considering whether to make some comment. He decided against it. Instead he rattled out a series of further questions: slave or free? Occupation? Financial status? State of health? Age?

'I am a slave, a secretary. I have some savings. My health is good. I am nineteen.' Demetrius answered truthfully.

'When did you have the dream?'

'Six nights ago,' Demetrius answered, counting inclusively, as everyone did.

'At what hour of the night?'

'In the eleventh hour of darkness. The effects of the previous evening's wine had long since passed off. It was well after midnight when the door of ivory through which the gods send false dreams shuts and the door of horn through which pass true dreams opens.'

The blind man nodded. 'Now tell me your dream. You must tell me the truth. You must add nothing, nor must you omit anything. If you do, the prophecy will be false. The fault will not be mine, but your own.'

Demetrius nodded in turn. When he had finished recounting his dream the *oneiroskopos* held up a hand for silence. The hand trembled slightly and was marked with the liver spots of age. Time stretched on. The *agora* was emptying fast.

Suddenly, the old man began to speak. 'There are no male vultures; all are female. They are impregnated by the breath of the east wind. As vultures do not experience the frenzy of sexual desire, they are calm and steadfast. In a dream they signify the truth, the certainty of the prophecy. This is a dream from the gods.'

He paused before asking, 'Does your *kyrios* inhabit the *agora*?' On being told that he did not, the old man sighed. 'Just so. A pity. A busy *agora* would have been an auspicious sign but, as it is . . .' he shrugged, 'it is not good. It is a symbol of confusion and tumult because of the crowds that flock there. There are Greeks, Romans and barbarians in your dream. There will be confusion and tumult caused by all these, experienced by all these.

'At the heart of it is the statue.' He winced slightly as if in discomfort. 'Did the statue move?' Demetrius murmured that he did not think so. The aged man's hand shot out and, with a bony, hard grip, grabbed the youth's arm. 'Think! Think very carefully. It is of the greatest importance.'

'No – no, I am certain it did not.'

'That, at least, is something.' A drool of saliva hung from the dream-diviner's lips. 'The statue was of gold. If your *kyrios* were a poor man, it would have indicated future riches, but your *kyrios* is not a poor man, he is a wealthy and powerful man. The golden statue indicates that he will be surrounded by treachery and plotting, for everything about gold incites designing people.'

Without warning, the old man rose. Standing, he was surprisingly big. Peremptorily he croaked that the session was over. He was sorry the prophecy had not been better. He started to shuffle off towards the alley.

'Wait,' called Demetrius. 'Wait. Is there not anything else? Something you are not telling me?'

The old man turned at the entrance to the alley. 'Was the statue larger than life?'

'I am not sure. I . . . do not think it was.'

The old man laughed a horrible laugh. 'You had better hope that you are right, boy. If it *was*, it spells death for your beloved *kyrios* Ballista.'

Once again it was being brought home to Maximus that, natural fighter though he was, he would never make an officer. It was the boredom, the sheer grinding bloody boredom of it. The last two days had been bad enough. Watching the artillery shoot had been all right, if a bit repetitive. Undoubtedly it was more fun when there was someone on the receiving end. But looking at them making the missiles had been insufferable. And, as for the walls, if you've seen one big wall you've seen them all. Yet all that had been as nothing compared with this morning.

As every good Roman commander with something on his mind should, Ballista had summoned his *consilium*, his council. It consisted of just Mamurra, Acilius Glabrio and Turpio, with Demetrius and Maximus in attendance. In a way fitting to antique Roman virtue, they had met very early in the morning, at the first hour of daylight. Since then, they had been discussing the size of the population of Arete. At great length. At the last census there had been 40,000 men, women and children registered in the city and, of these, 10,000 were slaves. But could these figures be trusted? The census had been taken before the Sassanids seized the town and since then many would have died or fled. Some would have returned, and with the invasion next spring, many would flood in from the villages. Perhaps it all balanced out.

Just when Maximus thought he might scream, Ballista said they would have to assume this and use the figures as a guide. 'Now, the real question. How do we feed everyone from March to November when we are besieged? Let us start with existing food reserves.' He looked at Acilius Glabrio.

'Legio IIII has stockpiled grain and oil to last our thousand men twelve months.' The young aristocrat was careful not to look smug. There was no need.

'Things are far from so good with the nearly thousand men of Cohors XX,' said Turpio with a wry smile. 'There are dry supplies for three months and wet for just two.'

Ballista looked at Demetrius. The youth's eyes were unfocussed, his mind elsewhere. 'Demetrius, the figures for the municipal reserves and those of the three caravan protectors.'

'Sorry, *Kyrios*.' In his confusion, the boy lapsed momentarily into Greek, before continuing in Latin. 'Sorry, *Dominus*.' He consulted his notes. 'The caravan protectors all say the same, that they have enough supplies for their dependants, including their mercenaries, for twelve months. Incidentally, all three claim to have about three hundred mercenaries. The municipal reserves hold enough grain, oil and wine for the whole population for two months.'

'Obviously we have to make sure all our troops are supplied. And while the civilians must ultimately take responsibility for themselves, I think that we should try to provide a half ration to them throughout the siege,' said Ballista. Forestalling the expected objection from Acilius Glabrio, he continued, 'No law says we must feed them, but we will want volunteers to fight. We will press others into work gangs. Starving, desperate men are liable to turn traitor and open the gates. And of course there is basic humanity.'

'Could we not arrange for supplies to be shipped to us down-river?' Mamurra asked.

'A good point. Yes, we should try that. But that relies on others, and on the Persians neither getting any boats nor besieging the places upriver that would be sending us supplies. I would rather keep our fate in our own hands.' Everyone agreed. 'Anyway, let us think about it as we inspect the storehouses.'

At least they were close, just by the palace in the north-east corner of the city. Seen one Roman army granary, seen them all, thought Maximus. Raised on a farm, the Hibernian rather admired the practicality of the great, long buildings. The Romans had taken the risk of fire, the need to keep rain and damp away from the walls and the need for air to circulate into account in their design. But he had never understood why they always built granaries in pairs.

A *contubernium* of ten legionaries under the eye of a centurion was unloading a wagon at the adjacent loading bay. As Ballista and his *consilium* climbed the steps into the first granary, two of the legionaries quietly but perfectly audibly howled like wolves.

'Silence in the ranks,' yelled Acilius Glabrio. 'Centurion, put those men on a charge.' The young patrician gave Ballista an odd look. The northerner glowered back.

The cool, airy dark of one granary succeeded another and another, and Maximus drifted off into thoughts of the woman who had given birth to a monkey. It was still occupying his mind after they had left the army granaries and arrived at the great caravanserai near the Palmyrene Gate which housed the municipal supplies. It was unlikely to be any form of portent or warning from the gods, he thought. Either she had looked at a monkey, or possibly a picture of one, at the moment of conception, or she had actually fucked a monkey. The idea that she had given birth to a very hairy baby that happened to look a bit like a monkey never occurred to the Hibernian.

'Right,' said Ballista, 'here is what we are going to do. We commandeer this caravanserai and everything in it. We place guards both here and on the military granaries. We issue an edict of maximum prices for foodstuffs – Demetrius, can you find out a list of reasonable prices in this town? Anyone selling for more will be fined and what they are selling confiscated. We will announce that the *Dux* will buy foodstuffs at ten per cent over the fixed price. We keep on buying, using promissory notes if necessary, until we have enough to feed a full ration to our troops, plus however many militia we raise, and a half ration for the rest of the inhabitants for nine months.'

Ballista was livid, so furiously angry he found it hard to concentrate. That little bastard Acilius Glabrio had not wasted any time telling the story of the barbarian *Dux*'s werewolf father. He had grabbed the opportunity to undermine Ballista in the legionaries' minds.

He forced his mind to focus on the matter of water supply. Almost every building with any pretensions to size in the city of Arete boasted a cistern into which the carefully collected rainwater was channelled. This was all very good as a reserve but, on its own, it would never hold out for more than a few weeks. High on its plateau, the town was way too far above the water table for wells of any sort. Its main supply of water had always arrived, and would always arrive, on the backs of donkeys and men, via the steep steps that led from the banks of the Euphrates to the Porta Aquaria or a series of winding passages and tunnels cut into the living rock. While the eastern walls were held, those that reached out into the Euphrates from the foot of the cliff, this supply could not be denied. These walls were short, each either side of a hundred paces. The approaches to them, along the floors of the ravines, were difficult and completely open to missiles from the main walls of the town. It should be safe enough, but it was to inspect it all that the angry northerner now set his feet.

Ballista climbed down the steps from the Porta Aquaria. He looked around the narrow plain between the cliffs and the water. He studied the entrances to the tunnels: two had gates and three were boarded up as unsafe. He considered the short walls and was reassured to note how each was dominated by a tower overhead on the circuit wall. Finally, he ran his eye over the wharves and those boats present. Back at the top, puffing slightly, he issued his orders.

No one was to draw water from a cistern without official authorization. All water used was to come up from the Euphrates. Guards were to be set on all the major cisterns in military buildings, and also on those in the caravanserai and the major temples. A century of Legio IIII was to be based in the Porta Aquaria. Among other duties to be assigned later, its men were to oversee the bringing up of water and the security of the tunnels. Those deemed unsafe were either to be repaired or securely sealed.

It was to the tunnels that Ballista, with serious disquiet, now turned. Lamps were produced, bolts drawn and a gate to one of the supposedly safe tunnels opened. Hoping that his extreme reluctance was not obvious, Ballista stepped into the rectangle of darkness. He stopped for a moment just inside, waiting for his eyes to become accustomed to the gloom. A short flight of steps ran away from him. Each one dipped in the centre where generations of feet had worn it down. After about a dozen steps the passage turned sharp right. Ballista repeated the line that had got him through many bad things: do not think, just act.

Stepping carefully, he walked down the steps. Turning the corner, he was confronted by another short flight of steps and another right-hand bend. Past this things changed. Underfoot, the steps gave way to a slippery ramp which fell abruptly away. Putting out a hand to steady himself, Ballista found the walls rough and streaming with moisture. No light from the gate penetrated this far. Ballista held up his lamp, but the passage seemed to stretch on for ever. Out of sight something squeaked and scuttled away.

Ballista very much wanted to get out of this tunnel. But he knew that, if he turned round, by nightfall every man under his command would know that their new big tough barbarian *Dux* was afraid of confined places. Suddenly the air round the northerner's head was full of wheeling and flitting black shapes. As quickly as it had appeared the colony of bats vanished. Ballista wiped the sweat from his palms on his tunic. There was only one way that he could get out of this horrible tunnel. Gritting his teeth, he pressed on down into the cold, clammy darkness. It was like descending into Hades.

Ballista was tired, dog-tired. He was sitting on the steps of a temple at the end of Wall Street at the south-west corner of the town. Just Maximus and Demetrius were still with him but neither were talking. It was nearly dusk. It had been a long day.

Every day has been long since we got here, Ballista was thinking. We have been here only eight days, the work has barely started, and I am exhausted. What was it Bathshiba had said when he first saw this place? 'Is it worth it?', or something like that. Right now, the answer was no and it always had been in Ballista's mind. But he had been sent by the emperors, and no would lead to death or imprisonment.

Ballista missed his wife. He felt lonely. The only three people in this town whom he could call friends were also his property, and that created a barrier. He was very fond of Demetrius; years of shared dangers and pleasures had drawn Maximus and him close together; Calgacus had known him since he was a child. Yet still, even with these three, there was the constraint of servitude. He could not talk to them as he could to Julia.

He missed his son. He felt an almost overwhelming, almost unmanning ache when he thought of him: his blond curls, so unexpected given his mother's black hair, his green-brown eyes, the delicate curve of his cheekbone, the perfection of his mouth.

Allfather, Ballista wished he was at home. As he formed the thought he wished that he had not. As night follows day, the next insidious thought slid unwanted into his mind: where was home? Was it Sicily – the brick-built, marble-inlaid house high on the cliffs of Tauromenium? The elegant urban villa whose balconies and gardens gave views of the Bay of Naxos and the smoking summit of Aetna, the home that he and Julia had made and shared for the last four years? Or was home still far to the north? The big thatched longhouse, painted plaster over wattle and daub. The house of his father, built on rising ground just inland from the sand dunes and the tidal marshes where the grey plovers waded and the *kleep kleep* call of the oystercatchers sang through the reeds.

A middle-aged man wearing just a tunic and holding a writing block turned into Wall Street. When he saw Ballista waiting, he broke into a run.

'*Kyrios*, I am so sorry to be late.'

Ballista was dusting down his clothes. 'You are not late. We were early. Do not trouble yourself.'

'Thank you, *Kyrios*, you are very kind. The councillors said that you wanted to be shown the properties on Wall Street?'

Ballista agreed that it was so, and the public slave gestured at the temple on whose steps the northerner had been sitting. 'The temple of Aphlad, a local deity who watches over the camel trains. The interior has recently been repainted at the expense of the noble Iarhai.' The man walked backwards up the street. 'The temple of Zeus, *Kyrios*. The new façade was provided by the generosity of the pious Anamu.' They reached the next block without the slave turning away from Ballista. 'Private houses, including the fine home of the councillor Theodotus.'

You poor bastard, thought Ballista. You are a slave of the council of Arete. These people own you, probably don't even know your name, yet you are proud of them, of their houses, the temples on which they lavish their wealth. And that pride is the only thing that gives you any self-respect. The northerner looked sadly down Wall Street. And I am going to take it away. In a couple of months, by the *kalends* of February, I will have destroyed all this. All will be sacrificed to the great earth bank to shore up the defences of Arete.

A legionary hurtled round the corner. Seeing Ballista, he skidded to a stop. He sketched a salute, and tried to speak. He was out of breath, and the words would not come. He gasped in a lungful of air.

'Fire. The artillery magazine. It's on fire.' He pointed over his left shoulder. The strong north-east wind was blowing the leading edge of a pall of thick black smoke over the many roofs of Arete, straight at Ballista.

Ballista pounded through streets filling with excited people. Swerving round the crowds, pushing past them, Maximus and Demetrius ran with the northerner. The already out-of-breath legionary soon fell behind.

By the time he reached the artillery magazine Ballista's lungs hurt, his left arm ached from holding the scabbard of his long *spatha* away from his legs – and the building was well ablaze. Mamurra and Turpio were already there. The strong north-eastern wind which had been drying out the rain-sodden land was fanning the fire, driving it remorselessly onward. Flames were licking out of the barred windows and around the eaves, sparks flying high then being whipped dangerously away towards the town. Turpio was organizing a work party to clear a fire break and douse the houses to the south-west. Mamurra had a chain of legionaries passing material out of the doomed magazine. To encourage the men, he was conspicuously running the same risks they were, darting in and out of the southern door.

Ballista knew he could not expect his officers and men to do what he would not. He followed Mamurra into the building. It was so hot the plaster was peeling from the walls and, on the beams above their heads, the paint seemed to be bubbling and boiling. Scalding droplets fell on the men below. There was little smoke in the room, but that was probably deceptive. The fire was surreptitiously outflanking them, creeping high, unseen, and into the cavities of the walls. At any moment the beams could give, the roof come crashing down, trapping them, choking them, burning them alive.

Ballista ordered everyone out, shouting above the inhuman roar of the fire. He and Mamurra fled only when the last legionary reached the threshold.

Outside, all busied themselves moving the rescued stores to a position of safety upwind. Then they watched the fire rage. The building did not collapse immediately. Sometimes the fire appeared to be dying down, before bursting forth into ever more destructive life. At last, with a strange groan and a terrible crash, the roof gave way.

Ballista woke to a beautiful morning, clear and crisp. Wrapped in a sheepskin, he watched the sun rise over Mesopotamia. The vast bowl of the sky turned a delicate pink; the few tattered shreds of clouds were silvered. Pursued by Skoll the wolf, as it would be until the end of time, the sun appeared on the horizon. The first wash of gold splashed over the terrace of the palace of the *Dux Ripae* and the battlements of Arete. At the foot of the cliff the wharves and whispering reedbeds remained in deep blue shadow.

Ballista had had only a very few hours' sleep but, surprisingly, they had been deep and restful. He felt fresh and invigorated. It was impossible not to be full of well-being on such a morning – even after the disaster of the previous evening.

Behind him, Ballista could hear Calgacus approaching across the terrace. It was not just the uninhibited wheezing and coughing, there was also some very audible muttering. Unshakably loyal, in public the aged Caledonian was silent to the point of being monosyllabic about his *dominus*. Yet when they were alone he presumed on a lifetime's acquaintance to say what he pleased, as if he were thinking aloud – usually a string of criticism and complaint: 'Wrapped up in a sheepskin . . . watching the sunrise . . . probably start quoting fucking poetry next.' Then, at the same volume but in a different tone, 'Good morning, *Dominus*. I have brought your sword.'

'Thank you. What did you say?'

'Your sword.'

'No, before that.'

'Nothing.'

'Beautiful morning. Puts me in mind of Bagoas's poetry. Let me try some in Latin:

> 'Awake! For Morning in the Bowl of Night
> Has flung the Stone that puts the Stars to Flight:
> And Lo! The Hunter of the East has caught
> The Great King's Turret in a Noose of Light.

What do you think?' Ballista grinned.

'Very nice.' Calgacus's mouth pursed thinner, more shrewish, than ever. 'Give me that sheepskin. They are waiting for you at the gate.' His mutterings – 'time and place . . . not find your father spouting poetry at the sunrise like a lovesick girl . . .' – diminished in volume as he retreated into the palace.

Ballista walked with Maximus and Demetrius to the burnt-out shell of the magazine. Mamurra was already there. Possibly he had been there all night.

'We will do what is ordered, and at every command we will be ready.' The *praefectus fabrum* saluted smartly. His face and forearms were black with soot.

'How does it look?'

'Not good, but could be worse. The building will have to be demolished. Almost all the artillery bolts are burnt. All the spare fittings for the *ballistae* – washers, ratchets and the like – are buried under that lot.' He ran a hand across his face, the gesture of a tired man. 'But all the shaped stones for the *ballistae* were stored outside, so they are all fine. I am going to have ropes rigged to try and pull the walls down outward. We may be able to salvage some of the metal fittings, some of the metal tips of the bolts – depends how hot the fire got in there.' Mamurra paused, took a long drink of water and tipped some over his head. The soot ran, leaving strange black streaks. 'Anyway, not quite the total disaster someone wanted.'

'You are sure that it was arson?'

'Come with me.' Mamurra led them to the north-east corner of the building. 'Don't get too close to the walls. They could come down at any moment. But have a smell.'

Ballista did, and his stomach turned. He saw again the pole slowly beginning to turn, the *amphora* above his head start to tip, remembered the screams, and the other smell – the smell of burning flesh.

'Naptha.'

'Yes, once you have smelt it you never forget. Not if you have seen it in action.' Mamurra pointed to a small, blackened ventilation louvre high up in the wall. 'I think they poured it in there. Then probably threw a lamp in.'

Ballista looked around, trying to picture the attack in his mind: Last hour of daylight; no one around. One man, or more? And would he have run or tried to mingle with the gathering crowd?

'There are witnesses. Two of them.' Mamurra pointed to two men sitting unhappily on the ground, guarded by two legionaries. 'They both saw a man in the street of the sickle-makers running away to the south-east.'

'A good description?'

Mamurra laughed. 'Yes, both excellent. One saw a short man with black hair wearing a rough cloak, and the other saw a tall man with no cloak, bald as a coot.'

'Thank you, Mamurra. You have done very well. Carry on and I will be back when I have talked to the witnesses.'

The two men looked cowed and resentful. One had a black eye. Ballista well knew the mutual antipathy between Roman soldiers and civilians, but he was surprised by the stupidity of the troops. These two men had come forward to volunteer information. By some misplaced process of guilt by association, they had been bullied, possibly beaten up. There was no way they would help in the future.

Ballista, having asked Maximus to go and fetch him some fresh water, spoke gently to the civilians. Their stories were as Mamurra had said. It was just possible they had seen two different men.

There was some uncertainty about timing. But it was equally likely that they just remembered things differently. Neither had recognized the man. The questioning was leading nowhere. Ballista thanked them and asked Demetrius to give them a couple of *antoniniani* each.

Ballista returned to Mamurra. 'Right, here is what is going to happen.' He spoke quickly, confidently. 'Mamurra, have this building torn down and rebuilt about twice the size, with a wall round it and plenty of guards. There is nothing like shutting the gate after the horse has bolted.' Mamurra smiled dutifully. 'You are also going to form and command an independent unit of *ballistarii*. The twenty-four specialist *ballistarii* already in Legio IIII will be transferred to you, as will another ninety-six ordinary legionaries. Each *ballistarius* will be responsible for training four legionaries. By the spring I expect a unit of 120 specialist *ballistarii*.' Mamurra started to say something, but Ballista cut him short.

'Also by then I expect your men to have built, tested and sited another twenty-one bolt-throwers – there is room for two bolt-throwers on every tower that now contains just one. You can requisition any civilian labour, carpenters, blacksmiths that you need. Select the legionaries yourself. Don't let Acilius Glabrio pass off his worst cases on you.'

A slow grin spread across Mamurra's square face.

As Ballista walked away, Maximus spoke quietly to him in Celtic. 'If your young patrician did not hate you before, he sure will now.'

The *telones*, seeing them coming down the main street, knew that this was no time for jocular anecdotes, about philosophers or anything else. Certainly it was no time for officiousness, let alone extortion. The *boukolos* straight away started to herd a family of tent-dwellers and their donkeys out of the way, roughly pushing animal and human off the road, cursing them foully for dawdling. Warned by an urchin who ran errands for them, the *contubernium* of ten legionaries hurriedly stopped playing dice and tumbled out of the guardroom. Pulling their equipment into order, they came to attention.

The *Dux Ripae* gently pulled up his horse. He held up his hand, and his entourage of four halted behind him.

The customs official watched the northerner look over the Palmyrene Gate. Gods, but he was huge; huge and fierce, like all his kind.

'Good day, *Telones*,' said the barbarian in good Greek, an agreeable expression on his face. He repeated the affable greeting to the *boukolos* and the legionaries, then indicated to his men that they should move on, and rode out of the city of Arete.

'Nasty-looking brute, isn't he?' The *telones* shook his head. 'Very nasty. I wouldn't like to cross him. Savage temper – they all have.'

About half a mile from the gate, where the necropolis ended, Ballista reined in Pale Horse. He studied the tower tombs. There had to be at least five hundred of them. Apart from at Palmyra, he had never seen anything like them. Each stood on a square stepped plinth as tall or taller than a man. Above the plinth was a first storey, two or three times as tall again, decorated with plain columns sculpted in relief. Looming above this were another two or three storeys, each resembling a flat-roof house and diminishing progressively in size.

The dead were placed in niches in the walls inside with the precious possessions they would take to the next world. Grieving relatives entered via the sole door and ascended an internal staircase up to the roof to eat a funeral meal. The sealing of the niches and the securing of the tomb were left to the undertakers.

It must have taken generations to build them all, thought Ballista, and we have three months to pull them down. Left standing, they could shelter an attacker from missiles from the walls, act as observation posts, be converted into artillery towers or destroyed by the Persians to provide materials for siege works. The citizens of Arete would hate it, but the eternal resting place of their ancestors had to be razed to the ground.

'Demetrius' – as he started to speak, Ballista saw that his secretary had his stylus poised – 'we will need cranes with wrecking balls. We will need haulage – lots of ox carts for the bigger debris, donkeys for the smaller.' Ballista paused to make sure that the

Greek could keep up. 'And lots of labour. There are said to be 10,000 slaves in the town. We will requisition every able-bodied male – that should give us at least 2,500. Then we will impress citizens and employ the troops – hard work, but the soldiers do enjoy knocking things down. In areas where no one is working at the time the *ballistae* can use the tombs for target practice.' The northerner detected a qualm on his secretary's part. 'Oh, of course, we will let the families remove their loved ones first.'

Ballista played with Pale Horse's ears. 'And would you make a note about security at the gates? The northern and southern postern gates are to be closed unless I order them opened. The guards at the Palmyrene Gate and the Water Gate are to be doubled. Everyone entering or leaving is to be searched, not just for weapons but for messages. I want the searches to be thorough: shoes, seams of tunics and cloaks, bandages, horse furniture – messages can be stitched into bridles as easily as into the sole of a sandal. Let Acilius Glabrio know that I hold him responsible for carrying out these orders.'

Demetrius stole a glance at his *kyrios*. He seemed to draw energy from violent action, from physical danger. Fighting the Borani in the Aegean, rushing into the burning magazine yesterday – after both, the northerner had seemed invigorated, more purposeful, somehow more fully alive. Long may it stay that way. Gods hold your hands over him.

Demetrius could not stop his thoughts returning to the dream-diviner. The encounter had shaken him. Was the old man a fraud? He could have worked out that he was Ballista's secretary logically. Demetrius had given away the fact that he habitually used dream-diviners when he talked of the doors of ivory and horn through which the gods send false and true dreams. As Demetrius had never consulted the old man before, it could be assumed that he was new to town – and who but Ballista had recently arrived in town with a young well-spoken Greek secretary in tow?

The old man had predicted tumult and confusion, treachery and plotting, possible death. Were the dreams divinely inspired, or was their interpretation more prosaic – a warning, designed to unsettle and undermine? Was it in some way connected to the sabotage of the magazine? Should he tell Ballista? But Demetrius felt obscurely guilty about the whole episode and, more than that, he feared Ballista's laughter.

Yet at that moment Ballista's thoughts were also of treachery; he was also trying to divine the future. If he went over to the Persians and were appointed general, what would be his plan of attack?

He would pitch camp about here; five hundred paces out, just beyond artillery range. In his imagination, Ballista removed all the tombs from the approach, saw the defences as they would be that coming April. He would launch an assault straight away. It would go in across the flat plain – no cover of any sort. From four hundred paces out, artillery bolts and stones would start to fall, his men would begin to die. In the last two hundred, arrows and slingshots would kill many more. There would be traps underfoot, pits, stakes. Then a ditch, more stakes, more traps. The men would have to climb the steep glacis, ghastly things hurled and tipped on to them from the battlements, crushing, blinding, burning. Once the ladders were against the wall, the survivors would climb, hoping against hope that the ladders would neither break nor be pushed over, that they would not be hurled to the bone-breaking ground. And then the final few would fight hand to hand against desperate men. The assault might succeed. More likely, it would fail. Either way, thousands of the attacking warriors would die.

A plain covered in dead and dying men, a failed assault – what would Shapur do? Ballista thought of everything Bagoas had told him about the Sassanid. It was vital to understand your enemy, to try and think like him. Shapur would not be deterred. He was king by the will of Mazda; it was his duty to bring the *bahram* fires to be worshipped by the whole world. This town had played him false before, opened its gates then massacred his garrison. This latest rebuff would be but another sign of the evil nature of its inhabitants. He was Shapur, King of Kings, not some northern barbarian warlord little better than the warriors he led, not some Roman general terrified of the emperors' disapproval. Casualties would not be an issue: the men who died would be blessed, their place in heaven assured. Shapur would not desist. He would not rest until everyone in the town was dead or in chains, until only wild beasts slunk through the ruined streets of Arete.

The party moved on to the entrance to the southern ravine. Here they dismounted and led their horses down the stony slope. Ballista went first, boots sliding on loose stones, slipping in the mud. At the bottom it was wider and they could remount and descend further. By the time the walls of Arete loomed high on the left they were deep indeed.

It was obvious at a glance that no one in their right mind would try and storm the southern wall of the town. It would take an age to ascend for the slope was long and steep and, apart from the occasional small thorny shrub, the side of the ravine was completely bare. Open to any missiles from above, it was a perfect killing ground.

Not that the side of the ravine could not be climbed at all. There was a postern gate at the top, and it was crisscrossed with paths or goat tracks. A guard would have to be kept. Many towns had fallen because the attackers had climbed difficult places that the defenders had neglected to watch. But only surprise or treachery could get the enemy into the town here.

As they rode on, the ravine opened out in front of them. From this distance, the city walls were invulnerable to attack by *ballistae*. Ballista noticed a large number of caves high up the slope just under the walls. Several vertiginous paths led to them.

'They are tombs, *Dominus*,' one of the cavalrymen said, 'Christian catacombs.' He spat. 'They don't want to be buried with the rest of us in our necropolis, and we don't want their corpses there.' He spat again. 'If you ask me, they are the cause of all our problems. The gods have looked after us, held their hands over the *imperium* for centuries. Then along come these Christians. They deny the gods exist, will not offer sacrifice. The gods are annoyed, withdraw their protection, and you get the time of troubles. Stands to reason.' Thumb between index and forefinger, he averted the evil eye.

'I know little of them,' said Ballista.

'May the gods keep it that way, *Dominus*,' replied the trooper, getting into his stride. 'As for their "Thou shall not kill" bollocks, I would like to see how they feel about that when a bloody great barbarian has his prick up their arse – begging your pardon, *Dominus*.'

Ballista made a negating gesture as if to say, Think nothing of it, I am often of a mind to inflict anal rape on members of minority religious sects.

The ravine narrowed somewhat, then opened out as it reached the floodplain of the Euphrates. Away to the right were thick groves of tamarisk, the occasional poplar and wild date palm. Turning left, they came to a gate set into a wall in such a way that it was necessary to turn to the left to enter, thus exposing one's right, unshielded side. The gate was a simple affair, and the wall a feeble enough thing, not more than twelve foot high but Ballista was not at all worried by the paucity of these defences. To approach them, the Persians would either have to come from the river – unlikely, given that the defenders would have requisitioned or sunk every boat on the middle Euphrates – or follow the route Ballista's party had just used – and that would be foolhardy as it would mean marching over poor going for several hundred yards, continually exposed to missiles from the town.

'Demetrius, please make a note: we will position heavy rocks on the lip of the southern ravine, to be released on any Persians foolish enough to approach from there.'

The gate sprang open, and a *contubernium* of legionaries saluted. Ballista and his men dismounted and chatted to them. Inside the wall at the foot of the cliffs more legionaries were tearing open the entrance to one of the boarded-up tunnels. Ballista looked up at the cliff face. It was closely stratified, line after close line of rock ruled across like a ledger. He suppressed a shudder at the thought of what lay behind, of the dripping dark tunnel he had edged down anxiously two days earlier.

They continued north along the water's edge. Everywhere was bustle and activity. Skins of water were raised from the river by means of ropes running over rickety-looking wooden frames and pulled by donkeys. Donkeys and men then carried the skins up the steep steps to the Porta Aquaria. Boats pulled in from the rich fields across the river, their decks full of figs, dates and trussed and indignant chickens. Farmers carrying or driving their wares added to the jostling on the steps to the town. The smell of grilling fish drifted from the market.

It was some time past midday, well past lunchtime. Ballista's party made its way over and one of the troopers ordered their meal.

Their horses fed, watered and tethered in the shade, the five men sat and drank wine and ate pistachios. The winter sun was as warm as a June day in Ballista's childhood home. Men busied themselves preparing the meal. The gutted fish were grilled in a metal cage hung over the fire from the branch of a tree. Juices spat and sizzled and smoke eddied.

At the foot of the steps, a goat escaped its owner and a furious burst of shouting in Aramaic ensued. Ballista couldn't understand a word. The irony struck him that he could speak the languages of these people's conquerors, the Romans, and of their would-be conquerors, the Persians, but not that of those whose freedom had been entrusted to him.

The sunlight glinted off the Euphrates as they rode on, full of goodwill. Ballista wondered how firm was the footing on the nearest island. If the Persians did not acquire boats, it might make a refuge, if the city fell, albeit a transient one. It was vital to have some form of exit strategy. He would do everything in his power to defend this town, but he had no intention of Arete being the scene of his last stand.

Having paused for a few words with the guards, the party rode out through the gate to the north, a twin to its southern counterpart. The slopes of the northern ravine were also steep but there were no paths on its bare flanks. The figures far away and high up on the battlements above the postern gate were tiny.

The rains had brought down a section of the cliff under the town walls and the fallen rock and earth stretched out into the ravine like a poorly made siege ramp. It looked unstable, its surface treacherous. Some attackers could climb it but, with use, it would most likely soon give way and resume its temporarily halted descent into the floor of the ravine. Still in high spirits, Ballista knew that had he been at the top he would have been sorely tempted to set Pale Horse at it, just to see if they could make it down in one piece.

'Onager,' said one of the troopers quietly.

The wild ass was grazing about a hundred paces further up the ravine. Its head was down, its white muzzle searching out camel thorn.

One of the troopers passed Ballista his spear. Ballista had never hunted onager. The cornel-wood shaft of the spear felt smooth and solid in his hand. A gentle pressure of his thighs, and Pale Horse walked slowly forward. The ass looked up. With a rear hoof, it scratched one of its long ears. It stared at the approaching horseman, then spun round and, gathering its quarters under it, sprang away. Ballista pushed his mount into a canter. While nowhere near full gallop, the onager was moving fast, supremely confident on the rough going of the partially dried-out bed of the torrent. Its yellow-brown back with its distinctive black-edged white stripe was pulling ahead. Ballista moved Pale Horse into a gentle gallop. Sure-footed as the gelding was, Ballista did not want to risk his mount flat out on shaky ground. There was plenty of time. This would be a long chase. There was nowhere for them to go except up the ravine.

The ravine closed in around them. Ballista could sense Maximus and the others falling behind. The onager came to a fork. With no hesitation, it bounded into the right-hand passage. Easing Pale Horse, Ballista looked around. The sides of the cliffs were sheer here. He must be about level with the western defences but he was out of sight of the walls of the town and the plain. A bend in the path hid him from those following. On his own initiative, Pale Horse followed the ass into the right-hand passage.

Down here, the heat of the summer still seemed to reflect out of the rocks. Clouds of gnats, washed by the rains out of the air up above, stung Ballista's face, got in his eyes, invaded his mouth. On and on, up and up the path climbed. The onager's hoofs raised puffs of mud as it bounded tirelessly on. Pale Horse was tiring. Ballista steadied his pace.

Suddenly, Pale Horse shied violently. Hooves fighting for purchase, he stopped dead and dived to the left. Given no warning, Ballista was thrown forward. All that stopped him disappearing over the gelding's right shoulder was his stomach punching into the front right-hand horn of the saddle. The horse, eyes wide with panic, was spinning in fast, tight circles. The motion was forcing Ballista ever further out, pushing him beyond the point of no return where he must fall. Instinctively, he still gripped the spear in his right hand, its point banging and clattering over the stones. Clinging with all the strength in his thighs, Ballista reached out and caught the nearest saddle horn with his left hand. With a convulsive effort born of desperation he began to haul himself back on. He felt the saddle slip, the girth coming loose.

Nothing else for it: Ballista threw the spear clear, let go his grip on the saddle and kicked hard with his legs. With a sickening wrench, his left boot caught on the horns. As the horse turned, Ballista was spun almost horizontally through the air. He tried to kick his leg free. His head was inches from the sharp stones. Fighting against the centrifugal force, he kicked again. His foot came out of the boot and he crashed, rolling to the unyielding ground.

His right arm was skinned, his shoulder jarred. He did not stop to check his injuries. He saw the spear and scrambled over to it, half on his knees. The weapon in both hands, he got into a crouch and turned warily around, looking for whatever had panicked the horse.

The great yellow eyes, blank yet cunning, looked at him from about twenty paces away. A lion. A male. Fully grown; it must have been eight foot long. Ballista could hear it breathing. He could smell its hot fur, thought he could smell its rank breath. The lion swished its tail, showed its teeth. It snarled: low, rumbling, terrifying – once, twice, three times.

Ballista had seen lions many times, safely confined in the arena. One had been despatched in the morning beast hunt in Arelate on the day he had first seen Maximus fight. Now would be a good time for the Hibernian to arrive and pay off his debt by saving my life, thought Ballista.

He had seen lions kill before – criminals, as well as a few beast-hunters in the arena. They used their momentum to knock the man down, pinned him with their weight and wide-spread, razor-sharp claws and sank their long, long teeth, almost delicately, into his windpipe.

Ballista knew he had just one chance. He assumed a side-on crouch and, gripping the shaft of the spear tightly in both hands, he wedged the butt under his still-booted right foot.

The lion moved, accelerating faster than Ballista thought possible. One bound, two, three, and it landed, front paws together, for the pounce. Head forward, it launched itself into the air at Ballista.

The spear took the lion in the chest. Its jaws opened. Its momentum forced the spear out of the northerner's hands, out from under his boot. Ballista threw himself backwards. A paw caught him a glancing blow, claws raking his upper arm, and sent him spinning back.

The lion landed, paws together, chest moving down, driving the spear deeper into its body. The shaft broke. The lion tipped over, slid on its back, legs splayed.

It got to its feet. Ballista pulled himself up, tugging his *spatha* free of its scabbard. The lion collapsed.

Maximus and the Christian-hating trooper clattered into view. 'You are the man!' The Hibernian was beaming. 'You are the man!'

A group of some twenty peasants had appeared from nowhere. They formed a chattering circle around the body of the lion.

'They may well want to worship you,' Maximus called over. He was still beaming. 'Your lion has been terrorizing their village.' He jerked his thumb over his shoulder. 'We've come all the way to the villages in the hills to the north-west of the city.'

Maximus having been set the tasks of seeing to the skinning of the lion and the transportation of the pelt into town, Ballista walked over to Demetrius, who was now standing with Pale Horse.

'What is wrong?' Ballista looked up from inspecting the gelding's feet.

'Possibly it may be unwise to make too much of killing the lion.' The boy looked unhappy. 'Back in the reign of the emperor Commodus, one of the ruling family of Emesa, one Julius Alexander, brought down a lion with his javelin from horseback. The emperor sent *frumentarii* to kill him.'

'Commodus was mad. Valerian and Gallienus are not.' He squeezed the boy's shoulder. 'You worry too much. It will be fine. And if I tried to keep it quiet and news got out, it might look suspicious.' Ballista turned away, then stopped. 'What happened to the man?'

'He had to flee to the Euphrates, to the enemy.'

Demetrius did not add that Julius Alexander had fled with a young favourite. The boy could not keep up. The man had dismounted, cut the boy's throat, then plunged the sword into his own stomach.

Four days had passed since he had killed the lion. It seemed to Ballista that every waking moment of those days had been devoted to meetings. The cast had varied – sometimes a small group, just his *familia*; at others more, when he had summoned his *consilium*. Once, he had asked the three caravan protectors Iarhai, Anamu and Ogelos to attend. The scene and the props had remained constant: a large plan of Arete spread out on the dining-room table in the palace of the *Dux Ripae*; the current general registers of Legio IIII and Cohors XX, both now accurate, propped open near by; writing blocks, styluses and sheets of papyri everywhere. Out of the endless talk and calculations, Ballista had formed his plan for the defence of Arete. Now it was time to tell it to the *boule*, the council, of the city – or at least as much of it as they needed to know.

It was the *kalends* of December, the first of the month. Ballista waited in the quiet of the courtyard of the temple of Artemis. It struck him again where power lay in this town. In any city where democracy was more than a word the *bouleuterion* faced on to the *agora*, where the *demos*, the people, could keep an eye on the councillors. In Arete the council met in a closed building tucked away in the corner of a walled compound. It was a democracy guarded from its own citizens by armed men.

Watching Anamu step out into the sunshine, Ballista experienced the strange certainty that he had done all this before. A sinner in

Hades, he was condemned to repeat this unenviable task for eternity. He would wait in the courtyard, be greeted by Anamu and tell the councillors some hard truths, some things they did not want to hear, things that would make them hate him. Perhaps it was a fitting punishment for a man who had killed an emperor he had sworn to protect, for the killing of Maximinus Thrax.

'Marcus Clodius Ballista, greetings.' The down-turned corners of Anamu's mouth moved. Probably it was intended as a smile.

Inside the *bouleuterion* it was as before, some forty councillors arranged on the U-shaped tiers of seats. Only Anamu, Iarhai and Ogelos on the first tier, sitting far apart. There was a deep, expectant silence in the small room.

Ballista began. 'Councillors, if Arete is to survive, sacrifices must be made. The priests among you can tell you how to make things right with your gods.' Taking their lead from Ogelos, those priests nodded their approval. The hirsute Christian smiled broadly. 'I am here to tell you how we can make things right among men.' Ballista paused and looked at his notes, written on a piece of papyrus. He thought he caught a look of disappointment, possibly shifting into contempt, on Anamu's face. To Hades with that – the northerner needed clarity, not rhetorical effect.

'You all know that I am stockpiling food – prices are fixed, only agents of the *Dux Ripae* can pay more. Again, you all know that the water supply has been taken over by the military: all water consumed is to come from the Euphrates; the cisterns are not to be drawn on.' Ballista was softening them up, telling them things they knew, things to which they had no great objection.

'Various things will be requisitioned: all boats on the river, all stocks of timber for building and a great deal of firewood. Also requisitioned will be large terracotta storage jars and metal cauldrons, all cowhides and all the chaff in the town.' The northerner noticed that one or two of the councillors looked at each other surreptitiously and grinned. If they were still alive when the time came, they would see that the last few requisitions were anything but the odd whims of a barbarian.

'Again, you know that everyone and everything entering and

leaving the city is being searched.' There was a quiet murmur from the back benches. 'It causes delays. It is inconvenient. It is an invasion of privacy. But it is necessary. Indeed, we must go further. From today there will be a dusk-to-dawn curfew. Anyone on the streets at night will be arrested and may be killed. All meetings of ten or more people must obtain permission from the *Dux Ripae*. Anyone flouting this order, for whatever reason, will be arrested and may be killed.' The murmuring was a touch louder but, so far, the councillors found little to which they could really object: if a few of the common people got killed in the streets at night so be it.

'Some soldiers are billeted in private houses.' The muttering ceased. Now he had their attention. Given as soldiers were to wanton destruction, theft, violence and rape, the billeting of troops was always deeply unpopular. 'So that troops can reach their posts quickly, billeting will have to be extended. Buildings in the second blocks in from the western wall and the first blocks in from the other walls may be affected. A reasonable compensation will be paid to the owners of the buildings.' There was silence. The councillors were the great property-owners. Providing they could keep the soldiers out of their own homes, they might do well out of this. 'Also, the caravanserai near the Palmyrene Gate will be taken over by the military. Compensation will be paid to the city.'

Sunlight was pouring into the room from the door behind Ballista. Motes of dust swirled in the golden air. Maximus and Romulus came in and stood behind him.

'The nine hundred mercenaries of the three caravan protectors will be formed into three *numeri*, irregular units, of the Roman army. They will be joined by the same number of conscripted citizens. The troops will be paid by the military treasury. Their commanders will hold the rank and draw the salary of a *praepositus*.' Iarhai grinned. The other two tried to look as if it were all a noble self-sacrifice, Ogelos rather more successfully than Anamu. It was a windfall: their private armies were to be doubled in size and paid for by the state.

'There is a terrible need for manpower. All able-bodied male slaves – and we estimate that there are at least 2,500 of them in the town – will be requisitioned into labour gangs. They will not be nearly enough. Some 5,000 citizens will be pressed into labour gangs as well. Some occupations will be reserved. Blacksmiths, carpenters, fletchers and bowyers will be exempt from the labour gangs but will work exclusively for the military. The *boule* will draw up the necessary lists.' The three caravan protectors betrayed nothing but, behind them, the other councillors exclaimed with barely suppressed anger. They were to have to organize the handing over of large numbers of their fellow citizens to slave-like labour.

'These labour gangs will assist the troops in digging a moat in front of the western, desert wall, and building a glacis, an earthen ramp, in front of it. They will also help construct a counter-glacis behind the wall.' Here goes, thought Ballista, unconsciously touching the hilt of his *spatha*.

'To make room for the counter-glacis, the internal earthen ramp, the labour gangs will assist in demolishing all the buildings in the first blocks in from the western wall.' For a moment there was a stunned silence, then men at the back began to shout in protest. Against the rising noise, Ballista pressed on.

'The labour gangs will also help the troops to demolish all the tombs in the necropolis outside the walls. Their rubble will be used as the filling of the glacis.'

Uproar. Almost all the councillors were on their feet, shouting: 'The gods will desert us if we pull down their temples . . . You want us to enslave our own citizens, destroy our own homes, desecrate the graves of our fathers?' The cries of sacrilege were echoing back off the walls.

Here and there were isolated islands of calm. Iarhai was still seated, his face unreadable. Anamu and Ogelos were on their feet but after initial exclamations they were silent and thoughtful. The hairy Christian still sat, smiling his beatific smile. But all the other councillors were up and shouting. Some were jeering, waving their fists, incensed.

Over the uproar Ballista shouted that, from now on, for ease of communication, his engagements would be posted up in the *agora*. No one seemed to be listening.

He turned and, with Maximus and Romulus covering his back, walked out into the sunshine.

Ballista thought it best to let the dust settle after his meeting with the *boule*. Syrians were notorious for acting and speaking on the spur of the moment and there was no point in risking an exchange of harsh, ill-considered words. For the next two days he remained in the military quarter, planning the defence of the city with his high officers.

Acilius Glabrio was smarting from losing 120 of his best legionaries to the new unit of artillerymen. And although they were not present, doubtless he was not pleased to think of Iarhai, Anamu and Ogelos, yet more barbarian upstarts in his view, being catapulted into command in the Roman army. He retreated into a patrician vagueness and studied unconcern. Yet the others worked hard. Turpio was keen to please, Mamurra his usual steady considered self and, as *accensus*, Demetrius seemed less distracted. Gradually, from their deliberations a plan began to form in Ballista's mind – which sections of wall would be guarded by which units, where they would be billeted, how their supplies would reach them, where the few – so very few – reserves would be stationed.

A lower level of military affairs also demanded his attention. A court-martial was convened to try the auxiliary from Cohors XX who had been accused of raping his landlord's daughter. His defence was not strong: 'Her father was home, we went outside, she was saying yes right up until her bare arse hit the mud.' His centurion, however, provided an excellent character statement. More pertinently, two of the soldier's *contubernales* swore that the girl had previously willingly had sex with the soldier.

The panel was divided. Acilius Glabrio, the very incarnation of Republican virtue, was for the death penalty. Mamurra voted for leniency. Ultimately, the decision was Ballista's. In the eyes of the law, the soldier was guilty. Quite probably his *contubernales* were lying for him. Ballista guiltily acquitted the soldier: he knew he could not afford to lose even one trained man, let alone alienate his colleagues.

Another legal case occupied him. Julius Antiochus, soldier of the *vexillatio* of Legio IIII Scythica, of the century of Alexander, and Aurelia Amimma, daughter of Abbouis, resident of Arete, were getting divorced. No love was lost; money was involved; the written documents were ambiguous; the witnesses diametrically opposed. There was no obvious way to determine the truth. Ballista found in favour of the soldier. Ballista knew his decision was expedient rather than just. The *imperium* had corrupted him; Justice had once more been banished to a prison island.

On the third morning after his meeting with the *boule*, Ballista considered that enough time had elapsed. The councillors should have settled down by now. Volatile as all Syrians were, it was possible they might even have come round to Ballista's way of thinking. Yes, he was destroying their homes, desecrating their tombs and temples, dismantling their liberties, but it was all in the cause of a higher freedom – the higher freedom of being subject to the Roman emperor and not the Persian king. Ballista smiled at the irony. Pliny the Younger had best expressed the Roman concept of *libertas*: You command us to be free, so we will be.

Ballista sent off messengers to Iarhai, Ogelos and Anamu inviting them to dine that evening with him and his three high officers. Bathshiba, of course, was invited too. Remembering the Roman superstition against an even number at table, Ballista sent off another messenger to invite Callinicus the Sophist as well. The northerner asked Calgacus to tell the cook to produce something special, preferably featuring smoked eels. The aged Hibernian looked as if he had never in his very long life heard such an outrageous request and it prompted a fresh stream of muttering: 'Oh, aye, what a great Roman you are . . . what next . . . fucking peacock brains and dormice rolled in honey.'

Calling Maximus and Demetrius to accompany him, Ballista announced that they were going to the *agora*. Ostensibly they were going to check that the edicts on food prices were being obeyed but, in reality, the northerner just wanted to get out of the palace, to get away from the scene of his dubious legal decision-making. His judgements were preying on his mind. There was much he admired about the Romans – their siege engines and fortifications, their discipline and logistics, their hypocausts and baths, their race-horses and women – but he found their *libertas* illusory. He had had to ask imperial permission to live where he did, to marry the woman he had married. In fact his whole life since crossing into the empire seemed to him marked by subservience and sordid compromise rather than distinguished by freedom.

His sour, cynical mood began to lift as they walked into the north-east corner of the *agora*. He had always liked marketplaces: the noises, the smells – the badly concealed avarice. Crowds of men circulated slowly. Half humanity seemed to be represented. Most wore typically eastern dress, but there were also Indians in turbans, Scythians in high, pointed hats, Armenians in folded-down hats, Greeks in short tunics, the long, loose robes of the tent-dwellers and, here and there, the occasional Roman toga or the skins and furs of a tribesman from the Caucasus.

There seemed a surfeit of the necessities of life – plenty of grain, mainly wheat, some barley; lots of wine and olive oil for sale in skins or *amphorae*, and any number of glossy black olives. At least in his presence, Ballista's edicts on prices appeared to be being observed. There was no sign they had driven goods off the market. As the northerner and his two companions moved along the northern side of the *agora* the striped awnings became brighter, smarter, and the foods shaded by them moved from Mediterranean essentials to life's little luxuries – fruit and vegetables, pine kernels and fish sauce and, most prized of all, the spices: pepper and saffron.

Before they reached the porticos of the western side of the *agora* the luxuries had ceased to be edible. Here were sweet-smelling stalls with sandal- and cedarwood. Too expensive for building materials or firewood, these could be considered exempt from Ballista's edict on the requisitioning of wood. Here men sold ivory, monkeys, parrots. Maximus paused to examine some fancy leatherwork. Ballista thought he saw a camelskin being quietly hidden at the rear of the shop. He was going to ask Demetrius to make a note but the boy was staring intently over at the far end of the *agora*, once more distracted. Many of the things that men and women most desired were here: perfumes, gold, silver, opals, chalcedonies and, above all, shimmering and unbelievably soft, the silk from the Seres at the far edge of the world.

In the southern porticos, to Ballista's distaste, was the slave market. There, all manner of 'tools with voices' were on display. There were slaves to farm your land, keep your accounts, dress your wife's hair, sing you songs, pour your drinks and suck your dick. But Ballista studied the merchandise closely; there was one type of slave he always looked to purchase. Having inspected all that was on offer, the northerner returned to the middle of the slave pens and called out a short simple question in his native tongue.

'Are there any Angles here?'

There was not a face that did not turn to gaze at the huge barbarian warlord shouting unintelligibly in his outlandish tongue but, to Ballista's immense relief, no one answered.

They moved past the livestock market to the eastern portico, the cheap end of the *agora* where the rag-pickers, low-denomination money lenders, magicians, wonder workers and others who traded on human misery and weakness touted for trade. Both Ballista's companions were looking intently back over their shoulders at the alley where the prostitutes stood. It was to be expected of Maximus, but Demetrius was a surprise – Ballista had always thought the young Greek's interests lay elsewhere.

Allfather, but he could do with a woman himself. In one sense it would be so good, so easy. But in another sense it would be neither. There was Julia, his vows to her, the way he had been brought up.

Ballista thought bitterly of the way some Romans, like Tacitus in his *Germania*, held the marital fidelity of the Germans up as a mirror to condemn the contemporary Roman lack of morality. But traditional rustic fidelity was all very well when you lived in a village; it was not designed for those hundreds of miles, weeks of travel, away from their woman. Yet Ballista knew that his aversion to infidelity stemmed from more than just his love for Julia, more than the way he had been brought up. Just as some men carried a lucky amulet into battle, so he carried his fidelity to Julia. Somehow he had developed a superstitious dread that, if he had another woman, his luck would desert him and the next sword thrust or arrow would not wound but kill, not scrape down his ribs but punch through them into his heart.

Thinking now of his companions, Ballista said, 'For the sake of thoroughness, perhaps we should check what is on sale in the alley? Would you two like to do it?'

Demetrius's refusal was immediate. He looked indignant but also slightly shifty. Why was the boy acting so strangely?

'I think I am qualified to do it on my own,' said Maximus.

'Oh yes, I believe you are. But, remember, you are just looking at the goods, not sampling them.' Ballista grinned. 'We will be over there in the middle of the *agora*, learning virtue from the statues set up to the good citizens of Arete.'

The first statue Ballista and Demetrius came to stood on a high plinth. 'Agegos son of Anamu son of Agegos,' read Ballista. 'It must be the father of our Anamu – a bit better-looking.' The statue was in eastern dress and, unlike Anamu, he had a good head of hair. It stood up in tight curls all around his head. He sported a full short beard like his son but also boasted a luxurious moustache, teased out and waxed into points. His face was round, slightly fleshy. 'Yes, better-looking than his son, although that is not hard.'

'For his piety and love of the city' – Ballista read out the rest of the inscription – 'for his complete virtue and courage, always providing safety for the merchants and caravans, for his generous expenditure to these ends from his own resources. In that he saved the recently arrived caravan from the nomads and from the great dangers that surrounded it, the same caravan set up three statues, one in the *agora* of Arete, where he is *strategos*, one in the city of Spasinou Charax, and one on the island of Thilouana, where he is *satrap* (governor). Your geography is better than mine' – Ballista looked at his *accensus* – 'Spasinou Charax is where?'

'At the head of the Persian Gulf,' Demetrius replied.

'And the island of Thilouana is?'

'In the Persian Gulf, off the coast of Arabia. In Greek we call it Tylos.'

'And they are ruled by?'

'Shapur. Anamu's father governed part of the Persian empire. He was both a general here in Arete and a satrap of the Sassanids.'

Ballista looked at Demetrius. 'So which side are the caravan protectors on?'

In the afternoon, about the time of the *meridiatio*, the siesta, it started to rain. The man watched the rain from his first-floor window while he waited for the ink to dry. Although not torrential like the first rains of the year, it was heavy. The street below was empty of people. Water ran down the inner face of the city wall. The steps which ran up to the nearest tower were slick with water, treacherous. A lone rook flew past from left to right.

Judging that the ink was dry, the man lit a lamp from the brazier. He leant out of the window to pull the shutters closed. He secured them and lit another lamp. Although he had locked the door when he entered the room, he now looked around to check that he was alone. Reassured, he picked up the inflated pig's bladder from where he had hidden it and started to read.

> *The artillery magazine has been burnt. All stocks of ballistae* bolts are destroyed. The northern barbarian is gathering stocks of food for the siege. When he has gathered enough, fires will be set against them. There is enough naptha for one more spectacular attack. He has announced that the necropolis will be flattened, many temples and houses destroyed, his troops billeted in those that remain. He is freeing the slaves and enslaving the free. His men strip and rape

women at will. The townsmen mutter against him. He has conscripted townsmen into army units to be commanded by the caravan protectors. Truly the fool has been made blind. He will deliver himself bound hand and foot into the hands of the King of Kings.

His moving finger stopped. His lips ceased inaudibly shaping the words. It would do. The rhetoric was pitched a bit high, but it was not part of his plan to discourage the Persians.

He picked up two oil flasks, one full and one empty, and placed them on the table. He untied the open end of the pig's bladder and squeezed the air out. As it deflated, his writing became illegible. Taking the stopper out of the empty flask, he pushed the bladder inside, leaving its opening protruding. Putting his lips to the bladder and silently giving thanks that he was not Jewish, he reinflated it. Then he folded the protruding swine's intestine back over the spout of the flask and bound it in place with string. When he had trimmed away the excess with a sharp knife, the bladder was completely concealed within the flask, one container hidden within another. Carefully he poured oil from the full flask into the bladder in the other. As he replaced the stopper in both, again he looked round to check he was still alone.

He looked at the oil flask in his hands. They had stepped up the searches at the gates. Sometimes they slit open the seams of men's tunics and the stitching of their sandals; sometimes they stripped the veils from respectable Greek women. For a moment he felt dizzy, light-headed with the risk he was running. Then he steadied himself. He accepted that he might well not survive his mission. That was of no consequence. His people would reap the benefits. His reward would be in the next world.

In the queue at the gate, the courier would know nothing. The flask would arouse no suspicion.

The man took out his stylus and started to write the most innocuous of letters.

My dear brother, the rains have returned . . .

From the colonnade at the front of his house Anamu regarded the rain with disfavour. The streets were again ankle-deep in mud: the rains had put him to the expense of hiring a litter and four bearers to take him to dinner at the palace of the *Dux Ripae*. Anamu did not care to be put to unnecessary expense, and now the litter-bearers were late. He tried to smooth down his irritation by summoning up a half-remembered line from one of the old Stoic masters: 'These four walls do not a prison make.' Anamu was not sure he had it word perfect. 'These stone walls do not a prison make.' Who had said it? Musonius Rufus, the Roman Socrates? No, more likely the ex-slave Epictetus. Perhaps it wasn't a Stoic at all – perhaps he had written it himself?

Warmed by this secret fantasy of other men quoting his words, men completely unknown to him drawing comfort and strength from his wisdom in their time of troubles, Anamu looked out at the rainswept scene. The stone walls of the city were darkened by the water running down them. The battlements were empty; the guards must be sheltering in the nearby tower. An ideal moment for a surprise attack, except that the rains would have turned the land outside the town into a quagmire.

The litter-bearers having eventually arrived, Anamu was handed in and they set off. Anamu knew the identity of the other guests due at the palace. Little happened in the town of Arete that Anamu did not quickly hear about. He paid good money – a lot of good money – to make sure it was that way. It promised to be an interesting evening. The *Dux* had invited all three of the caravan protectors, all of whom had complaints about the barbarian's treatment of the town. Iarhai's daughter would be there too. If ever a girl had a fire burning in her altar, it was her. More than one paid informer had reported that both the barbarian *Dux* and the supercilious young Acilius Glabrio wanted her. And the sophist Callinicus of Petra had been invited. He was making a name for himself – he'd add culture to the mix of tension and sex. With the latter in mind Anamu got out the scrap of papyrus on which earlier, in privacy, he had written a little crib for himself from Athenaeus's *Deipnosophistae, The Wise Men at Dinner*. Anamu was widely known to be very fond of mushrooms and it was most probable that, as an act of respect, the *Dux* would have instructed his chef to include them in the menu. To be prepared, Anamu had lifted some suitably esoteric quotes from the classics about them.

'Ah, here you are,' said Ballista. 'As they say, "Seven makes a dinner, nine makes a brawl." ' Since his rather impressive rhetorical display at the gates, Ballista had gone down and down in Anamu's estimation. The northerner's bluff welcome did nothing to restore the position. 'Let us go to the table.'

The dining room was arranged in the classical *triclinium*, three couches, each for three people, arranged in a U-shape around the tables. Approaching, it became clear that at least the *Dux* had had the good sense to abandon the traditional seating plan. The northerner took the *summus in summo*, the highest place, at the extreme left. He placed Bathshiba on his right, then her father; on the next couch were Callinicus the Sophist, then Anamu and Acilius Glabrio; and on the final one reclined Ogelos, Mamurra and then, in the lowest place, *imus in imo*, Turpio. Traditionally, Ballista would have been where Ogelos now was. The problem would have lain in who would have reclined on the northerner's left, *imus in medio*, the traditional place for the guest of honour. As it was, the caravan protectors were each on different couches and none of them was either next to the host or in the place of honour. Anamu grudgingly admitted to himself that this was cleverly done.

The first course was brought in: two warm dishes – hard-boiled eggs and smoked eel in pine resin sauce and leeks in white sauce; and two cold – black olives and sliced beetroot. The accompanying wine was a light Tyrian, best mixed two to three with water.

'Eels. The ancients have much to say about eels.' The voice of a sophist was trained to dominate theatres, public assemblies, thronged festivals so Callinicus had no problem in commanding the attention of those gathered. 'In his poetry Archestratus tells us that eels are good at Rhegium in Italy, and in Greece from Lake Copais in Boeotia and from the River Strymon in Macedonia.' Anamu felt a surge of pleasure to be part of such a cultured evening. This was the right setting for one such as himself, one of the *pepaideumenoi*, the highly cultured. Yet at the same time he experienced a pang of envy: he had not been able to join in – so far, there were no mushrooms.

'On the River Strymon Aristotle concurs. There the best fishing is at the season of the rising of the Pleiades, when the waters are rough and muddy.'

Allfather, it was a terrible mistake to invite this pompous bastard, thought Ballista. He can probably keep this stuff up for hours.

'The leeks are good.' A caravan protector's voice might not be as melodious as that of a sophist but it was accustomed to making itself heard. It broke the flow of Callinicus's literary anecdotes. Nodding at the green vegetables, Iarhai asked Ballista which chariot team he supported in the Circus.

'The Whites.'

'By god, you must be an optimist.' Iarhai's battered face creased into a grin.

'Not really. I find continual disappointment on the racetrack philosophically good for my soul – toughens it up, gets me used to the disappointments of life.'

As he settled to talk racehorses with her father, Ballista noticed Bathshiba smile a small, mischievous smile. Allfather, but she looked good. She was more demurely clothed than in her father's house, but her dress still broadly hinted at the generous body beneath. Ballista knew that racing was not a subject which was likely to interest her. He wanted to make her laugh, to impress her. Yet he knew he was not good at such small talk. Allfather, he wanted her. It made things worse, made it still harder to think of light, witty things to say. He envied that smug little bastard Acilius Glabrio, who even now seemed to be managing a wordless flirtation across the tables.

The main course arrived: a Trojan pig, stuffed with sausage, *botulus*, and black pudding; two pike, their flesh rendered into a pâté and returned to the skins; then two simple roast chickens. Vegetable dishes also appeared: cooked beet leaves in a mustard sauce, a salad of lettuce, mint and rocket, a relish of basil in oil, and *garum*, fish sauce.

The chef flourished his sharp knife, approached the Trojan pig and slit open its stomach. It surprised no one when the entrails slid out.

'How novel,' said Acilius Glabrio. 'And a good-looking *porcus*. Definitely some *porcus* for me.' His pantomime leer left no doubt that when he repeated the word he was using it as slang for cunt. Looking at Bathshiba, he said, 'And plenty of *botulus* for those who like it.'

Iarhai started to rise from his couch and speak. Quickly Ballista cut him off.

'Tribune, watch your tongue. There is a lady present.'

'Oh, I am sorry, so very sorry, utterly mortified.' His looks belied his words. 'I meant to cause no embarrassment, no offence.' He pointed at the *porcus*. 'I think that this dish led me astray. It always puts me in mind of Trimalchio's feast in the *Satyricon* – you know, the terrible obscene jokes.' He gestured to the pike. 'Just as *porcus* always leads me astray, this dish always makes me homesick.' He spread his hands wide to encompass the three couches. 'Do we not all miss a pike from Rome caught as they say "between the two bridges", above Tiber island and below the influx of the *cloaca maxima*, the main sewer?' He looked around his fellow diners. 'Oh, I have been tactless again – being Roman means so many different things these days.'

Ignoring the last comment, Ogelos jumped in. 'It would be hard for anyone to catch a pike or anything else here in the Euphrates now.' Talking fast and earnestly, he addressed himself to Ballista. 'My men tell me that the fishing boats I own have all been taken by the troops. The soldiers call it requisitioning; I call it theft.' His carefully forked beard quivered with righteous indignation.

Before Ballista could reply, Anamu spoke. 'These ridiculous searches at the gates – my couriers are kept waiting for hours, my possessions are ripped apart, ruined, my private documents displayed to all and sundry, Roman citizens are subjected to the grossest indignities . . . Out of respect for your position, we did not speak out at the council meeting, but now we are in privacy we will – unless that freedom is to be denied us as well?'

Again Ogelos took up the running. 'What sort of freedom are

we defending if ten people, ten *citizens*, cannot meet together? Can no one get married? Are we not to celebrate the rites of our gods?'

'Nothing is more sacred than private property,' Anamu interrupted. 'How dare anyone take our slaves? What next – our wives, our children?'

The complaints continued, the two caravan protectors raising their voices, talking over each other, each drawing to the same conclusion: how could it be worse under the Sassanids, what more could Shapur do to us?

After a time, both men stopped, as if at a signal. Together they turned to Iarhai. 'Why do you say nothing? You are as much affected as us. Our people look to you as well. How can you stay silent?'

Iarhai shrugged. 'It will be as God wills.' He said nothing more.

Iarhai gave an odd intonation to *theos*, the Greek word for god. Ballista was as surprised as the other two caravan protectors by his passive fatalism. He noticed that Bathshiba glanced sharply at her father.

'Gentlemen, I hear your complaints, and I understand them.' Ballista looked each in the eye in turn. 'It pains me to do what must be done but there is no other way. You all remember what was done here to the Sassanid garrison, what you and your fellow townsmen did to the Persian garrison, to their wives, to their children.' He paused. 'If the Persians breach the walls of Arete, all that horror will look like child's play. Let no one be in any doubt: if the Persians take this town there will be no one left to ransom the enslaved, no one left to mourn the dead. If Shapur takes this town it will return to the desert. The wild ass will graze in your *agora* and the wolf will howl in your temples.'

Everyone in the room was staring silently at Ballista. He tried to smile. 'Come, let us try to think of better things. There is a *comoedus*, an actor, waiting outside. Why don't we call him in and have a reading?'

The *comoedus* read well, his voice true and clear. It was a beautiful passage from Herodotus, a story from long ago, from the days of Greek freedom, long before the Romans. It was a story of ultimate courage, of the night before Thermopylae, when the incredulous Persian spy reported to Xerxes, the King of Kings, what he had seen of the Greek camp. The three hundred Spartans were stripped to exercise; they combed each other's hair, taking not the least notice of the spy. It was a beautiful passage, but an unfortunate one given the circumstances. The Spartans were preparing to die.

Reaching out to pick up the carcass of one of the chickens, Turpio spoke for the first time that evening. 'Don't the Greeks call this bird a Persian Awakener?' he asked of no one in particular. 'Then we will treat the Sassanid Persians as I treat this.' And he pulled the carcass apart.

There was a smattering of applause, some murmurs of approval.

Unable to bear another, let alone a rough ex-centurion, getting even such muted praise, Callinicus cleared his throat. 'Of course I am no expert in Latin literature,' he simpered, 'but do not some of your writers on farming refer to a valiant breed of fighting cock as the Medica, that is to say the bird of the Medes, who are *the Persians*? Let us hope that we do not meet one of those.' This ill-timed scholarship was met with a stony silence. The sophist's self-satisfied chuckle faltered and died away.

The desert that now appeared consisted mainly of the usual things – fresh apples and pears, dried dates and figs, smoked cheeses and honey, and walnuts and almonds. Only the *placenta* in the centre was unusual: everyone agreed they had never seen a larger or finer cheesecake. The wine was changed to the sort of forceful Chalybonian said to be favoured by the kings of Persia.

Watching the Persian boy Bagoas anointing Mamurra with balsam and cinnamon and placing a wreath of flowers on his head, a gleam of malevolence shone in Acilius Glabrio's eyes. The young patrician turned to Ballista, a half-smile playing on his face.

'You are to be congratulated, *Dux Ripae*, on the close way in which you follow the example of the great Scipio Africanus.'

'I was not aware that I followed directly any illustrious example of the great conqueror of Hannibal.' Ballista spoke lightly, with just a trace of reserve. 'Unfortunately I am not favoured with nocturnal visits from the god Neptune, but at least I have not been put on trial for corruption.' Some polite laughter greeted this display of historical knowledge. At times it was too easy for people to forget the northerner had been educated in the imperial court.

'No, I was thinking of your Persian boy here.' Without looking, Acilius Glabrio waved a hand in his direction.

There was a pause. Not even the sophist Callinicus said anything. At length, Ballista, suspicion in his voice, asked the patrician to enlighten them.

'Well . . . your Persian boy . . .' The young nobleman was taking his time, enjoying this. 'Doubtless some with filthy minds will provide a disgusting explanation for his presence in your *familia*' – now he hurried on – 'but I am not one of those. I put it down to supreme confidence. Scipio, before the battle of Zama which crushed Carthage, caught one of Hannibal's spies creeping round the Roman camp. Rather than kill him, as is normally the way, Scipio ordered that he be shown the camp, taken to see the men drilling, the engines of war, the magazine.' Acilius Glabrio left time for this last to register. 'And then Scipio set the spy free, sent him back to report to Hannibal, maybe gave him a horse to speed him on his way.'

'Appian.' Callinicus could not contain himself. 'In the version of the story told by the historian Appian, there are three spies.' Everyone ignored the sophist's intervention.

'No one should mistake such confidence for overconfidence, let alone for arrogance and stupidity.' Acilius Glabrio leant back and smiled.

'I have no reason to mistrust any of my *familia*.' Ballista had a face like thunder. 'I have no reason to mistrust Bagoas.'

'Oh no, I am sure that you are right.' The young officer turned his blandest face to the plate in front of him and delicately picked up a walnut.

The morning after the ill-starred dinner given by the *Dux Ripae*, the Persian boy walked the battlements of Arete. In his head he was indulging in an orgy of revenge. He completely slid over such details as how he would gain his freedom or find the tent-dwellers who had enslaved him, let alone how he would get them in his power. They stood already unarmed before him – or rather, one at a time they grovelled on their knees, held out their hands in supplication. They tore their clothes, tipped dust on their heads, they wept and begged. It did them no good. Knife in hand, sword still on hip, he advanced. They offered him their wives, their children, begged him to enslave them. But he was remorseless. Again and again his left hand shot out, his fingers closed in the rough beard and he pulled the terrified face close to his own, explaining what he was going to do and why. He ignored their sobs, their last pleas. In most cases he pulled up the beard to expose the throat. The knife flashed and the blood sprayed red on to the dusty desert. But not for those three. For the three who had done the things they had done to him, that was not enough, nowhere near enough. The hand yanked up the robes, seized the genitals. The knife flashed and the blood sprayed red on to the dusty desert.

He had reached the tower at the north-east angle of the city walls. He had walked the northern battlements from near the temple of Azzanathcona, now the headquarters of the part-mounted and part-infantry Cohors XX Palmyrenorum, current effective strength 180 cavalry, 642 infantry. Repetition helped in memorizing the details. It was a stretch of about three hundred paces and not a single tower. (Silently he repeated 'about 300 paces and no towers'). He climbed down the steps from the wall walk before the sentry at the tower had time to challenge or question him.

The dinner last night had been dangerous. That odious tribune Acilius Glabrio had been right. Yes, he was a spy. Yes, he would do them all the harm he could. He would learn everything in the heart of the *familia* of the *Dux Ripae*, unravel their secrets, find where their weaknesses lay. Then he would escape to the advancing all-conquering Sassanid army. Shapur, King of Kings, King of Aryans and Non-Aryans, beloved of Mazda, would raise him from the dirt, kiss his eyes, welcome him home. The past would be wiped clean. He would be free to start his life as a man again.

It was not that he had been treated in any way badly by Ballista or any of his *familia*. With the exception of the Greek boy, Demetrius, they had almost welcomed him. It was simply that they were the enemy. Here in Arete the *Dux Ripae* was the leader of the unrighteous. The unrighteous denied Mazda. They denied the *bahram* fires. Causing pain to the righteous, they chanted services to the demons, calling on them by name. False in speech, unrighteous in action, justly were they *margazan*, accursed.

He was now approaching the military granaries. All eight were the same. The loading platforms were at one end, the doors the other, both closely guarded. At the sides there were louvres, but set high up under the eaves, too high to gain access. There were, however, ventilation panels below waist level – a slight man might be able to squeeze through; any man could pour inflammable materials through. The granaries were brick with stone roofs but the floors, walls and beams inside would be made of wood, and food stuffs, especially oil and grain, burnt well. One incendiary device would, at best, burn only two granaries, and only then if the wind was in the right direction or the fire fierce enough to jump the narrow eavesdrip between the target and its immediate neighbour. But then simultaneous attacks would cause more confusion, and lead to greater loss.

Bagoas had been unable to discover the quantities of supplies currently held in the granaries. He was hoping to get some idea by looking through the doors now.

Moving between the first two pairs of granaries, he saw that all the doors to his left were shut, but that the first two to his right were open. As he passed he tried to see inside. There were two legionaries on guard up by the door, four more off duty lounging at the foot of the steps. They were staring at him. Hurriedly, he looked away.

'Hey, bum boy, come over here. We'll teach you a thing or two.' The Persian boy tried to walk past normally, as if unconcerned. Then the comments stopped. Out of the corner of his eye he could see one of the legionaries talking low and earnestly to his friends. He was pointing. Now they were all looking more intently at him; then they started to follow him.

He did not want to run, but he did not want to dawdle; he

wanted to walk normally. He felt himself quicken his pace. He could sense that they quickened theirs as well.

Perhaps they just happened to be going the same way; perhaps they were not following him at all. If he turned down one of the alleys separating the pairs of granaries, maybe they would just walk on by. He turned into the alley on the left. A moment later they turned into the alley too. He ran.

Sandals slipping on the dust, kicking up odd pieces of rubbish, Bagoas sprinted as fast as he could. Behind him he heard running feet. If he turned right at the end of the alley and past the loading bays, he had only to turn that final corner and he would be in sight of the northern door of the palace of the *Dux Ripae*.

He skidded round the first corner and almost ran straight into an ox cart. Sidestepping the lumbering vehicle, he put his head down and sprinted once more. Behind him he heard a commotion; shouting, cursing. He was pulling clear. There were just a few paces, just one corner to go.

As he cleared the corner of the granary he knew there was no escape. Two legionaries were pounding towards him. The lane was narrow, no wider than ten paces. There was no way he could dodge and twist past both of them. He stopped, looking round. There was the northern door to the palace, only some thirty or forty paces away – but it was the other side of the legionaries. To his left was the blank wall of the palace, to his right the unscalable side of a granary. Despite his speed, despite the ox cart, the other two would be on him in a moment.

Something hit him hard in the back, sending him sprawling forward into the dirt. His legs were seized. He was dragged backwards. Face down, his arms were being skinned on the surface of the lane.

He kicked out with his right leg. There was a grunt of pain. He jerked half to his feet, yelling for help. He saw the two *equites singulares* on guard duty at the palace door look uninterestedly at him. Before he could call again a heavy blow struck his right ear. His world swam around him. His face hit dirt again.

'Traitor! You dirty little traitor.' He was manhandled into the narrow eavesdrip that ran between the nearest two granaries, hauled to his feet, pushed into one of the bays formed by the buttresses projecting from each storehouse. He was slammed back against a wall.

'Think you can walk around as you like, do you? Walk right past us as you spy on us?' One of the legionaries got the boy's neck in a painful grip, brought his face inches from the boy's. 'Our *dominus* told us what you are – fucking spy, fucking bum boy. Well, your barbarian isn't around to save you now.' He punched Bagoas hard in the stomach.

Two legionaries pulled the boy upright and held on to him as the other two hit him repeatedly in the face and stomach.

'We're going to have some fun with you, boy. Then we're going to put a stop to your games for ever.' There was a flurry of blows, then they let him go. He fell to the ground. Now they took it in turns to kick him.

Bagoas curled into a ball. The kicking continued. He could smell the leather of their military boots, taste the sharp iron tang of his own blood. No, Mazda, no . . . don't let this be like the tent-dwellers, no. For no reason that he could follow, a fragment of poetry came into his mind.

> I sometimes think that never blows so red
> The Rose as where some buried Caesar bled.

The kicking paused.

'What the fuck are you looking at?'

Through his bruised, half-closed eyes, the Persian boy saw Calgacus outlined at the end of the eavesdrip.

'Oh, aye, you are hard men – the four of you on one boy. Maybe you think you could take on one old man as well.'

To the Persian boy's eyes, Calgacus looked younger and bigger than ever before. But it could end only one way. The youth wanted to shout, wanted to tell the old Caledonian to run, tell him that it would do no good him being beaten, maybe killed, as well, but no words came.

'Don't say we didn't warn you, you old fucker.' The legionaries were all facing Calgacus.

There was an exclamation of surprise and pain. One of the legionaries shot forward, tripping over the Persian boy's outstretched legs. The other three looked stupidly down at their friend. As they started to turn the youth saw Maximus's fist smash into the face of the legionary on the left. The man wore an almost comical look of shock as he slumped back against the wall, his nose seemingly spread right across his face, fountaining blood.

The legionary that Maximus had knocked forward had landed on his hands and knees. Calgacus stepped forward and kicked him sharply in the face. His head snapped back and he collapsed motionless, moaning quietly.

The two legionaries still on their feet glanced at each other, unsure what to do.

'Pick up these pieces of shit and get the fuck out of here,' said Maximus.

The soldiers hesitated, then did as they were told. They supported their *contubernales* down the eavesdrip. When they reached the road, the one with the badly broken nose called back that it was not over, they would get all three of them.

'Yeah, yeah,' muttered Maximus as he bent over Bagoas. 'Give a hand, Calgacus, let's get this little bastard home.'

> I sometimes think that never blows so red
> The Rose as where some buried Caesar bled.

The fragment was running through the Persian boy's thoughts just before he passed out.

At a gesture from Ballista the soldier again knocked on the door. So far it had been a very trying day. Ballista had set out at the second hour of daylight accompanied by Demetrius, two scribes, three messengers, Romulus, who today did not have to carry the heavy standard, and two *equites singulares*. As the ten men had walked to the southern end of Wall Street, some legionaries in the distance, far enough away not to be recognizable, had howled like wolves.

Ballista and his party were inspecting all the properties near the western desert wall that would soon be destroyed, encased in rubble and mud. The complaints voiced at dinner the previous night by the caravan protectors were on the lips of all the residents. This morning they seemed to have added meaning. They were being voiced by the priests whose temples would be torn down, whose gods would be evicted. They were being voiced by the men whose houses would be razed, whose families would be made homeless. Some of these were defiant; others fought back tears, their wives and children peeping round the doors from the women's rooms. Whether they saw him as an irresponsible imperial favourite, a power-drunk army officer or just a typically stupid barbarian, none of them saw Ballista's actions as anything but a cruel and thoughtless whim.

With some irritation, Ballista again gestured for the soldier to knock on the door of the house. They did not have all day, and they were only at the end of the third block out of eight. This time, as soon as the soldier finished hammering, the door opened.

In the gloom of the vestibule stood a short man dressed as a philosopher: rough cloak and tunic, barefoot, wild long hair and beard. In one hand he held a staff, the other fingered a wallet hanging from his belt.

'I am Marcus Clodius Ballista, *Dux* –'

'I know,' the man rudely interrupted. It was hard to see clearly, as Ballista was looking from the bright sunlight into the relative darkness, yet the man seemed very agitated. His left hand moved from his wallet and began to fidget with his belt buckle, which was shaped like a fish.

Allfather, here we go again, thought Ballista. Let's try and deflect this before he starts ranting.

'Which school of philosophy do you follow?'

'What?' The man looked blankly at Ballista as if the words meant nothing to him.

'You are dressed like a Cynic, or possibly a hardline Stoic.

Although, of course, the symbols are appropriate for almost all the schools.'

'No . . . no, I am no philosopher . . . certainly not, nothing of the sort.' He looked both offended and frightened.

'Are you the owner of this house?' Ballista pressed on. He had wasted enough time.

'No.'

'Will you fetch him?'

'I do not know . . . he is busy.' The man looked wildly at Ballista and the soldiers. 'I will get him. Follow me.' Suddenly he turned and led the way through the vestibule into a small, paved central atrium. 'Inspect what you will,' he said then, without warning, vanished up some steps to the first floor.

Ballista and Demetrius looked at each other.

'Well, one cannot say that philosophy has brought him inner peace,' said the Greek.

'Only the wise man is happy,' quoted Ballista, although in all honesty he was not certain where the quote came from. 'Let's have a look around.'

There was an open portico off to their left. Straight ahead they entered a long room which ran almost the length of the house. It was painted plain white and furnished only with benches. It looked like a schoolroom. There was an almost overwhelming smell of incense. Re-entering the atrium, they looked into another room, opposite the portico. Empty but for a few storage jars in one of the far corners. Again the room was painted white. Again the almost choking smell of incense masked every other.

There was one final room on the ground floor, separated from the vestibule by the stairs up which the man had vanished. Entering, Ballista stopped in surprise. Although, like the rest of the house, almost empty of furniture, this room was a riot of colour. At one end was a columned archway, painted to resemble marble. The ceiling was sky-blue and speckled with silver stars. Under the arch was a bath, big enough for one and, behind it, a picture of a man carrying a sheep.

Ballista gazed about him. Wherever he looked there were pictures. He found himself staring at a crude painting of three men. A man on the left was carrying a bed towards a man on the right, who was lying on another bed. Above them a third man stood, holding his hand out above the reclining figure.

'Fucking odd,' said one of the soldiers.

Just to the right of this picture, a man dressed as a peasant was hovering over the sea. Some sailors looked at him in amazement from a well-rigged ship.

'Greetings, Marcus Clodius Ballista, *Vir Egregius, Dux Ripae*.' The speaker had entered quietly behind them. Turning, Ballista saw a tall man dressed in a plain blue tunic with white trousers and simple sandals. He was balding, hair cropped close at the sides. He sported a full beard and an open smile. He looked very familiar.

'I am Theodotus son of Theodotus, Councillor of the City of Arete, and priest to the Christian community of the town.' He smiled pleasantly.

Annoyed with himself for not recognizing the Christian priest, Ballista grinned apologetically and thrust out his hand.

'I hope that you will forgive any rudeness in welcoming you on the part of my brother Josephus. You understand that, since the persecution launched by the emperor Decius a few years ago, we Christians get nervous when Roman soldiers knock on our doors.' He shook Ballista's hand and laughed heartily. 'Of course things are much better now, under the wise rule of Valerian and Gallienus, and we pray that they live long, but still old habits die hard. We find it best to remain discreet.'

'No, if anything I was unintentionally rude. I mistook your brother for a pagan philosopher.' Although Theodotus seemed amiably enough disposed, Ballista thought it best to forestall any trouble if he could. 'I am very sorry, so very sorry that it is necessary to destroy your place of worship. I assure you that it would not happen were it not absolutely necessary. I will try my utmost to get you paid compensation – if the city does not fall, obviously.'

Rather than the storm of protest and complaint that Ballista was expecting, Theodotus spread his hands wide and smiled a beatific smile.

'It will all fall out as God wills,' said the priest. 'He moves in mysterious ways.'

Ballista was going to say something else, but a waft of incense caught the back of his throat and set off a fit of coughing.

'We burn a lot of incense for the glory of the lord,' said Theodotus, patting the northerner on the back. 'As I came in I saw you looking at the paintings. Would you like me to explain the stories behind them?'

Still unable to speak, Ballista nodded to indicate he would. Mercifully, today he was not attended by the Christian-hating trooper.

Theodotus had only just begun when a soldier burst through the door. '*Dominus*.' A quick-sketched salute and the legionary rushed through the army greeting. '*Dominus*. We have found Gaius Scribonius Mucianus.'

Gaius Scribonius Mucianus was dead.

Violent unexpected death in peacetime always draws a crowd. A dense throng of soldiers and civilians, old and young, clustered under the eastern wall by the entrance to one of the old water tunnels.

Romulus shouted something in Latin, then Greek, and finally Aramaic and reluctantly the crowd shuffled sideways, opening a small path to let Ballista and his entourage through. Mamurra, Acilius Glabrio and a centurion from IIII Scythica stood over the body. They turned and saluted.

Ballista looked inquisitively at Demetrius, who leant close and whispered 'Lucius Fabius' in his ear.

'Lucius Fabius, would you get the crowd to move back, at least thirty paces?'

The centurion rapped out orders and his legionaries used their heavy javelins as herdsmen use their crooks to herd the bystanders away.

Scribonius Mucianus lay on his back, arms and legs sprawling, head twisted sideways at an unnatural angle. His clothes were stained with long-dried blood and green mould. His face was a mottled yellow-green turning black. Ballista had seen more corpses than he wanted. Five years earlier, the siege of Novae had given him the unwanted opportunity to observe the dead decompose. In front of the walls defended by the northerner and his general Gallus thousands of Goths had lain unburied under the summer sun for nearly two months. Ballista guessed that the tribune had been dead for at least two months. Quietly he asked Demetrius to fetch a local doctor and an undertaker to make independent estimates.

'How do you know it is him?' Ballista directed the question to all three men still close to the corpse.

'Of course it is him,' Acilius Glabrio replied. 'Not that his looks have improved.'

Ballista said nothing.

'One of the soldiers recognized his seal ring,' said Mamurra. The *praefectus fabrum* thought for a while. 'And he wears the gold ring of an equestrian, the sword belt is fancy, the clothes expensive . . . There were thirty silver coins near the body.'

'Near the body?'

'Yes, his purse had been cut from his belt, the coins tipped out on the floor.' Mamurra handed over the purse.

'Not robbery then.'

'No, not unless they were disturbed.' Mamurra slowly shook his head. 'He was searched. The seams of his tunic and his sandals were slit. Searched but not robbed.'

There were stentorian shouts, loud military oaths. Again the crowd, which was growing by the moment, reluctantly nudged apart. Through the narrow passage opened to the corpse strode Maximus and Turpio.

'Well, he did not burn our artillery magazine,' said Maximus straight away. All the group, except Ballista and Turpio, turned to look intently at the Hibernian. 'Come on, it must have crossed everyone's mind. Now we know he didn't do it. He has been dead too long. By the look of him he was dead before we even reached Seleuceia.'

All the time his bodyguard was talking, Ballista was watching Turpio. The latter's usually humorous, mobile face was very still. He didn't take his eyes off Scribonius Mucianus. Finally, very low, he said, 'You poor bastard, you poor fucking fool.'

Ballista got down on one knee by the corpse and studied it

intently, starting at the head and working down, his nose inches from the corrupt flesh. Demetrius, his gorge rising, wondered how his *kyrios* could bring himself to do such a thing.

'He was robbed of something if not of money.' Ballista pointed at the ornate sword belt. 'See – here and here, two sets of thongs which have been cut. These ones secured this purse.' The cut ends he held up matched. He picked up the other thongs. 'And from these hung a –'

'A writing block,' said Turpio. 'He always had a writing block with him, hanging from his belt. He was always fiddling with it.' A wry smile passed across the ex-centurion's face. 'He was always opening it to do sums and write figures down.'

'Was it found?' Ballista asked. The centurion Lucius Fabius shook his head.

'Would someone get me some water and a towel?' Ballista didn't look but heard someone moving away. Allfather, power is corrupting me, he thought. I give orders and expect them to be obeyed. I do not even know or care *who* obeys. The corruption of power is as certain as the natural corruption in this corpse.

Steeling himself, fighting his natural repugnance, Ballista gripped the decaying corpse with both hands and rolled it over on to its face. He resisted the impulse to wipe his hands. Life in the *imperium* had taught him not to show weakness.

'Well, at least it is easy enough to see how he was killed.' Ballista pointed to a savage wound to the side and back of Scribonius Mucianus's left thigh. 'That brought him down. He had his back to his killer. Maybe he was running away. A sword cut from a right-handed man and, from the size of the wound, probably a standard military sword, a *spatha*.'

A pitcher of water and a towel were placed on the ground. Ballista shifted to look at what was left of the back of Scribonius Mucianus's head. The mess of congealed flesh and brains was totally black. Liquid oozed out. The wounds resembled coal tar and seemed to have its faint iridescence. Ballista was beginning to feel sick. He forced himself to tip water on the wounds, to wash them with his bare hands.

'Five, six, seven . . . at least seven sword cuts to the back of the head. Quite probably the same sword. What every master at arms likes us to do – get your man down with a leg wound, on all fours, on the ground, then finish off with as many hard blows to the head as it takes, as many as you have time for.' Gratefully Ballista let one of his scribes, the one with the Punic accent, pour water over his hands. He thanked him and took the towel. 'Who found him?'

The centurion waved a legionary forward.

'Gaius Aurelius Castricius, soldier of the Vexillatio of Legio IIII Scythica, century of Lucius Fabius, *Dominus*. We will do what is ordered, and at every command we will be ready, *Dominus*.'

'Where did you find him?'

'*Dominus*, in a side gallery of this disused tunnel. *Dominus*, down there.' He pointed to some steps leading down to a black hole.

'What were you doing down there?'

'Ordered to search all the side passages and galleries, *Dominus*.' The legionary looked vaguely embarrassed.

'Castricius here had the skills for the job,' his centurion interjected. 'On account of his having plenty of experience in tunnels before he took the *sacramentum*, the military oath.'

The legionary looked more embarrassed. No one went down the mines by choice. As a civilian, Castricius must have been convicted of something bad to end up there.

'Well, Castricius, you had better show me where you found him.' Telling Maximus to attend him and everyone else to wait above ground, Ballista followed the legionary. Just inside the tunnel they paused to light lamps and let their eyes adjust. The soldier was making small talk. Ballista was not listening; he was praying.

This tunnel was worse, far worse, than the other one. The footing was rougher and more slippery. There were reasons it had been boarded up. Several times they had to climb over piles of rock fallen from the ceiling or collapsed from the walls. Once they had to crawl through a gap little wider than the northerner's shoulders. It must have been hell getting the corpse out of here. Down and down. It was very dark. It was very wet. There was water underfoot, water running down the walls. It was like a living descent into

Niflheim, Misty Hell, the bitter-cold realm of unending winter, the realm of the dead, where the dragon Nidhogg gnawed at the roots of Yggdrasill, the World Tree, until the end of time.

'Here. I found him here.' They were in an abandoned side gallery, a dead end, too low to stand up in.

'Exactly where was he?' Ballista asked.

'Just here.'

'What position was he in?'

'On his back. Arms outstretched against the walls. Feet together.'

'Maximus, would you mind lying down in the position of the corpse?' Filthy as all three men already were, the bodyguard shot his *dominus* a look that suggested he minded quite a lot. Nevertheless, the Hibernian got down on the floor and let Castricius arrange him in precisely the right position.

'Scribonius Mucianus was certainly not killed here. Maximus, would you get on your hands and knees?'

The bodyguard looked as if he were going to make a joke, but decided against it. Ballista drew his *spatha*. He tried to mime a cut at Maximus's head. The ceiling of rock was far too low.

'It must have been hell getting the corpse down here,' said Ballista. 'It must have taken more than one man.'

'Almost certainly. But maybe one very strong man might just have been able to do it,' Castricius replied.

Emerging into the sunlight, they were confronted by a ring of faces. At the front were the army officers, Mamurra, Acilius Glabrio and Turpio. They had been joined by the three caravan protectors, on the grounds that, as commanders of units of *numeri*, they were also army officers now. Behind them, still kept back by the legionaries, the crowd had grown yet bigger. It was fronted by the other councillors, Theodotus the hirsute Christian well to the fore. The ordinary people, the *demos*, were further back and further back still were the slaves. At any gathering, the people of the *imperium* tended to arrange themselves by status, as if they were at the theatre or the spectacles.

'The poor fool, the poor fucking fool,' said Turpio. 'As soon as he heard of your appointment he started acting more and more strangely. Just before he disappeared, two days before I set out to meet you at the coast, he had taken to talking to himself. Several times I heard him mutter that now everything would be all right, he had found something out that would make everything all right.'

'What did he mean?' Ballista asked.

'I have no idea.'

Ballista was fighting the urge to leave his desk. He had a vague sense of unease, a strong feeling of restlessness. Several times in the past hour he had given way. Pacing about did no good. Yet it could have been worse. It was not as if he had received a nocturnal visit from the big man. Indeed, thankfully, the late emperor Maximinus Thrax had not made an appearance since that night on the *Concordia* off the Syrian coast. Did this undermine Julia's Epicurean rationalism, her view that the daemon was nothing more than a bad dream brought on by fatigue and anxiety? Since Ballista had reached Arete he had been dog-tired, and no one could deny he had been under great stress – one of his chief officers missing then discovered murdered, the other insubordinate and insufferable; the loyalty of the leading locals questionable; the artillery magazine burnt down. And at least one murderous traitor loose in the city.

It was the military dispositions for the defence of the town that were troubling him now. As a Roman general should, he had summoned his *consilium*, heard their opinions, taken advice. But ultimately the decisions were his alone. His plans had been finalized, making the best use of the pitifully inadequate manpower at his disposal, and were ready to be unveiled to his staff and put into operation. Yet he worried that he had missed something obvious, that there was some terrible logical flaw in them. It was ridiculous, but he was less worried that the thing he had overlooked would cause the fall of the town, lead to bloody ruin, than that the omission would be obvious to one of his officers straight away, that he would be exposed to the mocking laughter of Acilius Glabrio. A large part of him remained the barbarian youth of sixteen winters dragged into the *imperium* of the Romans. He still feared ridicule above all things.

Ballista got up from his desk and walked out on to the terrace of the palace. The sky was a perfect Mesopotamian blue. It was winter, the sixth of December, ten days before the *ides* of the month. Now the sun had burnt off the early morning mist, the weather was that of a glorious spring day in Ballista's northern homeland. He leant with his back to the wall of the terrace. From the river far below the sounds of the water carriers and the fish market, now all under military supervision, floated up. Nearer at hand, off to his left beyond the cross wall which separated the terrace from the battlements, he heard children playing. Turning to look, he saw four small children throwing a ball. One clambered up and stood precariously on the crenulations. Without thinking, Ballista started towards him. Before he had gone more than a few paces a woman in the flowing robes of the tent-dwellers snatched the boy to safety. Her scolding carried in the clear air.

Ballista thought of his son. Marcus Clodius Isangrim he had named him. No one could object to the first two names: nothing could be more conventional than the first son taking the good Roman *praenomen* and *nomen* of his father. Julia, however, had objected as vociferously as only an Italian woman can to her son carrying a barbarian *cognomen*.

Ballista knew that it was only their exquisite good manners, the manners that came with generations of senatorial birth, that had stopped Julia's relatives sniggering at the naming ceremony. Yet it was important to Ballista. Fear ridicule although he did, it was important that the boy grew up knowing his northern heritage. As he had tried to explain to Julia, it was not sentiment alone that had decided the choice. The *imperium* used diplomatic hostages as tools in its diplomacy. At any time, if the emperors became dissatisfied with Ballista's father, they would without a moment of hesitation uproot Ballista, send him back to the north and, backed by Roman arms and money, attempt to install him as the new *Dux* of the Angles. If Ballista were dead, they would send his son. Such things seldom worked out well, but neither Ballista nor his son would have any choice in the matter. So the boy was called Isangrim after his grandfather and he was learning the native language of his father.

They called him Isangrim. He was very beautiful, his hair a mass of blond curls, his eyes a green-blue. He was three years old, and he was playing hundreds of miles, several weeks' journey away.

And what of his *familia* here? Bagoas had taken a bad beating. He would be laid up for some time. Calgacus had been right that the boy should be followed. It did seem that, in his naive way, the boy was playing at being a spy. It was lucky that Maximus had been there. Calgacus was tough, but it was unlikely that the old Caledonian could have dealt with four legionaries on his own. There were two particularly worrying features to the incident. First, the legionaries had been encouraged, at least indirectly, by Acilius Glabrio. Second, two of the *equites singulares* had watched and not intervened as the boy was dragged off. And what should Ballista do with Bagoas when he recovered? Yet another cause of an uneasy mind.

The usual coughing, wheezing and muttering heralded the arrival of Calgacus.

'That hot-looking Syrian girl you want is here. I said you were busy, but she said she needed to see you *badly*.' The stress on 'badly' was accompanied by a lascivious leer of epic proportions. 'I hope you can give her what she *badly* needs.'

'Thank you for your concern. I will do my best. Would you show her in?'

'Dressed as a boy she is, trousers and the like.' Calgacus showed no sign of moving. 'Turn her round and you can have the best of both worlds.'

'Thank you for the advice. If you could show her in, you can get back to whatever appalling things you get up to in your own quarters.'

The Caledonian moved off in no great hurry, muttering at his customary volume. 'Whatever I get up to . . . looking after you morning, noon and fucking night, that's what I get up to.'

Ballista drew himself to his full height. Chin up, shoulders back, he willed himself to appear attractive.

Bathshiba walked out into the sunshine with Calgacus and one of her father's mercenaries.

'The *Dux Ripae* will see you now,' the Caledonian said with some ceremony, and left.

Bathshiba walked across to Ballista. The mercenary stayed where he was.

'*Ave*, Marcus Clodius Ballista, *Vir Egregius*, *Dux Ripae*,' she said formally.

'*Ave*, Bathshiba, daughter of Iarhai,' Ballista replied.

'My father wishes to extend his condolences to you on the death of your officer Scribonius Mucianus, and to offer what help he can give in catching the murderer.'

'Thank your father for me. Did he send you with this message?'

'No. He sent Haddudad there. I told Haddudad I would come with him.' She laughed, her teeth very white, her eyes very black. 'People get very nervous confronting barbarians in their lair. Who can tell what they will do?'

Ballista wished very badly to say something light and witty. Nothing came. There was just the hollow feeling of desire. As real as a waking dream, he pictured himself taking her arm, leading her back into the palace, to his room, to his bed, throwing her down on it, unbuckling her belt, dragging down . . .

She shifted on her feet and brought him back to reality.

'Would you like a drink?'

'No, I cannot stay long. Even with Haddudad here it would not be good for my reputation.' There was a naughtiness, a hint of wantonness about her smile that further unsteadied Ballista.

'Before you go . . . there was something I wanted to ask you.' She waited. 'I saw a statue in the *agora* the other day.'

'There are many statues there. Most set up by the grateful inhabitants of the town to celebrate the virtues of caravan protectors like my father.'

'This one was of Anamu's father. He was called Agegos.' She did not speak. 'The inscription said that Agegos was satrap of Thilouana. The island of Thilouana is in the Persian gulf. It is part of the empire of the Persians. It is ruled by Shapur.'

For a moment Bathshiba looked puzzled, then she laughed a laugh of genuine amusement. 'Oh, I see what you are thinking.

You are wondering how loyal to Rome can a man be whose father was a satrap for the Persians.' She laughed again. 'My father will be furious that I have thrown away an opportunity to blacken one of his rivals to the new *Dux Ripae* . . . although he has been strangely pacific recently, even towards them.' She thought for a moment then continued. 'It is all perfectly normal for a caravan protector. The wealth of other rich men in the *imperium* ultimately depends on land. The caravan protectors own land around the villages to the north-west and across the river. They receive rents from their tenants, and from the properties they own in town. Although it is seldom mentioned, they lend money out on interest. But their real wealth comes from escorting caravans between Persia and Rome. To protect the caravans as they cross the frontier they need contacts, connections in both empires. They have many connections also with the tent-dwellers of the deep desert who acknowledge neither Persia nor Rome.'

'Thank you,' said Ballista. 'But one thing puzzles me. How does this protection generate their wealth? The inscription spoke of Anamu's father protecting caravans from his own resources.'

'You have a lot to learn.' She gave the big northerner a very different look from before, possibly a look of uncomplicated affection. 'Possibly there is some truth in the image of the . . . naive barbarian from beyond the north wind. My father and his like act out of the generosity of their souls. No merchant would dream of offering *payment*, and a caravan protector would be offended for it to be offered, but a suitable *gift*, a completely voluntary *contribution*, is quite a different matter. Merchants are *grateful* for protection.'

They were standing close together. She was looking up at him. He began to lean forward. She stepped away, the look of mischief back in her eyes.

'Don't forget that you have a wife – and Haddudad has a sharp sword.'

Winter advanced on the town of Arete.

It was nothing like the iron-bound winters of the land of the Angles. There, the snows could lie heavy on the fields, over the huts of the peasants and the high-roofed halls of the warriors for months on end. Beyond the stockades the freezing fogs enfolded the improvident and the unwary. Men and animals died in the cold.

Winter in Arete was a different beast, gentler but capricious. Most nights in December and January there was a frost. On the days that it rained, many as the old year died but fewer after the solstice, it rained hard. The ground turned into a sea of mud. The air remained chill. Then the strong north-eastern winds would blow away the clouds, the sun would dawn in splendour, warm as a spring day by the northern ocean, and the land would dry – before it rained again.

In some ways life in Arete continued as normal. The priests and the devout celebrated the festivals of their particular gods – Sol Invictus, Jupiter, and Janus, Aphlad, Atargatis and Azzanathcona. Criers preceded the processions through the streets warning those of less, different or no faith to lay down their tools lest the priests and their deities catch the ill-omened sight of men at work on the holy day. Ballista had bowed to popular pressure and rescinded his edict banning gatherings of ten or more. He hoped that this concession might make the other stringencies he had introduced more bearable. Certainly this concession was welcome at the two great festivals of the winter, at the Saturnalia, the seven days of present-giving, gambling and drinking in late December when slaves dined like their masters, and again at the Compitalia, the three days in early January when extra rations, including wine, were issued to the servile.

As ever, the first of January, the *kalends*, saw the garrison and those provincials eager to impress the authorities renew their oath of loyalty to the emperors and their family. On the same day, new magistrates took up office, Ogelos replacing Anamu as *archon* in Arete. As ever, the soldiers looked forward to the seventh of January: pay day, with a roast dinner to follow the sacrifices – to Jupiter Optimus Maximus an ox, to Juno, Minerva and Salus a cow, to Father Mars a bull. As ever, rents had to be paid on the first of January; debtors fretted at the approach of the *kalends*, *nones* and *ides* of each month, when interest on loans became due; and the superstitious feared the unlucky 'black days' that followed.

Yet in many, many ways this winter in Arete was abnormal. Day by day the city became more like an armed camp. Under the slow but careful eye of Mamurra the physical defences of the town began to take shape. Gangs of impressed labourers tore down the proud tower tombs of the necropolis and teams of oxen and donkeys hauled the debris to the town. More labourers heaped the rubble against the inner and outer faces of the western wall, slowly shaping it into the core of huge ramps – the glacis and counter-glacis. Once padded with reeds and faced with mud brick it was hoped these ramps would keep the walls standing in the face of whatever the Sassanids could throw at them. As each area of the *necropolis* was cleared, further gangs of workmen started to dig the wide ditch that would hinder approach to the desert wall.

The interior of the town was likewise loud with activity. Blacksmiths beat ploughshares into swords, arrow points and the heads of javelins. Carpenters wove osiers and wood to make shields. Fletchers worked flat out to produce the innumerable arrows and artillery bolts demanded by the military.

In every home, bar and brothel – at least when there were no Roman soldiers within earshot – the abnormality of the winter was discussed. On the one hand, the big barbarian bastard was roundly condemned: homes, tombs and temples desecrated, the slaves freed, the free reduced to the state of the servile, civic liberties stripped away, the modesty of wives and daughters compromised. On the other, only the *Dux* offered any hope: perhaps all the sacrifices would prove worth while. Round and round the arguments went, down the backstreets and the muddy alleys from the little sanctuary of the Tyche of Arete behind the Palmyrene Gate to the stinking lean-tos down by the waterside. The citizens of Arete were both outraged and scared. They were also tired. The *Dux* was driving them hard.

The soldiers were also working hard. On New Year's day Ballista had unveiled his dispositions for the defence of the town. No one, not even Acilius Glabrio, had laughed. The northerner had concentrated his manpower on the western wall facing the open desert. Here the battlements would be manned by no fewer than eight of the twelve centuries of Legio IIII Scythica and all six centuries of Cohors XX Palmyrenorum. The arrangement was that each section of battlement for two towers would be defended by one century of legionaries and one of auxiliaries. An additional century from IIII Scythica would be stationed at the main gate. At the extreme north of the wall only one century of Cohors XX would be available to cover the last four towers, but here the northern ravine curled round to provide additional defence and the towers in any case were closer together.

The other walls were far less well defended. The northern wall facing the ravine was held by only one century of IIII Scythica and two dismounted *turmae* of Cohors XX. The eastern wall facing the Euphrates would be guarded by the irregular *numerus* of Anamu, with one century of IIII Scythica seeing to the Porta Aquaria, the tunnels and the two gates down by the water. Finally, the garrison of the southern wall above the ravine would consist of the *numeri* of Iarhai and Ogelos, with just one dismounted *turma* of Cohors XX guarding the postern gate.

The real weakness of the plan was the small number of reserves – just two centuries of IIII Scythica, one stationed around the *campus martius* and one in the great caravanserai, and two *turmae* of Cohors XX, one guarding the granaries and one the new artillery magazine. At current levels of manning, that amounted to a mere 140 legionaries and 72 auxiliaries.

Yet the plan won guarded approval. Surely the main danger did lie on the western wall. It would be held by no fewer than 560 men from IIII Scythica and 642 from Cohors XX. The auxiliaries were bowmen and the legionaries expert hand-to-hand. They would be backed by twenty-five pieces of artillery, nine throwing stones and sixteen bolts.

The senior officers had been further reassured when Ballista outlined the additional measures that would be put in place when the glacis, counter-glacis and ditch were complete. The last two hundred yards to the western wall would be sown with traps. There would be thousands of caltrops, spiked metal balls. No matter which way a caltrop landed, a wicked spike always pointed upwards. There would be pits. Some would contain spikes, others the huge jars which had been requisitioned, filled with the limited stockpile of naptha. Stones to drop on the enemy would be stockpiled on the walls. There would be cranes equipped with chains, both to drop the larger stones and to hook any Sassanid rams which neared the wall. Large metal bowls of sand would be heated over fires. At the siege of Novae, white-hot sand had proved nearly as effective as had the naptha at Aquileia.

On the sixth of January, his plans well in hand, Ballista decided he needed a drink. Not an effete Greek or Roman *symposium*, but a proper drink. He asked Maximus if he could find a decent bar – does the Pontifex Maximus shit in the woods? – and tell Mamurra that he was welcome to join them. It was the day after the *nones* of January, one of the 'black days', but Ballista had not grown up with the superstitions of the Romans.

'This looks all right.' Ballista ran his eyes over the bar. The room and the girls looked clean. On the wall opposite him was a painting of a couple having sex balanced on two tightropes. The girl was on her hands and knees, the man taking her from behind and drinking a cup of wine. He looked out at the viewer with a complacent air.

'I chose it because I heard that Acilius Glabrio had ruled it off limits for his legionaries,' said Maximus.

'Why?' Mamurra asked.

'Oh, because when he comes here he likes some privacy to be buggered senseless by the barmen,' replied Maximus.

Mamurra looked owlishly at the Hibernian before starting to laugh. Ballista joined in.

A pretty blond girl with big breasts, few clothes and a fixed smile came over with their drinks and some things to eat. Maximus asked her name. As she bent over, the Hibernian slid his hand down her tunic and played with one of her breasts. He tweaked her nipple until it was erect. 'Maybe see you later,' he called after her as she left.

'Poor girl. Working here must be like walking round with her tunic pulled up, endlessly being pawed by bastards like you,' said Ballista.

'Just because you're not getting any,' Maximus replied. 'Not even from Bathshiba.'

'Do you want to talk about Massilia?' Ballista's words closed the exchange and the three men drank in silence for a while.

'Right, let's talk about the two things we have to talk about. Get them out of the way so we can relax.' Ballista paused, and the others looked expectantly at him. 'Who do you think killed Scribonius Mucianus?'

'Turpio,' Maximus replied with no hesitation. Ballista looked sharply at Mamurra, who quickly swore he would not speak of this conversation to anyone else. 'He had motive: Scribonius was blackmailing him. He had opportunity: he was Scribonius's second-in-command. The timing fits: on Turpio's own account Scribonius *disappeared* two days before Turpio left to meet us. And without Scribonius around to mess up his story, Turpio has done well. Rather than being punished he has been promoted to Scribonius's position. We have not traced the money Scribonius embezzled; Turpio probably has that too. He's a five-to-one on certainty.'

'If he did it, he had an accomplice,' said Mamurra. 'It would take at least two men to drag a body down there.' Seeing the look Ballista was giving him, Mamurra continued, 'After you left, I got Castricius to take me.'

'But in the days before he was killed Scribonius talked about having found out something that would make everything all right,' said Ballista, 'maybe something to make me overlook his corruption and his running his unit into the ground. It would have to be something so important that someone would kill to keep it a secret. They killed him and searched his body to check he had nothing on him to implicate them. They took away his writing block. The evidence was written there.'

'We only have Turpio's word for the last mutterings of Scribonius,' said Maximus. Ballista acknowledged this and asked the Hibernian to check if anyone in Cohors XX could confirm Turpio's account, and to be discreet, very discreet.

'Right, what about the other thing? Who burnt down our artillery magazine?'

'Bagoas.' Again there was no hesitation before Maximus spoke. 'All the legionaries and some others are saying that it was Bagoas.'

'And do you think he did it?'

'No. He was with Calgacus at the time. Sure, the Persian boy hates Rome – although not as much as he hates tent-dwellers – but he does not see himself as an underhand saboteur. He sees himself as a scout – one brave man venturing alone into the camp of his enemies, collecting information, ferreting out their deep secrets, then returning openly in a blaze of glory to the bosom of his people to point out where to place the battering rams, where to dig the mines, how to overthrow the walls.'

'The boy must be nearly recovered from the beating,' said Mamurra. 'What are you going to do about him when he is up and about?'

'Either make sure he does not escape, or help him on his way making sure he takes the *intelligence* we want the Persians to have with him.' Ballista took a long drink before continuing. 'Well, if he did not burn the artillery, who did?'

This time Maximus did not jump in. He remained silent, his quick eyes darting from one to the other of his companions. Mamurra's mouth stayed tightly closed. His massive, almost cubic head tipped slightly to the right as he studied the ceiling. No one spoke for quite some time. Eventually Ballista started trying to answer his own question.

'Whoever it was wanted our defence to fail. They wanted the Persians to take the town. So, who here in Arete, soldier or civilian, might want the Persians to take the town?'

'Turpio,' Maximus said again. Seeing the scepticism on the faces of the other two, he hurried on. 'Somewhere out there is evidence – evidence he cannot suppress – that he killed Scribonius. He knows this evidence will come to light at some point. So Turpio prefers the promises of a new life under the Sassanids to the certainty of ultimate disgrace and death under Rome.'

'Well . . . it is possible,' said Ballista, 'but there is nothing to support it.' Mamurra nodded.

'Right, if you do not like Turpio, I give you Acilius Glabrio, patrician and traitor.' This time both Ballista and Mamurra smiled straight away.

'You just don't like him,' said Ballista.

'No . . . no, I don't like him – I cannot stand the odious little prick – but that is not the point.' The Hibernian pressed on. 'No, no . . . listen to me' – he turned to Ballista – the point is that he does not like you. Our touchy little aristocrat cannot bear to take orders from a jumped-up, hairy, thick, unpleasant barbarian like you. The Sassanids play on the little bugger's vanity, offer to make him satrap of Babylon or Mesopotamia or something, and he sells us all down the river. After all, what do a bunch of ghastly barbarians, Syrians and common soldiers matter compared with the *dignitas* of one of the Acilii Glabriones?'

'No, you are wrong.' For once there was no pause for reflection before Mamurra spoke. The great square face turned to Ballista. 'Acilius Glabrio does not dislike you. He hates you. Every order of yours he has to obey is like a wound. He wants to see you dead. But he would like to see you humiliated first. I agree with Maximus that he could be behind the fire – but not that he would go over to the Persians. What is the point in being an Acilius Glabrio if you are not in Rome? Possibly he wants to hamstring your defence of this town. Then, when you have been exposed as a stupid blundering barbarian – sorry, *Dominus* – he steps in to save the day.'

'It could be,' said Ballista. 'But I can think of about forty thousand other potential traitors – the whole population of this town. Let's be honest, they have little reason to love us.'

'If the traitor is a townsman, we need only look to the rich,' said Mamurra. 'The fire was started with naptha. It is expensive. Only the rich here in Arete could afford it. If the traitor is a townsman, he is on the *boule*, the council.'

Ballista nodded slowly. He had not thought of that, but it was true.

'And who are more important on the council than the caravan

protectors?' Maximus interrupted. 'And all three of them have links to the Sassanid empire. And now all three of them are entrusted with defending the walls. We are all completely fucked, fucked beyond belief!'

The blond girl came over with more drinks. Her smile became more fixed than ever as Maximus pulled her on to his lap.

'So,' said Ballista, turning his gaze to Mamurra, 'a rogue officer or an alienated councillor – we don't know which.'

'But we know that it has only just begun,' Mamurra added.

'If it were you, what would you do next?' Ballista's question hung for some time as Mamurra thought. With an ease born of practice the blond girl giggled like she meant it and parted her thighs to admit Maximus's hand.

'I would poison the cisterns,' Mamurra finally replied. There was a long pause. In the background the girl giggled again. 'I would contaminate the food stocks . . . sabotage the artillery.' Mamurra was speeding up. 'I would make sure I had a way of communicating with the Sassanids, then one dark night I would open a gate or throw a rope over an unguarded stretch of wall.' The girl sighed. 'Oh, and there is one other thing that I would do.'

'What?' said Ballista.

'I would kill you.'

Obsessio

(Spring–Autumn AD256)

'"Beware the *ides* of March."' The *telones* shook his head sadly as he watched the cavalcade pass. '"Calpurnia turned in her sleep and muttered . . . beware the *ides* of March."'

After the last horseman had jingled out from under the tall arch of the western gate, there was an unnatural silence, as if everything were holding its breath.

'What the fuck are you on about?' The *boukolos* often sounded put out when confronted by things outside his limited experience.

'That is poetry that is. That old centurion, the one who was always drunk, always quoting that he was . . . you know the one, the Sassanids got him somewhere downriver, cut his balls off, and his cock – shoved them down his throat.' The *telones* shook his head again. 'Poor bastard. Anyway, today is the *ides* of March. The day Julius Caesar was murdered by some of his friends. Not a good day to start out on something, not what you would call a day of good omen.'

Just beyond the Palmyrene Gate Ballista had halted his small mounted force to reorder for the march. Two *equites singulares* were put on point duty in front, and one at each side and the rear. The northerner did not intend to be surprised if he could help it. Ballista would lead the main body with Maximus, Romulus and Demetrius. The two scribes and two messengers would ride next, then the five servants leading the five packhorses. The other five *equites singulares* would form the end of the column. Ordered like a miniature army, scouts out and baggage in the middle, the force was as ready as it could be for any trouble – not that trouble was expected.

This was a straightforward tour of inspection. The small fort of Castellum Arabum, garrison to twenty camel-riding *dromedarii* from Cohors XX, lay to the south-east, some thirty miles as the crow flies, some forty-five by road. Castellum Arabum was now the furthest south of Rome's possessions on the Euphrates. It was the tripwire that was intended to warn of the coming of the Sassanids. No enemy had yet been seen. Local experts assured Ballista that it took time for the Sassanids to assemble their forces in the spring; they would not come until April, when there was grass for their horses and no danger of rain ruining their bowstrings. No hostile encounters were expected on this trip: two days' easy ride down, a day to look at the defences and make a speech to hearten the *dromedarii*, and two easy days' ride back.

As the men on point duty rode off to take up their positions, Ballista looked back at Arete. Bricklayers still plied their methodical trade, facing the earth, rubble and layers of reeds that formed its core but the great glacis that fronted the western wall was in essence complete. The 500 paces that separated Ballista from it was now a wasteland. Scattered low piles of broken bricks and smashed stones were all that remained of the once proud tower tombs of the necropolis.

Looking at the wasteland he had created, Ballista wondered what he should feel. A good Roman would probably be meditating on something like the immutability of fate. To his surprise, Ballista's main feeling, rather than pity or guilt, was one of pride: I, Ballista son of Isangrim, did this – look on my works and tremble. He smiled to himself. Everyone knows we barbarians enjoy destruction for its own sake. And maybe not just us. He half-remembered a line from the *Agricola* of Tacitus: 'Rome creates a desert and calls it peace.' Tacitus had put the words into the mouth of a Caledonian chief called Calgacus. Isangrim's sense of humour had not deserted him all those years ago when naming the Caledonian slave who would look after his son.

The point men were in position. Ballista signalled the advance. The small column set off at a walk towards the south. The cool of the night was giving way before the early morning sun. Only down in the ravines and on the surface of the river was the mist still clinging. Soon it would be hot – or hot by northern standards.

The road was unpaved but, created by millennia of caravans, it was mainly broad and easy to follow. For the most part it kept on the plateau away from the river. Sometimes it even diverted quite some distance inland to go round the ravines that ran down to the Euphrates; at others it descended into these *wadis*, sometimes climbing straight out the other side, sometimes following the floodplain until the gradient allowed it to climb back to the plateau.

Down by the river they stopped for lunch in the shade of a grove of wild date palms. It was peaceful in the dappled sunlight, listening to the river slip by. Ballista had ordered that the scouts remain on the look-out above them on the plateau. After he had eaten the cold pheasant, bread and cheese that Calgacus had packed for him, he lay back and closed his eyes.

It was good to be out in the country, slightly stiff and tired after a morning in the saddle. It was good to be away from the endless interruptions and irritations of organizing the defence of Arete. Sunlight coming through the palm fronds made shifting patterns on his eyelids. The south wind was getting up; he could hear it moving through the stands of tamarisk. But even in this almost idyllic setting his mind would not rest. Castellum Arabum had a garrison of twenty. It was too few to mount a defence, and more than was needed for a look-out post. He had inherited this arrangement from the previous *Dux Ripae*. So far he had not found time to visit Castellum Arabum. Now, maybe it was too late to start altering things.

Ballista sat up and looked around at his men. They should start moving. Again it struck him how easy it was to slip into other people's ways of doing things. Twenty-three men and twenty-eight horses just to transport him to look at a small fort less than fifty miles away. Like the garrison of Castellum Arabum, the column was the wrong size. It was too small to fight off any determined

Sassanid war party and too large to move quickly. The size of Ballista's entourage, somehow without any intention on his side, had expanded to fit Roman expectations. A *Dux* on the move needed scribes, messengers, guards. It was lucky he had not found himself saddled with a masseur, pastry cook and a hairy Greek philosopher as well. Ballista felt he should have ridden down to Castellum Arabum with just Maximus and Demetrius. Moving fast, they could have kept away from any trouble. It would be a foolish tent-dweller who decided to try to rob Maximus.

The tethered horses had eaten their hay and were either sleeping or desultorily searching the ground for anything edible. The sun was hot but in the shade of the stand of trees it was still cool. The men were resting or lying down talking quietly; there was all the time in the world. Ballista lay back down and shut his eyes. A sudden childish fantasy came over him. Why not just saddle Pale Horse, slip away and all alone ride west, never to return to the bustling irritations of Arete? But straight away he knew it was impossible. What about Maximus and Demetrius – and Calgacus? And then the big question: where would he go? To sit in his sun-drenched garden on the cliffs of Tauromenium or to drink by the fire in the high-roofed hall of his father?

At length it was Romulus who started them moving again, pointing out somewhat reproachfully that now they would not reach the ruined caravanserai that marked the half-way point by nightfall. Ballista said it did not matter. Maximus loudly and repeatedly said that it was a blessing in disguise: such places were undoubtedly crawling with snakes; the open air was far, far safer.

The afternoon followed the pattern of the morning, the river to the left, the wide emptiness of the sky and the land, the broad road along the plateau always unrolling to the south. As in the morning, sometimes they followed the road down into ravines, the horses' hooves sending showers of stones ahead, sometimes the road climbed straight out again, and sometimes it took its time, meandering down to the river and running along the floodplain, through the tamarisks and date palms, until a suitable opportunity appeared to regain the plateau.

The low winter sun was throwing long shadows to their left, making strange elongated beasts of horses and riders, when something happened. It started quietly. Maximus leant over, touched Ballista's knee and jerked his head back in the direction they had come. Ballista pulled his mount round to one side to see better. The cavalryman on rear point duty was in sight. He was a long way off but rapidly catching them. He was galloping, although not flat out. The south wind was making the dust his horse kicked up stream out behind them. The column came to a halt. Realizing he was observed, the cavalryman gathered the ends of his cloak in his right hand and waved them in the air, the usual signal for Enemy in Sight.

He was still some way off. They waited, all eyes not on the cavalryman but looking beyond him to see what might appear. The five *equites singulares* with the column fanned out into a line. Behind them the servants waited phlegmatically with the pack animals. The scribes and messengers talked rapidly among themselves. They all looked very frightened, except the scribe with the Spanish accent, who waited as impassively as any of the soldiers.

Nothing had shown itself by the time the cavalryman brought his horse to a halt before Ballista.

'*Dominus*, Sassanid light cavalry, bowmen – about fifty or sixty of them – about three miles away.'

'Which direction are they heading?'

'They were coming from the west, down from the hills to the river.'

'Did they see you?'

'Yes.'

'Did they chase you?'

'Not straight away. They waited until their lead group had reached the river, then they started to follow me, but at a walk.'

'Lead group?'

'Yes, *Dominus*. They were split into five groups stretched out over the three or four miles between the hills and the river.'

'Had they seen the rest of us?'

'I don't think so, *Dominus*.'

Allfather, but this looks bad, thought Ballista. Everyone was looking at him, waiting. He tried to block them out and think clearly. He looked around. Still nothing to be seen.

The man on point to the left, the east, was only a couple of hundred paces away; beyond him was the cliff down to the river. To the west the scout was about 400 paces out. Straight ahead to the south neither of the scouts could be seen, but the fresh wind was carrying a wide line of dust towards them from some miles away.

'Romulus, where exactly are we?' Ballista worked hard at making his voice sound calm, possibly even slightly bored.

'Just under twenty miles out of Arete, *Dominus*, just over twenty-five short of Castellum Arabum. The disused caravanserai is about three miles ahead.'

'Is there any shelter up in the hills to the west – a fort or settlement, occupied or not?'

'Only the village of Merrha to the north-west. It is occupied and walled, but the Sassanids are between us and it.' Romulus brightened. 'But we can go to the disused caravanserai. Its walls still stand, and we can reach it long before the Persians catch up with us.'

'Yes, it is tempting. But I think that it is possibly the last thing we should do.' Ballista circled his arms, calling in the men from left and right. 'Romulus, which of the *equites singulares* here has the best mount?'

Before the standard-bearer could answer, another cheekily cut in. 'No question about that, *Dominus*, me.' The man grinned. Demetrius whispered in Ballista's ear: 'Antigonus.'

'Right, Antigonus, I want you to go and bring in the two scouts from out in front. Meet us back at the last grove of date palms we passed through, down by the river. We will wait for you there. If we are not there, the three of you are to make your own way either to Arete or Castellum Arabum. Save yourselves as best you can. There is not a moment to lose. I will explain when you return. Take care.'

While Antigonus set off to the south at a gallop, the column retraced its steps to the north, also at a gallop. Once they were in the stand of trees, Ballista rattled out orders to put them in a new formation, his voice little above a fierce whisper. They were to form a wedge, an arrowhead. Ballista was to be the point, Maximus close to his right and half a length behind him, three *equites singulares* beyond and behind him. Romulus and the other four *equites singulares* were to comprise the left side of the formation. Demetrius and the Spanish scribe were to ride right behind Ballista, then the rest of the staff and the servants with the packhorses.

Ballista quietly, and he hoped calmly, explained what he was about. The aim could not be simpler: they were to break through the group of Sassanids closest to the river. With luck, the Persians would be taken by surprise as they charged out of the shelter of the date palms. Again with luck, this group of Persians down by the river would at that moment be out of sight of the others up on the plateau, buying the Romans just a little time. Anyway, once through the nearest group, the Romans would ride flat out for Arete and safety. With yet more luck, the night would hide them from the pursuing enemy.

It was growing dark among the date palms. The shadow of the cliff stretched out across the Euphrates. The temperature was dropping quickly. The wind worried at the palm fronds and tamarisks. The waters sucked at the banks. It was hard to hear anything clearly and difficult to see in the gathering gloom. Somewhere on the other side of the river a jackal barked.

'How do you know we are in a trap?' Maximus whispered, his mouth very close to Ballista's ear. The northerner took his time replying, wondering how to put his suspicions into words.

'The Sassanids between us and Arete are not acting like a normal scouting party looking for information. If that is what they were they would have chased the one of us they saw, chased him flat out – catch him and they could go home, out of danger. Instead they are moving south at a slow walk, strung out across the plain between the river and the hills. They have been sent on a flank march to catch any of us who escape from the main ambush. That line of dust in the sky to the south – it might just be the wind, but to me it looks all too like the sort of dust raised by a lot of cavalry moving fast.'

The sound of a scatter of stones and the first of the Persian horsemen appeared. They rode out of the *wadi* and on to the floodplain, advancing in the gathering gloom. As the scout had said, they were light cavalry, horse archers. Dressed in tunic and trousers, they were unarmoured. One or two had metal helmets, but the majority were bareheaded or wore just a cloth cap or bandana. Each had a long cavalry sword on his left hip, some had a small round shield on their left arm. There seemed to be at least fifteen of them. If they had ridden in any particular order, it had been dissipated by the descent into the ravine. Now they rode in a loose group, three horses across and four or five deep. They came on at a walk, their horses stepping delicately.

The Sassanids were getting close. Even in the gloom Ballista could make out their long hair, the glitter of their dark eyes. They were getting too close. Any moment now one of them would see the immobile forms waiting in the deeper shadow of the palm grove. Ballista could feel his heart beating as he sucked in air to fill his lungs.

'*Now!* Charge! Charge!' he yelled, kicking his heels into Pale Horse's flanks. There was a second's pause as the gelding gathered his quarters and then they were crashing through the reeds which fringed the grove and hurtling towards the Persians. There were exclamations of surprise, shouts of warning. The enemy tugged swords from scabbards. Their horses had come to a halt, some wheeling pointlessly. Ballista aimed at a point between two of the leading Sassanids. As he shot between them the northerner directed a vicious cut at the head of the Persian on his right. The man blocked the blow. The shock jarred Ballista's arm.

There was virtually no gap between the next two Sassanids in front of the northerner. He jabbed his heels into Pale Horse and set him at them. The gelding's left shoulder crashed into the withers of the Persian horse to the left. It staggered back. A gap opened, but the impact had robbed Pale Horse of all momentum. Ballista kicked furiously. His mount responded, leaping forward. To his right he saw Maximus's blade topple first one then another Persian out of the saddle.

They were nearly through; just one line of Persians still ahead. Maximus was no longer right on his shoulder. Ballista drew his *spatha* back over his left shoulder and aimed a mighty downward cut at the Sassanid to his right. Somehow the man blocked it with his shield. Ballista wrenched his blade free of the splintered wood and cut horizontally over Pale Horse's ears at the man on his left. This time he felt the blade bite home. There were no more enemy in front.

The force of the blow smashed Ballista's head forward. His nose crunched into Pale Horse's neck and blood poured from it. It was broken. He could feel more blood running down the back of his neck. Instinctively he twisted round to the right, bringing his *spatha* up in an attempt to parry the next blow he knew would come, the blow meant to finish him.

There was the Sassanid, sword arm raised. The bastard smiled – and looked down, clutching his side, staring stupidly at the sword wound.

Ballista waved his thanks to the Spaniard and kicked on. The scribe grinned back and flourished his sword – then the look on his face changed to shock. His horse disappeared from beneath him. He seemed to hang for a moment, then he went down into the tumbling, sliding mass of his own horse and under the hooves of the following Roman and Sassanid mounts alike.

There would be time for pity or guilt later. Ballista could not have stopped Pale Horse in any case. They rushed on, up the *wadi*, up its steep bank. As they emerged on to the plateau it grew much lighter. Up here the sun had not quite set. Without looking to see who was still with him, Ballista set the pace at a hell-for-leather gallop. He angled away from the road towards the north-west. It was vital that they pass inland of the next ravine.

The northerner looked over his left shoulder. There was the next group of Persians, about twenty of them. They had turned and were now riding hard to cut Ballista and his men off. Their long shadows flickered over the plain. The other groups of Persians had also turned, but they could not possibly reach the ravine in time; for now they were of no concern.

Ballista heard Maximus shout something. He ignored him; he needed to think. Despite the growing ache in his head, his mind was clear. He was calculating the distances and the angles. He saw it all as if watching from a great height: the fixed point of the head of the ravine, the two moving bodies of horsemen converging on it. He leant forward in the saddle, pushing Pale Horse for just that last bit of effort, that last pace or two of extra speed.

Ballista and his men made it with a little bit to spare. They skidded round the mouth of the ravine with the Persians still fifty paces away. They pushed on, but some of the urgency seemed to have gone out of the pursuit. Soon they were a couple of hundred paces ahead. Ballista slackened the pace. It was now twilight. There was something that had to be done. He did not want to do it, but it could not be deferred. He looked round to see who had fallen.

Maximus was there. Demetrius was there. Romulus was there, and four *equites singulares*, one scribe, both messengers and three servants, the latter commendably still leading their packhorses. The butcher's bill could have been higher – three soldiers, one Spanish scribe and two servants. It could yet mount higher, much higher.

The moon was up, but the strong south wind was pushing tattered clouds across its face.

'Are you all right? You look terrible,' Maximus called.

'Never better.' Ballista replied sourly. 'Like a slave at *Saturnalia*.'

'Do you think they will give up?' Demetrius asked, trying but failing to keep the desperate wishful thinking out of his voice.

'No.' It was Maximus who firmly crushed his hopes. 'They are settling in for the long haul. They intend to run us down during the night.'

As the Hibernian spoke, a series of twinkling lights appeared strung out between the river and the hills.

'Do we still have a lantern?' Having been assured by one of the servants that they still had two, Ballista ordered one of them to be lit. The order was obeyed amid unvoiced horror. Bright golden light spilled out around them.

'I do not want to appear stupid, but does not your lamp make it just a bit easier for your Persians to follow us?' Maximus asked.

'Oh yes, and that is just what I want.' Ballista asked a servant to tie the lantern securely to the saddle of one of the packhorses. They rode on in silence for a time, travelling no faster than an easy canter. The clouds were building up, the moon ever more obscured. Now it was pitch dark outside the pool of lantern light.

'Romulus, you know where the village of Merrha lies?'

'Yes, *Dominus*. Off in the hills to the north-west, not far now, four miles maybe.'

'I want you to lead the packhorse with the lantern in that direction. When you think that you have gone far enough or the Sassanids are getting too close, set the packhorse running free and ride for Arete.'

The standard-bearer smiled enigmatically. 'We will do what is ordered, and at every command we will be ready.' He spoke ruefully. He took the horse's leading rein and set off diagonally across the dark plain.

'Now we ride flat out again.'

In complete silence the small group rode hard. Off to their left, the light of Romulus's lantern bobbed across the plain towards the just distinguishable darker mass of the hills. Beaded across the wide plain were the lights of the Sassanids. Soon they altered course and surged after the lone Roman lantern. Ballista and his remaining twelve men rode north into the darkness to safety.

Not one was looking back when the line of Sassanid lights converged on the solitary lantern making vainly for the hills.

They were found by the patrol just after dawn; Turpio was working Cohors XX hard these days: the first patrols set out early, always in the dark. When Ballista and his party were found they were still a couple of miles from town, and in a bad way. Horses and men were completely exhausted. The flanks of the horses were covered in a white foam of sweat, their nostrils wide, mouths hanging open. The men were ashen-faced, almost insensible with fatigue. Apart from a servant more dead than alive who was slung over a packhorse, they were walking, stumbling along by their mounts. The *Dux Ripae* looked terrible, his face masked in dried blood, staggering, hanging on to the near-side pommel of his horse's saddle.

Before they reached Arete the *Dux* called a halt. He washed as much as he could of the blood from his face. He put on a hooded cloak borrowed from one of the troopers. He climbed back on to his horse and pulled the cloak up to hide his injuries. He rode into town with a straight back.

After the battered cavalcade had passed through the Palmyrene Gate the *telones* looked at the *boukolos* with an air of smug vindication.

'Calpurnia mutters . . . There is truth in poetry, boy – looks like that old centurion knew a thing or two: the *ides* of March did not do our barbarian *Dux* any good.'

'And knowing poetry didn't do your fucking centurion much good either; he still had his bollocks cut off,' replied the *boukolos*. 'Now this is what *I* call an omen: first time our commander meets the Persians they nearly kill him. Bloody bad omen that.'

From this first conversation discussions of the events at Castellum Arabum spread out across the town of Arete.

An hour or so after their return, Ballista, Maximus and Demetrius were lying in the *tepidarium* of the private baths attached to the palace of the *Dux Ripae*. The doctor had come and gone. He had put a couple of stitches in a gash on Maximus's thigh and five or six in the scalp wound on the back of Ballista's head. Demetrius had come through untouched.

They were lying in silence, dog-tired, aching. Ballista's head throbbed.

'No one to blame but yourself . . . your own fucking fault,' Calgacus grumbled as he brought in some food and drink. Ballista noted that now the Caledonian felt free to express his opinions before Maximus and Demetrius.

'Those notices you keep posting up in the *agora*: "the *Dux Ripae* will be virtually on his own riding down to some fly-blown piece of shite in the middle of nowhere; why not send a message to the

Sassanids so they can ambush him?" Never listen . . . just like your bloody father.'

'You are right,' Ballista said tiredly. 'There will not be any more notices, no more advance warning of what we are going to do.'

'Surely it could just be chance, bad luck? Their patrol just happened to be there and we just happened to run into them. Surely there does not have to be a traitor?' Demetrius's tone could not be mistaken. He desperately wanted one of them to say he was right, it was unlikely to happen again.

'No, I am afraid not,' said Ballista. 'They knew we were coming. That dust cloud in the south was the main force. It was intended to take us as we camped at the disused caravanserai. We were behind schedule. We were never meant to see the ones we ran into. They were just a screen to catch any of us who managed to escape the massacre.'

'So,' said Maximus, 'you see the virtue in sloth – a good long *meridiatio* saved our lives.'

Four hours after the *Dux Ripae* rode through the Palmyrene Gate the *frumentarii* were in their favourite bar in the south-east of the city.

'Left him to die like a dog in the shand.' The emotion was not counterfeit; the North African was packed full of anger.

'Yes,' said the one from the Subura. He kept his voice neutral. He was sorry for the Spaniard, Sertorius as he had dubbed him, but what else could the *Dux Ripae* have done – stop and get the whole party killed?

'Like a dog . . . hope the poor bashtard was dead before they got to him.'

'Yes,' repeated the one from the Subura. The North African's Punic accent was becoming stronger, the volume louder and, although the bar was almost empty, the Roman did not want attention drawn to them.

'I will fix that bashtard barbarian . . . write a report that will fix him, write such a report on him, the bashtard. I just wish I could be there when the *princeps peregrinorum* hands the report to the emperor – see the look on Valerian's face when he hears how his barbarian boy has fucked up – the fucking bashtard.'

'Are you sure that is a good idea?'

'Godsh below it is . . . fix that bashtard good and proper.'

The Persian rug which curtained off the inner room was drawn back. Mamurra walked through and over to the table of the *frumentarii*. He leant down, bringing his great slab of a face close to them.

'My condolences on the loss of your *colleague*.' He spoke softly, and walked on without waiting for a reply. The two *frumentarii* looked at each other in some consternation. How long had the *praefectus fabrum* been there? What had he heard? And was there something in the way he had pronounced 'colleague' that implied more than the Spaniard being a fellow member of the staff of the *Dux Ripae*?

Seven days after the events at Castellum Arabum Antigonus rode in on a donkey led by a peasant. He told the *telones* and *boukolos* to fuck off, made himself known to the centurion from Legio IIII in charge at the Palmyrene Gate and, within half an hour, he was in the palace. Sitting in the private apartments of the *Dux Ripae*, food and drink to hand, he told his story.

Yes, Antigonus had found the two troopers on point duty. The Sassanids had been *questioning* them, the poor bastards, as he rode past. Oddly, no one had pursued him. There was a line of Persian cavalry coming up from the south, a lot of them. Antigonus had turned his horse loose – excellent horse it was too – hidden most of his kit in a ravine and swum out to an island in the Euphrates. He told them proudly that he was a Batavian from the Rhine. The whole world knew that the Batavians were great swimmers. As everyone in the party of the *Dux* had taken the standard three days' rations with them, he had sat on his island for two days. He had not seen a Persian after the first day. Then he had swum ashore, picked up as much of his kit as he could carry and walked south to Castellum Arabum. It had not been pretty. Eighteen heads were mounted over the gate and on the walls. The other two *dromedarii* might have escaped but, more likely, they had been taken for further questioning.

'Anyway,' Antigonus continued, 'I found a peasant who, out of the kindness of his heart, offered to let me have his donkey and bring me home to Arete.' In response to a sharp look from Ballista he hurried on. 'No, no, he is fine. In fact, he is waiting in the first courtyard for the huge reward I said the *Dux Ripae* would pay him.' Ballista nodded to Demetrius, who nodded back to say he would deal with it.

'There is more. On my way back I came across Romulus, or what was left of him. Nasty – he had been mutilated, hopefully after he was dead.'

The ever-changing stories spread out far beyond the city of Arete. Ten days after the reality had played out in darkness and fear by the Euphrates, a messenger prostrated himself in the magnificent throne room in the Persian capital of Cetisiphon and told a version of the story to Shapur, the Sassanid King of Kings. Twenty-six days after that, a messenger prostrated himself in the palace high on the Palatine Hill and told the first of several versions of the story that Valerian Imperator of the Romans would hear. Another three days elapsed before a messenger tracked down Gallienus, Valerian's son and fellow Augustus, by the cold banks of the Danube. By then, many more things had happened at the city of Arete and, for most there, the events at Castellum Arabum were a fading memory.

From the walls of Arete, for a long time the only sign of the approach of the Sassanid horde was the thick black cloud looming up from the south. On the morning of the fourteenth of April, the day after the *ides* of the month – always an unlucky day – Ballista, accompanied by his senior officers, staff and *familia*, took his stand on the battlements above the Palmyrene Gate. There was the cloud downriver, coming up from the realms of Shapur. Dark and thick, it was still some way off, at least as far as the disused caravanserai, if not as far as Castellum Arabum. No one needed to ask what caused it. It was impossible to escape the thought of the tens of thousands of marching men, horses and other, terrifying beasts kicking up the dust, of the smoke writhing up oily from the innumerable fires consuming everything in the path of the horde from the east.

At twilight a line of campfires could be seen burning no more than a couple of miles from the city. The Sassanid scouts were settling in for the night. Later, in the depth of the night, more fires flickered into life, stretching round in an arc along the hills to the west. After midnight a terrible orange glow lit the sky to the north-west as the Persian outriders reached the villages. By cock crow smudges of fire and smoke had appeared on the other side of the river to the east. Everyone within the walls of the town of Arete knew they were surrounded, cut off by land from help or flight. And yet, so far, they had not seen a single one of the warriors of Shapur.

At dawn the *Dux Ripae* and his men were still at their post. Most had left to try and rest for an hour or two but, to Ballista, sleep seemed impossible on a night so obviously momentous. Wrapped in a sheepskin, he leant against one of the two pieces of artillery on the roof of the gatehouse, a huge twenty-pounder *ballista*. His eyes ached with fatigue as he peered out on to the western plain. He thought he saw movement but, unsure his tired eyes weren't playing tricks on him in the grey light, he waited until one of the others shouted and pointed. There they were. About where the necropolis used to end, dark shapes were moving fast through the early morning mist. The small amorphous groups of mounted scouts, dividing, reuniting, crossing each other's tracks, reminded Ballista of animals running before a forest fire, until the inappositeness of the image struck him. These animals were not fleeing anything, they were hunting, hunting for a means to attack the northerner himself and all those it was his duty to protect. They were wolves looking for a way into the sheepfold.

The sun was well clear of the horizon and it was towards the end of the third hour of daylight when the vanguard of the Sassanid army finally came into view. Ballista could make out two long dark columns which seemed, like enormous snakes, to crawl towards him infinitesimally slowly across the face of the land. Above each hung a dense isolated cloud of dust. The base of a third cloud had not yet come into sight. The northerner could make out that the nearer column was composed of cavalry, the further of infantry. He thought back to his training in fieldcraft: this meant that the columns must be within about 1,300 paces. But, as he could not yet make out any individuals, they must still be more than 1,000 paces away. If he had not known of their advance toward him, the rays of sunlight flashing perpendicular off spear points and burnished armour would have told him.

Time passed slowly as the columns continued to crawl towards the city. When they were about 700 paces away (the distance at which a man's head can be made out as a round ball) they began to incline away to the north. Ballista moved to the parapet and called Bagoas to his side. By the time the columns reached the beginning of the wasteland where the furthest tower tombs had once stood, they were moving parallel to the western wall. The third column was now revealed as the baggage and siege train. The nearest column, the cavalry, was close enough for Ballista to be able to see the lighter-coloured spots of the men's faces, their costumes and weapons, the bright trappings of their mounts, the banners above their heads: about 500 paces away, just out of artillery range.

Speaking in Greek, Ballista asked Bagoas if he could identify the units of the Sassanid horde and their leaders.

'Excellent, how very cultured our siege will be. We can begin with our very own *View from the Wall*.' Although Acilius Glabrio had interrupted in Latin, he used the Greek word '*teichoskopia*' for the *View from the Wall*. To any educated person in the *imperium*, the word instantly summoned up the famous scene in the *Iliad* of Homer where Helen looked down from the walls of Troy and identified each of the bronze-armoured Achaeans come to tear her from her lover Paris and take her home to her rightful husband, the broad-shouldered Menelaus. 'And who better than this delightful Persian boy to play the *Queen* of Sparta?' Acilius Glabrio smiled at Ballista. 'I do hope our Helen does not feel the need to criticize the manliness of *her* Paris.'

Bagoas's grasp of Latin might still be rudimentary, and Ballista had no idea if the boy knew anything of the *Iliad*, but it was obvious that he realized he was being mocked, that his masculinity was being questioned. The boy's eyes were furious. Before he could do anything, Mamurra spoke to Acilius Glabrio.

'That is enough, Tribune. This is not a time for dissension. We all know what happened to Troy. May the gods grant that these words of ill omen fall only on the man who utters them.'

The young nobleman spun around looking dangerous. He brought his well-groomed face inches from that of the *praefectus fabrum*. Then he mastered himself. Clearly it was beneath one of the Acilii Glabriones to bandy words with sordid plebeians like Mamurra. 'The men of my family have always had broad shoulders.' With patrician disdain, he brushed an imaginary piece of dirt from his immaculate sleeve.

Ballista pointed to the enemy and indicated to Bagoas to start talking.

'First ride some of the non-Aryan people subject to my lord Shapur. See the fur cloaks and long hanging sleeves of the Georgians, then the half-naked Arabs, the turbaned Indians and the wild nomadic Sakas. From all the corners of the world, when the King of Kings calls, they obey.' The boy shone with pride. 'And there . . . there are the noble Aryan warriors, the warriors of Mazda, the armoured knights, the *clibanarii*.'

All the men on the gate tower fell silent as they regarded the serried ranks of the Sassanid heavy cavalry, the elite of Shapur's army. Five deep, the column seemed to stretch for miles across the plain. As far as could be seen were armoured men on armoured horses. Some looked like living statues, horse and man clad in iron scales, iron masks covering any humanity. The mounts of others were armoured in red leather or green-blue horn. Many wore gaudy surcoats and caparisoned their horses similarly – green, yellow, scarlet and blue. Often man and beast wore abstract heraldic symbols – crescents, circles and bars – which proclaimed their clan. Above their heads their banners writhed and snapped – wolves, serpents, fierce beasts or abstract designs invoking Mazda.

'Can you tell who leads each contingent from their banners?'

Ballista had had this moment in mind when he purchased the Persian youth.

'Of course,' Bagoas replied. 'In the van of the *clibanarii* ride the lords from the houses of Suren and Karen.'

'I thought that those were great noble houses under the previous regime. I assumed they would have fallen with the Parthian dynasty.'

'They came to see the holiness of Mazda.' Bagoas beamed. 'The King of Kings Shapur in his infinite kindness restored their lands and titles to them. The path of righteousness is open to all.'

'And the horsemen behind them?'

'Are the truly blessed. They are the children of the house of Sasan – Prince Valash the joy of Shapur, Prince Sasan the hunter, Dinak Queen of Mesene, Ardashir King of Adiabene.' Pride radiated from the boy. 'And look . . . there, next in the array, the guards. First the Immortals, at their head Peroz of the Long Sword. Then the Jan-avasper, those who sacrifice themselves. And see . . . see who leads them – none other than Mariades, the rightful emperor of Rome.' The boy laughed, careless of the effect his words were having, the punishments they might bring. 'The path of righteousness is open to all, even to Romans.'

Out of the swirling dust kicked up by many thousand horses, enormous grey shapes loomed. One, two, three . . . Ballista counted ten of them. Bagoas literally jumped for joy, clapping his hands. 'The earth-shaking elephants of Shapur. Who could think to stand against such beasts?'

Ballista had seen elephants fight in the arena but had never himself faced them in battle. Certainly they looked terrifying, not altogether of this world. They had to be at least ten foot high at the shoulder, and the turrets on their backs added yet more height. Each turret was packed with armed fighting men. At the bidding of an Indian who sat astride behind their ears, the elephants moved their great heads from side to side. Their huge tusks, sheathed in metal, dipped and swung from side to side.

'Frightening, but inefficient.' The experience in Turpio's voice was reassuring. 'Hamstring them, or madden them with missiles.

Kill their drivers, their *mahouts*, and they will run amok. They are as likely to trample their own side as us.'

The Sassanid army had halted and turned to face the city. A trumpet rang out, clear across the plain.

From the left a small group of five unarmed horsemen appeared, moving at an easy canter. In their midst an enormous rectangular banner embroidered in yellow, red and violet and embedded with jewels that flashed as they caught the sunlight hung from a tall crossbar. The banner was topped by a golden ball, and bright strips of material streamed out behind it.

'The Drafsh-i-Kavyan, the royal battle flag of the house of Sasan.' Bagoas almost whispered. 'It was made before the dawn of time. Carried by five of the holiest of *mobads*, priests, it goes before the King of Kings into battle.'

A lone horseman appeared from the left. He rode a magnificent white horse. His clothes were purple and on his head was a golden domed crown. White and purple streamers floated out behind him.

'Shapur, the Mazda-worshipping divine King of Kings of Aryans and Non-Aryans, of the race of the gods.' Bagoas prostrated himself on the battlements.

When Shapur reached the Drafsh-i-Kavyan standard at its station in front of the centre of his army, he reined his horse to a halt. He dismounted, seemingly using a kneeling man as a step. A golden throne was produced and Shapur sat on it. A large number of other men ran about.

'Enemy numbers?' Ballista threw the question open to his *consilium* gathered on the roof of the gate tower.

'I estimate about 20,000 infantry,' Acilius Glabrio answered promptly. 'Then about 10,000 heavy cavalry, 8,000 of them Sassanid *clibanarii* and 1,000 or so each from the Georgians and Sakas. There seem to be roughly 6,000 barbarian light cavalry at the front of the column, maybe 2,000 each from the Arabs and Indians and 1,000 each from the Georgians and Sakas.' Whatever one thought of the young patrician, it could not be denied that he was an extremely competent army officer. The estimates mapped almost exactly on to those Ballista had made.

'The Sassanids' own light cavalry?' The northerner kept the question short, business-like.

'Impossible to say,' answered Mamurra. 'They are scattered all over the countryside burning and plundering. There is no way for us to estimate their strength. However many there are, the majority will be on our side of the river. There will be just a few across the river – the nearest ford is about 100 miles downstream and we have commandeered every boat for miles. They will not have committed many men across the river.'

'What the *praefectus fabrum* says is true,' said Turpio. 'We cannot know their numbers. At Barbalissos there were somewhere between five and ten light cavalrymen to every *clibanarius*, but at other times their numbers have been said to be about equal.'

'Thank you,' said Ballista. 'So it seems the enemy have somewhere between 40,000 and 130,000 men to our 4,000. At best we are outnumbered ten to one.' He smiled broadly. 'It is very lucky for us that it is a bunch of effeminate easterners who get scared at the sound of a noisy dinner party let alone a battle. We would not want to fight anyone with any bollocks at these odds.' The army officers all laughed. Demetrius tried to join in.

Ballista noted that the baggage train had caught up with the other columns, and that its first task was to erect a spacious purple tent just behind the centre of the army. The tent, which could be none other than Shapur's, was being set up directly along the western road out of Arete, about 600 paces from the Palmyrene Gate.

Men continued to rush around Shapur.

'What is going on?' Ballista asked Bagoas, who was still prostrate.

'The King of Kings will make sacrifice of a kid to ensure that Mazda smiles on his works here, to ensure that this town of unbelievers falls to the army of the righteous.'

'Get up off your belly, and mind what you say. You might push our patience too far,' snapped Ballista.

Despite his tone, the northerner was actually pleased with his Persian slave. Just as he had hoped, he was learning a lot about his enemy from the boy. There was the voluble religious fervour, linked to the awe of the king, and the fact that Bagoas had not considered the Sassanid infantry even worth mentioning. So, an army of fanatics of whom only the cavalry were any good at fighting. Ballista just had to hope that this individual Persian was not totally unrepresentative of his countrymen.

As the boy got up, he briefly put his arms behind his back as if they were bound. Ballista knew that this was the Persian gesture of supplication – possibly the boy was begging Shapur not to blame him for being a slave of the King's enemies.

The sacrifice having been made, Shapur could be seen issuing orders to the nobleman known as the Suren. On being asked to explain, Bagoas said that the King of Kings would now send the Suren to Ballista. If Ballista and his men submitted and converted to the most righteous path of Mazda, their lives would be spared.

As he watched the Suren walk his horse along the road towards him, Ballista's thoughts were racing. While the horseman was still about 200 paces away, Ballista quickly issued orders to two of his messengers. All the *ballistae* on the western wall were to prepare to shoot at the enemy army. They were to take maximum elevation as if going for their greatest range but their crews were to loosen the torsion springs by two turns of the washers so that their missiles fell well short of their maximum range. Hopefully it would deceive the enemy about the true range of the *ballistae*. The messengers ran off along the wall walk; one south, the other, the one with the heavy accent from the Subura, north. With the Suren about a hundred paces away, Ballista told Mamurra to go below to the first floor of the tower and train one of the bolt-throwers on the approaching messenger. On Ballista's command, a bolt was to be shot just over the head of the Suren.

He was riding a beautiful Nisean stallion. It was jet-black, deep-chested, no less than sixteen hands tall. Good job it was light cavalry that ambushed us, Ballista thought. Pale Horse would never knock a beast like that back on its hocks.

The Suren reined in his horse. He had stopped about thirty paces from the gate. Ballista was relieved. The enemy nobleman would have detected two of the traps that Ballista had set. He had crossed over two pits in the road, one at a hundred and one at fifty paces from the gate. The pits were concealed from view, boarded over with sand thickly spread on top, but the hollow ring of his stallion's hooves would have warned the Persian. Yet so far he should know nothing of the final pit, the crucial one, just twenty paces from the gate.

The Suren took his time taking off a tall helmet in the shape of a predatory bird, possibly an eagle. His own features, once revealed, did not look greatly different. With the assurance of a man whose ancestors have owned broad pastures for generations without number, he looked up at the men on the battlements.

'Who is in command here?' The Suren spoke in almost unaccented Greek. His voice carried well.

'I am Marcus Clodius Ballista, son of Isangrim, *Dux Ripae*. I command here.'

The Suren tipped his head slightly to one side, as if better to study this blond barbarian with a Roman name and title. 'The King of Kings Shapur bids me tell you to heat the water and prepare his food. He would bathe and eat in his town of Arete tonight.'

Ballista tipped his head back and laughed.

'I am sure that the bum-boy who passes for your *kyrios* would love to get in the bath and offer his arse to anyone interested, but I fear that the water would be too hot and my soldiers much too rough for his delicate constitution.'

Seemingly unmoved by the obscenity, the Suren methodically began to undo the top of the quiver that hung by his right thigh.

'What the hell is he doing?' Ballista demanded of Bagoas in a whisper.

'He is preparing formally to declare war. He will shoot the cane reed that symbolizes war.'

'Like fuck he will. Quietly pass the word for Mamurra to shoot.'

The order was muttered from man to man across the gate-house roof and down the stairs.

Having extracted presumably the correct symbolic arrow, the Suren pulled his bow from its case. He was just notching the arrow when came the terrifying loud twang, slide, thump of a *ballista* being released. To his credit, the Suren barely flinched as the bolt shot a few feet above his head. Composing himself, he drew his bow and sent his arrow high over the walls of the town. Then he made his horse rear. The glossy coat of the stallion shimmered as it turned on its hind legs. The Suren called over his shoulder.

'Do not eat all the smoked eel, northerner. My *kyrios* is very fond of smoked eel.'

Ballista called for the rest of the artillery to shoot. As the Suren and his magnificent mount disappeared back up the road, the missiles arched over their heads but fell some way short of the watching Sassanid army.

'Clever,' said Acilius Glabrio. 'Very clever to pre-empt their barbarian declaration of war with an impromptu version of our very own Roman ceremony of throwing a spear into enemy territory.' The ever-present sneer dropped from the tribune's voice as he went on. 'But if you have tricked them into thinking the range of our artillery is only about 300 paces, that is far cleverer.'

Ballista nodded. Actually, he had been thinking of something else, of Woden the Allfather casting his spear into the ranks of the Vanir in the first ever war. And, from the very first war, it was a very small step to thinking of Ragnarok, the war at the end of time, when Asgard will fall and death come to man and gods alike.

Ballista was leaning on the wall of the terrace of the palace of the *Dux Ripae*. He was looking down and across the river. He was looking at something horrible.

Where had the woman come from? He had had cavalry methodically sweep the opposite bank, driving everyone they found down to the boats and back across the river. Peevishly he thought that it had not been easy getting two *turmae* of cavalry ferried back and forth across the Euphrates. Of course, some fools will always stay in the false delusional safety of their homes, no matter with what certainty you tell them of the horror that man or gods are about to visit on them. Maybe the Sassanids had brought her with them.

Every now and then the horse archers would pretend to let her get away. She would run towards the river. Before she got there, the horsemen would ride her down. They would throw her to the ground and another two or three of them would rape her. There were about twenty of them.

With none of his usual noises, Calgacus leant on the wall beside Ballista. 'They are all inside. For once Acilius Glabrio was on time. So were Turpio, Antigonus and the four centurions you told to come. It was Mamurra who was late.'

Both men looked across the river.

'Bastards,' said Ballista.

'Don't even think of trying to save her,' said Calgacus. 'It is just what they want. She would be dead by the time you got any troops into a boat, and then your men would land into an ambush.'

'Bastards,' said Ballista.

They both continued to look over the river.

'It's not your fault,' said Calgacus.

'What?' The silence of the Caledonian's arrival should have warned Ballista that something was coming.

'What is happening to that poor girl over there . . . the fact that this city is being besieged and, no matter what, lots of its people are going to suffer and die . . . what happened to Romulus and those scouts . . . none of it is your fault.'

Ballista briefly pulled an unconvinced face but his eyes remained fixed over the river.

'You have always thought too much. Since you were a child. I am not saying it's a bad thing in itself, but it is no help to a man in your position.' Ballista did not respond. 'All I am saying is that if you give yourself over to sentiment, then you will not be thinking clearly, and then things will get still fucking worse.'

Ballista nodded and straightened up. As he unclenched his hands from the wall, he saw his palms had brick dust embedded in them. He rubbed them together.

On the other side of the river the men had encircled the woman. One of them was on top of her. Ballista looked away.

'I suppose you are right.' He looked up into the sky. 'Only just over an hour to nightfall. Let's go in and talk to the others. We have a lot to organize for the unpleasant surprise that is going to befall the King of Kings tonight.'

It was dark under the high barrelled arch of the Palmyrene Gate. The outer gate was still closed and, although the inner was open, little light found its way in. The larger-than-life personification of the *Tyche* of Arete painted on the northern wall was nothing but a blur to Turpio, and he could see nothing of the graffiti thanking her for safe journeys he knew to be scrawled below.

Turpio had always had a particularly developed sense of smell. The prevailing smell here was of the cool, possibly even damp, dust which lay in the shade of the gatehouse and which the sun never reached. There was also the smell of the worked wood of the great gate in front of him and, surprising because it was so out of context, there was a strong, a very strong scent of perfume: oil of myrrh. The hinges of the gate were soaked in it to prevent them squeaking.

Turpio was tense, but he was glad to be there in the dark waiting to lead the raid. He had had to argue his case hard in the *consilium*. Acilius Glabrio had pointed out that two centuries of his legionaries amounted to 140 men, while two *turmae* of Turpio's auxillaries came only to 72 troopers so, in fairness, it should be Acilius Glabrio himself who commanded. Turpio had been reduced to appealing to Ballista on the grounds that, while the northerner could not afford to risk the patrician commander of the legionaries in his garrison, an ex-centurion who commanded auxiliaries was more expendable. Eventually the *Dux Ripae* had given his assent.

Turpio was aware that everyone in the *consilium* had known why he was just so keen to lead this raid: he still needed to prove his worth after the stain that Scribonius Mucianus had left on his character. Over the winter he had trained Cohors XX well. Certainly there was no corruption now. It was an efficient unit, a unit of which one could be proud. But if Turpio were to do well here in Arete, win the trust of Ballista, do everything that he wanted, he needed more. He needed a chance to prove himself in action. What could be better than a straightforward, desperate night raid into the heart of the enemy camp? Of course the risks were enormous, but so was the possibility of glory. '*Decapitate the Persian reptile. Aim for the huge purple tent in the centre of the Sassanid camp. Catch the King of Kings sleeping or with his baggy trousers down. Bring me his head. No one will ever forget your name.*' Turpio was not the only one to have been stirred by Ballista's words.

Turpio detected another scent – cloves, or possibly carnations; a clean pleasant smell. It had to be Acilius Glabrio. The young patrician moved slowly, carefully, along the passageway. Turpio spoke his name quietly and held out his hand. The two men shook hands. Acilius Glabrio handed over some burnt cork, wished Turpio good luck, and left. As Turpio blackened his face and forearms, he wondered if he had misjudged the young nobleman.

He smiled to himself in the dark. No, he had not totally misjudged him. The young nobleman was still a prick. Turpio could feel laughter bubbling up in his chest as he thought of the meeting of the *consilium*. When Ballista walked in Acilius Glabrio had approached him full of patrician self-importance. 'A word if you please, *Dux Ripae*.' The northerner had slowly turned on him his unsettling barbarian blue eyes. He looked as if he had never seen the speaker before. His reply had been couched in terms of the frostiest civility: 'With pleasure, *Tribunus Laticlavius*, in just a moment.' Ballista had asked his new standard-bearer, Antigonus, to attend him and had led the Batavian to the far corner of the room. There he had spoken in low, emphatic sentences. At the end Antigonus had saluted and left. Walking back, Ballista's face was open and guileless. 'What was it you wanted, *Tribunus Laticlavius*?'

The wind having been taken from his sails, the fuming young patrician had muttered that it could wait.

A muted commotion in the passageway behind Turpio indicated the approach of the *Dux Ripae*. Against the gloom, the greater darkness of the northerner's height and bulk, the strange bird crest above his helm could just be distinguished. The northerner seemed to have no smell at all. In his heightened, pre-battle state, Turpio wondered for a moment if that were like casting no shadow.

'Everything is ready. Time to go,' Ballista said quietly.

'We will do what is ordered, and at every command we will be ready.'

They shook hands. Ballista half turned, raised his voice slightly. 'Try not to get too many of the boys killed.' The nearer soldiers chuckled. Turning back, Ballista dropped his voice. 'Remember, Turpio – straight in and straight out. If you reach Shapur's tent, excellent, but if not no problem. Do not get into a fight. You have a couple of hundred men. They have about 50,000. If you can, surprise them, kill a few, burn a few tents, shake them up. But then get out quickly. Do not get trapped. At the first sign of organized resistance, head for home.' They shook hands again. Ballista stepped back to the side of the passage just below the pale shape of the *Tyche*. He called softly over the heads of the waiting soldiers.

'Time to go, boys, time to start the *venationes*, the beast-hunts.'

Despite the oil of myrrh the gates seemed to creak alarmingly as they ponderously opened. Turpio set off.

As good luck would have it, it was the night before the new moon. Yet even lit just by starlight, the western plain looked very bright after the darkness of the gate. The road shone very white as it stretched arrow-straight ahead. The flickering campfires of the Persians seemed infinitely distant.

For a time Turpio just concentrated on walking quickly. Soon he was breathing more deeply. The road under his feet felt smooth but unnaturally hard. Behind him the 140 legionaries of Legio IIII Scythica marched as quietly as Roman soldiers could. They were not talking and were taking care not to clash their weapons and armour. Some had even tied rags around their military boots to deaden the sound of their hobnails. Yet there was a steady series of small chinking sounds. Nothing could ever completely persuade Roman soldiers of the necessity of removing all the good-luck charms from their belts.

Once he had remembered to do so, Turpio counted off 200 paces and then stepped to one side and looked around to take stock. Ten wide and fourteen deep, the small column of legionaries appeared tiny in the immensity of the plain. Turpio looked back at the town. True to his word, Ballista had managed to persuade the priests to organize a religious ceremony at the Temple of Bel. Designed to draw any sleepless Sassanid eyes and ears, a big procession with bright lights and loud chanting was making its way slowly along the extreme northern end of the city wall. To help the raiding party orientate itself, a single torch burnt over the Palmyrene Gate and another on the last tower to the south. The rest of the wall was in darkness.

Turpio had to run to regain his position at the front of the column. Like him, the legionaries wore dark clothes and had blackened their equipment and exposed skin. To Turpio, they seemed hideously exposed on the gleaming white road.

Ahead, quite widely separated individual fires marked the Sassanid picket line. Behind them was the more general glow of the camp, spreading as far as the eye could see. The picket lines suddenly were much nearer. Surely the Persian sentries could not fail to notice the legionaries? Turpio's own breathing seemed loud enough to carry across the plain and wake the dead.

Nearer and nearer to the picket on the road. Turpio could make out the single rope tethering the nearest horse, individual flames in the fire, dark shapes swathed in blankets on the ground. Without a word he broke into a run, faster and faster, drawing his sword. Close behind him heavy footfalls, laboured breathing.

Turpio vaulted over the first sleeping sentry and swerved around the fire to reach the far side of the picket. The sentry nearest the Sassanid camp sat up, his mouth forming an 'O' to shout, and Turpio smashed his *spatha* down on his head with all his force. It needed a boot on the man's shoulder to withdraw the blade. Behind, a brief flurry of grunts, cut-off yells and a series of sounds that always reminded Turpio of knives cutting through cabbages. Then near-silence. Just 140 men panting.

He took stock. There were no shouts, no trumpet calls, no shadowy figures fleeing across the dark plain to raise the alarm. The nearest picket fires on either side were at least a hundred paces away. There was no movement around them. All was quiet. Ballista had been right; the big barbarian bastard had been right. The Sassanids lacked discipline, good old-fashioned Roman *disciplina*. Tired after the march, contemptuous of the small numbers of soldiers against them, the Persian pickets had laid down to sleep. The first night of the siege, and no Sassanid nobleman had yet taken it on himself to impose a routine.

Turpio mastered his breathing and called softly. 'First Century, form *testudo*.' He waited for the shuffling to subside and a dense knot of overlapping shields to form. 'Second Century to me.' More shuffling, then silence. 'Antoninus Prior, make the signal to the *Dux*.' The centurion merely grunted, and three legionaries detached themselves from the *testudo*. There was a brief flurry of activity and three lanterns hung in a row, their blue-leaded lights winking their message back across the plain.

Turpio turned to the column of the second century drawn up close behind him. 'Swords and torches to hand, boys.' Turpio looked at the Sassanid camp and at the royal tent looming up massive in its centre. He spoke to the centurion beside him. 'Ready, Antoninus Posterior? Then let's go and decapitate the reptile.'

Ballista had been waiting to see the signal. How he had been waiting. When the two centuries had set off down the road they had looked horribly exposed, surely visible for miles. But soon they had become an indistinct moving blur then vanished into the dark. Time's arrow had gone into reverse. Ballista prayed that he had not sent them all to their deaths. The noises of the two waiting *turmae* of cavalry had floated up to him on the roof of the gatehouse; the jingle of a bridle, the stamp of a hoof, a horse coughing abrupt and loud.

The three blue lights appeared. Ballista's heart leapt. So far so good. Demetrius whispered the name of the senior *decurion* in his ear. Ballista leant over the battlements. 'Paulinus, time to go. Good luck.'

Seventy-two horsemen in two columns, the *turmae* of Paulinus and Apollonius, clattered out into the night one after another, quickly picking up speed. They also vanished into the moonless night.

Time dragged.

Allfather, Deep Hood, Raider, Spear-Thruster, Death-Blinder, do not let me have sent them all to their deaths. Do not let them be killed in the darkness out there like Romulus. Yet so far the plan was going well. To avert the evil eye, Ballista started to clench his fist, thumb between index and forefinger. If this carried on he would end up as superstitious as Demetrius. He completed the gesture anyway.

The plan was straightforward. Having overwhelmed the picket on the road, one century of legionaries was to remain there to cover the retreat, while the other century aimed for the jugular, rushing into the enemy camp, aiming to cut their way into the very tent of the King of Kings. To help them by spreading maximum confusion, the two *turmae* of cavalry were to fan out left and right and ride between the picket lines and the Sassanid camp proper shooting fire arrows at everything in sight. The *turma* heading south, that of Paulinus, was to make its escape by descending into the southern ravine and riding all the way to the wicket gate by the Euphrates. If any Persians were foolish enough to follow them down into the ravine, so much the worse for them. Hundreds of paces of bad going exposed to missiles from the walls of Arete would deal with them. The other *turma*, that of Apollonius, had a trickier task. It was to ride north for a short way then turn about and form up on the road back to town to aid the century which was to cover the retreat.

The plan had seemed so straightforward in the meeting of the *consilium*. Ballista was praying that it would not all become terribly confused and fall apart in the terrifying reality of a dark night.

Time continued to drag. Just when Ballista was beginning to wonder how much longer the hiatus could possibly last, someone needlessly called out – *There! There!* – and was promptly shushed.

Lights could be seen moving in the heart of the Sassanid camp. The first fragmented sounds of alarm drifted back to the town of Arete. Turpio and the legionaries were about the real work of the night, just seventy men challenging the beast in its lair.

Now things were speeding up. Time's arrow had resumed its course. Events came tumbling one after another. Ballista could see yellow flames winking into life as the troopers of the *turmae* kindled their torches from the picket fire directly ahead. Then two strings of torches could be seen moving fast away from the centre of the Persian camp, one north, one south. The first fire arrows were arcing through the sky. Like a beast angered at being disturbed from sleep, a great roaring came from the Sassanid camp. The noise rolled across the plain to those on the high walls and towers of Arete.

More and more lights – red, yellow, white – flickered into life as fire arrows, thrown torches and kicked-over lamps set fire to tents, soft bedding, stacked fodder, piled-up provisions, jars of oil. Shapes flitted across the fires, gone too quickly to tell what they were. The noise, like that of a great forest fire, bounced back and forth around the plain. Above the general background rose sharp screams, human and animal, and the strident call of trumpets attempting to restore some order to the Persian horde.

As Ballista watched, the string of lights heading south winked out one by one. This should be a good sign – Paulinus's troopers jettisoning the last of their torches and riding hell for leather through the darkness for safety. But, of course, it could be bad – the Sassanids surging around them, cutting them down. Even if it were good, the *turma* was far from home safe. Riding flat out on a moonless night, would they find the entrance to the ravine? It had been an easy enough descent for Ballista and four others at a comfortable pace on a bright, sunlit day, but they had dismounted. It might be a very different proposition for nervous men on panting, labouring horses in the pitch dark.

By the time Ballista looked to the north the chain of lights that marked Apollonius's *turma* had also vanished. Hauled from their horses by blades and hands or riding unmolested to their rendezvous, there was no way of telling.

Allfather, The Wakeful, The Wanderer, The Crier of the Gods, what is happening? What of Turpio?

Roaring. Head far back, roaring, laughing. Turpio had seldom felt so happy. It was not the killing, not that he had any objection to killing: it was the sheer ease of it all. The first thing they had come to in the camp was the horse line of a unit. It had been the work of moments to cut the tethers, slap the horses with the flat of their blades and send them stampeding ahead into the camp. Consternation spread rapidly as the animals thundered through the tightly packed tents, overturning cooking pots, bringing down small tents. A Persian head appeared from one. A swing of Turpio's *spatha* and the head fell back bloodied.

Yelling at his men to keep together, Turpio pounded through the Sassanid camp. Once, a guy rope caught his foot and he went sprawling on his face. The metal-studded sole of the boot of one of his own men stamped into his back before strong arms dragged him to his feet and they were off again. Pounding through the camp, trying always to keep the looming royal tent in sight. Isolated Persians, individuals or small groups, popped into view. They ran or fell where they stood. There was no organized opposition.

In what seemed no time they were there. Several large standards hung limply from tall poles. Half a dozen guards, their gilded armour glinting in the light of the fires, made a stand in front of the huge purple tent. Leaving some of the legionaries to deal with them, Turpio ran a few yards to one side and used his blade to slice through the side of the tent. He emerged into what appeared to be a corridor. Rather than follow it, he cut through the inner wall. Now he was in an empty dining room. Some of the remains of the evening meal had not been cleared away. Turpio swept up a drinking flagon and tucked it safely in his belt.

'No time for looting,' he bellowed and, swinging his *spatha*, tore through the next wall. This time he emerged into pandemonium – high-pitched screams, female voices. He swung round, knees bent, sword at the ready, seeking out any threat, trying to make sense of the sweet-smelling, soft-lit room.

'Fuck me, it's the King's harem,' said a legionary.

Women and girls wherever one looked. Dozens of beautiful girls. Dark, blond. Clad in silk, kohl round their eyes, cowering in corners, behind pieces of soft furniture, they called out in Persian. Turpio could not tell if they were calling for help or begging to be spared.

'I must be dead and in the Elysian fields,' said a legionary.

Looking round, Turpio spotted an ornate doorway. A fat eunuch dithered indecisively in front of it. Turpio kicked him out of the way. Shouting for the legionaries to follow him, he dived through the opening.

The room was nearly dark. It was empty. There was a smell of balsam, a smell of sex. Turpio went over to the wide, rumpled bed. He put his hand on the sheets. They were warm. *Jupiter Optimus Maximus, we were that fucking close.*

A small movement caught the corner of Turpio's eye. In a flash, he whirled his sword out. The girl was in the corner of the room, trying to hide behind a sheet. Her eyes were very wide. She was naked. Turpio smiled, then realized it might not be altogether reassuring.

Tyche! A few moments earlier and everything would have been different. Turpio noticed a gold bangle on the bed. Without thought he picked it up and slid it on his wrist. *Tyche.*

His reflective mood was shattered when a legionary barrelled through the door. 'The bastards are coming for us, *Dominus*.'

Outside, a group of Sassanid *clibanarii* on foot had banded together. They were edging forwards from the right. A tall nobleman was haranguing them.

'Close ranks.' As soon as he sensed the legionaries around him, Turpio filled his lungs and began the call and response. 'Are you ready for war?'

'Ready!'

'Are you ready for war?'

On the third response and with no hesitation the legionaries surged forward. Turpio saw a shiver run through the enemy ranks. Some of them edged sideways, trying to get closer into the protection of the shield of the man on their right. Some gave a step or two backwards.

Excellent, thought Turpio. Momentum against cohesion, the age-old equation of battle. We have momentum, and they have just sacrificed their cohesion. Thank the gods.

Tucking his shoulder into his shield, Turpio slammed into one of the enemy. The Sassanid staggered back, knocking the man behind him off balance as well. Turpio brought his *spatha* down on the first man's helmet. The helmet did not break, but it buckled, and the man fell like a stone. The next man gave ground. Turpio lunged forward. The man gave more.

'Hold your position. Re-form the line. Now, keep facing the reptiles, and step back. Step by step. No hurry. No panic.'

The Sassanids stayed where they were. The gap between the combatants widened. Soon the legionaries were back where they had entered the king's pavilion. Turpio ordered the nearest musician, a *bucinator*, to sound the recall.

'Right, boys, on my command we turn around and get out of here at the double.'

Getting out of the Sassanid camp was harder than getting in. There was no organized pursuit, no systematic resistance, the camp was in uproar – but this time the Persians were awake. Three times, smallish ad hoc bands of Sassanid warriors, twenty or thirty men, blocked their path and made a stand. Each time the Romans had to check, re-form, charge and fight hard for some moments before they could resume their escape. Once, Turpio called a halt because he feared that they were lost. He had himself hoisted up on a shield. When he could see in which direction the walls of Arete lay, they resumed their headlong flight. On and on they pounded, down the alleyways formed by thousands of close-packed tents. Sometimes they turned left or right; usually they just forged straight ahead. Out of the gloom whistled missiles launched by both soldiers and camp followers. Now and then a man went down. Turpio affected to ignore the swift rise and fall of a Roman *spatha* when it dealt with those too wounded to keep up. Legio IIII Scythica was not leaving her own to be tortured by the enemy.

At last there were no more tents in front. There was the road to Arete, just off to the left, and there, about one hundred paces down, was the picket fire behind which waited their friends, the century of Antoninus Prior supported by the *turma* of Apollonius. Turpio and his men seemed to cover the ground in no time.

Turpio rattled out orders, his voice rough from shouting. The raiding party, the century of Antoninus Posterior, was to carry straight on, stick together but make all speed to the Palmyrene Gate. They had done more than enough for one night. Turpio joined the other century. In moments he had Antoninus Prior redeploy it from *testudo* to a line ten wide and seven deep. Then they set off towards safety at the double, the cavalrymen of the *turma* of Apollonius trotting about fifty paces ahead, ready to shoot over the heads of the legionaries at any approaching threat.

Four hundred paces. Just 400 paces to safety. Turpio started to count, lost his place, started again, gave up. He had taken his place in the rear rank which, when the enemy caught them, would be the front. Over his shoulder he saw the first dark shapes of horsemen leaving the camp, spurring after them. There would be no chance of reaching the gate unmolested. Ahead, still at some distance, he could see through the gloom hard by the side of the road the short stretch of wall that Ballista had left standing and painted white. It marked 200 paces, the limit of accurate effective artillery shooting from the walls. More important now for Turpio, the ground on either side of the road for the last 200 paces was sown with a myriad of traps. If they could reach that white wall they would be a little bit safer. From then on, the Persian cavalry could only charge them straight down the road. Out here there were but a few pits and caltrops. Out here it was possible for the enemy to outflank then surround them.

Looking back, Turpio saw that the Sassanid horsemen had coalesced into two groups. One was forming up on the road, the other setting off to the north in a wide sweep that would bring them behind the fleeing Romans. There looked to be at least two or three hundred horsemen in each unit. More cavalry were emerging from the camp all the time.

Turpio ordered a halt. The cavalry on the road were moving forward. They were going to charge without waiting for the outflanking manœuvre to be completed. The legionaries turned to face their pursuers. With a high trumpet blast the Persians put spurs to their horses and came on. These were *clibanarii*, the Sassanid elite heavy cavalry. Backlit by the fires in the Persian camp, they looked magnificent. For the most part, the men had had time to put on their own armour – it flashed and flickered – but not that of their horses. They came on, moving from a canter to a loose gallop. Turpio could feel the thunder of the hooves of their huge Nisean chargers reverberating up from the ground. He sensed the legionaries around him just begin to waver. Gods below, but it was hard to stand up to a charge of cavalry. In a moment or two some of the legionaries might flinch, open gaps in the line, and then it would all be over. The *clibanarii* would be in amongst them, horses sending men flying, long cavalry swords scything down.

'Hold your positions. Keep the line unbroken.' Turpio did not think it would do much good. The enormous Nisean horses were getting larger by the second.

Over the heads of the legionaries whistled the arrows of Apollonius's troopers. At least they have not abandoned us, thought Turpio. We will not die alone.

A lucky arrow must have hit a vital part of a Sassanid horse. It fell, skidding forwards and sideways. Its rider was thrown over its head. He remained airborne for an improbably long time before smashing into the road, his armour ringing and clattering around him. The horse took out the legs of its neighbour. It too went crashing. The horse on the other side swerved away and barged into the next horse, which lost its footing. The second rank of horses could not stop quickly enough. They had no option but to plough into the fallen. Within moments, the magnificent charge had been transformed into a tipping, thrashing line of chaos, of men and horses writhing in pain and surprise.

'About turn, at the double, let's get as far from them as possible.' They would have to sort the chaos out. It had bought Turpio and his men a few moments, a few yards nearer to safety.

Jogging down the road, Turpio anxiously looked to his left to see what had become of the party of Sassanid cavalry riding to outflank his men from the north. He could see no sign. He felt his fear rising. Hercules' hairy arse, how could they have got between us and the gate so quickly? Then his spirits lifted. They were not between Turpio and the gate; they were drawing off towards their camp. A group of figures with torches looking down at a fallen horse indicated why. A single horse had fallen into one of the sparse traps set in the band between 200 and 400 paces from the wall. A single horse had fallen, and they had given up.

Now there was only one threat to face. But probably it was too much. Turpio felt that, the next time Sassanid *clibanarii* thundered down the road at them, the legionaries would break. It had been a very long, frightening night. Men's nerves can only take so much.

'Halt. About turn. Prepare to receive cavalry.'

This time the *clibanarii* were taking their time. They had formed up in a column seven wide, and Turpio could not see how many men deep. The front rank consisted of seven who had somehow found the time to armour their horses as well as themselves. They were riding knee to knee, big men on big horses. They formed a solid wall of iron, hardened leather, animal horn, the chilling steel points of their lances catching the starlight above them.

Turpio felt a ripple run through the legionaries around him. He could hear feet shuffling nervously, hobnails scraping on the surface of the road. The man on his right was glancing back over his shoulder, looking at the safety of the town. Turpio caught the rank smell of fear. Theirs or his, he was not sure.

'Hold the line. Keep steady. Stand tall. Horses will not run into formed infantry.' Turpio was shouting himself hoarse. He would not be able to speak tomorrow. He grinned as the other unfortunate implication of this struck him. He turned to encourage the ranks behind him.

'If we don't budge they cannot touch us. Keep the line and we will be all right.' Jupiter's bollocks, but the gate looked close. Anyone could imagine turning, running and getting into safety. It was only about 150 paces away. So near you felt you could be there in a moment. 'Do not think of running. You cannot outrun a horse. Run and you are dead. Hold the line and we all live.' The men were not meeting his eye; it was not going to work.

A trumpet shrilled, cutting through the ambient noise of the disturbed night. The *clibanarii* dipped their awful lances and began to advance down the road at a walk. There was the jingle of armour, the ringing of their horses' hooves on the road, but no sound of humanity. They came on like a long serpent, scale-armoured and implacable.

Twang – slide – thump. The noise of a *ballista* shooting. Twang – slide – thump. Another. Then another. Louder than anything in the night, all the artillery on the western wall of the town of Arete was shooting – shooting blind into the dark night.

A terrible silence after the first volley. The *clibanarii* stopped. The legionaries froze. Everyone knew that the *ballistae* were re-loading, the greased winches turning, the ratchets clicking, the torsion springs tightening. Everyone knew that within a minute at most the *ballistae* would shoot again, that again with superhuman speed and power, missiles would rain down across the plain, falling on friend and foe alike.

Twang – slide – thump. The first of the second round of *ballistae* was heard. 'Stand up. Stand up. Stand your ground.' Turpio's men were cowering, shields held pathetically above their heads in a useless attempt to protect them from incoming artillery bolts or stones.

Turpio turned to look down the road at the Sassanids, and started to laugh.

'Right, boys, now get up and RUN!'

There was a shocked pause, then they all realized that the *clibanarii* were cantering away into the night, back to their camp, out of range of the artillery on the walls of Arete. The legionaries turned and ran.

Turpio saw Ballista waiting in the gateway. The torchlight made the northerner's long hair shine golden. He was smiling. As he ran up to him, Turpio again started laughing. They shook hands. They hugged. Turpio was slapping his *Dux* on the back.

'Brilliant. Absolutely fucking brilliant,' Turpio panted.

Ballista tipped his head back and laughed. 'Thank you. I liked it. Not such a stupid northern barbarian then?'

'Brilliant . . . mind you, obviously I realized straight away that the *ballistae* were not loaded, that the mere sound would scare the reptiles off.'

The young *optio* was prepared to be most helpful. The matter reflected well on Legio IIII Scythica, and it reflected well on the young *optio*. The latter was a not inconsiderable factor for a junior officer with a career to make.

'Gaius Licinius Prosper, of the *vexillatio* of Legio IIII Scythica, *Optio* of the Century of Marinus Posterior. We will do what is ordered, and at every command we will be ready.' The salute was smart.

'Tell me exactly what happened.' Ballista returned the salute. Almost certainly the 'exactly' was redundant. Prosper clearly intended to have his moment, to take his time telling the story before he would lead them to the corpse. Ballista sniffed. He could smell the corpse, or at least what had killed him, from here.

'Last night, as the *turma* of Apollonius was withdrawn from guard duties at the military granaries so that it could take part in the raid on the Sassanid camp – many congratulations on the success of the raid, *Dominus*, a piece of daring worthy of Julius Caesar himself, or of –'

'Thank you.' Ballista spoke quickly before they were sidetracked into lengthy comparisons between himself and any daring generals from Rome's past whom the *optio* could recall. 'Thank you very much. Please continue.'

'Of course, *Dominus*. As I was saying . . . as the *turma* of Apollonius was not guarding the granaries, you ordered Acilius Glabrio to select thirty-two legionaries drawn from the centuries of Naso, Marinus Prior, Marinus Posterior and Pudens to take over the guard duties.' Ballista stifled a yawn. It was the third hour of daylight. He had had no sleep the previous night and, now the excitement of the raid had drained out of him, he was very tired. 'You did me the honour of choosing me to be the *optio* in command of the guard detail.'

Ballista was careful not to smile. He had merely told Acilius

Glabrio to put a small but adequate guard on the granaries last night. Until a few moments ago he had not been aware of the existence of the young *optio*. It is easy to collapse all hierarchies above oneself into one almost undifferentiated rank, to assume that your superiors know each other and that your commander-in-chief knows about you. 'You have more than repaid that honour by your diligence,' he said. 'Now please tell me what happened.'

The youth smiled broadly. 'Well, I thought it best to station two legionaries at the doors at each end of the granaries. I thought that, if there were always two legionaries together, there would be far less risk of them being overpowered or one of them falling asleep.' He looked suddenly embarrassed. 'Not that legionaries of IIII Scythica would ever fall asleep on guard duty.'

No, but I might at any moment, if you don't get a move on. Ballista smiled. 'Very good,' he said encouragingly.

'Of course this left only myself as a mobile patrol.'

Ballista reflected that the young *optio* – Prosper, must remember his name – might recount a lot of information that was unnecessary, but that was better than one of those tongue-tied witnesses you were always having to prompt and chivvy along, especially when he was as dog-tired as he was now.

'I first saw him in the fourth watch, at the end of the tenth hour of the night, just before you had the artillery shoot, when I was proceeding south towards the palace of the *Dux Ripae*, that is, towards your palace.' Ballista nodded weightily as if at the insight that he was the *Dux Ripae* and the palace was his. At least they were finally getting somewhere. 'He was walking north between the town wall and the eastern four granaries. Of course there is a curfew, so he should not have been there anyway. Yet there are always soldiers or their slaves out and about at night. He was dressed as a soldier – tunic, trousers, boots, sword belt – but I was suspicious. Why would a soldier be off duty last night of all nights? And he looked wrong somehow. Now I realize it was his beard and hair. They were far too long. No centurion would have let him get away with it, not even in an auxiliary unit. Not that you could tell now, not with the condition he is in.' The young man shuddered slightly.

'And he was acting suspiciously. He was holding a big jar in one hand, holding it away from his body, as if it were very precious, as if he were terrified of spilling a drop. And he was holding a shuttered lantern in the other hand. Again holding it unnaturally far from his body.'

'Excellent observation, *Optio*.'

'Thank you, *Dominus*.' The *optio* was in full flow now. 'As I walked towards him he saw me and turned into the gap between the first and second granaries. I called for him to stop, but he ignored me. I shouted the alarm. I ran after him and yelled to the legionaries on guard at the other end that there was an enemy coming down the eavesdrip and to cut him off.' The young *optio* paused as if to take questions. None came. He continued. 'When I turned into the alley I could not see him at first. I could see Piso and Fonteius blocking the far end, but he was out of sight. I knew that he must be hiding in one of the alcoves formed by the big buttresses of the granaries.'

One of those alcoves in which Bagoas had been beaten up, thought Ballista.

'As he was cornered, I thought that he might be dangerous. So I called Scaurus from my end to come with me. We drew our swords and started off very cautiously down the alley.' Ballista nodded to indicate that the course of action was both thoughtful and courageous. 'It was very dark. So we were going slowly, covering both sides, waiting to be attacked. Suddenly there is a noise of splintering wood up ahead. Then I am almost blinded by a bright light two alcoves down. There is a sort of whooshing sound, and a ghastly smell. When we can see again, we run forward. Piso and Fonteius are running towards us from the far end. We all get there at once. I will never forget it. Never.' He stopped talking.

'*Optio?*'

'Sorry, *Dominus*. It was horrible. I hope I never see anything like it again.'

'Please continue.'

'The bastard was crawling into the little ventilation opening at the foot of the wall. I don't know if he got stuck or if the pain stopped him, but he was just sort of writhing when we got there, writhing and screaming. Never heard anything like it. He must have torn away the wooden slats over the ventilator with his sword, emptied the jar of naptha over himself and, with the lantern, quite deliberately set light to himself. Then he tried to crawl into the ventilator. He turned himself into a human missile. It smelt like . . . like roast pork.'

'What did you do?'

'There were flames everywhere. The naptha had set the remains of the ventilator on fire. There were flames licking up the brick walls. Even the mud around him seemed to be on fire. Gods below, it was hot. It looked as if it would spread into the granary, get in the ventilator and under the wooden floor. The whole place was about to go up. It was Scaurus who thought what to do. He got his entrenching tool, stuck it in the poor bastard's thigh, and dragged him to the middle of the alley, where we left him. We threw soil on the fires until they were smothered.'

The young *optio* led Ballista down the alley and introduced him to the legionaries Scaurus, Piso and Fonteius. The northerner praised them all, especially the rather singed Scaurus, and promised they would be rewarded. He asked Demetrius to make a note of it. The Greek boy was looking sick.

The scene was as Ballista had expected. The corpse was twisted, shrivelled, its hair and clothing gone, its features melted. Beyond the fact that he had been a short man, the corpse was completely unrecognizable. The *optio* was right: disgustingly, it smelt of roast pork. It smelt of Aquileia. It had an entrenching tool, the wooden handle burnt away, sticking out of its leg.

'Did you find anything interesting on the body?'

'Nothing, *Dominus*.'

Ballista crouched next to the corpse, willing his gorge down. The man's sword was a military-issue *spatha*. It signified little. There were many available on the open market. The man's boots did not have hobnails, but nor did the boots of a lot of soldiers these days.

'You were right. He was not a soldier.' Ballista grinned. 'Nothing can persuade a soldier to take his ornaments, awards for valour, his lucky charms off his sword belt. All that is left of this man's belt is the buckle.' The northerner pointed to an unremarkable buckle in the shape of a fish. 'Definitely not a soldier.'

From a little way away came the sound of retching. Demetrius was throwing up.

'What could make a man do such a thing?' the young *optio* asked.

Ballista shook his head. 'I cannot begin to imagine.'

Everyone was waiting for the sun to rise. Already the eastern sky was a pale bronze. A cool steady breeze blew from the south. Ducks were flighting over the Euphrates and the smell of baking bread wafted around the town. If you did not look too far away or you kept your eyes on the heavens, you could imagine that Arete was at peace.

One glance over the battlements shattered any pacific illusions. True as the light advanced, the western desert for once showed green. There were grasses and wild flowers in every little depression. Birds sang. But beyond the delicate spring scene was a black line about a thousand paces wide. The Sassanid host stood shoulder to shoulder. Thirty, forty ranks deep, it was impossible to tell. Above their heads the south wind tugged at the banners. Serpents, wolves, bears, abstract symbols of fire, of righteousness, of Mazda, snapped in the breeze.

Behind the ranks of men loomed the instruments of war. A line of siege mantlets, tall shields mounted on wheels, could be made out running almost the length of the force. Here and there the wooden frames of *ballistae* stuck up; the keenest eyes counted at least twenty of them. And there, quite widely spaced and unmistakable behind the line, were the City Takers, the three tall, tall siege towers.

Ballista was impressed despite himself. It was just seven days since the Persian horde had descended on Arete. They had found nothing useable; there was no timber for miles: Ballista's men had stripped the countryside in advance. It had done no good. The Sassanids had brought with them everything they needed. Somehow they had transported upriver all the instruments of siege warfare in prefabricated form, almost ready to use. For six days they had laboured. Now, on the seventh day, they were ready. Although he would not admit it to anyone else, would barely concede it to himself, Ballista was worried. These Sassanids were like no barbarians he had fought before. Goths, Sarmatians, Hibernians or Moors – none could have done such things, none could prosecute a siege with such vigour.

Ballista and the defenders had not been idle in the seven days since the night raid. Turpio's foray may have failed to kill Shapur but still must be counted a success. Roman casualties had been very light. Five troopers were missing from the *turma* of Paulinus, none at all from that of Apollonius. Of the legionaries, there were twenty empty places in the century that had actually entered the Persian camp, that of Antoninus Posterior, and one from that of Antoninus Prior – oddly, as it had not actually been engaged. The latter, although no one said so out loud, was widely considered to have deserted. Overall the raid had raised Roman morale, and it was safely assumed to have shaken that of the Persians. Yet such a large-scale raid had not been repeated. Ballista knew that the Sassanids would now be on guard. He was waiting for the next phase of the siege, the next predictable turn of the dance. He was waiting for an all-out Persian assault.

The Romans had not made another big foray yet the Sassanids were unlikely to have been sleeping soundly in their tents. The very night of the main raid Antigonus had returned in the early hours from across the river. He had found the girl who had been raped. She was dead; she had been mutilated. Antigonus left her there but returned with a Persian head. Two nights later he had gone south by boat and returned with another head, wrapped in a Persian cloak. The next night he had slipped out of the northern wicket gate down by the river and this time returned with two heads. Finally, last night he had gone across the river again and brought back yet another grisly bundle. In a sense five casualties meant nothing in a horde probably 50,000 strong. Yet morning after morning the news of finding yet another inexplicably decapitated corpse in yet another place was bound to summon up the very worst fears in the Persian army: a traitor turning his hand against his friends or, worse, far worse, a daemon able to strike at will throughout the sleeping camp.

Ballista was pleased with his new standard-bearer. He took little pleasure in the ghastly trophies, but he solemnly unwrapped each one, solemnly thanked its bringer. Each one was a mark of revenge for both Romulus and the unknown girl. Antigonus had a gift for this sort of thing. Ballista was glad they were on the same side.

Beyond Antigonus's nocturnal forays, beyond the normal activity of the besieged, the main activity of the seven days had been the construction of three huge mobile cranes. Every carpenter in the town had been seconded to work on them; likewise, every blacksmith had been forging the giant chains and implements they would deploy. With their completion, Ballista had the last major items necessary for when the Sassanids attempted to storm the town. Looking up and down the wall, the air already shimmering with heat where the large metal cauldrons hung over their fires, Ballista felt that he had done his best. He was far from sure that it was good enough, but he had done his best.

The sun was rising over Mesopotamia. A wash of gold splashed over the bright Sassanid banners, picked out their gorgeous costumes, the jewels in the headdresses. As one, every man in the vast host sank to his knees then prostrated himself in the dust of the desert. Trumpets blared, drums boomed, and across the plain rolled chants of 'Maz-da, Maz-da' as they hailed the rising sun.

The sun had now risen clear of the horizon. The chanting stopped, and the Persian army got to its feet. They waited in silence.

High on the battlements of the Palmyrene Gate, Ballista also waited and watched. The twenty-first day of April, ten days before the *kalends* of May: it was the *Parilia*, the birthday of eternal Rome. From the right of the Sassanid army, preceded by the Drafsh-i-Kavyan, the great battle flag of the house of Sasan, came the now familiar figure clad in purple riding a white horse.

'Shah-an-Shah, Shah-an-Shah.' A new chant rolled across the plain.

Shapur halted in front of the centre of the line. The great jewel-encrusted banner moved above his head, catching the sunlight, flashing yellow, violet, red. His horse stamped its foot, tossed its head and neighed, high and clear across the plain.

On the battlement Bagoas gave a small whimper of pleasure. 'The sure sign. When the charger of the King of King's does thus before the walls of a town, that place will surely fall.'

'Silence, boy.' Ballista would not have his slave spreading despondency. 'It is an easy enough omen to create.'

'What are they doing now?' Maximus asked. A line of seven roped men were being driven towards the priests, *magi*, around the Drafsh-i-Kavyan. 'This does not look good.'

Bagoas said nothing. He cast his eyes down. For once he looked rather shamefaced.

The men were wearing Roman uniforms. They were struggling, but being beaten forward. One fell. He was kicked back to his feet. They were driven to where a small fire was burning. A pot was hanging on a tripod, heating over the fire. The Romans were forced to their knees and held tightly. Their heads were forced back. One of the *magi* unhooked the pot from the tripod, lifted it free of the fire.

'Gods below, the barbarian bastards.' Maximus looked away.

The priest stepped over to the first of the prisoners. Two *magi* held the man's head. The priest tipped the pot. The man screamed.

'What is it?' Ballista tried to keep his voice level. 'What are they doing to them?'

'Olive oil.' Bagoas answered very quietly. 'They are blinding them with boiling olive oil.'

A single trumpet call was picked up by innumerable others. The vast Sassanid horde stirred itself and began to form up for its slow advance.

Gangs of men began to push the *ballistae*, mounted on squat carts or moved on rollers forward, to within effective range, about 200 paces of the walls. From there the stone-throwers would aim to destroy the defenders' artillery and knock down the battlements while the bolt-throwers swept Roman soldiers from the wall walks.

The mantlets were pushed to the fore. These would travel to

within effective bow shot, about fifty paces from the town. Forming an unbroken line of reinforced wood, the mantlets were intended to shield both the Persian archers and the storming parties as they assembled.

Most ponderously of all, hauled by hundreds of men each, the three City Takers began to inch forward. These monstrous wheeled siege towers were made of wood but entirely clad in plates of metal and damp skins. Water was frequently poured down their sides from the top to try to prevent the enemy setting fire to them. They had *ballistae* on their upper levels, but these were only secondary to their main purpose. The City Takers were designed to creep up to and overtop the walls of the town, let down a drawbridge and release on to the battlements a mass of screaming warriors. As the drawbridges came down, a host of storming parties carrying ladders would burst forth in support from the line of mantlets.

Ballista looked at them. They were the key to the assault. Everything else would revolve around them. They were quite far apart. One was on the road, heading straight for the gate where Ballista stood. The others were aimed to hit the wall beyond, three towers away north and south. Travelling at about one mile an hour, in theory they could strike the wall in about half an hour. Ballista knew that was not going to happen. The City Takers would make many stops, to change the crews of men hauling them, to test, smooth and reinforce the ground ahead, as well as to fill in Ballista's traps – if, of course, the latter were detected.

Ballista judged that the assault would probably not come until midday. Unfortunately, that would be good for the attackers in several ways. The morning sun would no longer be directly in their eyes as it was now. It would give plenty of time for the City Takers to reach the walls and for subsidiary attacks to be ready to go in on the other walls.

Clouds of horsemen had been spotted the day before on the other sides of the northern and southern ravines. Ballista had altered his order of battle, ordering 300 men, 100 mercenaries from each of the *numeri* of the caravan protectors, to join the defence of the dangerously undermanned north wall. It was odd that this weakness had been spotted by his *accensus*, the completely unmilitary Demetrius, not by himself nor any of his army officers. Sometimes one got too close to things. As Ballista's people said: you could not see the wood for the trees.

Midday. The northerner turned the timing over in his mind. Midday. The time when Romans ate their first substantial meal of the day. Bagoas had told him that Persians ate later, towards late afternoon. At midday the Persians would not be hungry, but the Romans would. Ballista was about to issue orders to bring forward the time of the soldiers' lunch when he saw something that might prove to be terribly important.

The distinctive figure clad in purple riding a white horse was on the move. Although now accompanied by a glittering entourage of the high nobility and client kings, there was no mistaking the high, domed golden helmet, the long purple and white streamers that indicated the King of Kings.

Ballista had been waiting for this moment, had been praying that it would come. In the Roman army, at the start of a siege it was customary for the commander to ride forward into range of the defenders' artillery. It was a tradition that served two goals. At a purely pragmatic level, it gave the commander a fine chance to observe the state of the defences. At an altogether more intangible but possibly far more significant level, it allowed the general to rouse the spirits of his troops by demonstrating his studied contempt for the weapons of their enemies. A fine tradition, one which killed two birds with one stone. The only problem was that it sometimes killed the besieging general as well.

Until this moment Ballista had not known if the Sassanids held to a similar practice. Asking Bagoas had produced no useful answer – 'Of course, Shapur, the beloved of Mazda, has no fear of the weapons of his foes.' More and more the northerner wondered just how much or how little the Persian boy knew about war. Bagoas clearly came from the Persian elite, but was it becoming ever more likely that he was from a family of scribes or priests than one of warriors?

Shapur and his men reined in just outside artillery range. Animated conversation could be seen. The King of Kings was doing most of the talking. Informing his high-status audience of his view of the direction the assault should take, Shapur made wide arcs and sweeps with his arms, the streamers flying behind him.

Ballista stared intently not at Shapur but at two distinctive humps of stone left on either side of the road. The sides facing the wall were painted white. They marked 400 paces, the maximum range of his artillery. Come on, you cowardly eastern bastard. Come on, just have the balls to get within range.

Forcing his mind away, Ballista issued orders for the men to take their lunch no less than two hours earlier than usual. As the messengers moved away, the northerner realized with a nasty lurch that he had not issued the far more pressing orders for every piece of artillery to aim at the Persian king but not to shoot until the *Dux Ripae* gave the command. As the next batch of messengers moved away, Ballista was slightly reassured by the thought that their message most likely was redundant – it would be a very poor *ballistarius* indeed who had not already trained the weapon on the man on the white horse.

The trick of turning the washers, slackening the torsion and decreasing the apparent range of the weapons was an old trick, an obvious one. Had it worked? And even if it had, would the traitor have betrayed it? Was the Sassanid mocking him?

Shapur kicked on, and the white horse moved down the road towards the Palmyrene Gate. Past the whitewashed piles of stone, with his meteor trail of the powerful, Shapur came on. *Allfather, Deceitful One, Death-Bringer, deliver this man to me.*

Ballista was painfully aware of the expectation surrounding him. The dead silence on the battlements was broken only by the small noises of well-oiled machinery being subtly adjusted as the *ballistae* tracked their target. *Wait until he stops moving. Do not snatch at this. Wait until the right moment.*

Nearer and nearer came Shapur; closer and closer to the white-painted section of wall at 200 paces.

He stopped.

Ballista spoke.

Antigonus hoisted the looked-for red flag.

Twang – slide – thump: the great twenty-pounder by Ballista hurled its carefully rounded stone. A moment later it was joined by its twin on the gatehouse roof. Then, twang – slide – thump, twang – slide – thump: all the artillery along the western battlements joined in. For a couple of seconds the northerner admired the geometry of it all – the fixed line of the wall, the moving triangle of missiles all converging on the fixed point of the man on the white horse.

The rider in fur next to Shapur was plucked from his horse. Arms wide, the empty sleeves of his coat flapping, the man looked like a large six-limbed insect as the bolt threw him backwards. Towards the rear of the entourage two, maybe three horses and riders went down as a stone reduced them to a bloody shambles.

After the strike there was a shocked near-silence. Only muted sounds could be heard: the click of ratchets, the groan of wood and sinew under gathering pressure, and the grunting of men working frantically. The near-peace was broken by a rising roar of outrage from the horror-struck Sassanid horde.

Shapur took both sides by surprise. Putting spurs to his mount, he kicked it into a gallop straight ahead. Thundering towards the Palmyrene Gate, he pulled his bow from its case, took an arrow from his quiver and notched it. About 150 paces from the gate he skidded to a halt, drew and released the arrow.

Ballista watched its flight. With a superstitious dread he felt that it was coming straight for him. As they always do, it seemed to gain pace as it grew nearer. It fell just short and to the right of the northerner, clattering off the stone of the wall.

Shapur's mouth was moving. He was yelling his outrage, his anger, but the words could not be made out on the wall. Two horsemen drew up on either side of the king. They were shouting. One went so far as to try to grab his reins. Shapur used his bow as a whip to knock the hands aside. The white horse was spun around and, with a shake of his fist, the King of Kings was racing back towards safety.

Twang – slide – thump: the artillery pieces started to speak again.

At this distance, against a fast-moving target, Ballista knew there was next to no chance of a projectile finding its mark.

Back in safety, Shapur could be seen riding along the front of the line haranguing his men. They began to chant: 'Sha-pur, Sha-pur.' Along the walls of Arete spread a counter chant: 'Ball-is-ta, Ball-is-ta.'

The *Dux Ripae* took off his helmet. The south wind caught his long fair hair and blew it out behind him. He waved to his men. 'Ball-is-ta, Ball-is-ta.'

'So, who was it we just killed?' He spoke conversationally.

'Prince Hamazasp the son of Hamazasp the King of Georgia.' Strong but hard-to-read emotions played across Bagoas's face. 'If his spirit is not avenged it will forever more be a stain on the honour of the King of Kings. Now there can be no quarter.'

With a child-like spontaneity Ballista threw his helmet in the air and caught it. 'That should concentrate the boys' minds.' Laughing, he turned to the soldiers on the gatehouse. 'I don't know about you, but I don't fancy letting those *magi* get their hands on me.' The men laughed in turn. By nightfall, the exchange, often altered and embellished, would have reached every corner of the city.

'How long until their line comes into extreme artillery range?'

'At least a quarter of an hour, maybe more.' As was only right, Mamurra, the *praefectus fabrum*, the man who was meant to know siege machinery, answered his *Dux*.

'Then, Calgacus, can you find us some food? Trying to kill the despot of half the known world has made me very hungry.'

Demetrius watched his *kyrios* eating bread and cold pheasant, talking and joking with the other men: Mamurra, Turpio, Maximus, Antigonus, the crews of the artillery pieces. They were passing a jug from hand to hand. The young Greek had never admired Ballista more. Did the *kyrios* plan these things or did they just come to him in a divinely inspired flash? Did he always know what he was doing? However it was, it made no difference: it was an act of genius. The hideous actions of the *magi*, the death of the Georgian prince and the exchange with Bagoas came together to tell a story that anyone could follow. By nightfall every soldier in Arete would be stiffened by the knowledge of what would happen to him if he fell into the hands of the Sassanids: capitulation meant torture and death; better to die on one's feet, weapon in hand.

Soon enough the Persians drew near the line of signs that marked 400 paces from the wall, maximum artillery range. The *Dux Ripae* had repeatedly stressed the need for these range markers, and those at 200 paces, to be inconspicuous. They were to be visible to the artillerymen but not to attract the attention of the besiegers. The majority of artillery crews had gone for carefully arranged, hopefully natural-looking low humps of dun-coloured rocks. There was not an artilleryman in the town who had not laughed, although only surreptitiously – never when the big man or his vicious-looking bodyguard were around – at the markers opposite the Palmyrene Gate chosen by the *Dux* himself: 'well, brother, that is a northern barbarian's idea of inconspicuous: two bloody great piles of stone followed by a bloody great wall, the whole lot painted white.'

The Persians were advancing sensibly, coming on in good order. The main body was advancing at the speed at which the *ballistae* could be moved. The mantlets, which could be transported considerably faster, were staying with the artillery to try to shield them. The three great siege towers were lagging quite some distance behind.

Ballista's eyes were concentrated on the two white stones 400 paces away. He held a piece of bread and cheese in one hand and a jug in the other, both completely unconsidered. When the Persians passed the stones, they would have to advance for 200 paces into the teeth of the artillery on the town wall. Hauling their artillery forward, for those 200 paces the Sassanids would be unable to hit back. The northerner had ordered his artillery to concentrate exclusively on the enemy *ballistae* and the men moving them. Initially, little could be expected – the range was too great for any accuracy – but things should improve as the slow-moving targets came closer. *Knock out as many of them as we can before they can get at us*. With luck, the stone-throwers would wreck some enemy engines. The bolt-throwers could not damage the *ballistae* themselves, but they could kill and alarm the men moving them and this would slow down their progress, keep them longer unable to strike back, longer exposed to the stone-throwers on the town wall.

Ballista nodded to Antigonus. The standard-bearer raised the red flag. Twang – slide – thump, twang – slide – thump: up and down the wall the artillery opened up.

The first volley achieved nothing and after a couple of minutes there was no semblance of volley shooting. The crews of the artillery pieces worked at different speeds. Ballista was far from convinced that the quickest were necessarily the best – better to take a little extra time and aim well. It cost him some effort not to take over the laying of the big twenty-pounder next to him. The northerner went to scratch his nose, found a jug in one hand, food in the other. He drank and ate.

Cheers, loud cheers, from the wall off to the right. Ballista looked just in time to see a wheel spinning in the air like a tossed coin. A cloud of dust rose from the plain. Small, brightly clad figures staggered out of it. One of the stone-throwers towards the north of the wall had scored a direct hit. One Sassanid *ballista* down, nineteen to go.

More cheers, this time off to the left. Ballista could not see the cause. Maximus pointed. 'There! There! Gods below, that's fucked him.' Ballista followed the direction of the Hibernian's outstretched arm. Way, way out from the wall, way out behind the main body of the Persians, was the southernmost of the three siege towers. The great Sassanid City Taker was leaning drunkenly forward, its front wheels deep in the ground.

'*Tyche*,' said Mamurra. 'I do not think that we dug any pits that far out. Its weight must have made it go through into one of the very furthest out of the old underground tombs. Anyway, they will not get that brute out again today.'

Any battle, like anything in nature, goes in phases. Now for a time the tide was with the defenders, and good news flowed in. As Ballista finished his bread and cheese two messengers treading on each other's heels ran up the steps to the top of the gatehouse.

While the first spoke Ballista passed the jug from his own hand to the other waiting messenger.

The Sassanid attack on the north wall had come to nothing. A great mass of men – it was reckoned there were about 5,000 of them – had been drawing up on the plateau north of the ravine. They were still a very long way off, at the very limits of artillery range, when Centurion Pudens ordered the bolt-thrower on the postern tower to try a shot at them. The *ballistarius*, more in hope than expectation, had aimed at the leading rider, a richly clad man on a gloriously caparisoned horse. The bolt had taken the Sassanid off the horse easy as could be, left him pinned to the ground. Their leader dead, the reptiles had swarmed away.

Ballista thanked the messenger, and gave him some coins. The other handed the jug over to his colleague and told his news.

The Persians, from somewhere, had got together five boats and crammed about 200 men into them. Stupidly, they had followed the western bank of the river down to Arete. As soon as the boats came into range of the bolt-throwers on the two north-eastern towers, the boatmen, local men who had been pressed into service, dived over the sides, swam to shore and deserted. From then on the boats were in utter confusion. They were little better than drifting while being shot at from the elevation of the walls by bolt-throwers and bowmen. When eventually they tried to land near the fish market, they were easy targets for at least ten artillery pieces and no fewer than 500 archers from the *numerus* of Anamu. Three of the boats capsized; one foundered just short of the nearest island in the Euphrates; one drifted away downriver. Most of those not killed by missiles were drowned. Only about twenty seemed to have escaped downriver, and another twenty or so were stuck on the island.

As the tale ended, with the Sassanids on the island, Antigonus looked enquiringly at Ballista, who enigmatically said yes, adding, if they were all still around that night. The northerner thanked the messenger and again parted with some coins.

But the tide cannot flow one way for ever. All too soon, and at the cost of only one more *ballista*, the Sassanid artillery had crossed their zone of impotence. They had reached their intended shooting positions just within effective range. Persians swarmed about, dismounting the artillery from their rollers, setting up protective screens, putting the ammunition to hand, winching back the sliders, placing the missiles, aiming and releasing.

Ballista felt a slight tremor run through the gatehouse as a stone struck. The time of carefree observation was over. Now the air had become a thing of menace; everywhere the tearing, ripping noises of missiles. To the right a man screamed as a bolt shot him from the wall walk. To the left a short section of battlements exploded in stone splinters as a missile struck. A man lay in the middle of the debris moaning. Another lay silent. Passing the word for carpenters to erect a makeshift battlement, Ballista reflected that, other things being equal, the defenders should win this exchange of artillery. They had twenty-five *ballistae* to eighteen, and the advantages of a higher position, as well as stone, not wooden, walls for protection.

Yet other things were not equal. The two City Takers remaining mobile had crept forward into maximum artillery range. Just when the enemy would be shooting back, the northerner was going to have to order his *ballistarii* to change targets. As they came in range, the huge siege towers would be the sole targets. Now it would be the turn of the defending artillerymen to endure shot without being able to return it; there can be little worse for any soldier. About to send off the runners to give the order, Ballista added that any *ballistarius* who aimed at anything other than one of the siege towers once they were within range would be flogged to death. *Allfather, the exercise of power has corrupted my soul.*

Leaving their *ballistae* 200 paces from the wall, the main body of Persians huddled as close as possible behind the line of mobile shields. Men fell to traps underfoot and arrows slicing down from above. Yet to the defenders it seemed no time at all before the line of mantlets was established a mere fifty paces from the walls and the Persian bowmen were bending their bows. Ten, twenty, thirty thousand arrows; it was impossible to guess. Like a shadow passing over the face of the sun, they made the day grow darker.

All along the wall, and behind it, the arrows fell as thick as hail in the deep midwinter. On the wall, and in the streets and alleys behind, men fell. The archers on the wall shot back. The defenders had some advantages: they were higher up, well protected by stone crenellations and the stout shields of the legionaries; almost all their arrows found their mark – so vast was the number of Sassanids that they formed a dense target and the mantlets could not shelter them all. But it was an unequal contest: fewer than 650 bowmen against innumerable thousands.

Sassanid arrows were striking home. Defenders were falling – far too many. Ballista wondered if all his planning, his clever ruses, would prove in vain. Would sheer numbers prevail? Would sheer weight of missiles clear the walls and leave the city open?

Endurance. They just had to endure. Ballista knew that only discipline, old-fashioned Roman *disciplina*, could get them through. For nine nights and nine days the Allfather had hung on the tree of life. His side pierced by a spear, voluntarily the Allfather had endured on the tree to learn the secrets of the dead. The northerner smiled. So much for the *romanitas* of the *Dux Ripae*.

The white *draco* hissing in the breeze attracted the full ferocity of the Sassanids. The air above the Palmyrene Gate was thick with missiles. Ballista was hunkered down behind the parapets in the midst of a makeshift shieldwall. It was hard to see or hear. Then, above the awful clamour of the storm of steel and stone rose the sound of cheering. Thin, half-swamped by the noise of battle, but exultant, came chanting: *'Ro-ma! Ro-ma!'*

Ballista peeked out around the crenellations. He jerked his head back into safety as an arrow snickered off the wall. He looked again. The northern half of the plain was enveloped in a great mushroom cloud of dust. Not wanting to tempt fate, Ballista retreated behind the parapet for a few moments. When he looked again the dust had cleared a little. He could see why his men were exulting. The northernmost City Taker was no more. In its place was a tortured tall frame of beams and girders. As Ballista watched, a man leapt from the top storey. The falling man, incongruously, looked as elegant as a pantomime dancer. Two, three, four more eastern men jumped to a certain death. Then, with a ponderous inevitability, the remains of the tower imploded.

A strange hush settled across the battlefield. The fighting slackened as both sides came to terms with the enormity of what had happened. The siege tower had been heading almost directly towards a tower housing one of the biggest pieces of artillery. The repeated impact of twenty-pound stones slamming in at a great pace must literally have shaken the City Taker apart.

Demetrius looked around. The fighting top of the Palmyrene Gate was littered, almost carpeted with spent missiles. As the fighting died down, defenders slumped down against the walls or the two enormous *ballistae*. Although he tried not to, the young Greek could not help repeatedly looking at the two corpses thrown in the corner. A slick pool of their mingled blood seeped out from under them. Demetrius both wanted and at the same time did not want to know their identity.

Was the fighting over? Zeus, Apollo, Athena and Artemis, please let it all be over, at least for today. Demetrius noticed some slaves carrying parcels and jars emerge from the trapdoor. They bent double as they moved. Stray missiles were still flying across the roof. For a moment the young Greek had no idea what the slaves were doing. Then, looking at the sky, he realized that it must already be towards the end of the fourth hour of daylight, the time that the *kyrios* had ordered the troops to take their early lunch. In one way the time had gone so quickly; in another, the screaming and the terror seemed to have lasted for days. Demetrius thought how Zeus, in the divine poetry of Homer, held back the day so that Odysseus and Penelope could enjoy their lovemaking and sleep. Today was nothing like that; Arete was nothing like Ithaka.

Earlier, when Ballista had called for his impromptu mid-morning snack, Demetrius had been unable to eat; there had been no saliva in his mouth. Now, as the fighting seemed to be dying down, he felt ravenous. Taking some bread, cheese and an onion, he started to wolf them down.

The *kyrios* was chewing in a desultory way. He was sitting on the floor with his back against the southern wall, Maximus and Antigonus either side of him. In quiet voices they were holding an intermittent technical discussion on the limits of depression of artillery pieces. Demetrius wondered at them. How could repetition ever so dull a man's senses that this morning of horror, this dealing in death, could become as mundane as reaping a cornfield? He began to giggle. Maybe it was because they were barbarians; an Angle, a Hibernian and a Batavian. To stop his giggling, Demetrius bit a large mouthful out of his onion.

Arete was in the eye of the storm. This isolated and previously insignificant town had been willed by the gods to become the latest focus of the eternal war between east and west. The conflict had always been there, from the earliest records. First, the eastern Phoenicians had kidnapped Io and the Greeks had responded by abducting first Europa then Medea. After the Trojans had taken Helen, things moved from girl-taking to war-making. The Achaeans burnt Troy, the Persians burnt Athens, and Alexander burnt Persepolis. The sands of the desert were sodden red with the wreck of Crassus's legions at Carrhae. Abandoned Roman corpses marked Mark Antony's retreat from Media. Julius Caesar was struck down on the eve of yet another war of revenge. Wars of revenge had repeatedly been undertaken by the emperors Trajan, Lucius Verus and Septimius Severus. Then came the Sassanids, and the east had struck back. Thousands of Roman dead at Meshike and Barbalissos. Antioch, the metropolis of Syria, and so many others burning in the time of troubles. East against west, the conflict that could never end.

Arete was the epicentre of a conflict of cosmic proportions; a never-ending clash of civilizations, an eternal clash of gods. The full might of the east was hurled against the west, and here eternal Rome – *humanitas* itself as some would have it, all of its arts and philosophy – was defended by three barbarians eating bread and cheese. Demetrius's stream of consciousness was broken by the sudden arrival of a soldier.

The messenger also trampled into Maximus's excellent reverie. The Hibernian had lost interest in the finer points of depressing artillery some time ago. His mind was running over the new girl at The Krater: nipples like a blind cobbler's thumbs, trim little delta, willing as you like. It was funny with girls – no matter what sort of nipples they had, they always wanted different ones. The girl from The Krater with her big brown aureoles like dinner plates said she would rather have small, neat little nipples. The girl from the bar at the north end of town, who had tiny, delicate pink nipples, wished hers were bigger. Maximus did not care; the girls were both lively well-built blondes. Certainly they would look good together.

The messenger was attempting to salute while bent double. Ballista and Antigonus saluted back without getting up. As a slave rather than a soldier, Maximus took pleasure in not feeling the need to join in.

'Good news, *Dominus*.' The soldier sat down with relief when Ballista indicated. 'The barbarian attack on the south wall has been driven off. There were about 5,000 of them. The reptiles formed up out of range on the plateau. But by the time they were descending into the ravine we had ten *ballistae* on them. The bastards were looking shaken when they started to climb our side of the ravine. When the bowmen of Iarhai and Ogelos started shooting and we rolled those bloody great stones you had us put out down among them the Sassanids ran like the true easterners they are – no stomach for it, no balls.'

Living in the moment, almost like a child, Maximus had actually forgotten all about the threat to the southern wall. But the news was welcome: things on the desert wall were bad enough on their own.

Ballista thanked the messenger and sent him back with an order for Iarhai to bring 300 of his archers round on to the desert wall.

Trumpets rang and drums boomed across the plain. Sassanid commanders shouted themselves hoarse trying to put the enthusiasm back into their men, to lift the tempo of the attack. The stream of incoming missiles picked up. Demetrius cowered closer to the floor. Wearily, Ballista, Maximus and Antigonus got to their feet and huddled behind the parapets, now and then looking out.

A terrible crash came from the tower to the north of the gate. Again a cloud of ominous dun-coloured dust billowed into the sky. It was followed by a rhythmic shout of pain like an animal bellowing. A Sassanid stone-thrower had scored a direct hit on one of the two Roman *ballistae* on the tower; the resulting jagged, fast-flying splinters of wood had reduced the platform of the tower to a charnelhouse.

Before Ballista could issue any orders, Mamurra had appeared on the stricken tower. The *praefectus fabrum* was organizing a work gang to throw the shattered remains of the bolt-thrower off the tower and sending men to drag a spare piece of artillery from the magazine. The corpses joined the remnants of the machine on the ground and the living were pushed into getting the remaining *ballista* working.

For the moment the defenders' main problem lay in the one Sassanid City Taker remaining operative. It had resumed its painful advance on the Palmyrene Gate. While it stood and was capable of movement, all the artillery of the defenders that could get an aim on it had no other choice. Only the towers at the extreme north of the desert wall were able to hit back at the Sassanid artillery tormenting them.

The last City Taker was taking a dreadful pounding. Again and again smooth round artillery stones, six-pounders and twenty-pounders, smashed at terrible speed into the tower. Bolts from *ballistae* and arrows caused havoc among the myriad men hauling the behemoth. The City Taker shook, seemed to stagger, but then, with new men on the ropes and with the terrible squealing of thousands of joints of wood under intense pressure, it advanced again.

Twice, work crews raced ahead of the siege tower to deal with Ballista's traps. The carefully concealed pits at one hundred and at fifty paces from the gate were filled in, but at frightful cost. The crews ran into an almost solid wall of tipped steel. The pits were partly filled with their bodies.

Inexorably the City Taker rolled on. If it reached the gate, if its drawbridge crashed down on the roof of the gatehouse, the siege was over, the town would fall. Ballista knew that now there was just one hope of stopping the siege engine reaching the gate. Did the Persians know that there was one more pit hidden a mere twenty paces from the gate? The Suren had not come that close. As far as Ballista knew, no Persian had come that close. But had the traitor warned them?

Nearer and nearer came the skin-clad tower. The smell of

uncured hides, wood and the sweat of men preceded it to the gatehouse. Thirty paces, twenty-five: no work crew racing ahead. Twenty paces. Nothing. Had Ballista miscalculated? Were the beams too strong? Would the City Taker cross unhindered over the trap?

There was a deep, deep groan. The surface of the road moved, the hidden boards over the pit began to buckle under the weight of the tower. A distinctive smell wafted up. One by one the boards snapped. The tower lurched forward. Men screamed.

Ballista snatched up a bow and arrow. The smell of pitch was strong in his nostrils. He touched the combustible material to a brazier. The arrowhead flared. Taking a deep breath, he stepped out from the shelter of the crenellations. He flinched as a Persian arrow shot past his face. He exhaled, and forced himself to lean out over the wall, to ignore the dangers, to concentrate on what had to be done. Dimly he was aware of missiles nicking off the stone around him. There was the dark opening of the trap. He filled his lungs, drew the bow and released. The arrow seemed to accelerate away, a smoke trail curling after it.

Other fire arrows darted into the pit, into the mouth of the large terracotta storage jar which had been hidden there. With a roar the naptha ignited. The flames shot up, curling and licking around the siege tower, darting up its companionways and the ladders inside. Men screamed. Ballista smelt something like roast pork.

'Ball-is-ta, Ball-is-ta.' The chants rang out from the walls. 'Ball-is-ta, Ball-is-ta.'

But the ordeal of the town of Arete was not yet over for the day. The sight of their tower and their men burning goaded the Sassanids. Trumpets called and drums thundered. Noblemen roared commands.

'Per-oz, Per-oz, Victory, Victory.' A proud chant came from the desert. 'Per-oz, Per-oz.'

Like a great wave driven against the shore by the frenzy of the sea, the easterners came out from behind their line of mantlets and set on towards the wall. The storming party was several thousand strong, each man clad in armour. The Sassanid knights, the *clibanarii*, had dismounted. The noblemen were even carrying their own siege ladders.

The human wave had fifty paces to cross, fifty, long, long paces. From the first step men fell, smashed backwards by the bolt from a *ballista*, curling round the shaft of an arrow, clutching a foot lacerated by a caltrop, screaming piteously as the stake concealed in its pit penetrated soft tissue, scraped down bone. Men fell in droves – as they crossed the open space, as they descended into the ditch, as they climbed out again. The Sassanids left lines of their dead and dying, but they reached the earth bank against the wall of Arete, they swung the siege ladders up against the battlements, and the first of them began to climb.

Now the simple but vicious devices honed by generation after generation of wicked, heartless human ingenuity were unleashed against the Sassanids. As the ladders banged against the wall defenders sprang forward with rustic pitchforks. Catching the uprights between the tines, the soldiers pushed the ladders sideways. Despite the arrows whistling past their ears, more defenders joined in; pushing, pushing ever harder. As one man fell another took his place. Those siege ladders not well secured at the base slid sideways, gathering momentum, shedding men, some crashing into neighbouring ladders. Sassanid warriors went spinning head over heels down to the unforgiving ground.

Great rocks, barely to be lifted by three or four men, were manhandled on to the parapet. They teetered for a second then tipped. Brushing men off the ladders, smashing the rungs, pushing the uprights irreparably apart, the stones plummeted to earth.

High out over the battlements soared the arms of Ballista's three new giant cranes. Levers were pulled and the great chains released their immense boulders. Where they struck, in the blink of an eye ladders became kindling, men were reduced to a pulp.

All along the wall walk were flurries of activity. Teams of four legionaries thrust well-wrapped metal poles through the handles of the big metal cauldrons hung over the fires. With haste, but carefully, they lifted the glowing bowls clear of the intense heat. Delicately they manœuvred their spitting, crackling burdens to the edge. Grunting with effort, they hoisted the poles on to their shoulders then, most dangerous of all, they carefully, so very carefully, tipped the contents over the parapet.

Men screamed. The white-hot sand flowed down the face of the wall, down the earth bank. The sand set fire to hair and clothes. The tiny grains penetrated the gaps in armour, the eye sockets in helmets, burning and blinding. Men ran, screaming, ripping off their armour, which had turned traitor, trapping the agonizing, scalding sand. Men rolled on the ground, beat at themselves, all unconscious of the arrows of the defenders, which continued to rain down.

The carnage below the walls was immense. Yet not all the Sassanid ladders were pushed aside or shattered. Still, gaily clad warriors, silk surcoats and streamers floating around steel armour, climbed unbroken ladders. There was no chanting now. They were saving their breath for climbing, for what was waiting for them at the top.

It is hard to climb a ladder and fight at the same time. For most of those Sassanids who reached the top all that awaited them was a series of blows from a Roman *spatha* which sent them crashing back down again. But in a few places warriors made it over the parapet and on to the battlements. Most of these footholds were overrun almost immediately, swamped while the numbers still overwhelmingly favoured the defenders.

'Look, *Kyrios*, over there.' Demetrius pointed to the wall walk just south of the gatehouse. A knot of four Sassanid *clibanarii* had made it over the crenellations. They stood, shoulder to shoulder, their backs to the ladder. Five or six bodies, Persian and Roman, lay at their feet. A ring of defenders had drawn slightly back from them. As the Greek youth watched, another eastern warrior scrambled over the parapet, then another.

'With me. Maximus, Antigonus, *equites singulares*, with me.' Without waiting to see if his order was being obeyed, Ballista drew his *spatha* and hurled himself through the trapdoor and down the stairs.

As the press of men on the roof thinned out Demetrius dithered.

He drew his sword. Should he follow his *kyrios*? He felt foolish holding the *gladius* that Maximus had given him. If he went down there he would just get himself killed, would get in the way and get the others killed.

Demetrius saw his *kyrios* emerge from the tower on to the wall walk below. The northerner set off at a run. With his left hand he unbuckled and tossed aside his black cloak. It fluttered and rolled down the inner earth ramp. Maximus and Antigonus were with him, six *equites singulares* right behind. The *Dux Ripae* was yelling some war cry in his native tongue.

There were eight Sassanids in the group by the time Ballista reached them. The nearest one swung overhand at the northerner's head. Ballista brought his sword across his body, rolling his wrist, forcing the blade of his opponent outward then, seemingly in the one motion, launched a backhanded cut which landed heavily in the Persian's face. As the first Sassanid fell sideways Ballista aimed a series of heavy blows at the next man, who covered up and cowered behind his shield.

Demetrius watched, heart in mouth; so much going on at once. Maximus killed a Persian. Then Antigonus another. One of the *equites singulares* went down. More Sassanids were falling than Romans. More Sassanids were falling than were getting off the ladder and on to the battlements. A group of Iarhai's mercenaries was attacking from the far side. Ballista unleashed a barrage of savage cuts which drove an easterner to his knees, battered his shield aside, thrust the *spatha* sickeningly into his face. As the *kyrios* put his boot on the man's chest to pull his sword out he half slipped. The walkway was slick with blood. A Sassanid seized the opportunity to lunge forward, catching Ballista's helmet a glancing blow. With his left hand the northerner swept off the damaged helmet. With his right he parried the next blow. One of Iarhai's mercenaries drove a sword into the Persian's back.

It was done. As if at a signal the three Sassanids still standing turned and scrambled for the elusive safety of the ladder. All three were cut down from behind.

Ballista rubbed the sweat from his eyes. He looked up and down the wall. There were no easterners still on the wall walk. Still taking care, crouching behind the battered crenellations, he looked over the wall. It was done. Panic was spreading through the Sassanid ranks. Where before individuals, the wounded, real or pretend, had been making their way back to the camp, now there were small groups. As Ballista watched, whole bodies of warriors turned and fled. The trickle had become a flood. Shapur's assault had failed.

'Ball-is-ta, Ball-is-ta.' The chants rang across the plain, taunting the retreating Sassanids. 'Ball-is-ta, Ball-is-ta.' Some of the legionaries howled like wolves, the story of the *Dux*'s father Isangrim turning from something to mock into a source of strange pride.

Ballista waved to his men, shook hands with or hugged those around him. As he was released from Maximus's bear hug, the northerner recognized the leader of the group of Iarhai's mercenaries.

'What the fuck are you doing here?' His voice was harsh. His concern for her was making him angry.

'My father was . . . indisposed. So I brought the men you asked for.' Bathshiba met his gaze. One of her sleeves was torn, a smear of blood showing.

'Allfather, but this is no place for a girl.'

'You did not object to my help just now.' She stared up at him defiantly.

'That was you?'

'Yes, that was me.'

Ballista mastered his anger. 'Then I must thank you.'

XIV

The stricken plain beyond the western wall of Arete was a ghastly sight.

From the roof of the gatehouse there was a panoramic view of the horror. Like flotsam thrown up on the shore after the storm has spent its fury, the Sassanid dead lay in distinct waves across the plain. The furthest wave was some 400 to 200 paces from the wall. Here the dead lay as individuals; crushed by a stone, skewered by a bolt, grotesquely half sunken in the ground in the trap which had killed them. The next wave ran almost to the wall. Here the dead at least had company, lots of company. They lay in lines, groups, even low hillocks. Here they had found another way of dying. The often brightly dyed feathers of arrows fluttered in the fresh southerly breeze. Bright, gay, like bunting at a festival, they added an inappropriate, macabre touch to the scene of devastation. Finally, there was the horror below the wall. Piled on top of each other, three, four, five high, they concealed the earth. Smashed, twisted and broken, the corpses here were almost all burnt.

For eighteen years, more than half his life, Ballista had had a particular horror of being burnt alive. Since the siege of Aquileia, everywhere he had served he had seen men die in flames. The High Atlas Mountains, the green meadows of Hibernia, the plains of Novae by the Danube, all had brought forth their crop of the burnt ones and here they were again at the foot of the wall of Arete;

hundreds, possibly thousands of Sassanids burnt by naptha and white-hot sand, their thick black hair and tightly curled beards reduced to charred wisps, their skin, turned orange, peeling away like singed papyrus, obscene pink flesh showing raw underneath.

Although there was the continuous low buzz of innumerable flies, the bodies looked strangely uncorrupted. It had been thirteen days since the assault. On comparable bloody fields in the west, Ballista knew that after four days the corpses would have begun to rot, fall apart, become unrecognizable. Here, the corpses of the Sassanids seemed to be drying up like dead tree trunks, without putrefaction. Turpio, boasting his local knowledge, put it all down to diet and climate; the easterners ate more frugally and were anyway desiccated by the dry heat of their native lands.

The Sassanids had not gathered their dead. Possibly they thought it would be interpreted as a sign of weakness if they asked for a truce to collect them. Maybe it was just unimportant, given that they would then expose the corpses to the birds of the air and the beasts of the fields. Ballista noted that religious scruples had not held them back from looting the dead. No one could leave the city of Arete; all the locals were refugees, in the town or elsewhere or – the gods have mercy on them – prisoners of the Persians – yet every morning more of the corpses were naked; armour, clothes and boots gone. The scavengers could only come from the Sassanid camp.

Thousand upon thousand of dead Persians; it was impossible to estimate their numbers. Demetrius told how the Persian king calculated casualties. According to Herodotus, before a campaign 10,000 men would stand packed as closely as possible together. A line would be drawn around them. They would be dismissed. A fence, about navel-high, would be constructed on the line. Ten thousand men at a time, the army would be marched into the paddock until all had been counted. At the end of the campaign the procedure would be repeated, and the King of Kings could find out how many men he had lost.

Bagoas laughed a bitter laugh. He claimed to know nothing of this Herodotus, but clearly the man was a liar or a fool. What good would it do to know casualties to the nearest 10,000? In reality, before Shapur, the beloved of Mazda, went forth to chastise the unrighteous, he had each warrior march past and drop an arrow. When the Mazda-worshipping King of Kings returned freighted down with fame and plunder from the lands of the non-Aryans he had each warrior pick up an arrow. Those arrows remaining gave the number of the blessed who had gone to heaven.

Demetrius shot the Persian boy a vicious look.

Ballista did not press the matter. He knew that the actual number of Persian dead was unimportant. Another hundred dead, another thousand dead – in itself, it made no odds. Given their overwhelming numerical superiority, it was not the Sassanid bodycount that mattered but their willingness to fight, and Shapur's willingness to commit them to fight. Ballista knew that to save the town of Arete he had to break one or the other. He suspected that the Persians would crack before their King of Kings.

Roman casualties were by comparison negligible. Yet they were higher than Ballista had anticipated, higher than was sustainable. The Sassanid arrow storm had been like nothing the northerner had experienced before. For a time he had thought it would empty the battlements of defenders unaided. If the easterners could be brought to repeat it for three or four days in a row, the defenders would simply run out of men. But Ballista knew that no troops in the world could stand before the walls of Arete day after day and take the casualties the Sassanids had endured.

On the Roman side, the bowmen had suffered most. The six centuries of Cohors XX Palmyrenorum had suffered over 50 per cent casualties. Each century was now down to just fifty effectives. The legionaries of Legio IIII Scythica had escaped more lightly. On average, each of the eight centuries along the western wall had lost ten men, bringing their numbers down now to about sixty each. Ten of Mamurra's artillerymen were absent from the standards. Extraordinarily, as they had been in the eye of the storm, just two of Ballista's bodyguard, the *equites singulares*, had fallen.

Of the combined Roman casualties of well over 400, about half were dead. They had been buried in the open area to the east of the artillery magazine, which had been designated an emergency cemetery. Ballista was very aware of the dangers of plague and disaffection if the bodies of the defenders were not treated with all due respect. Issues of health and religious sensitivities made the extra effort of burial more than worth while. The rest of the casualties were too badly injured to fight. The majority would eventually die; many of them in agony from blood poisoning. Before that happened, the military medical teams would be very busy. Every trained soldier who could return to the ranks would be very necessary.

When the Sassanid assault failed they had totally quit the field. They had dragged away out of range their mantlets and *ballistae*, and the luckiest of their wounded. The following day they had stayed in camp, given over to their mourning; high, wild music and wailing, barbaric to western ears. Then, their grief somewhat assuaged, they had turned their hands again to the siege.

The surviving siege tower, the southernmost City Taker, the one which had fallen through the roof of an underground tomb, was hauled back to the Sassanid camp, where it was promptly broken up. The majority of its timbers were reused to construct a very large wheeled shed; what the legionaries called a 'tortoise'. Bagoas was happy to tell everyone what the shed would shelter – no less than the illustrious Khosro-Shapur, the illustrious Fame of Shapur, the mighty ram that had battered down the double walls of the city of Hatra. For fifteen years since that glorious day, Khosro-Shapur had rested, dedicated to god. Now Mazda had put it in the mind of the King of Kings to bring the great ram forth to give anew evidence of its prowess. It would have been transported in pieces, and was now being reassembled to be hung from mighty chains under that shed. Nothing, Bagoas earnestly assured his listeners, nothing, neither gate nor wall, could stand against it.

Thirteen days since the assault, and now it was all going to happen again. Ballista looked out at the squat shape of the tortoise under which sheltered the Khosro-Shapur. He wondered if he had done enough to deny it, to keep it out. Certainly he had done what he could to replace the casualties. Two troopers had been transferred into the *equites singulares* from the *turma* of Cohors XX led by Antiochus on the north wall. Likewise, ten legionaries of Legio IIII had joined Mamurra's artillerymen from the century of Lucius Fabius at the Porta Aquaria on the east wall. Ballista had noticed that one of the replacements who appeared on the battlements of the Palmyrene Gate was Castricius, the legionary who had found the body of Scribonius Mucianus. Four hundred men from the *numerus* of Iarhai had been ordered to take their places on the desert wall. Ballista had made further specifications: 300 of them were to be trained mercenaries and only 100 recently recruited levies; the caravan protector was to lead his men in person; Bathshiba was not to be seen on the battlements. (Ballista put away, as something to consider later, whenever there was time, the strange, new reluctance to fight on the part of Iarhai.) The new arrangements meant that the western wall was nearly as well manned as before the assault. It did, however, mean that the other walls were each defended by only 200 mercenaries backed by a small number of Roman regulars and, in the cases of the east and south, a crowd of levies. Ballista knew that, as the siege went on and casualties mounted, he would be forced to rely more and more on the local levies. It was not a reassuring thought.

Across the plain the Drafsh-i-Kavyan, the battle standard of the house of Sasan, flashed red, yellow, violet in the early morning sun as it moved towards the great battering ram. It was followed by the now so familiar figure on the white horse. As Shapur arrived the *magi* started the sacrifice. Ballista was relieved to see that, despite their reputation for necromancy, it involved no people. There were no Roman prisoners in sight.

Two of the defenders' *ballistae* had been knocked out during the assault. One had been repaired, the other replaced from the arsenal. Mamurra had done well. Three of the enemy artillery pieces had been hit; two on the approach, one during the retreat. It could be seen that they had also been replaced. But no more had been constructed. Ballista's rigorous scorched-earth policy was bearing some fruit. There was no timber for miles. If they wanted to build more siege machines the Sassanids would have to fetch the materials from a great distance. Ballista felt reasonably sanguine about artillery; he still had twenty-five pieces on the western wall to the Persians' total of twenty.

Preceded by the Drafsh-i-Kavyan snapping in the wind, Shapur rode across to a raised tribunal, where he took his seat on a throne glinting with precious metals and jewels. Behind the throne loomed the terrifying, wrinkled bulk of his ten elephants. In front were the Immortals commanded by Peroz of the Long Sword and the Jan-avasper, 'those who sacrifice themselves', led by Mariades.

Ballista found it unsurprising that Shapur had not so far tried to use his tame pretender to the Roman throne to undermine the loyalty of the defenders of Arete. Who would follow an ex-town-councillor turned brigand then traitor like Mariades? It was as unlikely as anyone trying to elevate to the purple a barbarian warrior such as Ballista himself.

The battering ram was being cleared for action, camp followers, priests and their paraphernalia herded away. A chant began: 'Khos-ro-Sha-pur, Khos-ro-Sha-pur.' Here was the heart of the matter – the great ram, the Fame of Shapur and its protecting tortoise. From where it had been reassembled, Ballista assumed that it would advance straight down the road to the Palmyrene Gate. He had based his dispositions on this assumption. He hoped that he was right. Everything he could use to frustrate the ram was at the gate. The cowhides and chaff he had requisitioned were piled near by. Would the councillors remember sniggering when their barbarian *Dux* had announced their requisition? Ballista's three mobile cranes were stationed behind the gate. They were fitted with iron claws, a plentiful supply of enormous rocks to hand. And then there was his new wall. For four days the legionaries had laboured to finish the wall behind the outer gate. It was a pity that the painting of the *Tyche* of Arete had been obscured by it. The superstitious might read something into it – but Ballista was not superstitious.

Would the King of Kings send the Khosro-Shapur straight down the road into the teeth of the carefully prepared defences? Or would he have been warned by the traitor? Since the failed attack on the granaries, there was one fewer traitor in the town of Arete. But

Ballista was sure that there was at least one remaining. It had taken at least two men to burn the magazine, at least two men to murder Scribonius Mucianus and dispose of his body. Admittedly no traitor had told the Sassanids about the naptha-filled jar buried just before the gate that had trapped the central City Taker. But the northerner felt certain this was proof of a problem of communication rather than evidence that there was no traitor.

Shapur waved his arms, purple and white streamers flying. Trumpets blared and drums thundered. The great tortoise housing the Khosro-Shapur moved forward, as did the mantlets, the *ballistae* and innumerable hordes of bowmen.

'Do you think he practises that?' Maximus asked.

'What?' Ballista replied.

'Whirling those streamers about. Imagine what a prick he must look practising on his own. Pointless anyway. Not exactly a practical skill.'

'Why do you spend what little time you have when not rattling the bed practising those fancy moves with your *gladius*?'

Maximus laughed. 'It intimidates my enemies. I have seen grown men cry with terror.'

Ballista looked at his bodyguard without speaking.

'Oh, well, I see what you mean, but sure it is an entirely different thing,' Maximus blustered.

'One cannot help but think that on the whole it is a good thing that I own you, rather than the other way round.'

The great battering ram was coming straight down the road, the mantlets shielding the *ballistae* and bowmen flung out on either side.

Allfather, here we go again. Almost unconsciously Ballista ran through his pre-battle ritual: slide dagger out, snap it back, slide sword out, snap it back, touch the healing stone on the scabbard.

As the Sassanids came into range past the white-painted humps of rock Ballista nodded to Antigonus, who made the signal, and the artillery began to shoot. This time the northerner had instructed the *ballistarii* to aim exclusively at the enemy artillery. The Persians pushing the great battering ram would marvel at their luck, an unlooked-for piece of luck which Ballista thought might give Shapur and those around him pause for thought.

Practice was improving the skills of the artillerymen of Arete. By the time the Sassanid line reached the section of white-painted wall, three of their *ballistae* had been squashed by high-velocity missiles. As the ram, mantlets and bowmen carried on to cross the last 200 paces to the city wall, the Sassanid artillery unlimbered and began to shoot back. Honours were even: two of the defenders' and two of the attackers' *ballistae* were rendered inoperable. The *Dux Ripae* was happy enough. This was the only area of the siege where he would win a battle of attrition. Then another thought came to his mind: Disgraceful. Men are dying – my men as well as the enemy – and I am just calculating the numbers of machines destroyed and damaged, the effects on the rate of shooting. Disgraceful. Thank the gods that war can never be reduced to this impersonal machine-against-machine battle alone. If it could, what an inhuman business it would become.

The Sassanid officers had an admirable control over their troops. The archers held their fire until the mantlets were fixed in position just fifty paces from the walls. Not an arrow was loosed until the command. When it came, the sky darkened again. As, with a terrible whistling, the arrow storm hit, Ballista once more marvelled at the almost unbelievable enormity of the thing. The defenders hunkered down behind the battlements and below their shields to weather the storm. Shouts and cries showed that not all had done so unscathed. In the pause before the next wave the bowmen of Arete leapt to their feet and sent back an answering volley.

Crouched behind the parapet, shields held all around him, Ballista knew he had to ignore the arrow storm. It was an irrelevance. Stoic philosophers held that everything that did not touch a man's moral purpose was an irrelevance. For them, death was an irrelevance: fucking fools. Ballista's only purpose was to destroy the great ram, the Khosro-Shapur.

Judging by the tortoise, the ram was about sixty feet long. The head which emerged was capped with a metal sheath, fittingly enough in the shape of a ram's head. It was bound to the shaft with nailed-down strips of metal. The wooden shaft itself looked to be about two feet thick. Like the tortoise it was covered in dampened rawhides.

With suicidal courage, eastern warriors ran ahead to tear away the remains of the burnt siege tower and tip rubble to fill in the pit in which it had been trapped. The labourers were just twenty yards from the gate. It was hard for the Roman archers to miss. There was something deeply unnerving about the fanaticism with which the Sassanids leapt forward to replace men who had fallen – leapt forward to certain death. Were they drunk? Were they drugged?

The tortoise edged forward. The rubble in the pit shifted but took its weight. The ram neared the gate.

'Everyone, ready. Here they come. Now!' On Ballista's word legionaries stood up in the face of the arrow storm. Two near the northerner were punched backwards. Without a pause the survivors, grunting with effort, manhandled the huge, dripping-wet bags stitched together from uncured hides and stuffed with chaff over the battlement. The bags fell like massive soggy mattresses. The restraining ropes tied to the parapet snapped taut. The bags slapped wetly against the gate, held in place. Peering over, Ballista saw that he had calculated the length of the ropes exactly. The wood of the Palmyrene Gate was cushioned from the force of the ram. The sodden bags would not burn. Ballista had bought some time. Above the heads of the defenders, the arms of the three cranes swung out.

After only the briefest pause Sassanid warriors poured from the rear of the tortoise. They carried scythes tied to long poles. Through his disappointment Ballista felt a grudging admiration for Shapur and his men. They had been ready for this device. No wonder Antioch, Seleuceia and so many other towns had fallen to them in the time of troubles. These easterners were better at sieges than any barbarians Ballista had ever encountered.

Out in the open at the foot of the gate the Persians dropped like flies. As men fell others sprang out to snatch up the fallen scythes. Bloody fanatics, thought Ballista. One by one the ropes were cut. The bags began to sway and sag. He cursed himself for not thinking to use chains. Too late to worry about that now.

One by one the sodden stuffed hides fell ponderously to the ground. The wooden outer gate of Arete stood unprotected. The great ram surged forward, the horns of its head closing on the gate.

The northerner rose to his feet. He was met by a hail of missiles. With his right arm above his head, he began to guide the grapple of one of the cranes to its target; right a bit, a little more, stop, back a little, down, down, close the claws. Missiles whirled past him. An arrow embedded itself in his shield, making him stagger. Another hit the parapet and ricocheted past his face. The grapple caught the ram just behind its metal head. Ballista signalled for the crane to lift. The chains clanged rigid. The arm of the crane groaned. The grapple slipped a fraction, then held its grip. The head of the ram began to lift slowly, to point impotently towards the sky.

For a moment it looked as if it would work. Then suddenly the claws lost their grip. The grapple slid off. The head of the ram fell free. Again it pointed at the gate. Again the tortoise moved forward until it almost touched the gatehouse. There was no longer any room for a grapple between the two: the opportunity had passed; the device had failed. Ballista dropped back down behind the battlements.

The metal head of the ram drew back under the tortoise, then shot out. The whole gatehouse trembled. The crash echoed down the walls. The gate still stood. The ram drew back, then struck again. Another deafening crash. Again the gatehouse reverberated. The gate still held, but a strange tortured creaking indicated that it could not last long.

With his back to the parapet, Ballista watched Antigonus and another soldier guiding the other two cranes to their target. The massive boulders swung ominously at the end of the chains as they were traversed over the tortoise. A glance at each other and the two men signalled for the boulders to be dropped. As one, the grapples released their load. After a heartbeat there was an appalling crash.

Ducking out from behind cover, Ballista saw at a glance that the tortoise still stood. The boulders had bounced off. The arms of the two cranes were already swinging back over the wall to collect their next load. A Sassanid artillery stone took Antigonus's head off. Without even a fractional pause another soldier stood up to take his place.

The great ram struck again. The tremor came up through Ballista's boots. There was a terrible sound of rending wood. Khosro-Shapur had triumphed again: the outer Palmyrene Gate was reduced to firewood. A cheer started up from the Sassanids working the Fame of Shapur. It faltered and died. They had expected, they had been told, they would be looking down a corridor to another less strong wooden gate. They were not. They were looking at a closely cemented stone wall.

The arms of all three cranes, boulders swinging, arched back out over the gatehouse. Again Ballista stepped into the maelstrom to guide one – right, right, a bit further – Maximus and two of the *equites singulares* trying to cover him with their shields. An arrow caught one of the guardsmen in the throat. He fell back and his blood splashed over the group. It stung Ballista's eyes. The three grapples released their burden. A thunderous, splintering impact, and two of the boulders smashed through the roof of the tortoise, exposing its soft innards and the men below. Ballista dropped back into cover. There was no point in playing the hero unnecessarily. Maximus and the remaining guardsman landed half on top of him.

There was no need for further orders. Ballista could smell the pitch and the tar. Everything combustible that could be shot or thrown from the walls was being aimed at the yawning hole in the roof of the tortoise. Wishing they had some naptha left to make sure, Ballista closed his eyes, tried to steady his breathing and hands.

'Yes, yes, yes!' Opening his eyes, Ballista saw Maximus peering round the stone crenellations. The Hibernian was punching the air. 'It's burning – burning like a Christian in Nero's garden.'

Ballista looked up at his *draco* flying above the gatehouse. With the south wind hissing into its metal jaws, its white windsock body was writhing and snapping like a serpent. The incoming missiles had slackened. Maximus had been joined by Mamurra and they were looking over the battlements. Demetrius and Bagoas were huddled on the floor. The Greek boy was very pale. Ballista patted him, as if he were soothing a dog.

'They have had enough. They are running'. Maximus and Mamurra rose to their feet. Ballista stayed where he was.

Inexplicably, a group of girls appeared on the roof of the gatehouse. They were wearing very short tunics and a lot of cheap jewellery. There were no more incoming missiles. Ballista watched the girls walk to the battlements. They stood in a line giggling. All together they lifted their tunics around their waists. Baffled, Ballista stared at a row of fifteen naked girls' bottoms.

'What the fuck?'

Mamurra's slab-sided face cracked into a great grin. 'It is the third of May.' Seeing complete incomprehension on Ballista's face, the *praefectus fabrum* went on, 'the last day of the festival of the Ludi Florales, when traditionally the prostitutes of the town perform a striptease.' He jerked his thumb in the direction the girls were facing. 'These girls are honouring the gods and at the same time showing the Sassanids what they won't be enjoying.'

All the men on the gatehouse were laughing. Only Bagoas did not join in.

'Come on,' said Maximus, 'don't be prudish. Even a Persian like you must fancy a girl now and then, if only when he runs out of boys.'

Bagoas ignored him and turned to Ballista. 'Showing the bits that it is not proper to see is an omen. Any *mobad* could tell you. It portends the fall of this town of the unrighteous. As these women disclose their secret and hidden places to the Sassanids, so shall the city of Arete.'

For a day and a night a column of black oily smoke streamed away to the north as the Khosro-Shapur, the Fame of Shapur, burnt. The flames from the great ram and its tortoise lit the dark.

For seven days the Sassanids gave themselves over to their grief. Day and night the men feasted, drank, sang dirges and danced their sad dances, lines of men slowly turning, arms around each other. The women wailed, rent their clothes and beat their breasts. The sounds carried clear across the plain.

Then, for two months, the Persians did nothing – at least nothing very active in the prosecution of the siege. They did dig a ditch and heap a low bank around their camp; there was no wood to build a palisade. They stationed mounted pickets beyond the north and south ravines and on the far side of the river. Parties of cavalry rode out presumably to reconnoitre or forage. On occasional moonless nights, small groups would creep on foot close to the city and of a sudden release a volley of arrows, hoping to catch an unwary guard or two on the city wall or some pedestrians in the streets beyond. Yet, for two months, the Sassanids ventured no more assaults, undertook no new siege works. Throughout the rest of May, all of June and into July, it was as if the easterners were waiting for something.

What am I doing here? The thoughts of Legionary Castricius were not content. It is the twenty-fourth of May, the anniversary of the birthday of the long-dead imperial prince Germanicus – to the memory of Germanicus Caesar a supplication. It is my birthday. It is the middle of the night, and I am hiding in some damp undergrowth.

A cool breeze blowing across the Euphrates from the north-east rustled the reeds. There was no other sound but the great river rolling past, gurgling, sucking at the banks. There was a strong smell of damp earth and rotting vegetation. Up above, tattered clouds no more covered the moon than a beggar's cloak. Just in front of Castricius's face a spider's web was silvered in the moonlight.

It is my birthday, and I am cold, tired, scared. And it is all my own fault. Castricius shifted slightly, lifting one wet buttock from the ground, and was shushed by the man behind him. Fuck you, brother, he thought, settling down again. Why? Why am I always such a fool? A keen little *optio* like Prosper asks for volunteers – could be a bit dangerous, boys – and my hand goes up like a whore's tunic. Why do I never learn? Why do I always have to prove that I am the big man, up for anything, scared of nothing? Castricius thought back across the years and the many miles to his schoolteacher in Nemausus. You will end on a cross, the *paedagogus* had often said. So far he was wrong. But Castricius had been sent to the mines. He suppressed a shudder thinking about it. If I can survive the mines, I can survive anything. Moonlight or no moonlight, tonight will be a walk in a Persian *paradise* compared with the mines.

The soldier in front turned and, with a gesture, indicated that it was time to go. Castricius got stiffly to his feet. Crouching, they moved south through the reed beds. They tried to move quietly, but there were thirty of them: mud squelched under their boots, metal belt fittings chinked, a duck, disturbed by their passage, took off in an explosion of beating wings. And the wind is at our backs, carrying the noise down to the Persians, thought Castricius. Moonlight, noise and an inexperienced officer – this has all the makings of a disaster.

Eventually they reached the rockface. The young *optio* Gaius Licinius Prosper gestured for them to start climbing. If I die to satisfy your ambitions, I will come back and haunt you, thought Castricius as he slung his shield on his back and began to ascend. Since the young *optio* had foiled the plot to burn the granaries he had made little secret of his ambition. Down by the river the far cliff face of the southern ravine was quite steep. It was this that had attracted the attention of Prosper: 'The Sassanids will never expect a night raid from that quarter.' Well, we will soon find out if you are right, young man.

Castricius was one of the first to the top. Heights held no fears for him and he was good at climbing. He peered over the lip of the ravine. About fifty paces away was the first of the Persian campfires. Around it he could see the huddled shapes of men wrapped in cloaks sleeping. There was no sign of any sentries. From some distance came the sounds of talking, laughter, snatches of song. Nearby, there was no sign of anyone awake.

When the majority had caught up, Prosper just said, 'Now'. There were an undignified few moments as everyone scrambled over the edge of the ravine, rose to their feet, slid their shields off their backs, drew their swords. Miraculously, the Sassanids slept on.

With no further word of command, the ragged line of volunteers set off across the fifty moon-washed paces to the campfire. Maybe, just maybe, this is going to work, thought Castricius. Along with the others, he accelerated into a run. He chose his man: a red cloak, hat pulled down over face, still not stirring. He swung his *spatha*.

As the blade bit, Castricius knew that it was all about to go horribly wrong: they were in a trap, and he was very likely to die. The blade sliced through the man-shaped bundle of straw. Automatically, Castricius sank into a very low crouch, shield well up – and not a moment too soon, as the first volley of arrows tore through the Roman ranks. Arrowheads thumped into wooden shields, clanged off chainmail coats and metal helmets, punched into flesh. Men screamed.

A blow to his left temple sent Castricius sprawling. It took him a moment or two as he retrieved his sword and got back to his feet to realize that it was an arrow, that they were caught in a crossfire.

'*Testudo*, form *testudo*,' shouted Prosper. Bent very low, Castricius shuffled towards the *optio*. An arrow whipped past his nose. Near him a man was sobbing and calling in Latin for his mother.

A trumpet sounded, clear and confident in the confusion of the night. The arrows stopped. The Romans looked around. There were about twenty of them left, in a loose knot rather than a parade-ground *testudo*.

The trumpet sounded again. It was followed by a rising chant: 'Per-oz, Per-oz, Victory, Victory.' Out of the darkness swept a wave of Sassanid warriors. The firelight glittered on the easterners' armour, on the long, long blades of their swords, and in the murderous look in their eyes.

'Fuck me, there are hundreds of them,' said a voice.

Like a wave crashing on a shore, the Persians were on them. Castricius parried the first blow with his shield. He swung his *spatha* low, palm up in from his right. It swung under his opponent's guard, biting into the man's ankle. The impact jarred back up Castricius's arm. The Sassanid fell. Another took his place.

The new enemy swung overhead. As Castricius took the blow on his shield, he felt and heard it splinter. From his left a Roman sword darted forward and tried to take the Persian in the armpit.

Sparks flew and the point of the blade glanced off the easterner's mail. Before Prosper could pull back from the blow, another Sassanid blade flashed in and severed his right hand. Castricius watched horrified as the young *optio* spun round and sank to his knees, his left hand holding the stump of his right arm, his mouth open in a soundless scream. There was blood everywhere. The two Sassanids moved to finish the officer. Castricius turned and ran.

Boots stamping on the rock, Castricius flew back towards the edge of the cliff. He threw away his shield, dropped his sword. As he neared the lip of the ravine he threw himself sideways and down, sliding the last few yards, swinging his legs out first into space, twisting his body, his fingers scrabbling for purchase. For a moment he thought he had misjudged it, that he would slip backwards clear over the edge. The cliff had a hundred-foot drop here. If he fell he was dead. Sharp strong pain as his fingernails tore, but he had a grip. Sliding, scrabbling, boots missing toeholds, legs often dangling, he shinned down the face of the ravine.

High on the south-west tower of Arete, although he was at least 400 paces away, Ballista saw the trap close quicker than some of those caught in its jaws; the twang of bowstrings, the screams of men, the two clear trumpet blasts.

'Bugger,' he said succinctly.

'We must help them,' Demetrius blurted.

Ballista did not reply.

'We must do something,' the Greek boy continued.

'Sure it would be good,' said Maximus, 'but there is nothing to be done. It will all be over by the time we get any troops there. And, anyway, we cannot afford to lose any more men.'

Ballista watched for a while in silence, then said that they should go to the southern wicket gate, in case there were any survivors. Climbing down the steps from the Porta Aquaria, the northerner turned things over in his mind.

Ballista had been driven by the words dinned into him by his mentors in fieldcraft: a passive defence is no defence at all. An inactive defence not only hands all the initiative, all the momentum to the besiegers, it undermines the defenders' discipline, their very will to resist. So, since the burning of the ram, Ballista had quite frequently sent out small nocturnal raiding parties. But his heart had somehow not been in it.

The death of Antigonus had changed things. In Antigonus he had lost a master of clandestine operations. How the northerner missed him. Ballista thought back to the masterly way in which Antigonus had wiped out the Sassanids left stranded on the island in the Euphrates after the first failed assault on the city: twenty dead Persians, and not one Roman had fallen. Among the high reeds that night, death had come to the terrified easterners with bewildering speed and efficiency. The raiders Ballista had sent out since had tried their best, but the results had been mixed. Sometimes they were spotted and the mission abandoned near the start. As often as not they took as many casualties as they inflicted. And now, tonight, there was this unqualified disaster. Whatever the textbooks said, whatever the doctrines of his mentors, Ballista would send out no more raids.

Ballista stood by the open wicket gate and thought of Antigonus. It was strange how in a very brief time he had come to rely on him. It was one of the strange things about warfare – it quickly formed strong bonds between unlikely men, then with death it could even more suddenly break them. Ballista remembered the artillery ball taking off Antigonus's head; the decapitated corpse standing for a few moments, the fountain of blood.

Lungs burning, limbs aching, sweat running into his eyes, Castricius plunged on through the reed bed. He had hurled away his helmet, ripped off his mail coat when he reached the foot of the cliff. In flight lay his only hope of safety. On and on he ran, the date palms waving above his head, stumbling as roots twined round his legs. Once he fell full length in the mud, the breath knocked out of him. Fighting the exhaustion and despair that told him just to stay where he was, he struggled to his feet and plunged on.

With no warning, Castricius was clear of the reed beds. Ahead in the moonlight was the bare rock floor of the ravine; on the far side of it a group of torches along the low wall and around the wicket gate. There was no sound of pursuit. He set off at a run nevertheless. It would be a shame to get this far, so close to safety, and then be cut down.

They heard him coming before they saw him; the rasping breath, the dragging footfall. Into the circle of torchlight stumbled an unarmed man covered in mud. His hands were bleeding.

'Well, if it is not the tunnel rat Castricius,' said Maximus.

As spring turned to summer, deserters crawled through the ravines or slunk across the plain in both directions. It was a feature of siege warfare that never failed to amaze Ballista. No matter how futile the siege, some defenders would flee to the besieging army. No matter how doomed the fortress, some of the attackers would risk everything to join the encircled men. Demetrius said that he remembered reading in Josephus's *Jewish War* that there had even been deserters from the Roman army into Jerusalem just days before the great city was captured and burnt. Of course there was an obvious explanation. Armies consisted of a very large number of very violent men. Some of these would always commit crimes that carried the death penalty. To avoid death, or just postpone it for a short time, men would do the strangest things. Yet Ballista could not help but wonder why these men, especially among the besiegers, did not instead try to slip away and hide, try to find somewhere far away where they might be able to reinvent themselves.

There was a trickle of Sassanid deserters into Arete, never more than twenty, although it was suspected that others had been quietly despatched by the first guards they encountered. They were a great deal of trouble. Ballista and Maximus spent a lot of time interviewing them. Bagoas was emphatically not allowed to talk to them. It proved impossible to distinguish between the genuine asylum seekers and the planted spies and saboteurs. In the end, having had a few of them parade along the wall in an attempt to upset the besieging army, Ballista ordered all of them locked up in a barracks just off the *campus martius*. It was an unwanted extra problem. Ten legionaries from the century stationed there in reserve, that of Antoninus Posterior, had to be detailed to guard them. They had to be fed and watered.

Initially, larger numbers slipped out of Arete. This soon stopped. The Sassanids had a summary way with them. Along the plain, tapering wooden stakes were erected. The deserters were impaled on them, the spike through the anus. It was meant to be horrific. It succeeded. Some of the victims lived for hours. The Sassanids had placed the stakes just within artillery range, taunting the Romans to try to end the suffering of those who had been their companions. Ballista ordered that ammunition not be wasted. After the corpses had hung there for a few days the Sassanids took them down and decapitated them. The heads were shot by artillery back over the walls of the town, the bodies thrown out for the dogs.

If there was a motive beyond an enjoyment of cruelty for its own sake, Ballista assumed that the Sassanids wished to discourage anyone from leaving Arete to keep the demand for food in the town as high as possible. If the Persians hoped in this way to cause supply problems, they would be disappointed. Ballistas' stockpiling in the months before the siege had worked well. With careful management, there was enough food to last until at least the autumn.

The relative abundance of supplies was augmented by the arrival of a boat carrying grain. It was from Circesium, the nearest Roman-held town upriver. The passage of fifty or so miles had not been without incident. Sassanid horsemen were out in force on both banks. Luckily for the crew, the Euphrates, although winding, was wide enough to be beyond bowshot for most of its course here if one kept to the middle passage. The boat tied up opposite the Porta Aquaria on 9 June, ironically enough the festival of the *vestalia*, a public holiday for the bakers.

The crew was somewhat put out. Having run considerable risks, it had been hoping for a more voluble reception. Yet, in many ways, the arrival was something of a disappointment to the beleaguered garrison of Arete. Additional grain was welcome but not essential. When the boat was sighted the general expectation was that it was full of reinforcements. The crew of ten legionaries seconded from Legio IIII was a very poor substitute.

Never really having expected more men, Ballista had been hoping for letters. There was one. It was from the governor of Coele Syria, the nominal superior of the *Dux Ripae*. It was dated nearly a month earlier, written en route for Antioch – 'Well away from any nasty Persians' as Demetrius acidly commented.

The letter contained self-proclaimed wonderful news. The emperor Gallienus, having crushed the barbarians on the Danube, had appointed his eldest son, Publius Cornelius Licinius Valerianus, Caesar. The new Caesar would remain on the Danube while the most sacred Augustus Gallienius toured the Rhine. In Asia Minor the gods had manifested their love for the empire, a love engendered by the piety of the emperors, by raising the river Rhyndacus in flood and thus saving the city of Cyzicus from an incursion of Goth pirates.

There was nothing else in the governor's communication except platitudinous advice and encouragement: Remain alert, keep up the good work, *disciplina* always tells. Ballista had been hoping for a communication from the emperors, something in purple ink with the imperial seal that could be waved around to raise morale, something with some definite news of a gathering imperial field army, a relief column tramping towards them – possibly even something that contained a projected date for the lifting of the siege. Being informed that old-fashioned Roman *virtus* would always endure was less than enormously useful.

The wider picture grew worse after a private conversation over a few drinks with the legionaries from the boat put the 'wonderful news' into context. Far from crushing the barbarians on the Danube, Gallienus had had to buy peace from the Carpi, the tribe he had been fighting there, so that he was free to move to the Rhine, where the Franks and the Alamanni were causing havoc. The new Caesar was just a child, a mere figurehead left on the Danube, where real power was in the hands of the general Ingenuus. The flood waters of the Rhyndacus might have saved Cyzicus but nothing had stopped the Goths sacking Chalcedon, Nicomedia, Nicaea, Prusa and Apamea. The whole of Asia Minor was threatened. The general Felix, accompanied by the great siege engineer Celsus, had been sent to hold Byzantium. Valerian himself, with the main field army, had marched into Cappadocia to try to drive the Goths from Asia Minor.

Bad as the news of public affairs was, Ballista was more disappointed that there was no letter from Julia. He missed his wife very much. It had not been beyond the bounds of possibility that a letter written by her in Rome or from Sicily could have found its way to the eastern extremity of the *imperium*, to Circesium and on to the boat. With any letter Julia wrote she was bound to enclose a drawing by their son, a scribble of such abstraction that only the boy himself could tell what it depicted. It was ten months since Ballista had seen his son. Isangrim would be growing fast. Changing quickly, but hopefully not out of all recognition.

Battening down his disappointments, Ballista turned back to marshalling his meagre resources to defend the town. The ten new legionaries were assigned to the century of Lucius Fabius at the Porta Aquaria on the grounds that their experience as boatmen might be of more use there than elsewhere. Casualties had been surprisingly light on the day the great battering ram had been burnt and only a few had been lost to occasional Persian arrows or in unfortunate forays until the disaster in which the young *optio* Prosper died. The centuries of Legio IIII on the desert wall still mustered nearly fifty men each, the *turmae* of Cohors XX forty. Ballista had reinforced them with another hundred of the levy bowmen from the *numerus* of Iarhai. The northerner hoped that serving alongside the regulars would both instill resolve in the conscripted townsmen and encourage their expertise. He was very aware that it might go differently, that the lax discipline of the levies might infect the regulars. So far, things seemed to be going as Ballista wished, but he would have liked it if Iarhai would appear more often on the battlements. The grizzled caravan protector seemed ever less inclined to have anything to do with the military affairs of the siege.

As the season advanced to high summer the temperature grew ever hotter. From the walls of Arete mirages could often be seen shimmering out in the desert, making distances difficult to judge, masking the movement of the Persians. For a northerner, the heat was almost intolerable. As soon as clothes were put on, they were soaked in sweat. Sword belts and armour straps chafed, rubbing skin raw. But that was not the worst of it. There was dust everywhere. It got into eyes, ears, mouths, down into lungs. Everyone who was not a native of the town had a persistent hacking cough. The dust somehow penetrated into the very pores of your skin. And then there were the flies and gnats, continually buzzing and stinging, covering any morsel of food, swarming on the brim of every drink.

There were only two moments of the day when it was less than hellish to be outside. In the evening, the temperature dropped as a cooler breeze blew over the Euphrates and the sky turned briefly a lapis-lazuli blue. Just pre-dawn, the wild fowl flew and the bowl of the sky was a delicate pink before the sun was hauled free of the horizon to begin its task of punishing men.

At noon on 6 July, the first day of the festival of the Ludi Apollinares, Ballista was lying in the pool of the *frigidarium* avoiding the heat of the day. As the bathhouse was the private one attached to the palace of the *Dux Ripae*, the northerner was on his own. Castricius, his latest standard-bearer, walked in and saluted smartly.

'A large dustcloud has been spotted off to the south, our side of the river, heading this way.'

By the time Ballista had reached his accustomed post on the Palmyrene Gate the dustcloud was unmistakable. A tall, dense, isolated column, it could be caused by nothing but an enormous train of men and animals marching upriver. Most likely, the vanguard would reach the Sassanid camp by early afternoon the next day.

The Persian column made good time. By noon its forerunners could be seen approaching the camp. Line after line after line of camels stretched away as far as the eye could see. Swaying gently, all were heavily laden, some were hauling things along the ground. Ballista saw that there were next to no accompanying troops. The Sassanids were supremely confident.

'What is it? There seem to be very few armed men. That must be good.' Several soldiers smiled at Demetrius's words.

'Unfortunately not,' said Ballista. 'They already have all the warriors they need.'

'Probably more than they want,' said Mamurra. 'They outnumber us by so many they actually could do with fewer mouths to feed. And the danger of plague is always greater with a really large army.'

'Then those camels are carrying food?' Demetrius asked.

'I do not think that we are going to be that lucky.' Ballista wiped the sweat out of his eyes. 'I am very much afraid they carry timber.' The soldiers within earshot nodded gravely but, seeing that the young Greek seemed none the wiser, Ballista continued. 'One of the things that has kept us safe, kept the Persians so quiet for the last couple of months, is the lack of timber around here. What little there was we burnt before they arrived. You need wood for pretty much all siege works – to build artillery, siege towers, battering rams, ladders, mantlets, tortoises and all types of screens. You need wood for pit props if you are mining. Taking a town calls for lots of wood – unless, of course, you just offer the defenders big sacks of gold to go away.'

'If only, *Dominus*, if only,' said Castricius.

'Yes, indeed, *Draconarius*, it is a pity that the Sassanids are such bloodthirsty fuckers that they would rather impale us than bribe us.'

It took two full days before the last of the caravan arrived. The Persian camp now flowed over all the plain as far as the hills. Camels bellowed, men shouted, trumpets called. Although all seemed chaotic, some organizing principle must have been at work. Within a day, carpenters could be seen hard at work, the fires of mobile field forges were fired, and strings of unloaded camels were heading off to the north-west.

The camels returned a day later. Gangs of men could be seen unloading bricks. This time it was the *praefectus fabrum*, Mamurra, who explained the finer points of siege engineering to the young Greek.

'They are going to build a siege ramp to try to overtop the wall at some point. Now, a siege ramp, an *agger*, is mainly built up out of earth and rubble. But the soil round here is sand, spreads as easily as one of Maximus's women, so they need retaining walls. That is what the bricks are for. The reptiles have not been as idle as we thought. They have been making sun-dried bricks somewhere out of sight, probably up in one of the villages in the hills to the north-west. With all that wood they are making *vinae*, mobile shelters for the poor bastards who are going to have to build the *agger*, and artillery to try and fuck our *ballistae* and stop us killing them all.'

'Thucydides tells that it took the Spartans seventy days to build their siege ramp at Plataea,' said Demetrius hopefully.

'If we can delay them that long it would be good,' Mamurra replied.

'Is there nothing we can do to stop them?'

Ballista slapped a fly on his arm. 'No need for despair.' He looked closely at the squashed insect and flicked it away. 'I can think of something that might work.'

During the night of 20 July the Sassanids moved their artillery, thirty *ballistae*, into range opposite the southern end of the desert wall. Sunrise saw them emplaced behind stout screens some 200 paces out. The artillery duel began again. By lunchtime long chains of *vinae* were in place, making three long tunnels, at the front of which the beginnings of the ramp began to be evident. The long period of inactivity was over. The siege of Arete had entered a new and deadly phase.

'You look like a man offering a bun to an elephant. Come on, hand it over.' Although Ballista spoke with a smile, the doctor was plainly terrified. He was a civilian. His shabby tunic suggested that he was not at the peak of his profession. He held the arrow in both hands. Or rather, he had both arms held out, palms up, the arrow resting on them. His whole demeanour said, 'This is nothing to do with me.'

Seeing that the doctor was not going to move, Ballista slowly stepped forward. Making no sudden movements, as if the doctor were a nervous horse, he took the arrow. The northerner studied it closely. In most respects it was unremarkable, about two and a half foot long, with a three-bladed and barbed iron arrowhead about two inches long. On this, blood and human tissue were still evident.

As with most eastern arrows, the shaft consisted of two parts, a tapering wooden footing joined to a longer shaft of reed. For reinforcement, the join was bound with animal tendon. The shaft was decorated with bands of paint, one of black and two of red. What was left of the three feathers which made up the fletching appeared not to be coloured but a natural white. Possibly goose feathers, Ballista thought.

The arrow shaft bore various cuts and nicks, no doubt the legacy of whatever hooked and hideous instruments the doctor had employed during extraction. But what made this arrow so unusual and potentially so significant was the strip of papyrus unravelling from it. The papyrus had been bound around the very end of the shaft. The feathers of the fletching had been glued on top of it. The papyrus was some three inches long and about half an inch wide. Its inner face was covered with Greek characters written in a small, neat hand. There was no punctuation, but of course that was quite normal. Ballista tried to read it, but he could make out no words. All that emerged was a random-seeming sequence of Greek letters. He detached the coded message and handed it to Demetrius.

'Who did you dig this out of?'

The doctor swallowed hard. 'A soldier from the *numerus* of Ogelos, *Kyrios*, one of the conscripted townsmen.' The man stopped. He was sweating.

'Why did he come to you?'

'Two of his fellow soldiers brought him, *Kyrios*. They had taken him to the doctor of the *numerus*, but he was drunk.' The man stood straighter. 'I never drink to excess, *Kyrios*.' He beamed at Ballista. He was still sweating.

'And did you find out where he was when he was hit?'

'Oh yes, his friends told me. They said that he had always been unlucky. He was not on the wall, not even on duty. They had been drinking in The Krater all evening. They were on their way home, back to the tower just east of the postern gate. They were crossing that bit of open ground when, whoosh, out of the darkness, the arrow came down over the southern wall and hit him in the shoulder.'

'Did he survive?'

'Oh yes, I am a very fine doctor.' His tone betrayed his own surprise at this outcome.

'I can see that.' Ballista stepped towards him again. This time he came right up to him, using his size to intimidate. 'You will not mention this to anyone. If I hear that you have . . .' He let the threat hang.

'No, no one, *Kyrios*, no one at all.'

'Good. Give the soldier's name and that of his friends to my secretary and you are free to go. You have played the part of a conscientious citizen very well.'

'Thank you, *Kyrios*, thank you very much.' He virtually ran to Demetrius, who had his stylus ready.

There was a loud tearing sound of something big travelling fast through the air followed by a huge crash. The doctor visibly jumped. A fine trickle of plaster came down from the ceiling. The artillery duel had been going on for six days now. Clearly the doctor had no desire to be as near to it as this requisitioned house close behind the western wall. As soon as he had gabbled the names of the soldiers, he turned and fled.

Demetrius folded his writing block and hung it back on his belt. He picked up the papyrus again and studied it. To give him time, Ballista walked across the room and poured some drinks. He gave one each to Mamurra, Castricius and Maximus, put one down near the secretary and, sitting on a table, began to sip his own.

There was the awful sound of another incoming artillery stone, another crash, and again a fine drizzle of plaster. Mamurra commented that one of the Persian stone-throwers was overshooting. Ballista nodded.

At last Demetrius looked up. He smiled apologetically. 'I am sorry, *Kyrios*. I cannot make out the code. At least not straight away. Most codes are really very simple – you substitute the next letter in the alphabet for the one you mean and the like; sometimes even simpler: you make a small mark by the letters that are meant to be read, or you write them at a slightly different level from the others – but I am afraid that this does not seem to be so simple. If I may I will keep it and study it when I have no other duties. Maybe eventually I will unravel it.'

'Thank you,' said Ballista. He sat and drank, thinking. They all sat in silence. At intervals of about a minute there was another crash and more plaster drifted down to add to the fine dust which covered every surface.

Ballista once more felt the lack of Antigonus; he would have been ideal for what Ballista wanted done. Mamurra was already too busy; Ballista wanted Maximus with him . . .

'Castricius, I want you to talk to the three soldiers. Find out exactly when and where the man was hit. Swear them to secrecy. Threaten them a little to make sure they do not talk. You had better be quick talking to the wounded one before he dies of some infection.'

'*Dominus*.'

'Then pick three of the *equites singulares* and have them keep a discreet watch on the area. It is too much to hope that one of them will be hit by an arrow with a coded message tied to it, but I want to know who they see in that part of town.'

Again the standard-bearer simply said, '*Dominus*.'

'Anyone hanging around there might be our traitor looking for the message he was expecting but never received. At least now we have positive proof that we still have a traitor among us.'

A crescent moon hung low on the horizon. Above, the constellations slowly turned – Orion, the Bear, the Pleiades. It was the fifteenth of August, the *ides*. Ballista knew that, if they were still alive to see the Pleiades set in November, they would be safe.

It was deadly quiet on the battered south-west tower of Arete. Everyone was listening. Usually it seemed unnaturally quiet in the evening when the artillery duel ceased for the day but, now, as they strained to hear one particular sound, the night outside the tower was full of noise. A dog barked somewhere in the town. Nearer at hand a child cried. Faint noises drifted across the plain from the Sassanid camp: the whinny of a horse, a burst of shouting, snatches of a plaintive tune picked out on a stringed instrument.

'There, do you hear it?' Haddudad's voice was an urgent whisper.

Ballista could not hear it. He turned to Maximus and Demetrius. In the dim light they both looked uncertain. They all continued to strain their ears. The night grew quieter.

'There, there it is again.' The voice of Iarhai's mercenary captain was even softer.

Now Ballista thought he half heard it. He stilled his breathing. Yes, there it was: the chink, chink sound Haddudad had described, gone as soon as the northerner heard it. He leant out over the parapet, cupping his hand to his right ear. The sound was gone. If it had existed at all, it was covered by the noise of a Persian patrol making its way along the southern ravine. The scatter of stones dislodged in the near darkness, the creak of leather, the clang of metal on metal – all rang loud. They must have reached a picket. The listeners on the tower heard the low challenge 'Peroz-Shapur' and the answer: 'Mazda.'

Ballista and the others shifted their positions and breathed deeply as they waited for the patrol to pass out of earshot up on to the plain.

The volume of the night resumed its normal elusive texture. An owl hooted. Another answered. And in the silence that followed, there it was: floating up from somewhere down in the ravine towards the plain, the chink, chink, chink of pickaxe on stone.

'You are right, Haddudad, they are digging a tunnel.' Ballista listened some more until somewhere behind him in the town a door opened and a burst of laughter and raised voices obliterated any other sound.

'We should send out a reconnaissance party. Find out exactly where it starts. Then we can estimate the route it will take.' Haddudad still spoke in a whisper. 'I would be happy to go. I can pick the men in the morning and go tomorrow night.'

'Thank you, but no.' Ballista had been about to call for Antigonus. Then he remembered. He thought for some moments. 'We cannot wait until tomorrow night. If we make any preparations for a scouting party the traitor may find a way to warn the enemy. Our men would walk into a trap. No, it must be tonight, now. I will go with Maximus.'

There was a collective intake of breath, then several voices spoke at once. Quietly but determinedly Demetrius, Haddudad and his two sentries in their different ways said that this was madness. Maximus said nothing.

'I have made my decision. None of you will speak of this. Haddudad, you and your men will stay here. Demetrius, go and find me some ashes or burnt cork and meet Maximus and me at the southern postern gate.'

Haddudad and his men saluted. Demetrius hesitated for some time before going down the steps.

By the time Demetrius had fetched the camouflage from the requisitioned house that served as military headquarters and reached the postern gate, Ballista had told the plan to Cocceius, the *decurion* in command of the *turma* of Cohors XX stationed there. Ballista and Maximus were going to leave by the gate. It was to be left open until dawn. Then it was to be shut. It was not to be opened again unless the *Dux Ripae* and his bodyguard appeared before it in daylight, when the guard could be certain they were alone. In the event of them not returning, Acilius Glabrio was to assume command of the defence of Arete. Ballista had written a short order to this effect.

'Sure, is that not enlisting the wolf to be your sheepdog, thinking as you do that he himself might be the traitor?' Maximus had said in Celtic.

'If we do not come back, I think we will be past caring about that,' Ballista had replied in the same tongue.

Ballista prepared himself. He took off his helmet, mail coat and the two decorations on his sword belt – the mural crown and the golden bird that had been a parting gift from his mother. He tied his long fair hair in a dark cloth and, as he always wore black, had only to rub his face and forearms with burnt cork. Maximus took rather longer. He gave the many ornaments which festooned his belt to Demetrius, with a graphic threat of what he would do if the Greek boy lost any of them. As his tunic was white, he stripped it off and got help darkening his torso, heavily muscled and much scarred. With a minimum of fuss they stepped through the gate.

The two men stood just outside for a while, letting their eyes become accustomed to the light of the stars and the sliver of moon. Ballista punched Maximus softly on the shoulder. The Hibernian gently punched him back, his teeth flashing white in the darkness. A path, paler than the rock around it, snaked away down into the ravine.

With no words, they set off, Ballista in the lead, Maximus falling into step behind. They had known each other a long time; there was no need for any discussion. Maximus knew that, as was the custom among the tribes of Germania, Ballista on reaching puberty had been sent to learn the ways of a warrior with his maternal uncle. He had been a renowned war leader among the tribe of the Harii. Since Tacitus had written his *Germania*, the fame of the Harii as night fighters had spread far beyond the forests of the north. By preference, they fought on pitch-dark nights. With their blackened shields and dyed bodies, their shadowy and ghoulish appearance struck fear into the hearts of their enemies. Tacitus went so far as to claim that 'no enemy can endure a sight so strange and hellish'. Maximus knew that there were few more dangerous men in the dark of the night than his *dominus* and friend.

After a time the path turned to the right towards the plain and, still descending, ran along the flank of the ravine. Now Ballista and Maximus were among the tombs of the Christian necropolis. Above and below the path were the black entrances to the natural and manmade caves where the worshippers of the crucified god buried their dead. Ballista stopped and made a signal with his hand. Together they climbed up the side of the ravine to the nearest mouth of a cave. Some three feet in, the tomb was sealed with a wall of mud bricks. Still without speaking, the two men squatted down, leaning their backs against the wall. They listened and watched. Twinkling watch fires could be seen at the top of the far side of the ravine. Now and then sounds wafted across, so low as to be at the limit of hearing. From the floor of the ravine nothing could be seen or heard. The sounds of tunnelling had disappeared.

After what to Maximus seemed a very long time, Ballista rose to his feet. Maximus followed suit. Ballista turned to the wall, fumbled with his clothing and urinated on the wall.

'Do you not think it might bring bad luck, pissing on their tombs?' The Hibernian's voice was very quiet.

Ballista, concentrating on missing his boots, was slow to answer. 'Maybe, if I believed in their one god. But I would rather piss here in the darkness than out there in the open.' He rearranged himself.

'If I was frightened I would not do this,' said Maximus. 'I would go and till the soil, or sell cheese.'

'If you do not know fear, you cannot know courage,' replied Ballista. 'Courage is being afraid but doing what you have to do despite it – you could call it male grace under pressure.'

'Bollocks,' said Maximus.

They set off again down to the path.

Just discernible in the dim light, other narrow paths ran off to either side. Ballista ignored the first two to the left heading downhill. He stopped at the third. After looking all around to try to judge how far they had walked, he took the left-hand turning. They were still descending but were now travelling back towards the river. As they neared the bottom of the ravine, Ballista stopped more frequently. Eventually, he signalled that they were to leave the path and climb straight down the face of the ravine.

Maximus's boot dislodged a small avalanche of stones. Both men froze. There was no alarm. Far off in the distance a jackal barked. Others of its kind joined in. Ballista had judged the risk of making a noise while climbing on hands and knees, swords slung behind their backs, less than that of walking straight down one of the paths. If he had been in command of the Sassanid guard, he would have placed a watch where the paths reached the floor of the ravine.

They reached the bottom with no further incident. Without pausing, Ballista set off to cross to the southern wall of the ravine. There was no time to lose. They already knew that Persians carrying no lights sometimes patrolled here. Holding their swords away from their bodies, they moved at a slow jog.

As soon as they reached the opposite side they began to climb. The cliff face here was steeper. They moved slowly, searching for handholds. They had not been ascending long before the gradient lessened. Ballista signalled a halt. They lay on their backs, looking all around, listening hard. There it was again, coming from their left, from further up the ravine towards the plain, the chink, chink, chink of pickaxes on stone.

Crabwise they crawled along the cliff face, taking the greatest care where they put their hands and feet. Without being told, Maximus could appreciate Ballista's thinking. The entrance to the mine would be in the north face of the ravine, tunnelling towards the wall of the town. The attention of any sentries should be directed the same way. By crossing the ravine Ballista had in effect put them behind the enemy lines. With luck, no one would notice them as they approached from an unexpected direction.

Maximus was concentrating so hard on not making a sound that he failed to see Ballista's signal and bumped into him. There was a grunt from Ballista as a boot kicked him in the calf and a sharp intake of breath from Maximus. They made no other noise as they waited.

With infinite caution Ballista half turned and gestured down and across the ravine. Equally carefully, Maximus turned. The entrance to the Persian siege mine was about halfway up the northern face of the ravine. It was lit from within by torches or lamps. In their glow the black silhouettes of miners flitted back and forth, casting grotesquely elongated shadows. The sound of pickaxes was clear. Men working pulleys and winches to remove the spoil could just be made out at the lip of the mine. Instantly, Ballista's mind was full of memories of the distant north, stories of dwarves scheming mischief deep in their rock-hewn halls. He wondered what thoughts were in Maximus's mind. Probably what was usually there – women and drink. The men toiling at the pulleys ceased work and, abruptly, some form of screen was pulled across the mouth of the tunnel.

Ballista looked away into the darkness towards the river until his night vision returned. Then, using the faint chinks of light which escaped from the screen and the looming dark outline of the town defences, lit by just a few torches, he tried to estimate the exact position of the mine. He took great pains over this; distances are harder than ever to judge at night. He could sense that, beside him, Maximus was eager to go, but he took his time. There would be no second chance. Eventually, he patted the Hibernian's arm and signalled their withdrawal.

Crabwise again, they inched back along the cliff the way that they had come. Ballista was taking extravagant care. He feared that the relief of being on the homeward journey might lead him into a false move. When he judged that they were roughly where they had climbed up, he signalled to Maximus and they descended. This time, on reaching the floor of the ravine they waited, their senses probing the darkness. Across the void the great southern wall of Arete stood out black against the skyline. It was lit here and there by a torch. Their light and warmth beckoning, the massive solidity of the wall and towers gave Ballista a pang to be safe inside once more. He shrugged it off. Inside, his war was one of endless bureaucratic book-keeping, list after list of men and supplies. Out here in the darkness was the true way of the warrior. Out here his senses were fully alive, stretched to their limits.

Nothing threatening could be seen on the floor of the ravine. Nothing heard, and nothing smelt. Ballista gave the sign. As before, they set off at a slow jog.

The two men were halfway across when they heard the approaching Sassanid patrol. They froze. The sides of the ravine were too far to make a run for it. There was nowhere to hide. The noises were getting louder: the crunch of stones under numerous boots, the slap of weapons against shields and armour.

Leaning very close to his bodyguard, Ballista whispered. 'There are too many of them to fight. We will have to talk our way out of this. You had better not have forgotten your Persian.' The Hibernian did not reply, although Ballista was sure that he was grinning. The Persian patrol was emerging from the darkness that lay down towards the river, a dim blur, darker than its surroundings.

Suddenly, without warning, Maximus stepped forward. In a low voice but one pitched to carry he called 'Peroz-Shapur.' A surprised silence succeeded the noises of the advancing Sassanids. The patrol must have stopped. It had not been expecting to be challenged at this point. After a few moments a voice, slightly uncertain, called back, 'Mazda.' Without hesitation, Maximus called in Persian,

'Advance and identify yourselves.' The noises of armed men moving resumed.

Now the dark blur began to be recognizable as made up of individual warriors. Ballista noted two on either side detaching themselves from the main body and fanning out. Admiring as he was of Maximus's bold stroke, he did not intend to trust his life to the Hibernian's talking. When the patrol was about fifteen paces away, Ballista stepped to the front and called, 'Halt there. Identify yourselves.'

The Sassanids stopped. The four on the wings had arrows notched, their bows half bent. There looked to be about ten in the main body.

'Vardan, son of Nashbad, leading a patrol of the warriors of the Suren.' The voice was one used to authority. 'And who are you? You have a strange accent.'

'Titus Petronius Arbiter and Tiberius Claudius Nero.' At the sound of the Roman names the starlight glittered on the swords which the Sassanids drew, from the flanks bows creaked as they were pulled to maximum draw. 'Mariades, the rightful Emperor of the Romans is our master. Shapur the King of Kings himself decreed that his servant Mariades send men to reconnoitre by stealth the postern gate of the town of the unrighteous.'

There was silence for a while. Ballista could feel his heart beating, his palms sweating. At length Vardan replied. 'And how do I know that you are not deserters from the Great Emperor Mariades?' There was a wealth of scorn in 'Great Emperor'. 'Roman scum running to its own kind?'

'If we were fools enough to desert into a doomed town we would deserve to die.'

'There are many fools in the world, and many of them are Romans. Maybe I should take you back to camp to see if your story is true?'

'Do that and I will come and watch you impaled tomorrow morning. I doubt that the Mazda-worshipping Shapur, King of Aryans and Non-Aryans, will take kindly to his orders being countermanded by an officer of the Suren.'

Vardan walked forward. His men were clearly taken by surprise.

They started walking hurriedly after their commander. Vardan held his long sword at Ballista's throat. The others closed round. The commander put his sword aside and peered closely into Ballista's face. The northerner returned his gaze.

'Uncover the lantern. I want to see the face of this one.' A Persian behind Vardan began to move.

'No. Do not do that.' Ballista put all his experience of command into his voice. 'The great King's mission will fail if you show a light. The Romans up on the wall could not fail to see it. Shapur will not get the information, and we will meet our deaths at the foot of that wall.'

There was an awful moment of indecision before Vardan told the lantern-bearer to remain as he was.

Vardan brought his face so close that Ballista could smell his breath; a waft of some exotic spices. 'Even in the dark with your face blackened like a runaway slave I can still see you well enough to recognize you again.' Vardan nodded to himself. Ballista did not move. 'If this is a trick, if you are in the town when it falls, I will seek you out and there will be a reckoning. It will be I that watches you writhe on the stake.'

'Mazda willing that will not happen.' Ballista took a step backwards, keeping his hands well away from his sides. 'The night is advanced. If we are to return by dawn we must be going.'

Ballista looked over at Maximus, jerked his head towards the wall and walked to the edge of the circle of Sassanid warriors. The two blocking his way did not move. He turned back to Vardan. 'If we do not return tell our master Mariades that we did our duty. Remember our names: Petronius and Nero.'

Vardan did not reply. But at his sign the two men blocking Ballista's way moved aside. Ballista set off.

It is very difficult to walk normally when you think that someone is watching you and even more difficult when you think that someone might try to kill you. Ballista forced down an urge to break into a run. Maximus, Allfather bless him, had fallen in directly behind his *dominus*. The Hibernian would take the first arrow. Yet Ballista's back still felt terribly exposed.

Fifty paces was about the real limit of accurate bowshot, less in a dim light. How far had they walked? Ballista started to count his steps, stumbled slightly and went back to concentrating on walking as normally as possible. The walk seemed to last for ever. The muscles in his thighs felt twitchy.

In the end, the wall of the ravine came as almost a surprise. Both men turned, crouching, making themselves the smallest target possible. Ballista realized that he was panting. His tunic was soaked in sweat.

'For fuck's sake, *Petronius* and *Nero*?' Maximus whispered.

'It's your fault. If you ever read anything apart from the *Satyricon* some other names might have appeared in my mind. Anyway, let's get the fuck out of here. We are not home yet. The reptiles might change their minds and be after us.'

Demetrius was standing just outside the postern gate. He was surprised to find himself there. Admittedly Cocceius the *decurion* and two of his troopers were there as well. But even so Demetrius was surprised by his own bravery. Part of his mind kept telling him that he could hear and see just as well, maybe better, up on the tower. He pushed such thoughts away. There was a strange exhilaration in being outside the walls after so many months.

Demetrius stood with the three soldiers, listening and watching. The dark was alive with small sounds; the scurrying of nocturnal animals, the sudden rush of wings of a night bird. The gentle wind had moved round to the south. Fragments of sound, voices, laughter, the cough of a horse, drifted across from the Persian pickets on the far side of the ravine. Once, a jackal barked and others joined in. The chink of pickaxes came and went. But there was nothing that betrayed the progress of Ballista and Maximus.

The young Greek's thoughts drifted far away to the dark plain before the walls of Troy, to the Trojan Dolon slinging his bow across his shoulders, pulling the pelt of a grey wolf around him and stealing forth to spy out the Greek camp. Things had not gone well for Dolon. Out there across the dark plain he had been hunted down like a hare by cunning Odysseus and Diomedes of the great war cry. In tears, begging for his life, Dolon had revealed how the Trojan pickets lay. It had done him no good. With a slash of his sword Diomedes had cut through the tendons of his neck. His head dropped in the dust, and his corpse was stripped of his back-strung bow and the grey wolf-pelt.

Demetrius fervently prayed that Ballista and Maximus did not share the fate of Dolon. If the young Greek had had the poetry of Homer to hand he would have tried to see how things would fall out. It was a well-known method of divination to pick a line of the *Iliad* at random and see what light the divine Homer shed on the future.

The thoughts of Demetrius were dragged back to the present by the sounds of a Sassanid patrol making its way along the ravine up from the river. He heard the challenge 'Peroz-Shapur' and the response, 'Mazda', then a low exchange in Persian. Demetrius found himself, like the others, on the lip of the ravine, leaning forward, straining to catch the words. It was pointless. He did not know a word of Persian.

Demetrius physically jumped as a flood of light came from the postern gate. He spun round. In silhouette in front of the gate stood Acilius Glabrio. The torchlight caught the nobleman's gilded cuirass. It was moulded to resemble the muscles of an athlete or hero. Acilius Glabrio was bareheaded. The curls of his elaborate coiffure shone. His face was in shadow.

'What in the name of the gods below is happening here?' The patrician tones sounded angry. '*Decurion*, why is this gate open?'

'Orders, *Dominus*. Orders of the *Dux*.'

'Nonsense, his orders were that this gate remain shut at all times.'

'No, *Dominus*. He told me to keep the gate open until dawn.' The junior officer was cowed by the seemingly barely controlled anger of his superior.

'And why would he do that? To make it easy for the Persians to get in?'

'No . . . no, *Dominus*. He and his bodyguard are out there.'

'Are you mad? Or have you been drinking on duty? If you have I will have you executed with old-fashioned severity. You know what that entails.'

Demetrius did not know what that entailed, but presumably Cocceius did. The *decurion* started to shake slightly. Demetrius wondered if Acilius Glabrio's anger was real.

'Even our beloved *Dux* is not such a barbarian that he would desert his post to run around outside the walls in the middle of the night.'

Acilius Glabrio half turned. He pointed to the gate. 'You have moments to get inside and return to your post before I have this gate shut.'

Arguing with senior officers did not come easily to Cocceius. '*Dominus*, the *Dux* is still out there. If you close the gate he will be trapped.'

'One more word from you and it is mutiny. Inside now.'

The two troopers sheepishly went inside. Cocceius started to move.

'No.' Demetrius almost shouted. 'The *Dux* heard the sounds of tunnelling. He has gone to spy out where the Persian mine is being dug.'

Acilius Glabrio rounded on him. 'And what have we here? The barbarian's little bum boy.' He stepped close to Demetrius. He smelt of carnations. The torchlight highlighted the little ruffs of beard that were teased out in curls from his neck. 'What are you doing here? Selling your arse to this *decurion* and a few of his troopers so that they open the gate and let you desert?'

'Listen to the boy, *Dominus*. He is telling the truth,' Cocceius said.

The intervention attracted the full attention of Acilius Glabrio. Now the young patrician's anger was palpably genuine. Turning from Demetrius, he approached the *decurion*. 'Have I not warned you? Inside now.'

Cocceius dared a final appeal. 'But *Dominus*, the *Dux* . . . we cannot just abandon him out there.'

Forgetting the sword at his side, Demetrius bent down and picked up a rock.

'Are you disobeying a direct order, *Decurion*?'

Demetrius felt the rock sharp and gritty in his hand. The curls on the back of Acilius Glabrio's head shone in the torchlight.

'*Ave, Tribunus Laticlavius.*' A voice came from beyond the torchlight.

Acilius Glabrio whirled round. His sword rasped from its sheath. He crouched, his body tense.

Two ghostly figures, blackened and streaked with dust, emerged into the circle of light. The taller pulled a cloth from his head. His long fair hair fell to his shoulders.

'I must congratulate you, *Tribunus*, on your diligence. Patrolling the ramparts in the dead of night, most admirable,' Ballista said. 'But now I think that we should all go inside. We have much to discuss. We have a new danger to face.'

Ballista went to take a last look at the Persian siege ramp. He peered out from behind the makeshift parapet. Virtually every day the Sassanid artillery smashed the parapet to pieces. Then that night the defenders rebuilt it.

Despite the thick cloud of dust the progress of the ramp was clear enough. The Persians had begun work thirteen days before the *kalends* of August. It was now nine days before the *kalends* of September. Counting inclusively, that was thirty-six days' work. In thirty-six days the ramp had inched forward some forty paces and been slowly lifted up almost to the level of the parapet of the town wall. The ditch in front of the wall, which had taken the defenders such trouble to dig, had been packed with rubble. A gap like a canyon still separated the ramp from the defences. But the canyon was only about twenty paces wide, and it was partly filled by the defenders' own earth bank up against the wall. When the canyon was filled the Sassanid storming party would have a final approach over a level land bridge some twenty-five paces wide.

The progress of the siege ramp had been bought at the cost of the back-breaking labour of thousands. Every morning in the grey light of pre-dawn the Persian *vinae*, the mobile shelters, were pushed forward and joined together to form three long covered walkways. Under these, lines of men laboured to bring up the earth, rubble and timber that those at the front, protected by stout screens, dropped down into the space before the ramp. At the sides of the ramp more workers, again protected by screens, levered and mortared into place the mud bricks which formed the retaining walls.

The ramp's progress had been bought at the cost of the lives of many, many men in the Sassanid ranks. Soon after work had begun Ballista had sited the town's four twenty-pounder artillery pieces behind the wall in line with the ramp. Several houses had been demolished to create the new artillery emplacement. Those property owners that could be found had been promised compensation – should the town not fall. Every morning the *vinae* had to advance on the same lines, and then stay in place throughout the long day. Every morning the *ballistarii* in charge of the twenty-pounders, having checked the settings of their weapons, could fire blind at a high trajectory over the wall, reasonably confident that, sooner or later, with help from the spotters on the wall, one of their smooth round stones would hit one of the *vinae* at terrifying speed; would smash its wood and leather and reduce to a sickening pulp the men labouring in the illusory safety beneath.

As soon as the look-outs on the wall shouted, '*hit, hit,*' the defending bowmen would emerge from the shelters they had dug in the base of the town's internal glacis, sprint up to the battlements and pour a devastating hail of iron- and bronze-tipped arrows into those Sassanids exposed as they feverishly worked to repair or reposition the *vinae*.

Ballista had ordered that the two six-pounder artillery pieces sited on the towers at the threatened stretch of wall concentrate on the bricklayers working on the ramps' retaining walls. The *ballistarii* in charge of these had a clear line of vision. The screens could not withstand repeated impacts. Here again, over time, the slaughter was immense.

The Sassanid artillery had done what it could to destroy its counterparts. But so far they had been unable seriously to curtail the havoc caused by the defenders. Ballista had had to replace both the six-pounders and most of their crews twice, and one of the twenty-pounders had been smashed beyond repair. There were no further reserves of stone-throwers. Yet the volume of shooting had been little reduced.

As Ballista watched, a six-pound stone moving almost too fast to see crashed into one of the screens shielding the bricklayers. Splinters flew, a cloud of dense dust erupted, the screen seemed to buckle, yet it remained in place. Another one or two of those and that will be another gone: more dead reptiles, and another delay.

Ballista ducked back behind the parapet. He sat down, resting his back against it, thinking. Every night the Sassanids withdrew to start again the next morning. Why? Why did they not work through the night? They had the manpower. If Ballista had been their commander they would have done. The northerner had read somewhere that under the previous eastern empire, that of the Parthians, there had been a reluctance to fight at night. Maybe it was the same with their Persian successors. Yet they had been digging the mine from the ravine at night. Possibly it took something special to drive them to it. It was a mystery – but war was one long series of inexplicable events.

'I have seen all I need for now. Let us go down.' Crouching, Ballista moved to the stairwell in the roof of the tower, and down the stairs. He walked the few paces to the northern of his two mines. Castricius was waiting just inside. Ballista waved his entourage in first: Maximus, Demetrius, the North African scribe, two messengers and a couple of *equites singulares*.

'We can talk here.' Ballista sat down. Castricius squatted down next to him, Demetrius near by. Ballista noted the solid-looking lintel, the thick pit props. It was not too bad here, just near the entrance. The oppression of the enclosed space could not overwhelm him when it was but three or four steps from the open air.

On the other side of the mine a line of men passed baskets of spoil from hand to hand out of the tunnel.

Castricius produced several scraps of papyrus, all covered in his scrawled writing. He expounded with admirable clarity and brevity the course of his tunnel. It was under the wall, under the outer glacis, and was scrabbling like a mole towards the Persian siege ramp. Consulting one piece of papyrus after another, he outlined his projected needs for pit props and slats to hold up the sides and roof, lamps and torches to light the work, and various incendiaries and their containers for the ultimate purpose of the mine. As Ballista approved the figures, Demetrius wrote them down.

Castricius went to check on progress; Ballista sat in silence where he was. A Sassanid missile thundered into the wall above. A fine shower of earth fell from the roof. Ballista, from wondering if the opposite pit prop was slightly off centre, found himself thinking about Castricius and his changes of fortune. He must have committed a terrible crime to have been sent to the mines. He had survived that hell, which spoke of uncommon resilience; he had joined the army (was there a regulation that should have prevented that?); finding the corpse of Scribonius Mucianus had brought his knowledge of mines to the attention of his *Dux*; being one of the three survivors of the ill-fated expedition of the young *optio* Prosper had won him the post of standard-bearer to Ballista. Now, for a second time, his experience of the mines had aided him, bringing promotion to acting centurion to dig this tunnel.

Another stone hit the wall; more dust drifted down. From this mine and the mutability of fortune, Ballista's thoughts moved along unconsidered back roads to the question of treachery. Demetrius had not been able to unravel its secrets, but the mere existence of the coded message attached to the arrow showed that there was still at least one traitor in the city of Arete – or, at least that the Persians thought there was still a traitor active in the town. Ballista was sure they were right.

What did he know about the traitor? Almost certainly, he had murdered Scribonius Mucianus. He had burnt the artillery magazine. He had tried to organize the burning of the granaries. He was in communication, albeit sometimes interrupted, with the Sassanids. Clearly the traitor wanted the city to fall. Who could want such a thing, such a very monstrous thing? Could it be one of the townsmen, one of those who had lost their homes, family tombs, temples, slaves and all the liberties that were most precious to them because of the defensive measures Ballista had put in place?

And hadn't he played his own part? How far could one go before destroying the very thing one was trying to protect?

If it was one of the townsmen, it was a rich one. Naptha cost a lot of money; it stank: only the rich could afford it, and the luxury of space to conceal its noxious smell. If the traitor was a townsman, it had to be one of the elite, one of the caravan protectors – Anamu, Ogelos, even Iarhai – or one of the other town councillors, like that ever-smiling Christian Theodotus.

But was it a townsman? What of the military? Ballista was very aware that Maximus still mistrusted Turpio. Not without reason. The humorous-faced Turpio had a past of proven duplicity. He had done well out of the death of his commander, Scribonius Mucianus. Despite Maximus's urgings, Ballista had never pressed the matter of what it was that Scribonius had used to blackmail Turpio. Maybe he would say one day, but Ballista very much doubted that Turpio could be forced to tell. On the other hand, Turpio had done well throughout the siege. His raid into the heart of the Persian camp had called for exceptional courage: one might say that he had earned the right to be trusted. But yet again, as Maximus had reminded him, courage is useful for a traitor – and so is being trusted.

Then there was Acilius Glabrio. Ballista knew that he was prejudiced against him, extremely prejudiced against the *tribunus laticlavius*. The crimped hair and beard, the supercilious manner: the northerner disliked almost everything about him. He knew that the young patrician detested serving under a barbarian. If Turpio was the traitor, it would be for money or to prevent his ultimate exposure as the killer of Scribonius – so money again. But if Acilius Glabrio proved to be the traitor, it would be about *dignitas*, that untranslatable quality that gave a Roman patrician a reason to believe in his superiority, a reason to exist. Ballista wondered if serving under an eastern monarch would be better for the *dignitas* of a Roman patrician than the humiliation of obeying the orders of a northern barbarian. In a certain light, the easterner could be thought less of a barbarian than a savage from the northern forests like Ballista.

Although Castricius was now in charge of this mine, the watch was being maintained on the area of town where the arrow with the coded message had struck the unfortunate soldier – who had, of course, died a few days after the doctor had extracted the arrow. Four *equites singulares*, whom Ballista could ill spare, kept up a more or less discreet observation. So far it had yielded nothing of use. As was to be expected, both Acilius Glabrio and Turpio had been seen on their rounds. All three of the caravan protectors had properties in the area. The Christian church of Theodotus had relocated there.

Castricius returned. Again he squatted down, and again they talked of timber and olive oil and pig fat, of distances and density and momentum.

'Thank you, Centurion, thank you very much.' At Ballista's words, Castricius swelled with pride. He stood up sharply, but he was too old a hand to crack his head on one of the beams. He saluted smartly.

Stepping outside was like stepping into an oven. The heat sucked the air out of Ballista's lungs. Everywhere were shifting clouds of dust. The northerner could taste it gritty in his mouth, feel it sifting down into his lungs. Like everyone else he had a persistent cough.

As they walked to the southern mine there was a cry from the wall of 'baby on the way.' Most of the party threw themselves to the ground; Ballista and Maximus remained on their feet. The others might interpret it as coolness in the face of danger, but the two men knew that this was not true. Both stared upwards, thinking that if the missile were heading their way, they might get just a glimpse of it and have a split second to hurl themselves out of the way.

With a terrible tearing sound the stone ripped through the air above their heads and with a roar plunged into an already ruined house. A further cloud of dust rolled out.

Mamurra was waiting at the entrance to the other mine, which was hard up against the southernmost tower of the desert wall.

'*Dominus*.' His face broke into a smile.

'*Praefectus*.' Ballista smiled back. They shook hands then kissed on the cheek, slapping each other on the back. They had grown to like each other. Mamurra knew that, as far as the *Dux Ripae* was concerned, his conscience was absolutely clear. Nothing that he had said or written about him was unfair or malicious. The big barbarian was a good man. You could rely on him to do the right thing.

Ballista looked with distaste at the entrance to the tunnel – the big, roughly worked beams, the uneven floor, the jagged rock walls, the precarious hang of the roof. He stepped inside. The darkness stretched away in front of him, half-lit here and there by an oil lamp in a niche. It was strangely quiet in this mine after the noise of the other one.

'How goes it?'

'Good, so far.' Mamurra leant against a beam. 'As I said we would, we have dug deep; under the wall, the external bank, and the ditch. We have taken the tunnel out to about five paces beyond the ditch. There we have dug a short crosswise listening gallery. I found some old bronze round shields in one of the temples. I have put them up against the wall and have men listening at them.'

'Did the priests object?'

'They were rather unenthusiastic. But then, there is a war on.'

Although a slave should never initiate a conversation with the free, Demetrius could not contain himself. 'You mean it works? I had always thought that it might be just a literary conceit of the ancient writers.'

Mamurra's grin grew wider. 'Yes, it is an old trick, but it works. They amplify sound well.'

'And have you heard anything?' Ballista asked.

'Oddly, no, nothing at all. I am reasonably sure that if they were tunnelling near by we would have heard their pickaxes.'

'That must be good news,' Demetrius said. 'Either there has been a cave-in and they have abandoned their mine or it has wandered far off course and they are nowhere near our wall.'

'Yes, those are two possibilities,' Mamurra looked thoughtful, 'but unfortunately there is a third.' He turned to Ballista. 'When you and Maximus told me where their tunnel started out there in the ravine, I assumed – I think that we all assumed – that its purpose was to undermine the foundations of our southernmost tower, collapse it so that no artillery from there could interfere with their siege ramp. Now I am not so sure. It may well be more dangerous than that. Maybe they intend to dig clean under our defences and let their troops come up behind our wall. If so, they are waiting for the ramp to be near completion before they excavate the last part of the tunnel so that they can attack from two places at once.'

The whole party was silent, imagining an inexhaustible flow of Sassanid warriors pouring across the siege ramp while another erupted from the ground; imagining the sheer impossibility of the task of trying to stem both at once.

Ballista patted Mamurra on the arm. 'You will hear them coming. You will catch them.'

'What then?' Demetrius volubly clutched at this comfort. 'Will you smoke them out, throw bees or scorpions into their tunnel, release a maddened bear?'

Mamurra laughed. 'Probably not. No, it will be the usual – nasty work in the dark with a short sword.'

The arrow was coming straight for his face. With a convulsive twist, Ballista jerked himself back into cover. The side of his helmet hit the crenellation, the cheek piece scraping along the rough stone. He felt a muscle pull in his back. He had no idea where the missile had gone, but it had been far too close. He exhaled noisily, trying to will his breathing back to normal. Behind him he heard a low sob.

Keeping low, on his hands and knees, Ballista scrambled to the man who had been hit. It was one of his messengers, the one from the Subura. The arrow had gone in by the collarbone. Only the feathers still stood out. The man had his hands curled round them. His eyes were uncomprehending.

'You will be all right,' said Ballista. He ordered two of his *equites singulares* to carry the man to a dressing station. The guardsmen looked dubious at this fool's errand but obeyed anyway.

Back behind the parapet, Ballista steadied himself. He counted to twenty then peered out. There was the Persian ramp; there was the void between the ramp and the wall. But now the gap was less than five paces wide. From underneath the screens at the front, seemingly almost close enough for the defenders to touch, earth and rubble, the occasional tree trunk, fell into the drop.

It would be today. Even if he had not seen the Sassanid troops massing at the far end of the covered walkways he would have known that it would be today. The Persians had clearly decided not to wait for the ramp to touch the wall but to use some kind of boarding bridge. The race was on. One way or another it would be decided today.

Ballista looked round. The messenger's blood was already soaking into the brickwork, a film of dust dulling the bright-red pool. Ballista nodded to those with him and, again keeping very low, crawled to the trapdoor. Maximus, Demetrius and the three remaining *equites singulares* clattered down the stone stairs after him.

Castricius was waiting at the entrance to his mine. With no formalities, he told them to get ready.

Ballista had been dreading this moment. It had to come. It was inevitable. He had to do it. But he did not want to. *Don't think, just act.* 'Let's go.'

As they walked down into the northern mine the sunlight from the entrance soon gave out. They moved quietly, just them in the darkness. None of the oil lamps in the niches was alight. Before they entered, Castricius had checked that no one had hobnails in the soles of their boots. They had left their sword belts, armour, helmets – anything metal – above ground. A careless spark could bring on their greatest fear, a premature fire.

In the pitch-darkness they moved in single file. Castricius led the way, feeling his way with his right hand on the wall. Ballista followed, gripping the back of Castricius's tunic in his fist. Then came Maximus, then Demetrius.

The floor was uneven. Ballista's boot half-turned on a loose stone. He imagined twisting his ankle, breaking his leg, being trapped down here. He fought down a surge of panic. *Keep going. Don't think, just act.*

The walk defied time, defied logic. They had been walking for hours. They could have walked all the way across the plain to the Persian camp.

Something changed. Ballista could sense space opening all around him. Possibly it was the quality of sound. The echo of their footfalls came back more slowly. The air smelt strange. It brought to mind different things: a stable, a butcher's shop, a warship. But the air was less close than before.

Castricius stopped. Behind him, the others stopped. Carefully, very carefully, Castricius opened his shuttered lantern just a chink. The thin beam of light barely illuminated the far side of the cavern. He held up the lantern. The roof was lost in shadows. Bringing the lantern down again, he directed the light at the timbers which held up the roof. To Ballista's eye there seemed very few of them, and those there were impossibly slender.

'There are just enough to hold the roof,' said Castricius, as if reading the mind of his commander. 'The wood is good, well-seasoned, tinder-dry. I have coated the timbers in pitch.'

'Good,' said Ballista, feeling he had to say something.

Castricius directed the light downwards. Most of the floor of the cavern was ankle-deep in straw. Around the bases of the timbers were pigskins stuffed with pig fat. 'A few cooks may have a problem, but they will burn well.'

'Good,' said Ballista in a voice that sounded strained to himself.

'And here is the heart of the matter.' Castricius shone the light behind them. To the left of the mouth of the tunnel where they had entered there were three large bronze cauldrons raised on wooden blocks, straw heaped around them. A trail of straw ran from them back up the tunnel. 'I found some bitumen for the first cauldron. The others contain oil.'

'I see,' said Ballista.

'Is it good?'

'Very good.'

'The fuse leads two-thirds of the way out of the tunnel. When you are clear, call to me and, with your permission, I will light it.'

'You have my permission.'

'Then let's go.'

Back on the surface the sunlight was blinding. Tears ran from their eyes. Having got his breath back, Ballista called to Castricius to fire the mine. They stepped away from the entrance.

For some time nothing happened. Then they heard the sound of Castricius's boots dislodging stones as he ran. He shot out of the tunnel, bent double but running hard. He skidded to a halt, looked around and, blinking hard, walked over to the others.

'It is done. Now it is in the hands of the gods.'

They struggled back into their armour and sword belts and ran to the tower. Taking the steps two at a time, Ballista burst out on to the battlements. He dived behind the parapet and looked out.

Almost everything was as it had been before. Yet Ballista knew something was wrong. There was the void. There was the Persian ramp with the screens along its face. Further back, level with the base of the ramp, was the line of mantlets. Further back still were the Persian artillery emplacements. Ballista searched hard, but he could see no wisp of smoke escape from the ramp. There was no evidence of what should be happening. There was no sign of the conflagration that should be raging in the manmade cavern below, the terrible fire that should be burning through the props, bringing down the cavern roof and the whole ramp above it. Everything on the surface was completely still.

That was it: everything was completely still – no incoming artillery, no archery, no rubble being tipped into the void. It would be now: the assault would come any second now.

'Haddudad, get the men up on the wall. The reptiles are coming.' Even as he shouted to the mercenary captain, Ballista saw the screen at the front of the Persian ramp begin to tip up. Allfather, we are going to lose this race. So close – just a few minutes more was all we needed.

The screen was pulled horizontal. Ballista ducked back behind the crenellations. A volley of arrows like a swarm of hornets buzzed across the fighting top, snickering off the stone. A sentry howled. The arrow in his shoulder, he spun round, lost his footing and tumbled down the slope of the inner earth ramp, where he got in the way of some legionaries coming out of their dug-outs and beginning the climb.

The arrow storm stopped. Ballista quickly glanced out. The boarding bridge was being pushed towards him across the void. A vicious-looking spike stuck down from beneath its leading edge. Ballista looked back inside the town. The defenders were labouring up the inner glacis, Roman regulars, mercenaries and local levies combined: they would not make it in time.

The boarding bridge crashed down, its spike well over the parapet. Without thinking, Ballista grabbed it. The wood was warm and smooth under his right hand. He swung his legs up on to the bridge. His boots thumped hollowly as he landed. Side on, shield well out in front, he drew his sword. He heard Maximus's boots thump down just to his left, those of another defender beyond the Hibernian. The boarding bridge was not wide. If no one fell, three men might hold it – at least for a short time.

In front was a line of fierce, dark, bearded faces, mouths open, yelling hatred. Under a coating of dust were the bright colours of Sassanid surcoats and the shine of their armour. Their boots drummed on the boarding bridge.

The easterner hurled himself baying at Ballista, not even trying to use the long sword in his hand. He wanted to smash his shield into that of the northerner, simply drive the defender back and off the bridge.

Ballista let himself begin to be pushed backwards. He stepped away to the right with his rear foot – there was no railing to the bridge; his boot was far too near the edge – and brought his left foot back behind his right. The Persian's momentum drew him on. As Ballista's body turned, he brought his sword over and, palm down, he stabbed it into the easterner's collarbone. There was a momentary resistance from the mail coat, then the point slid in, cutting through the soft flesh, scraping down the bone.

As the first Sassanid fell, beside and behind Ballista, the next came on. Ballista dropped to one knee and swung the sword in a wide arc at the man's ankle. The Persian hastily dropped his shield to take the blow. Leaning over, off balance, the man had little chance. Ballista lunged forward and up, driving his shield into the man's chest, knocking him back and sideways. There was a momentary look of horror on the Persian's face as he realized that there was nothing under his boots, that he had been driven over the edge of the bridge; then he fell backwards, arms waving into the void.

For a second Ballista teetered on the edge, then he regained his balance. He glanced to his left. There were two Persians on the floor around Maximus. Beyond that, one of the *equites singulares* was down, but another had taken his place. Calling to the other two defenders to stay with him, Ballista carefully stepped back over the body of the first Sassanid he had killed.

The line of angry, contorted faces stopped. To get at the defenders they would have to risk the uneven footing of stepping on or over the bodies of four dead or dying men. The Sassanids were no cowards, but it would be a fool who would willingly put himself at a disadvantage in a fight like this.

Ballista felt a surge of confidence: he could do this; he was good at this. A perfect Thessalian feint followed by taking the man over the edge. The northerner's euphoria was broken by a vicious pain in his right thigh. There was a thin white line, which suddenly swelled into a red gash. As the blood ran down he shifted his leg. It hurt. It hurt a lot. But it would take his weight. The arrow had caused only a glancing flesh wound.

Crouching low behind his shield, arrows flying in from both sides, Ballista looked over the edge at the siege ramp. He thought he saw a wisp of smoke curling out of the mud bricks at the side of the ramp. It was gone before he could be certain. Sweat ran down his back. Maddeningly, a fly tried again and again to land on his eyes. His leg was throbbing; soon it would stiffen up.

A Sassanid nobleman was shouting at the storming party on the ramp. Any moment now they would recover their nerve. Ballista looked over the edge again.

There! There was a wisp of smoke. This time he was sure. Another, and another.

The Sassanids on the boarding bridge knew that something was wrong. They stopped yelling, stopped screaming at the defenders. They looked from one to another, puzzled. It was the noise, something beyond the sounds of men in combat, something deep, low and elemental, something like a wave crashing on a rocky shore.

As Ballista watched, smoke leaked out from all over the siege ramp. The noise changed to the deep rumble of an earthquake. The ramp seemed to quiver. The boarding bridge began to buck wildly. The looks on the Sassanid faces changed to terror. Slowly at first, then too sudden to follow, the centre of the ramp sank out of sight. The three side walls held for a moment. The boarding bridge swayed above the abyss.

'Jump!'

As he shouted, Ballista spun round and started to run. The wooden boards under his feet tipped up. He was scrabbling upwards on his hands and knees, his sword swinging dangerously from its wrist loop. The boarding bridge slid backwards down into the void. Its spike snagged for a moment on the parapet.

With a leap born of desperation, the leap of a salmon, Ballista just got the fingers of his right hand over the end of the bridge. There was a deafening roar. A mushroom cloud of choking dust and smoke blinded him. The parapet gave way. The boarding bridge began to slide down into the abyss.

A hand caught his wrist. The grip slipped, then held. It was joined by another hand. Then another. Haddudad and Maximus hauled Ballista up on to the fighting top.

For a time he lay on his back in the dust, holding both hands to the wound in his thigh. Through the darkness he could hear the groaning of thousands of tons of earth, wood and rock shifting, and hundreds, thousands, of men screaming.

Thick sweet coils of smoke meant to keep the swarms of insects at bay rose from the incense burners. Despite the clouds of gnats, evening was the one time of day Ballista still enjoyed in Arete. The artillery fell silent and a cool wind blew across the Euphrates. The terrace of the palace of the *Dux Ripae* was the best place to enjoy it. Here, the door guarded by the *equites singulares* and the waspish presence of Calgacus, Ballista could know some privacy.

The northerner picked up his drink and went and sat on the wall, one leg dangling. In the half-light bats flitted along the face of the cliff. Below him the great river rolled past, always changing, always the same. The green of the tamarisks provided a welcome relief for the eyes. Across the river came the bark of a fox.

Ballista put his drink down on the wall and looked again at the amulet that the two guardsmen had brought him. The messenger from the Subura had of course died. They had found the amulet on his body. In life he had worn it under his clothes. The leather thong on which it had hung around his neck was stiff with dried blood. The amulet was a circular disc, not more than two inches across. It was an identity tag, one side blank, the other stamped with two words: MILES ARCANUS. Ballista turned it in his hands.

The northerner's thoughts were interrupted by the approach of Calgacus. 'That hot Syrian bitch and her miserable father are outside. He says he wants to talk to you – probably wants to know why you haven't fucked her yet.'

'That should make for an interesting conversation.'

'What?'

'Never mind, would you show them in?'

Calgacus walked away. 'Your father would have had her on her back months ago. Any man in his right mind would.'

Ballista put the amulet in the purse on his belt and swung down off the wall. He brushed down his tunic. He had not yet had a chance to bathe or eat.

'*Dominus*, the *synodiarch* Iarhai and his daughter Bathshiba.' Calgacus could not have sounded more courtly.

Ballista had seen very little of Iarhai recently. For the last couple of months the caravan protector had seldom appeared on the walls. More and more he had entrusted the running of his troops to the mercenary captain Haddudad. Haddudad was a fine officer, but Iarhai's continuing absences were worrying.

As Iarhai advanced out of the gloom of the portico Ballista was struck by a change in him. He looked thinner, gaunt even. The broken nose and cheekbone looked more prominent. The lines on his forehead and at the sides of his mouth were deeper.

'*Ave*, Iarhai, *Synodiarch* and *Praepositus*.' Ballista greeted him formally, giving him his titles both as caravan protector and as Roman officer.

'*Ave*, Ballista, *Dux Ripae*.' They shook hands.

With a thickening in his throat Ballista turned to the girl. '*Ave*, Bathshiba, daughter of Iarhai.' Her eyes were black, very black. They smiled as she returned his greeting.

'Calgacus, would you bring some more wine, and something to eat, some olives and nuts?'

'*Dominus*.' The aged Caledonian left without a sound.

'If we sit on the wall we can catch the cool of the breeze.' Ballista watched Bathshiba's lithe movement as she sat, curling her legs beneath her. She was dressed as one of her father's mercenaries. She took off her cap and put it behind her on the wall. Her long black hair tumbled down around her shoulders. Allfather, but she had a body made to be against that of a man.

Ballista knew enough of easterners not to talk first to the daughter. He knew enough of easterners not to ask the father straightforwardly what he wanted.

'Your men have done good work, Iarhai, very good work.'

'Thank you. It is partly about them that I want to talk to you.' At Ballista's nod the caravan protector continued. 'They have taken many casualties. There are but 150 of the original 300 mercenaries left, and over 100 of the levies have died. I would like your authority to conscript another 100 civilians. While they are being trained they can be stationed on the southern wall, where it is usually quiet.'

'Yes, I have been thinking that something of the sort would soon be necessary. I think that you should try to conscript more, say 200. If suitable free men are hard to come by, we could offer some able-bodied slaves their freedom.'

'My fellow caravan protectors, Anamu and Ogelos, will not like it.'

'No, but as they are not placed on the desert wall, their troops have not suffered comparable casualties.'

'I will speak gently to them about it. I have no wish to upset them.'

Calgacus brought out the food and drink. Ballista took a sip of his own wine and pondered Iarhai's last words. More than his appearance seemed to have changed.

Iarhai, who was still standing, held his cup up towards Ballista. 'My congratulations on your destruction of the Persian siege ramp yesterday. It was a fine stroke.' As the northerner dipped his head in acknowledgement, Iarhai went on. 'The defence goes well. The end of the ramp was a turning point. Now the danger is less.'

Inwardly Ballista sighed. Iarhai could not believe that the danger was in any way passed, any more than Ballista himself did. The caravan protector was fully aware of the Persian mine from the ravine, the possibility of another all-out assault, the ever present threat of treachery.

'I think that it is a long road before we are safe.' Ballista smiled to try and take any sting out of contradicting his guest.

There was a short silence as they all took a drink.

'Things go well in the east. Your arrangements down by the river are good.' As there had been no repetition of the one failed Sassanid venture by water, Ballista had allowed some fishing boats to go out, under strict military supervision. At least one legionary from the Porta Aquaria went with each boat. The ten legionaries who had brought the grain boat down from Circesium had proved useful.

'Yes, it is good to eat fresh mullet and eel,' said Ballista. He was wondering where was this going. Iarhai had established his loyalty by talking about his soldiers, then pretended that the danger was past, and now he had brought up the river. The northerner took another drink. When he had first met Iarhai he had considered him wonderfully straightforward for an easterner. Quite a lot had changed.

A muscle twitched in Iarhai's broken right cheekbone. 'I own a few of the boats.' He looked away across the river to the approaching Mesopotamian night. 'One of them is called the *Isis*.' He pronounced the name of the goddess with distaste. 'She is large for a fishing boat. She has benches for ten rowers. Before all this I used to use her to go upriver for pleasure trips – fishing, hunting – sometimes as far as Circesium.'

'Everyone in the west believes that it is impossible to take boats up the Euphrates, the current is too strong,' Ballista said. He glanced at Bathshiba. She was sitting very still. Her face gave nothing away.

'The current is strong. Usually you row for short spells then come to shore. Taking a boat up the mother of all rivers is hard work. But it can be done. It would not be in the interest of the caravan trade for the authorities in Rome to know that it can be done.' Iarhai smiled. For a moment he looked like his old self.

'Well, I will not tell them unless it is necessary.' Ballista smiled too, but the warmth had gone from Iarhai's face.

'I would ask you a favour.' Iarhai stopped. He said no more.

'I will grant it if I can,' said Ballista.

'I want you to give the *Isis* back to me. I want your permission for ten of my men to take her to Circesium. I want them to take my daughter there.'

Ballista took care not to look at Bathshiba. He could sense her stillness. 'I am afraid that I cannot grant you this. It could not be done in secret. Once it was known that you had evacuated your family to safety, everyone would assume that the town is about to fall. It would cause panic. If I let you do this, how could I refuse the others? Anamu, Ogelos, the councillors – all would want a boat to take their loved ones, themselves, to safety.' Aware he was talking too much, Ballista stopped.

'I understand.' Iarhai's mouth was a thin line, like the mouth of a fish. 'I will not trouble you further. I have to do the rounds of my men. Come, daughter.'

Bathshiba got down from the wall. As they made their formal farewells, Ballista could read nothing in her face.

Calgacus appeared and led them out.

Ballista leant on the wall and looked out into the night. On silent wings an owl was hunting over the big island. Again he heard the bark of a fox, nearer now. There was a light footstep behind him. He turned fast, his hand going to his sword. Bathshiba stood there, just out of reach.

'That was not my idea,' she said.

'I did not think that it was.' They looked at each other in the pale moonlight.

'I am worried about my father. He is not himself. The fight has gone out of him. He hardly ever goes to the battlements. He leaves everything to do with the troops to Haddudad. He stays in his rooms. If you ask him his opinion about anything he just says that it will be as god wills. You must have seen. He is even being nice about Anamu and Ogelos.'

Ballista took a step towards her.

'No. My father is waiting at the gate. I left something.' She walked around Ballista and picked up her cap from the wall. She pushed it on her head, piling her long black hair under it. 'I must go.' She smiled and left.

Back sitting on the wall, Ballista took the amulet from his purse and turned it in his hands. MILES ARCANUS – literally secret or silent soldier. It was the mark of a *frumentarius*.

Ballista was sweating like a Christian in the arena. The air was very bad down here, close and fetid. It was hard to draw breath properly. At Mamurra's gesture, the northerner moved at a crouch to the far right of the gallery. The sweat was slick on his sides. Kneeling down, he put his ear to the first of the round shields held to the wall. The bronze was cold to his ear. He listened. He would have liked to shut his eyes to concentrate on listening, but he feared what would happen when he opened them again. He had done that once before, and he had no wish to relive that almost physical surge of panic that ran up through his body as his eyes told him that he was still in the tunnel.

After a time he looked at Mamurra and shook his head. He could hear nothing. Mamurra gestured to the next shield. His fear making him clumsy, Ballista shuffled along and put his ear to this one. He put his hand over his other ear. He tried to calm himself, tried to filter out the thumping of his heart, the small scratching noises as the shield moved imperceptibly against the rock. Yes, now he thought he heard something. He listened some more. He was not sure. He made a gesture of uncertainty, palms up. Mamurra pointed to the final shield. With this one there was no doubt. There it was: the steady, rhythmic chink, chink, chink of pickaxe on stone.

Ballista nodded. Mamurra pointed, his hand describing an arc from straight ahead to about forty-five degrees off to the left. Then, still without speaking, he held out the splayed fingers of his right hand, once, twice, three times. The enemy mine was approaching from the left; it was about fifteen paces away. Ballista nodded and jerked his head towards the entrance. Mamurra nodded back. Still crouching, Ballista turned to leave, hoping his pathetic relief was not too evident.

Back above ground, back from the realm of the dead, Ballista sucked air into his lungs. The hot, gritty, dust-laden air that hung over the town of Arete was like the coldest, cleanest air off the northern ocean of his childhood. Gulping it down, he used his scarf to mop the stinging sweat and dirt from his eyes. Maximus passed him a skin for water. He cupped a hand, filled it and bathed his face. Above him, the wind sail over the entrance to the mine hung limp. One of Mamurra's engineers was tipping a bucket of water over it to try and make it draw better.

'Now I can show it to you from up above,' said Mamurra.

In contrast to what had gone before, the view from the battlements of the south-west tower was Olympian. There off to the right was what remained of the Persian siege ramp. Broken-backed, it lay like a stranded whale. Beyond it was the broad sweep of the plain. Shattered missiles, scraps of clothing and bleached bones broke the wide, dun-coloured monotony that stretched all the way to the Sassanid camp.

They kept low behind the much-repaired parapet. Since the fall of the ramp shooting had been desultory, but a man in full view would still attract missiles. Mamurra borrowed a bow from one of the sentinels. He selected an arrow with bright fletching. He looked round the crenellations to find his mark, ducked back into cover, took a deep breath and stepped out to draw and release. Ballista noted that Mamurra drew the bowstring not with two fingers but with his thumb, like the nomads of the steppes.

'Hmm.' Mamurra grunted as the arrow embedded itself in the ground, its bright red feathers quivering. He considered for a moment or two. 'You see the arrow? Now move your eyes five paces to the right. Now almost ten paces away. Not as far as the scrap of yellow material. You see what looks like a large molehill?' Ballista saw it. 'Now move further away, twenty-five, thirty paces. You see the next one? Then, at a similar distance, the one beyond that?'

'I see them. That was not a great shot,' Ballista said.

'I have done better.' Mamurra grinned. 'It served its purpose. Now you can see the air shafts the reptiles have dug up from their mine. The Persian tunnel is considerably longer than ours so those air shafts are necessary. Ours is about forty paces long. Much further and the air gets bad at the head of the mine. The wind sail helps a little. If there had been time I would have dug another tunnel next to our mine: if you light a fire at the mouth of a parallel tunnel it draws out the bad air.'

Allfather, but he is a good siege engineer this one, a good *Praefectus Fabrum*. I am lucky to have him.

'I think that their tunnel will pass just to the left of our cross gallery. We will have to dig a little more to catch them,' Mamurra continued in answer to Ballista's unspoken question. 'There is a risk that they will hear us digging, that they will be ready for us. But we will dig and listen by turns. Anyway, it cannot be helped.'

Both were silent. Ballista wondered if Mamurra was also thinking that the traitor might already have warned the Sassanids of the Roman counter mine.

'When you intercept them, what will you do?'

As was often his way, Mamurra slowly mulled the question over. 'We could try and break into their tunnel from below, light a fire and smoke them out. Or we could come in from above, throw down missiles, maybe pour in boiling water, try to make their mine unworkable. But neither really answers. As I told the Greek boy when he talked of bears, bees, scorpions and such things, it will be nasty work in the dark with a short sword.'

'And then?'

'Collapse their mine. Preferably not with us still in it.'

'How many men will you need?'

'Not many. Numbers can be an encumbrance underground. When I ask, bring up the reserve century stationed on the *campus martius*. I will take twenty of them into the tunnel to add to my miners. Have the rest of the century around the entrance. Keep Castricius with you, in case things should work out badly.' The corners of Mamurra's mouth were turned down.

'I will tell the centurion Antoninus Posterior to have his men ready.'

Two days passed before a red-faced messenger sought out the *Dux Ripae*. Ballista collected Antoninus Posterior and his men. When they reached the mine Mamurra was waiting. There was no time for an extended farewell. Ballista shook the hand of his *praefectus fabrum*, and Mamurra led twenty legionaries into the tunnel.

Faced with a period of inactivity when nothing was required of him, Ballista did what all soldiers do: he sat down. There was no convenient shade from which he could see the entrance, so he sat with the hot sun on his back. He watched the awful black mouth of the mine. It was the twenty-ninth of September, three days before the *kalends* of October. It was autumn. In the north it would be cool. Here it was still very hot. He draped his cloak over his shoulders to keep the sun off the metal rings of his mail coat.

Calgacus arrived with some slaves from the palace. They handed round skins of water. Ballista took off his helmet and scarf. He took some water in his mouth, swilled it round and spat it out then, holding the skin away from his lips, poured a sparkling jet of the cool liquid into the back of his mouth.

Passing the water skin to Maximus, Ballista looked round and caught the eye of his latest standard-bearer, a lumpen-faced Macedonian called Pudens.

'*Dracontius*, take my standard to the Palmyrene Gate. Let the Persians see the white dragon flying there as usual.' Ballista picked one of his *equites singulares*, a Gaul with fair hair. 'Vindex, take my cloak. Put it on and show yourself by the standard. Play at being the *Dux Ripae* for a while. Let the Persians think it is just another day.'

*

Mamurra took his ear from the bronze shield. It was time. Holding it so that it did not clash on anything, Mamurra stepped between the two miners, then between the two men with bows. Putting the shield out of the way against the side wall, he squatted down. In the flickering light of the oil lamps everyone stared at him. Very quietly Mamurra said, 'Now.'

The two miners hefted their pickaxes, looked at each other, then swung. The noise was very loud after the silence in the enclosed space. Crash-crash, splinters flew. The two bowmen shielded their eyes. Crash-crash, crash-crash, the men with the pickaxes worked as a team, concentrating their blows in one place. Stripped to the waist, their bodies shone with sweat.

Mamurra drew his weapons, an old-fashioned short sword, a *gladius*, in his right hand, a dagger, a *pugio*, in his left. A lot depended on how quickly the axemen could make an entrance in the thin wall of the tunnel. Mamurra fervently hoped he had got it right. By all his calculations, by all his instincts, the Persian mine had advanced beyond the Roman counter mine. The breach should bring the Romans out some way behind the Persian pit face.

Crash-crash, crash-crash. *Come on, come on*. How thick was the wall? Mamurra was sure it would give at any moment. He found that he was humming under his breath, a legionary marching song as old as Julius Caesar:

> Home we bring our bald whore-monger,
> Romans lock your wives away!
> All the bags of gold you sent him
> Went his Gallic whores to pay.

One of the pickaxes went handle deep through the wall. The miners redoubled their efforts to enlarge the hole. Crash-crash, crash-crash.

'Enough,' shouted Mamurra. The men with the pickaxes stepped back. The bowmen stepped forward. They drew and released straight through the hole. The arrows could be heard ricocheting off the opposite wall. They drew again. They shot again, this time one to the left, one to the right. The arrows snickered down the rock walls. The bowmen stepped aside.

Mamurra and the man next to him hurled themselves through the hole and into the Persian mine. Crashing into the far wall, Mamurra turned right. The man next to him turned left. Mamurra took a couple of steps, then waited until another man joined him.

Together they moved forward. Mamurra kept low. Without his helmet or a shield he felt terribly vulnerable. In the distance, a shaft of light came down from one of the Persian air holes. Beyond it Mamurra could see the indistinct shapes of Sassanids. He caught a glimpse of a curved bow. He resisted the urge to flatten himself against the wall – arrows could follow walls. He crouched, making himself as small as possible. He heard the wisp, wisp sound of the feathers as the arrow spun through the air, felt the wind of its passing.

Straightening only a little – he had no desire to crack his head on the jagged roof of the tunnel – Mamurra ran at the Persians. The two eastern warriors at the front drew their swords, stood for a moment, then turned to run. One tripped. The legionary next to Mamurra was on the fallen Persian, a foot on the small of his back, stabbing repeatedly down at the man's head, neck, shoulders.

'Hold,' yelled Mamurra. 'Bring up the shields.' Wicker shields were passed forward. Four legionaries improvised a barrier. 'Where are the miners? Good, bring down those pit props and collapse the reptiles' mine.'

As the men with the pickaxes set to work Mamurra turned to find out what was happening in the other direction, at the head of the mine. He did not see what gave him the blow, he just felt the terrible dull impact. He stood for a moment stunned, feeling nothing but a vague surprise. Then a violent wave of nausea surged up from his stomach as the pain hit him. He saw the rough floor of the tunnel as he fell. Felt his face smash into the rock. He was conscious just long enough to hear the Persian counter attack, to feel a man stand on his ankle.

The first Ballista knew of the disaster below ground was when a legionary ran out of the entrance to the mine. His hands empty, the man stopped, looking around stupidly. Another legionary followed. He nearly ran into the first man.

'Fuck,' said Maximus quietly. They all rose to their feet. The soldiers around the entrance hefted their weapons. Antoninus Posterior started to get them into line. Now there was a stream of men running from the mine. Everyone knew what had happened. The Persians had won the underground fight. At any moment Sassanid warriors would burst out of the mine hard on the heels of the fleeing Romans. Castricius was standing by Ballista, waiting.

'Bring down the mineshaft,' said Ballista.

Castricius turned and issued a volley of orders. A group of men with crowbars and pickaxes fought their way into the mouth of the tunnel against the flow of panic-stricken legionaries. Others took up the ropes that were already tied around some of the pit props.

'No!' Maximus caught Ballista's shoulder, his grip tight. 'No. You cannot do this. Our boys are still down there.'

Ballista ignored him. 'As quick as you can, Castricius.'

'You bastard, you cannot do this. For fuck's sake, Mamurra is still down there.'

Ballista rounded on his bodyguard. 'You want us all to die?'

The noise of frantic work came from the dark mouth of the tunnel.

'You bastard, he is your friend.'

Yes. Yes, he is but, Allfather, I have to do this. *Don't think, just act*. Plenty of time later for recriminations, for guilt. *Don't think, just act*.

The men with crowbars and pickaxes sprinted back out of the mine. A couple more legionaries emerged with them. Castricius bellowed more orders. The men on the ropes took the strain and – one, two, three – began to pull.

Ballista watched. Maximus had turned away.

First one, then another of the gangs of men shot forward, stumbling, some falling as the strain came off their ropes. One by one the pit props were pulled away. There was a low groaning, then a strange roaring. A dense cloud of dust enveloped the mouth of the mine.

*

There was just enough light to see in the Persian tunnel. Although Mamurra kept his eyes shut, he could tell there was enough light to see. He was lying on his back. There was a crushing weight on top of him, a strong smell of leather. He could hear Persian voices. One of them was obviously shouting orders. Strangely, his ankle hurt worse than his head. The harsh, iron taste of blood was in his mouth.

Cautiously, Mamurra opened his eyes a fraction. There was a boot on his face. It was not moving. Clearly its owner was dead. There was a distant groaning, which changed to a roaring. There was a burst of shouting, the sound of men running, and the tunnel was filled with dust.

Mamurra shut his eyes and tried to breathe shallowly through his nose. He did not dare cough. When the moment passed it was quiet. He opened his eyes again. He tried to move, but only his right arm responded and, in doing so, the skin of his elbow scraped along the wall. He shifted the dead man's boot a little to make it easier to breathe.

He was at the bottom of a pile of bodies. Somehow that and the roaring and the dust told him everything. The victorious Persians had thrown him and the other casualties aside, out of the way. They had been following hot on the heels of the routed legionaries when Ballista had collapsed the Roman mine. Bastard. Fucking bastard. There would have been nothing else that the northerner could have done, but the fucking bastard.

It was very quiet. Biting his lip against the pain, Mamurra moved his right arm. Both his sword and dagger were gone. He rested for a moment. It was still quiet. Slowly, stifling a whimper of pain, he moved his right hand up and across, pushing it into the neck of his mail shirt, down under the collar of his tunic. Grunting with effort despite himself, he pulled free the concealed dagger. He let his arm drop, the dagger close by his right hip. He closed his eyes and rested.

Death did not worry him. If the Epicurean philosophers were right, everything would just return to sleep and rest. If they were wrong, he was not too sure what would happen. Of course there were the Islands of the Blessed and the Elysian Fields. But he had never really been able to tell if they were one place or two, let alone discover how you entered them. He had always had a talent for gaining access to places he was not meant to be – but not, he suspected, this time. It would be Hades for him. An eternity in the dark and cold, flitting and squeaking like an insentient bat.

It must be easier for the Sassanids. Fall in battle, become one of the blessed, and straight to heaven. Mamurra had never bothered to ask what their eastern heaven was meant to contain – probably shady arbours, cool wine and a never-ending supply of fat-arsed virgins.

It must be easier for a northerner like that bastard Ballista – for sure he had had no choice, but bastard anyway. The bastard and he had talked of it. Fight and die like a hero and the northerner's high god with the outlandish name might – just might – send his shield maidens to bring you to a glorified northern warlord's hall where, in a typical northern way, you would spend eternity fighting every day and, your wounds magically healed, drinking every night. No, not eternity. Mamurra half-remembered that, in Ballista's world, even the gods die in the end.

No, it was not death that Mamurra minded, it was not being alive. It seemed a monstrous, obscene joke that the world could continue and he not know anything about it. *Not knowing*. He, a man who had ferreted out so many things he was not meant to know.

He knew what being alive meant. Walking through a field of grain, running your hand through the heads of the wheat as the wind moved them; a sound horse between your legs as you rode into the valley, through the trees and down to the clear running water, and to the hills and trees on the other side – for him, that was not really being alive. No, it was waiting in the dark in an alley for the servant you had bribed or threatened to come and unlock the wicket gate, slipping inside, slipping inside to unravel the dirty secrets of the powerful, the fuckers who thought they were above the likes of him. It was lying in the dark, cramped behind the false ceiling, afraid to move a muscle, straining your ears to hear the drunken senators move from nostalgia to outright treason. That was being alive, more alive than at any other time.

The tune started rerunning in his head:

> Home we bring our bald whore-monger,
> Romans lock your wives away!

Mamurra heard the Persians returning. He moved his right hand back into his tunic. His fist closed around the hard metal disc. His fingers traced the words. MILES ARCANA. Very soon he would be a very silent soldier, very silent indeed. If it had not hurt so much he might have laughed. The sounds were getting nearer. He moved his hand back to the dagger by his hip. He had not yet made up his mind: try and take one of the bastards with him or end it quickly? One way or another, the fourth *frumentarius*, the one the others had not spotted, was prepared to die. The pommel of the dagger was slick in his hand.

The dried peas moved on the skin of the tambourine. Not much, but perceptibly.

Maximus did not like it. It was as if those left below were trying to attract attention. It was as if that great square-headed bastard Mamurra were trying to dig his way out. The poor bastard.

Castricius picked up the tambourine and moved it from the western to the northern wall of the tower. They waited for the dried peas to settle. They lay still for a time, then moved.

They walked outside and looked into the three large cauldrons of water along the wall which faced into the town. The waters were still.

Castricius led them to the north. Here, along the inner face of the town wall at intervals of about five paces, were three more cauldrons of water. The water rippled in the two nearest the tower; it was still in the one furthest away.

'It is clear what they are doing,' Castricius said. 'If poor old Mamurra was right that they originally intended to tunnel clean under the wall to bring troops into the town, they have changed their minds. They know we are expecting that, so they have decided to undermine the south-east tower and about ten paces of the wall to its north.'

He is good, thought Ballista. He is not Mamurra – may the earth lie lightly on him – but he is good. As Ballista framed the conventional line its sheer inappositeness struck him.

'Can we stop them?'

With no pause for thought Castricius replied, 'No, there is no time. They can spring their mine at any moment. When the peas and the waters stop moving, that will be the time. I will send word.'

In the event, Ballista and his entourage had only just reached the Palmyrene Gate when the word caught up with them. They turned and retraced their steps.

Nothing moved on the face of the waters. The dried peas stayed in place. The Persians had stopped digging. There was nothing to do but wait. The tower and the adjacent stretch of wall had been evacuated. Two volunteers had remained on the battlements of the tower. The terms were those usual if it had been a storming party. Should they survive, they would receive a large sum of money. Should they not, their heir would receive the money. Ballista had summoned both the reserve centuries of legionaries, that of Antoninus Prior from the caravanserai and that of Antoninus Posterior from the *campus martius*. The men were marshalled in the open space behind the tower. They were armed. They also carried entrenching tools. Piles of timber and mud bricks were at hand. That was all anyone could think to do.

Turpio, now acting *praefectus fabrum* in addition to commanding Cohors XX, stood on one side of Ballista. Next to Turpio was Castricius, now deputy to the new *praefectus fabrum*. On Ballista's other hand, as ever, were Maximus and Demetrius. The white *draco* hung limp behind them. They waited.

After an hour the indefatigable Calgacus appeared, followed by a train of slaves carrying water and wine. The *Dux Ripae* and his companions drank thirstily in silence. There was little to talk about. Even Maximus, out of sorts for the two days since the underground disaster, had nothing to say.

When it happened there was next to no warning. There was a loud crack. The wall near the tower shook. It seemed to ripple. Held in place by the great earth banks, unable to fall outward into the plain or inward into the town, it slid vertically about two paces into the ground. It shuddered, cracks zigzagged across its face, but it remained standing. A stunned silence. Another loud crack. The south-east tower lurched drunkenly forward. Its descent caught by the outer earth bank, it leant at an angle. It shook. Some of the makeshift parapet came away, bricks raining down. The tower remained upright.

Ballista thought that the two volunteers on the tower were screaming. But no, clinging to what was left of the battlements, they were howling, howling like wolves. The howling echoed along the whole wall as soldier after soldier joined in. Then a chant began: 'Ball-is-ta, Ball-is-ta.'

The tall northerner laughed. Men slapped him on the back. The defences of Arete still stood.

XVI

Ballista lay in the pool of the *frigidarium*. The cool water was scented with carnations or cloves. He was alone; both Maximus and Demetrius had asked for the evening off. To anyone who knew them it was no surprise after such a day. They would look for release in their different ways. Maximus would find his with a woman; Demetrius would opt for the less physical, the rather less tangible comforts offered by a dream-diviner, an astrologer, or some such charlatan. Ballista had been happy to grant their requests. Solitude was a rare commodity for a man in his position.

Putting his thumbs in his ears and blocking his nostrils with his forefingers, he submerged himself. Motionless underwater, his eyes shut, he listened to the beating of his heart, the plink, plink of water dripping. It had been a good day. Things had worked out well at the tower and the wall. But every danger surmounted brought on fresh dangers in its train.

Ballista surfaced, shaking water out of his hair, wiping it from his eyes. It had a taste of carnations or cloves too. Idly he wondered where Calgacus had got this new, unlikely scent. He lay motionless. The ripples in the pool died down. Ballista looked at his body, the forearms burnt dark brown by the sun, the rest pale white, the two long scars on the left of his ribcage a still paler white. He flexed his left ankle, felt the bone scrape and click. He yawned a big yawn, the right-hand side of his jaw scrunching where it had been broken.

He was thirty-four. Sometimes he felt much older. His body had taken a battering in the thirty-four winters he had walked the middle earth between the gods above and Hell below.

Ballista started to think of the siege. He pushed the thoughts away, keen to hang on to the momentary feeling of peace the bath had brought. He thought of his son. It was over a year – thirteen months – since he had left Isangrim in Rome. The boy had turned four in March. He would be growing fast, changing fast. Allfather, do not let him forget me. Deep Hood, Fulfiller of Desire, let me see him again. Ballista felt crushed by longing, by sadness. Unwilling to give way to tears, he plunged under again.

Standing up abruptly, the water sluiced off his heavily muscled, battered body. Stepping out of the pool, he wrung the water from his long fair hair. From nowhere Calgacus appeared and handed him a towel. The northerner began to dry himself. Somehow he had never got used to the Roman habit of having others towel you down.

'Did you like the *perfume*?' Calgacus asked, his intonation showing what he thought of it.

'It's fine.'

'It was a present. From your mincing little *tribunus laticlavius*. Seeing how fond you and Acilius Glabrio are of each other, I tested it on one of the house slaves. He did not die, so it must be safe.' Both men smiled. 'And here is the robe you asked for; the finest sheer Indian cotton – you sensitive little flower,' wheezed Calgacus.

'Yes, I am, renowned for it.'

'What?'

'Nothing.'

Although he spoke at the same volume, Calgacus as ever affected to believe that a change of tone rendered the asides he came out with when they were alone completely inaudible.

'I have put some food and drink out on the terrace for you. It is in the shade of the portico. There is a cover over it to keep the flies off.'

'Thank you.'

'Will you need me again tonight?'

'No. Go off and indulge in whatever frightful drunken lechery your vices demand.'

With no word of thanks Calgacus turned and walked away. As his domed head receded, his complaints floated behind him. 'Lechery . . . vices . . . and when would I find the time for them, working my fingers to the bone all hours looking after you?'

Ballista pulled the soft robe around himself and walked out on to the terrace. In the gathering gloom under the portico he found the food up against the back wall. Lifting the heavy silver cover by its handle, he poured himself a drink, scooped up a handful of almonds. Having replaced the cover, he went over to his accustomed place on the wall of the terrace.

It was the best time of the day. To the west the farmland of Mesopotamia was purple-hazed as night advanced. A cool wind blew over the Euphrates. The first stars shone. Bats hunted across the face of the cliff. But none of it brought back to Ballista the fleeting peace of the bathhouse.

Things had gone well today. But that was luck. Ballista had had the earth banks built to protect the walls and towers from artillery and from rams; that they had saved the defences from undermining was luck. Yet, Ballista smiled ruefully in the dark, if others put it down to his farsightedness, that was no bad thing for morale. He had issued orders to capitalize on his luck. Throughout the night men would labour, packing the leaning tower with earth. By the morning the parapets of tower and wall should have been replaced or shored up.

The Persians had thrown all the instruments of siege warfare at the city of Arete: siege towers, the great ram – the Fame of Shapur – the siege ramp, the mine. All had failed. The defences had held. Now it was the first of October. The rains should come in mid-November. There was not enough time for the Persians to gather the materials and begin new regular siege works. But only those defenders of very little understanding could believe that the danger was passed. The King of Kings would have no intention of slinking away defeated. The frustrations, the losses, the stain on his glory – all would have increased his resolve. Shapur would have no intention of lifting the siege. If his siege engineers could not deliver the town to him, he would punish them – probably savagely – and revert to a simpler strategy. He would decree another attempt to storm the town.

Five and a half months of siege had taken their toll on the defenders. Casualties had mounted. When the Sassanids launched another assault, Ballista wondered if there would still be enough defenders to deny them. The storm would not come tomorrow; there was not enough time for Shapur and his nobles to whip their men up to fighting frenzy. It would come the day after. Ballista had one day. Tomorrow he would send more men to the desert wall. He would go among them. He would speak to them, try to encourage them. Tomorrow evening he would hold a last supper for his officers and the leading men of the town; try to put heart in them. Inauspiciously, he thought of the final dinner in Alexandria of Antony and Cleopatra. What had they called the diners? 'Those inseparable in death' – something like that.

Finding that he had finished his drink, Ballista wondered for a second if he could throw the heavy earthenware beaker all the way over the fish market far below and into the black waters of the Euphrates. He did nothing of the sort. Instead he walked back to the portico. It was very dark behind the columns. He only found the food because he already knew where it was.

There was a noise of something scraping on brickwork. He froze. The noise came again, from the south of the terrace. Ballista crouched down low. From over the south wall a shape appeared. Compared with the darkness under the portico where Ballista waited, it was reasonably light out on the terrace. Ballista could make out the black-clad figure that dropped down over the southern wall, the wall that led into the town. More sounds of scraping on brickwork and two more black-clad figures joined the first. There was a quiet rasping as the three drew their weapons. Starlight glittered on the short swords.

Ballista reached for his own sword. It was not on his hip. *You fool, you stupid fucking fool.* He had left it in the bathhouse. So this was how it was going to end: betrayed by his own stupidity. He had let down his guard and he was going to be punished. *You stupid fucking fool*. Even that poor bastard Mamurra warned you of this.

The three black-clad assassins moved slowly forward. Ballista pulled the robe up half over his head to cover his face, his long fair hair. If by some miracle he survived, he must thank Calgacus for finding a robe of the finest Indian cotton in the black that his *dominus* customarily wore. The dark figures advanced down the terrace. Moving ever so gently, the fingers of Ballista's left hand found the big silver food cover. He gripped the handle. His right hand found the heavy earthenware beaker from which he had been drinking. As weapons they were not much but they were better than nothing. He stilled his breathing and waited.

A fox barked away across the river. The three assassins stopped. They were a few paces short of Ballista. One of them waved, gesturing the one nearest Ballista to go under the portico. The northerner raised himself up ready to spring.

The door to the terrace opened. A rectangle of yellow light shone across to the wall, plunging everything outside it into a deeper darkness. The assassins stopped.

'*Kyrios? Kyrios*, are you out here?' the voice of Demetrius called. After a moment, when there was no answer, the young Greek could be heard going back into the palace. His shadow disappeared from the rectangle of light.

One of the assassins spoke softly in Aramaic. All three crept silently towards the open door. The one just inside the portico, his night vision spoilt by looking into the light, passed no more than four paces from Ballista. At the edge of the patch of yellow they stopped, drawing close together. Again one whispered in Aramaic, so low that Ballista probably would not have made out the words even had he spoken the language.

The first assassin slipped through the door.

Safe, thought Ballista. Let them come inside, run across the terrace, over the north wall, drop down into the alley, a few paces to the two guards on the north door, collect them, run to the main courtyard, collect the five *equites singulares* from the guardroom, pick up a sword, and then back through the main door into the living quarters. Take one of the bastards alive, and then we can find out who sent them.

The second assassin slipped through the door.

But – Demetrius. The Greek boy would be killed, maybe Calgacus too.

Ballista moved. As the third assassin stepped through the door, Ballista came up behind him. The northerner smashed the heavy beaker into the back of the man's head. There was a sickening thud, the sound of breaking crockery. With a gasp of pain the man turned. Ballista ground the broken crockery into his face, twisting the edges into his flesh. The man fell back, his face a bloody ruin.

Just outside the doorway Ballista assumed a fighting crouch, side on, the food cover held out as an improvised shield, the shards of the beaker drawn back to strike.

One of the assassins dragged the injured man out of the way. The third man leapt forward, stabbing underhand with his sword. Ballista took the blow full on the food cover. He felt the soft metal buckle. The impact jarred up his arm to his shoulder. He lunged with the broken beaker. The lunge was too short and the black-clad man swayed back out of reach. The man stabbed again. Ballista angled his improvised shield to deflect the blow. Again his counter-stroke failed to bite home.

The other uninjured assassin was crowding behind Ballista's assailant, bobbing about, desperate to be in a position to attack their quarry. Ballista knew that, as long as he held the doorway, they could come at him only one at a time. Another thrust sliced a chunk out of the northerner's inadequate shield. Ballista found that he was yelling, a deep, wordless roar of rage. Again and again his opponent's sword bit into his increasingly tattered shield. The food cover was awkward, offering less defence and feeling heavier with each blow it took.

The assassin unable to gain access to Ballista stopped hopping from foot to foot. He looked down at the three inches of steel protruding from his stomach. He opened his mouth. Blood came out. He was hurled sideways. Realizing something was wrong behind him, the assassin fighting Ballista ducked, turned and swung a cut at Maximus's head. The Hibernian parried the blow, rolling his wrist to turn the blade aside, and stepped inside to drive his own weapon up into the assassin's throat.

'Don't kill the other one. Take him alive,' Ballista shouted.

The injured man had crawled to the side of the room. There was a smear of blood across the chequered tiles. Before Ballista or Maximus could act, the final assassin got to his knees, put the point of his sword against his stomach, braced the pommel against the tiles and threw himself forward. There was an awful sound as the sword tore through his guts. He collapsed sideways, curled around his own blade, twitching in his death agony.

From the start things did not bode well for Ballista's dinner party.

It was not the setting: the great dining room of the palace of the *Dux Ripae* was splendidly decked out. The windows opening on to the terrace were open to catch the evening breeze blowing across the Euphrates. Hangings of fine material were in place to keep out insects. The polished cedarwood tables were arranged in an inverted U. Flouting the convention that diners should not outnumber the nine Muses, places were laid for thirteen. As much a council of war as a social gathering, it was to be an all-male affair. Dining with Ballista were his senior commanders Acilius Glabrio and Turpio, and the three caravan protectors turned Roman officers Iarhai, Anamu and Ogelos. Some less exalted officers were present, the two senior centurions from the two cohorts of Legio IIII, Antoninus Prior and Seleucus, the one from Cohors XX, Felix and Castricius, as deputy *praefectus fabrum*. The numbers were made up with three of the more influential town councillors – the bearded Christian Theodotus, a nondescript little man called Alexander and, most unusually of all, a eunuch called Otes. As poor Mamurra had often pronounced, things were very different in the east.

It was not the food, the drink or the service. Despite months of siege there was a sufficiency of meat, fish and bread. In truth the fruit was limited – just a few fresh apples and some dried plums, and the vegetables were few and far between ('How much for a fucking cabbage?' as Calgacus had been heard eloquently to exclaim) – but there was no danger whatsoever of the wine running out and the guests being reduced to the unhappy expedient of drinking water, and the servants came and went with silent efficiency.

All the way through, from the hard-boiled eggs to the apples, there was a spectre at the feast. Never spoken of but seldom far from mind were the three naked corpses nailed to crosses in the *agora* and the treachery they represented. At dawn Ballista had had the assassins stripped and publicly exhibited. On each cross beneath their feet was nailed a placard offering a large reward to the man who would identify them. The face of one was mutilated, but the wounds on the other two were to the body. They should have been easily recognizable. So far no one except one madman and two time-wasters had come forward. The soldiers had given them a beating for their temerity.

Near the end of the meal, as Ballista broke another loaf of unleavened bread and passed half to Turpio, he knew he could not be alone in thinking that the traitor had to be in the room. Pledging the health of his fellow diners, dipping his bread in the communal bowls had to be the man who had organized the attempt on Ballista's life the previous night, the man who would if he could betray the town to the enemy.

Ballista studied his fellow diners. On his right hand, Acilius Glabrio gave the impression that he would far rather be in other company as he drank deeply of his host's wine. To his left, Turpio gave the impression that he was privately enjoying the follies of mankind in general and those round the table in particular. The three caravan protectors, brought up in the hard school of their mutual loathing, betrayed nothing of their feelings. There was little to learn from the appearance of the town councillors: the Christian Theodotus looked beatific, the eunuch Otes fat, and the one called Alexander virtually anonymous. The four centurions wore suitably respectful expressions. Together the company looked as far from '*those inseparable in death*' as could be imagined – a group of disparate men thrown together by *Tyche*, and one of them a traitor.

Unsurprisingly, the evening had passed slowly, the conversation had flagged. It was not the place of the less important members of the party, the centurions and town councillors, to initiate conversation. The others, to avoid the topic of the crucifixions and everything they entailed, had chewed over again and again the likely course events would take the next day.

No one doubted that the Persians would make another assault in the morning. All day Sassanid noblemen had been seen riding to and fro in their camp haranguing their men. No attempt had been made to conceal the distribution of the siege ladders, the hasty repairs to the mantlets. All agreed, with more or less conviction that, after their terrible losses, the hearts of the Persians would not be in it, that they would not press their attack home: stand firm for just one more day and at last Arete and everyone left alive in the town would finally be safe.

All were agreed that the latest disposition of the defenders' meagre supply of men was the best that could be envisaged. As the nine centuries of Legio IIII on the western wall now averaged only thirty-five men each and the six of Cohors XX just thirty, Ballista had ordered that all the surviving mercenaries of the three caravan protectors be stationed there. They were to be joined by some levy bowmen nominally commanded by Iarhai; given the latter's now customary lack of involvement, they were really in the charge of Haddudad. In addition, Ballista had brought the number of artillery pieces there up to the original number of twenty-five by the expedient of taking them from elsewhere. All this seemed to put the defence of the desert wall on a sound footing. Some 1,300 men, composed of 500 Roman regulars, 500 mercenaries and 300 levies, supported by artillery, would face the Persian attack. Of course this came at a price. The other walls were now held only by conscripted citizens very sparsely supported by a few Roman regulars and an inadequate number of artillery pieces.

Over the cheese course, the silence was broken by the eunuch councillor Otes who, possibly surprised by his own daring, addressed himself directly to Ballista. 'So, you say that, if we stand firm for just one more day, we are safe?' One or two of the army officers failed to suppress a smile at the eunuch's use of the collective 'we stand firm' – they had never seen him on any of the battlements. Ballista ignored the look on his officers' faces. He tried to override the prejudice against eunuchs instilled in him by both his northern childhood and his Roman education. It was not altogether easy. Otes was grossly fat and sweating profusely. The cowardice was evident in his high, sing-song voice.

'Broadly speaking, yes.' Ballista knew it was not true except in the very broadest of terms, but this occasion had been intended to put heart into the men of importance in the town of Arete.

'Unless, of course, our mysterious traitor takes a hand – our very own Ephialtes shows Xerxes the path along the spine of the mountain and outflanks our Thermopylae so we all go down fighting bravely like the 300 Spartans against the countless thousands of the eastern horde.' Acilius Glabrio's reference to the most infamous traitor in Greek history (Ephialtes' notoriety had been immortalized by Herodotus) brought a shocked silence, which the young patrician affected to ignore for a time. He took a drink, then looked up, his face a picture of assumed innocence. 'Oh, I am sorry. I seem to have pointed out that Hannibal is at the gates, that there is an elephant in the corner of the room – to have let the cat clean out of the bag.'

Ballista saw that, while Acilius Glabrio's hair and beard were as elegant as ever, there were unhealthy-looking pouches under his eyes and his clothes were slightly disarrayed. Possibly he was drunk. But before Ballista could intervene, he continued.

'If tomorrow we are to share the fate of the Spartans, possibly we should pass our last night as they did, combing each other's hair, oiling each other's bodies, finding what solace we can.' Acilius Glabrio rolled his eyes at Demetrius as he spoke. The young Greek, standing behind the couch of his *kyrios*, kept his eyes demurely on the ground.

'I would have thought it better, *Tribunus Laticlavius*, if one of the Acilii Glabriones, a family which I understand claim to go back to the founding of the Republic, took examples of antique *Roman* virtue as his model – Horatius, Cincinnatus or Africanus, say – staying up all night doing the rounds, checking the sentries, staying sober.' Ballista had no idea if the Roman heroes that he named had a reputation for shunning sleep for duty, if they cut their wine with plenty of water. He did not care. He could feel his anger rising.

'*Claim* to go back to the founding of the Republic. *Claim!* How dare you! You jumped-up –' Acilius Glabrio's face was flushed, his voice rising.

'*Dominus!*' The voice of the *primus pilus* Antoninus Prior was used to carrying across a *campus martius*. It stopped the commander of his unit in mid-flow. '*Dominus*, it is getting late. We should take the suggestion of the *Dux Ripae*. It is time we checked the sentry posts.' Antoninus ploughed on, giving his superior no time to speak. '*Dux Ripae*, the officers of Legio IIII Scythica thank you for your hospitality. We must go.' As he spoke the centurion had risen to his feet and moved to Acilius Glabrio's side. The other centurion from the legion appeared on his other side. Together Antoninus and Seleucus gently but firmly got their young commander on his feet and propelled him towards the door.

Acilius Glabrio suddenly stopped. He turned and jabbed a finger at Ballista. The nobleman was shaking, all the colour drained from his face. He seemed too angry to speak.

Taking an elbow each, the two centurions got him out of the door with no further words spoken.

The party did not last long after that. Turpio with Felix and Castricius, the centurions under his command, were the next to leave, followed in rapid succession by the caravan protectors and the councillors.

As soon as he had said farewell to the last of his guests, the eunuch Otes – 'Most enjoyable, *Kyrios*, a great success' – Ballista, Demetrius at his heels, retired to his private quarters. Maximus and Calgacus were waiting.

'Did you get the things I asked for?'

'Yes, *Dominus*,' replied Maximus.

'And bloody expensive they were too,' added Calgacus.

On the bed were spread two sets of clothing. Gaudy red, blue, yellow and purple tunics, trousers and caps, striped, hemmed and embroidered in contrasting colours in the local style.

'Let's get on with it.' Ballista and Maximus began to strip off their normal clothes and pull on the eastern garments.

'*Kyrios*, this is madness,' said Demetrius. 'What good can it do?'

Ballista, having removed the two ornaments from his belt, the mural crown and the gilded bird of prey, was looking down, concentrating on attaching a new decoration which spelt out FELIX, good luck. 'There is a danger that junior officers tell their superiors what they think they want to hear: "the men are in good spirits, full of fight." Imagine what the King of Kings is told. I am no Shapur, but it is always more pleasant to bring good news than bad.' Ballista scooped his long hair up under the Syrian cap.

'Please, *Kyrios*, think of the dangers – if not to yourself, then to the rest of us if something should happen.'

Ballista was wondering if he should remove the amber healing stone from the scabbard of his sword. He decided against it. 'Stop worrying, boy. There is no better way of testing the morale of the men. At their posts, unsupervised, they talk intimately of their hopes and fears.' The northerner patted Demetrius on the shoulder. 'It will be fine. I have done this sort of thing before.'

'No one seems all that concerned about me,' said Maximus.

'You are expendable,' said Calgacus.

Ballista hung a combined bow case and quiver over his shoulder, draped a wolfskin around himself and looked at himself in the mirror that Calgacus held out. Then he looked at his bodyguard. 'Maximus, rub some soot on your nose. Apart from that gleaming white cat's arse, no one could recognize us. We look like a couple of the most villainous mercenaries employed by the caravan protectors.'

A quiet word with the guards, then the two men slipped out of the northern door of the palace. They turned left and walked down through the military quarter towards the desert wall. At the *campus martius* they were challenged by a picket of legionaries from the century of Antoninus Posterior stationed there: *Libertas*. They gave the password – *principatus* – and went on their way.

They climbed up to the battlements at the north-west angle of the wall by the temple of Bel. Having been challenged again –

Libertas–Principatus – they stood by the parapet for a time looking out over the ravine to the north and the great plain to the west. In the distance the myriad fires of the Sassanid camp cast a ruddy glow in the sky. A low hum of noise drifted across the desert. A Persian horse neighed and, near at hand, a Roman one answered.

Along the wall torches guttered. From somewhere in the town came the ringing of a hammer as a blacksmith worked late, closing up the rivets of a sword or the sprung rings of a mail coat. Up on the tower above, a sentry called Antiochus talked lengthily and monotonously of his recent divorce: his wife had always been a shrew, vicious tongue on her, and gods below did she talk, worse than being married to your own stepmother.

Ballista leant close to his bodyguard. 'I think that you did enough last night to pay back your debt and claim your freedom.'

'No. It has to be the same. Last night, sure those three may have soon killed you, but I cannot be certain. When you saved me there was no room for doubt; on my back, weapon knocked out of my hand, one more second and I was dead. Certain, it has to be the same.'

'Some religions hold pride to be a terrible sin, I believe.'

'More fool them.'

Ballista and Maximus drifted south along the wall walk. Here and there as they passed in and out of the pools of torchlight, they were challenged by sentries, lean-cheeked men in war-worn tunics: *Libertas–Principatus*, *Libertas–Principatus*.

At the fourth tower they came to the sentries were playing dice. They were legionaries from IIII Scythica. Their oval shields, red with blue victories and a golden lion, were piled near by. Ballista and Maximus stayed in the shadows watching the firelight play on the men's faces, listening to their talk.

'*Canis*,' a player groaned as his four dice landed in the 'dog', the worst throw possible.

'You have always been unlucky.'

'Bollocks. I am saving all my luck for tomorrow, fuck knows we will need it.'

'Bollocks to you. Tomorrow will be a walk in a *paradise*. We have whipped them before and we will whip them again.'

'So you say. There aren't that many of us left. Most of the men on this wall are just fucking civilians playing at soldiers. I tell you, if the reptiles push it home tomorrow, we are fucked.'

'Crap. The big barbarian bastard has got us through so far. He'll see us right again tomorrow. If he says we can hold this wall, are you going to argue with him?'

Ballista grinned at Maximus in the shadows.

'I would rather argue with him than that fucking Hibernian bodyguard of his.'

Maximus's teeth flashed white in the shadows.

'You have got a point. You wouldn't want to meet him in a dark alley. Ugly bastard, isn't he?'

Ballista took Maximus by the arm and led him down the stairs.

By the time they had reached the Palmyrene Gate the night was creeping on and they had heard enough. The regular soldiers seemed solid enough; moaning furiously, their contempt was evenly divided between the enemy and the conscripts on their own side. The much-derided conscripts, especially those new to the desert wall, were either very quiet or boastfully loud – just as was to be expected from those who had not yet looked closely into the face of battle.

Ballista decided to return to the palace. They needed their sleep. Tomorrow was another day.

Demetrius finished dressing. Fussily he retied his writing block and stylus to his belt, getting them to hang just so. He looked at himself in his mirror. Despite the distortion in the polished metal, he could see that he looked awful. There was a network of fine blue veins under his eyes. He felt awful too. For the first half of the night he had remained fully dressed, pacing about. He had told himself that he would be unable to sleep until Ballista and Maximus returned from their foolish theatrical errand. When, some time after midnight, they had returned, in high spirits, laughing, teasing each other, Demetrius had gone to bed. He had still been unable to sleep. Stripped of his concerns for the others, he had had to face his fears for himself.

There was no escape from the thought that in the morning the Persians would come again. Demetrius had not been much reassured by Ballista's performance at the dinner. He knew his *kyrios* well: the big, bluff northerner was not good at lying. There had been a hollowness to his claims that the hearts of the Persians would not be in it. When that fat eunuch had asked if it was true that if they survived tomorrow they would be safe, what was it that Ballista had replied? Something like it being *broadly* true. The *kyrios* was not good at dissembling. But there again, privately, the *kyrios* was a worrier. It was part of what made him such a good soldier, the obsessive care for detail that made him such an excellent siege engineer. But this time surely he was right to be worried. This would be the Persians' last throw. Shapur and his nobles would have whipped their warriors into a lather of fanaticism and hatred. They would want to eat the defenders' hearts raw.

Although he did not want to, Demetrius kept remembering that first Persian assault. The fierce dark bearded men swarming up the ladders, long swords in their hands, murder in their hearts. And tomorrow it would happen again: thousand after thousand easterners over the parapets, laying about them with those terrible swords, cutting down those who stood in their way: an orgy of blood and suffering.

Needless to say, at *gallinicium*, when the cocks start crowing but in peacetime men are still fast asleep, that time well before dawn when the entourage of the *Dux Ripae* had been ordered to assemble, Calgacus had had to wake Demetrius from a troubled sleep, a sleep in which he endlessly chased an aged dream-diviner through the narrow, filthy back alleys of the town. Tantalizingly, the man had remained out of reach, while from behind had come the sounds of the pursuing Sassanids, the screams of men and women, the crackle of burning buildings.

'There is no time to lose,' the old Caledonian had said, not unkindly. 'They are all breakfasting in the great dining room. Everything will be all right. They are feeling good.'

Calgacus was not wrong. As Demetrius entered the dining room, where the lamps still burnt at this early hour, he was greeted with a wave of laughter. Ballista, Maximus, the centurion Castricius, the standard-bearer Pudens, the two remaining messengers, the one remaining scribe and ten of the *equites singulares* were crammed together eating fried eggs and bacon. Ballista called Demetrius over, shook his hand, had Maximus slide along to make him a space. If anything, Ballista and Maximus were in even higher spirits than they had been when they returned the previous night. They were laughing and joking with the other men. Yet Demetrius, the unwanted plate of food in front of him, wedged between the two men from the north, thought that he detected an underlying tension, a fragility to the humour. Maximus was teasing the *Dux* for drinking just water. Ballista said that he wanted to keep a clear head – a state he assured everyone that his bodyguard had never known; tonight he would drink until he sang maudlin songs, told them all he loved them as brothers, and passed out.

Breakfast finished, they trooped into the main courtyard of the palace to arm. They were quieter now; low conversations, short bursts of laughter. One after another men disappeared to the latrines. From the living quarters emerged Calgacus and Bagoas, carrying the parade armour of the *Dux Ripae*, unworn until now.

'If you are going to defeat the Sassanid King of Kings you should look like a real Roman general,' said Calgacus.

Ballista would have preferred his old war-worn mail shirt, but he did not argue. Calgacus always had a desire to send him off well turned out, a desire that Ballista all too often frustrated. He stood, arms outstretched, as Calgacus and Maximus buckled him into the breast and back plates of the muscled cuirass, fitted the ornate shoulder guards and the fringe of heavy leather straps designed to give protection to manhood and thighs. Ballista put on his sword belt then let Calgacus pin a new black cloak over his shoulders. Over the cloak Calgacus draped the wolfskin from the previous night against the chill of the early morning and handed Ballista his helmet. Ballista noted that the wolfskin had been cleaned, the helmet polished.

'If you don't defeat Shapur, sure you will turn up well dressed in Valhalla,' Maximus said in Ballista's native tongue.

'I hope that this is not the end of the long road for us, brother,' Ballista replied in the same language.

They set off from the main gate of the palace, silent now. In the darkness, torches flaring in the chill southerly breeze, they walked down through the military quarter, across the *campus martius* and to the northern end of the desert wall. As they climbed the steps by the temple of Bel to the north-west tower a sentry challenged them: *Isangrim*, the outlandish word correctly pronounced. Ballista gave the Latin response, *Patria*, fatherland or home.

Ballista greeted the men out on the battlements, a mixture of soldiers from Cohors XX and local conscripts, shaking each one by the hand. Then he climbed half up on to the artillery piece. He took off his helmet and his hair streamed away. The leather of his moulded cuirass gleamed in the torchlight. He addressed the men.

'*Commilitiones*, fellow soldiers, the time has come. Today is the final throw.' He paused. He had their full attention. 'The Persians are many. We are few. But their numbers will be nothing but an encumbrance. Our sword arms will have all the room they need.' There were rueful smiles in the torchlight. 'Their numbers do not signify. They are the effeminate slaves of an eastern despot. We are soldiers. We are free men. They fight for their master. We fight for our freedom, our *libertas*. We have whipped them before. We will whip them again.' Some of the soldiers drew their swords and began quietly to rap them against their shields.

'If we win today the noble emperors Valerian and Gallienus will declare this day a day of thanksgiving, a sacred day to be celebrated as long as the eternal city of Rome stands. The noble emperors will open the sacred imperial treasury. They will shower us in gold.' The soldiers laughed as one with Ballista. The elder emperor was not renowned for being open-handed. Ballista waited a moment, then, altering the tone of his voice, went on.

'Today is the last day of our suffering. If we win today we have won our safety with our own swords. If we win today we will have earned our fame, which will be remembered down the centuries. We will be remembered with the men who beat Hannibal at Zama, the men who beat the barbarian hordes of the Cimbri and Teutones on the plains of northern Italy, the men who beat the Asiatic multitudes of Mithridates the Great, humbled his oriental pride, and drove him to exile and a squalid suicide. If we win today we will be remembered from this day to the ending of the world.'

All the men cheered. The din of swords beaten on shields was deafening. The chant rang out: 'Ball-is-ta, Ball-is-ta.' It was picked up and, like a great wave, it rolled down the wall walks and towers of the embattled town.

When they left the tower it was the time of morning that the light of torches first turns a pale yellow then fades to nothing. They walked south the length of the wall. At every tower Ballista made a version of his speech. Always the listeners cheered; sometimes they chanted 'Ball-is-ta, Ball-is-ta'; sometimes they tipped their heads back and howled like wolves. By the time they had walked north again and taken their accustomed places high on the Palmyrene Gate the sun was hot on their backs.

'*Dominus*.' Two troopers of Cohors XX stood to attention. Between them stood a man in Persian dress. 'Marcus Antoninus Danymus and Marcus Antoninus Themarsas of the *turma* of Antiochus, *Dominus*. This here is a deserter. Came up to the north wall last night. Says his name is Khur. Says he can tell you all you want to know about the Persian plan of attack.'

At the sound of his name the Persian showed his teeth like a dog expecting a beating. The man's colourful clothes were grimed in dust. His loose long-sleeved tunic was unbelted. The belt must have been removed when he was searched and disarmed. Under the dirt his face was pale.

Ballista gestured him forward. The Persian came close, then prostrated himself. He bowed his forehead to the floor then got up to his knees, his arms out in supplication.

Demetrius watched the man with distaste as Ballista spoke to him in Persian. Before he replied the Sassanid prostrated himself again, covering his hands with his long sleeves. It was disgusting how these orientals abased themselves.

The man got to his knees again and lunged up at Ballista. The knife shone in the Persian's hand as he thrust it to stab below the northerner's cuirass. Quicker than Demetrius could follow, Ballista stepped forward and inside the blow. Seizing the Persian's arm with both hands, Ballista brought his knee up. There was a loud crack as the arm broke. The man screamed. The trooper called Danymus leapt forward and drove his sword between the shoulder blades of the Persian. The easterner fell forward. In a few seconds he had choked his life out.

'That was unnecessary, soldier,' Ballista said.

'Sorry, *Dominus*. I thought . . .' Danymus's voice trailed away.

'I take it he was searched?'

'Yes, *Dominus*.'

'Who by?'

'I do not know, *Dominus*.'

'Not by you?'

'No, *Dominus*.' Danymus dropped his eyes to where the blade of his sword was dripping blood on the floor. He was sweating heavily. His crestfallen manner was at odds with the jaunty ornaments on his military belt: a sunburst, a flower, a fish, a man carrying a lamb and a swastika. It struck Demetrius that the Persian's killer was the only one present with a drawn blade.

'Very well. Take the corpse away.'

Danymus sheathed his weapon and the two troopers, taking a leg each, dragged the Persian towards the stairs. The man's face scraped along the floor. He left a trail of blood.

'Pick that fucking corpse up. Someone could hurt themselves if they slipped in that blood,' Castricius roared.

Ballista and Maximus looked questioningly at one another. If he had been disarmed when he deserted, someone must have given the Persian the knife. There was no time to investigate that now. They could search for the culprit tomorrow, if they were still alive. Almost imperceptibly, Ballista shrugged and then turned to look up and down the wall.

Unable to take in the sudden eruption of extreme violence followed by the equally abrupt return to something like normality, Demetrius watched as his *kyrios* took off his helmet. As Ballista handed it over, Demetrius realized that his own hands were shaking.

The big northerner smiled a tight smile and said that he ought to show the boys that he was still alive. Demetrius became aware of the oppressive silence on the battlements, the sort of silence that precedes a thunderstorm. He watched Ballista climb up on to the frame of the nearest artillery piece and raise his arms above his head. Turning slowly so that all could see him, he waved. The southerly wind caught his sweat-flattened hair. The polished cuirass gleamed in the sunshine. There was a strange noise like a thousand men exhaling at once. Nearby a voice shouted, '*Flavius, Flavius.*' Along the wall walk soldiers laughed and took up the chant: '*Flavius, Flavius,*' 'Blondie, Blondie.'

'So that is what they really call me,' Ballista said as he climbed down.

'Among other things,' said Maximus.

When Demetrius tried to hand back the helmet, Ballista asked him to put it with the other things until it was needed. The young Greek went and placed the helmet on the carefully folded wolfskin next to the *kyrios*'s shield which, after some consideration, the young Greek had earlier put out of harm's way in the corner of the tower.

From the front parapet, Ballista inspected the defences. The men waited quietly. Above their heads, the banners snapped in the breeze. Two towers to the south, where Turpio was stationed, flew the green *vexillum* of Cohors XX, the unit's name picked out in gold, the image of its patron deity, a proud Palmyrene warrior god, shifting. On the southernmost tower was Iarhai's battle standard, the red scorpion on a white background. Haddudad would be standing there. Ballista wondered if Iarhai himself would be present. Away two towers to the north was the red *vexillum* of the detachment of Legio IIII, on it the personifications of victory in blue, the eagle, the lion and the lettering all gold. The young patrician Acilius Glabrio would have taken his stand under that. Beyond that flew the yellow-on-blue four-petal flower of Anamu. Beyond that again, near the north-west corner of the defences, was the banner of Ogelos, a golden image of the goddess Artemis on a purple background. And, in the centre, above the main gate, the white *draco* of the *Dux Ripae* hissed and snapped. Here and there along the wall the air shimmered where the fires were heating the sand to a crackling, spitting heat.

The city of Arete was as ready as it could be to face this ultimate test. This wall had become the final frontier of the *imperium*, where West met East, where *Romanitas*, even *humanitas* itself faced *Barbaricum*. The irony that four of the six standards that floated over the wall of Arete could in no real sense be described as Roman was not lost on Ballista.

He looked out across the blasted plain at the Sassanid horde. It was the fourth hour of daylight. The easterners had taken a long time getting arrayed for battle. Was this reluctance? Had it proved hard for Shapur, his client kings and nobles to have their men stand once again in the dreadful battle line? Or was it calculation, the desire for everything to be right? Were they merely waiting for the sun to be pulled clear of the eastern horizon, out of their eyes as they gazed on the stark, lonely wall of Arete?

The Sassanids were ready now, a dark line which stretched across the plain. The trumpets and drums fell silent. Thousand upon thousand warriors waited in silence. The wind kicked up dust devils out on the plain. Then the drums thundered, the trumpets shrilled. The sun struck the golden ball which topped the great battle standard of the house of Sasan as it was carried across the front of the army. The Drafsh-i-Kavyan glinted, yellow, red and violet. Thin at first then filling, the chant of 'Mazda, Mazda,' came across the plain. The chant faltered and died, then a new one began, this one stronger: 'Shapur, Shapur.' His white horse kicking up the dust, the purple and white streamers flowing behind him, the King of Kings rode to the front of his army. He dismounted, climbed on to the high raised dais, settled himself on his golden throne and signalled that the battle should begin.

The trumpets struck a different note. The drums hit a different rhythm. A slight hesitation, and the Sassanid army moved forward. The screens were pulled aside and the ten remaining Sassanid artillery pieces spat missiles. Ballista nodded to Pudens, who raised the red flag. The twenty-five *ballistae* of the defenders answered.

This phase of the day held few fears for Ballista. The odds in the artillery duel were heavily stacked in his favour.

As the Sassanid line began its long, long advance, Ballista called for his helmet and shield. Demetrius's fingers fumbled with the chin strap. Ballista leant forward, kissed Demetrius on the cheek, hugged him and whispered in his ear, 'We are all frightened.'

Armed, flanked by Maximus and Castricius, Ballista called the Persian boy Bagoas to his side to help identify the enemy.

When the Sassanid line crossed into extreme range of the defenders' artillery, Ballista nodded again to Pudens, who raised and lowered the red flag twice. The artillery of Arete switched its aim from the eastern artillery to their plodding infantry. Wicked iron-tipped bolts and carefully rounded stones shot away, seeking to pierce or smash the Persian mantlets and kill and maim the men who huddled behind them. As the first missiles struck, the Sassanid line seemed to ripple like a field of wheat when the wind gets up.

By the time the easterners passed the stretch of white-painted wall marking 200 paces from the town wall and came into the effective range of the defenders' artillery, their line had begun to fragment. Gaps had started to open between units. The gaudy banners under which marched the Sakas, Indians and Arabs, the men of King Hamazasp of Georgia and the warriors who followed the Lord Karen were falling behind. They still came on, but more slowly than the men under the banners of the scions of Shapur's family: Prince Sasan the hunter, Prince Valash, the Joy of Shapur, Queen Dinak of Mesene, Ardashir, King of Adiabene. The standard of the Lord Suren was still well to the front. In the forefront on the road which led to the Palmyrene Gate were the Immortals led by Peroz of the Long Sword, and the Jan-avasper, led by the Roman deserter Mariades.

'Shame, shame on those who dawdle,' muttered Bagoas. 'Truly they are *margazan*. They will be tormented in hell for eternity.'

'Quiet, boy,' hissed Maximus.

Ballista was lost in his own thoughts. The mere presence of the two guard units in the first wave of the attack was a double-edged weapon. It showed how furiously Shapur intended the attack to be pressed home. But, on the other hand, it showed that there were no reserves. If the first wave failed, there would not be another. 'So be it,' Ballista said under his breath.

When the leading Persian units were 150 paces from the wall, the red flag was raised and lowered three times and the archers among the defenders bent and released their bows. This time the Sassanids made no attempt to hold their shooting until they were just fifty paces from the town. As soon as Roman arrows struck, the Persians replied. The sky was darkened with their arrows. But Ballista noted with satisfaction that each Persian shot just when the mood took him: there were no disciplined volleys, and much of the shooting was very wild.

The Persian line was becoming ever more fragmented, the gaps between the units bigger. Now the men of the Lord Suren and those of Queen Dinak were falling behind – as were those of Mariades: 'Those who sacrifice themselves' were belying their name. Out in the plain, those who had already fallen behind were nearly stationary. Ballista watched a brightly clad horseman hectoring the Georgians. Bagoas confirmed that it was Hamazasp, their king. He had lost his son at the start of the siege. He had more reason than most to want revenge.

Ballista then saw something he had never seen on any field of battle. A line of men was deployed behind the Georgian warriors. They were wielding whips. A warrior turned to run. He was literally whipped back into position. Ballista looked at the other groups of warriors. Behind every one, even those still in the fore, was a line of men with whips. There was even one behind the Immortals. For the first time that day Ballista felt his confidence soar. He smiled.

Without warning, the warriors of Ardashir King of Adiabene hurled aside their mantlets and surged forward towards the wall. Ballista laughed for joy. This was not a charge born of courage or even bravado but of fear. Goaded and stung beyond endurance, the warriors of Ardashir just wanted to get it over one way or another. Throwing aside order and even their own protection, they ran forward. It was a classic flight to the front.

At an instant, the missiles of the defenders were concentrated on them. Hunched forward, stumbling as they carried their siege ladders, the Sassanids ran into the storm of iron and bronze. Men were falling. Ladders were dropped. More men were falling.

The first three ladders reached the wall. Up they swung, bouncing against the parapet. A simple rustic pitchfork pushed one ladder sideways. It fell, men jumping clear. A bronze cauldron appeared over another ladder and tipped white-hot sand down on those not quick enough to get away. The warriors around the foot of the third ladder looked at each other, then turned and ran.

The panic spread like fire on a Mediterranean hillside in high summer. Where before there had been an army, distinct units of warriors, now the plain was covered by an indiscriminate mass of running men, each with no thought but to save his skin, get away from the missiles which flashed towards him from the grim stone wall. The defenders did not spare them. Without any need for orders, they shot and shot again at the defenceless backs of their fleeing foes.

Along the battlements men laughed and roared. Competing chants broke out: 'Ball-is-ta, Ball-is-ta' – 'Rom-a, Rom-a' – 'Ni-ke, Ni-ke'. Some howled like wolves. The killing went on.

Ballista looked out across the plain. On the golden throne, high on the dais, Shapur sat immobile. Behind the King of Kings the great grey humps of his elephants stood impassive.

When the surviving Sassanids were out of range, all at once, as when a ship goes aground, any discipline vanished. Skins and jars of alcohol appeared as if by magic. Men tipped back their heads, gulping down the wine or local beer.

Maximus passed Ballista a jug of beer. The northerner found that his mouth was full of dust. He rinsed some of the thin, sour beer round and spat over the wall. The liquid landed on a Sassanid corpse. He felt disgusted. He drank some of the beer.

'I wonder how many of the fuckers we have killed – thousands, tens of thousands since they came here.' Castricius had his own jar of wine. Some of it was running down his chin.

Ballista did not know or care about the numbers of enemy dead.

He felt very tired. 'Castricius, I want the sentries doubled tonight.'

The centurion looked taken aback but quickly recovered. 'We will do what is ordered, and at every command we will be ready.' He saluted and, still holding his wine jar, went off to give the necessary orders.

Ballista's progress along the wall was slow. Every man wanted to shake his hand, thump him on the back, praise him. First he walked south. Two towers from the gate under the green banner of Cohors XX he thanked and praised Turpio. The ex-centurion's face carried a look of unalloyed pleasure. He took off his helmet, his hair flattened by sweat. He and Ballista embraced, Turpio's face bristly against that of Ballista. At the southernmost tower Haddudad stood under the red scorpion of Iarhai. The mercenary captain explained that the *Strategos* Iarhai had been indisposed. Ballista said it was no matter when the noble Iarhai had such a captain as Haddudad. The northerner looked round. He could see no sign of Bathshiba. Quite surprisingly, it seemed that she had heeded his orders to avoid the wall and the fighting line. There was a knot of Iarhai's mercenaries in one corner of the tower. Momentarily Ballista wondered if they were concealing her. Then he pushed the idea away.

The walk back to the north was even slower. The copious amounts of alcohol that were being consumed had transformed the defences into the sort of Bacchanalian orgy usually discreetly veiled by secrecy and the darkness of night. Soldiers leant drunkenly on the parapet. They lay in groups on the slope of the internal earth bank. They passed skins and jugs of wine and beer from hand to hand. They roared out jokes and obscenities. The prostitutes were out in force. With no shame one girl was on her hands and knees; her short tunic turned up, she accommodated one soldier from behind, another in her mouth. Another girl was on her back, naked. The soldier who was thrusting vigorously between her legs was raised up on his braced arms to let two of his colleagues get to her face. As they knelt she turned her head from side to side, taking first one then the other in her mouth. Three or four more soldiers stood around drinking, waiting their turn. Ballista noted she was blond, big breasts, very large dark-brown nipples. He felt a sharp stab of lust. Allfather, but he could do with a woman.

Two towers north of the Palmyrene Gate the red *vexillum* of the detachment of Legio IIII flew. When Ballista climbed to the fighting platform on the roof, he found Acilius Glabrio sitting on a stool drinking wine. A good-looking slave boy was holding a parasol over his head. Another was fanning him. He was holding court over his soldiers, talking to them and praising them in the manner of a patrician, affable but always letting them remain aware of a certain distance. The young nobleman made no hurry to rise and greet his superior officer.

'*Dux Ripae*, I give you joy of your victory,' he said when eventually he was on his feet. 'A wondrous result, especially given all the things against you.'

'Thank you, *Tribunus Laticlavius*.' Ballista ignored the ambiguous implications the other had opened up. 'A lion's share of the victory must go to you and your legionaries of Legio IIII Scythica.' The northerner's words brought a cheer from the legionaries present. Acilius Glabrio did not look pleased. He took another long drink of wine.

'Some idiot of a messenger came here. The fool claimed to come from you. I knew it was nonsense. He said you had ordered the sentries doubled tonight. I told him in no uncertain terms that our *Dux* would not have issued such a ridiculous order. I sent him on his way.' Acilius Glabrio took another long drink. He looked flushed.

'I am afraid there has been a misunderstanding' – Ballista tried to keep his voice neutral – 'the messenger was from me. I have ordered the sentries doubled for tonight.'

'But why?' Acilius Glabrio laughed. 'The battle is done and over. We have won. They have lost. It is over.' He looked round for moral support from his legionaries. Some nodded. More avoided his eye. They looked down at the ground, unwilling to be drawn into the escalating tension between these two senior officers.

'Yes, we have won today. But there are huge numbers of Sassanid warriors still out there. Shapur will now be desperate. He will know that we will celebrate hard. It would be an ideal time for him to strike, when we have let our guard down because we think we are safe.' Ballista could hear the anger creeping into his own voice. He was thinking angry thoughts: You may be a good officer, but do not push me too far, you perfumed and crimped little fucker.

'Pshhah.' Acilius Glabrio made a noise of dismissal and gestured with his wine cup. Some of the wine slopped over the edge. 'There is nothing whatsoever to fear. Shapur could never force them to attack again tonight.' Acilius Glabrio was swaying slightly. 'I see no reason to stop my boys having a good time.' He smiled round at his men. A few smiled back. Noticing that he was not receiving unanimous support, the young nobleman scowled.

'*Tribunus Laticlavius*, you will order your men to double the sentries tonight.' No one could now mistake the anger in the big northerner's voice.

'I will not.' Acilius Glabrio glared defiance.

'You are disobeying the direct order of your superior officer.'

'No,' Acilius Glabrio spat, 'I am ignoring the ludicrous whim of a jumped-up hairy barbarian who should have stayed in the squalor of his native hut somewhere in the woods.'

There was a deep silence on the fighting platform. From beyond the tower came the sounds of revelry.

'Acilius Glabrio, you are removed from command. You will disarm yourself. Go to your home and place yourself under house arrest. You will report to the palace of the *Dux Ripae* tomorrow at the fourth hour of daylight to face court-martial.'

Ballista sought out a centurion. 'Seleucus, you will inform the Senior Centurion Antoninus Prior that he is to assume command of the detachment of Legio IIII here in Arete. He is to ensure that enough of his men remain sober to double the sentries tonight. And tell him that I want a blue lantern prepared on every tower. They are to be lit at the first sign of any enemy activity.'

'We will do what is ordered, and at every command we will be ready.' There was no emotion in the centurion's words.

Acilius Glabrio looked round. No one caught his eye. Realizing that what he had said was irrevocable, he raised his chin and assumed a pose of nobility wrongly arraigned. He put down the wine cup, undid his sword belt, pulled the cross belt over his head and let it fall to the floor. Looking neither right nor left, he walked to the stairs. After a moment's indecision his two slave boys scampered after him.

XVII

'Nobody knows what the late evening may have in store,' Bathshiba said. She was laughing. Her eyes were very black.

How the hell did you get in here? Ballista was thinking. Obviously Demetrius was not near by. The young Greek disliked Bathshiba. He would have done all that he could to keep her away from his *kyrios*. But Maximus and Calgacus were definitely in the living quarters, through which she would have had to pass to reach the terrace of the palace. Ballista had no doubts about what had been in their minds when they let her through.

She walked across the terrace towards him. She was dressed as one of her father's mercenaries, but the tunic and trousers, the boots, the sword on her hip, did little to conceal that she was a woman. Ballista found himself watching the movement of her breasts, the roll of her hips. She stopped in front of him, just out of reach. Ballista felt a hollowness in his chest.

'Does your father know you are here?' As he spoke the words sounded ridiculous to Ballista.

Bathshiba laughed. 'He is part of the reason that I am here. But no, he does not know that I am here.'

'You did not cross town alone?' Ballista thought of what he had seen as he walked to the palace. By now, hours later, the whole town would resemble a wild Dionysian orgy. The celebrating soldiers would have no more trouble than Ballista in seeing through

Bathshiba's disguise. Many among them would have fewer qualms than the northerner in stripping that disguise from her. Ballista did not doubt that she could use the sword on her hip, but against a gang it would do her little good. Her resistance, the edge of danger, would only increase their pleasure in taking her.

'No. I'm not a fool. There are two well-armed men waiting in the great courtyard. By now they will be drinking in the guardroom.'

'And is one of them again your father's faithful captain Haddudad with his sharp sword?'

She smiled. 'No, I thought it better to bring others this time. Men whose discretion I think I can trust.'

Ballista stared at her. He could think of nothing to say.

Bathshiba took off her cap. As she shook out her long, tumbling black hair, her breasts swayed, heavy, full, inviting. 'Are you not going to offer a girl who is risking her reputation so much as a drink?'

'I am sorry. Of course. I will get Calgacus to bring some more wine.'

'Is that necessary?' She stepped round Ballista, just out of arm's reach, and picked up his cup from the wall. 'Do you mind?' She lifted the cup to her lips and drank.

'Why are you here?' He knew that his behaviour was awkward, even unwelcoming. He was unsure what he wanted, what he would do.

'As I said, in part because of my father. He did not go to the walls today. He stayed in the house, locked in his private rooms. I think he was praying. He has not been himself for some time. In part I am here to apologize.' She took another drink.

'There is no need. One more man would never have made a difference. He left his men in the hands of Haddudad. He is capable.'

She poured what remained in the jug and handed the cup to Ballista. He took it and drank. She was closer now. He could smell her perfume, her skin. Her long hair curled black round the olive skin of her neck, down over her tunic, over the swell of her breasts. 'Your soldiers know how to celebrate a victory. Do you?' She looked up at him. Her eyes were very black, knowing, full of promise. He said nothing. He did not move. 'Tell me, do you think that Shapur and his nobles would have restrained themselves had they taken the town?'

'I doubt it.' His voice was thick.

'Should the saviour of a town enjoy the same rights as a conqueror?'

Allfather, Ballista thought, if ever a woman has offered herself to me this is it. He was breathing hard. Her scent was strong in his nostrils. He could feel himself starting to get an erection. He wanted her. He wanted to rip the neck of that tunic, to expose her breasts. He wanted to pull down those trousers, lift her up on to the low wall, spread her legs and enter her. He wanted to take her there and then, her bottom on the wall, him standing in front of her, thrusting into her.

He did not move. Something stopped him. The fierce, smothering morality of his northern upbringing, the thought of his wife, the superstition that had grown in him about infidelity and battle – he did not know what, but something stopped him. He did not move.

Bathshiba stepped back offended. Her eyes were hard and angry. 'You fool. You may know how to defend a town, but I doubt that you could take one.' She swept up her cap, turned and walked furiously back across the terrace.

For a time after Bathshiba left Ballista stood by the wall. His desire slipped away and he was left with a feeling of frustration and an ill-defined sense of foreboding. The cup was still in his hand. He finished the wine.

At length he walked back into the palace. He called for Maximus. The Hibernian came clattering down the stairs from the flat roof.

'What were you doing up there?'

'I do not know to be sure. Certain, I was not spying on you. As always these days, fuck all to see there. I was just looking around. Sure, I cannot put my finger on it, but something is not right.'

'For once I know what you mean. Fetch a cloak. Tell Calgacus we are going out. We will walk the defences.'

The orders of the *Dux Ripae* had been obeyed to the letter. All along the wall walks and at every tower were twice the usual number of sentries. Blue warning lanterns hung ready on every tower. Looking mulish, the sentries paced slowly or leant against the parapets feeling resentful at their enforced sobriety and envious of their fellow soldiers' celebrations. From within the town came the noise of the celebrations: bursts of laughter, indecipherable shouts, girls' squeals, the sounds of running feet and cups being smashed – the distinctive cacophany of Roman soldiers baying for alcohol and women.

The sentries saluted Ballista and Maximus as they walked south along the desert wall. 'We will do what is ordered, and at every command we will be ready.' There was unhappy resignation, sometimes bordering on insubordination, in their voices. Ballista shook their hands, praised their *disciplina*, promised them three days' leave and a carefully unspecified sum of money as a donative. It did not seem to do an iota of good.

To the west the great dark plain stretched away. Beyond it were the lights of the Persian camp. There were men awake there. Lights flickered as they passed in front of the torches or fires. Yet it was strangely quiet. There was none of the keening mourning, the plaintive music and high-pitched wailing Ballista had expected. The silence of the Sassanids was unnerving. It added to Ballista's feeling of foreboding.

In the depth of the night Ballista and Maximus returned to the palace. They had a cup of warmed wine and Ballista retired to his sleeping quarters. He stripped off his clothes and lay down in the big, very empty bed. After a few moments' regret, he fell asleep.

It was well after midnight, maybe towards the end of the third watch, when Ballista heard the noise. Instinctively, his hand closed on the pommel of his sword. He knew it was pointless: somehow he knew what he would see. Ballista forced himself to look. There by the door was the big man, the great pale face under the deep hood of the shabby dark-red *caracallus*. The big man walked forward. He stood by the foot of the bed. The light of the oil lamp glittered on the thick golden torque and the eagle carved in the gem set in the heavy gold ring.

'Speak,' said Ballista.

'I will see you again at Aquileia.' The great grey eyes shone with malice and contempt.

'I will see you then.'

The big man laughed, a horrible grating sound. He turned and left the room.

The smell of the wax that waterproofed the hooded cloak lingered.

Ballista was sweating heavily. He threw back the covers, got out of bed and opened the window to let in the fresh night air. Naked, he stood by the window, letting the sweat dry on his skin. Outside, he saw the Pleiades low on the horizon.

It would all fall out as the Allfather willed.

Ballista went to the washbowl, splashed cold water on his face, towelled himself dry and got back into bed. After what seemed an eternity he fell into a deep sleep.

'Wake up! Wake up!'

Ballista struggled to the surface.

'Wake up, you lazy little shit.'

Ballista opened his eyes. Calgacus was standing by the bed shaking his shoulder.

'What?' Ballista felt drugged, stupid with sleep. Calgacus's sour, thin mouth was more pinched than ever.

'The Sassanids are in the town.'

Ballista swung himself out of bed. Calgacus talked as he handed the northerner his clothes and he dressed.

'I relieved Maximus up on the roof. I saw a blue warning lantern on one of the towers on the south wall. It shone for a moment, then went out. Pudens is raising the alarm. Castricius is turning out the guard. Maximus is saddling the horses. Demetrius and Bagoas are taking your armour down to the stables.'

'Which tower?'

'The one nearest the desert wall.'

Dressed, Ballista picked up his sword belt. 'Then we should go.'

The stables, when they reached them, were in a state of just controlled chaos. Grooms ran here and there carrying saddles, bridles and other bits of tack. The horses shook their heads, stamped their feet and called out in indignation or excitement at being woken at this unusual hour. In one of the further stalls a horse was misbehaving, rearing up and plunging against its headstall. Calgacus went off to find what had become of Demetrius and Bagoas.

Ballista stood still, a point of calm in the eye of the storm. He breathed in the familiar homely smell of the stables, the evocative mixture of horse, leather, saddle soap, liniment and hay. He was struck by the timelessness of the scene. Stables would always be much the same; the needs of horses did not change. Give or take the odd marble manger or bit of fine wood panelling, stables were the same in the *imperium* as anywhere else. They were the same in his homeland as they were in Sassanid Persia. Horses were not much affected by the culture of the men who rode them.

In the golden glow of the lamps Ballista saw Maximus making his way down the line of horses. The air was thick with dust raised from the straw by the boots of men and horses' hooves.

'I have saddled Pale Horse for you,' Maximus said.

'Thank you.' Ballista thought for a few moments. 'Thank you, but leave him in his stall – leave him saddled. I will ride the big bay gelding.'

Maximus did not question the order but went off to carry it out.

Calgacus appeared, chivvying along Demetrius and Bagoas, who were carrying Ballista's war gear. Ballista was pleased to see that they had not brought the fancy Roman parade armour of earlier that day but his old war-worn mail shirt. Asking just Calgacus to attend him, Ballista stepped into an unoccupied stall. As the aged Caledonian helped him into his armour Ballista spoke, his voice low so no one else could hear.

'Calgacus, old friend, I have a very bad feeling about this. When we are gone I want you to collect our essentials, saddle all the remaining horses, pack supplies on three of them: skins of water, army biscuit, dried meat. Wait here in the stables with Demetrius and the Persian boy. Have your sword drawn. Do not let anyone touch the horses. I will leave five of the *equites singulares* here in the palace. I will tell them to take their orders from you. Post one at each of the three gates, one on the terrace and one on the roof.'

Outside in the narrow alley between the palace and the granaries, Ballista rapped out orders. He organized his little mounted column and told his staff, the house slaves and the five guardsmen who were staying behind to do as Calgacus instructed. The latter received the command with a marked lack of enthusiasm.

Ballista squeezed the big bay gelding with his thighs and set off, around the small temple of Jupiter Dolichenus and down the wide road that led to the *campus martius*. The small column rode at a loose canter in single file. They kept well closed up. After Ballista came Maximus, Castricius, Pudens and the five *equites singulares*.

Trumpet calls echoed through the town. In the distance men were shouting. There were the sounds of crashing and banging. Yet the military quarter was strangely deserted. A few soldiers were running, some staggering, but not nearly the proper number were heading to their posts. In some doorways soldiers lay unconscious through drink. As he clattered past the military baths Ballista saw one soldier lying on the steps dead to the world, a half-naked girl next to him, one of her pale white legs across his. A large wine jar stood next to them.

Emerging on to the *campus martius*, Ballista saw Antoninus Posterior standing in the centre of the broad open space. The centurion was bareheaded, his helmet in his hand. He was shouting at his men. There were but ten of them. One or two appeared none too steady on their feet. Ballista rode over.

'We will do what is ordered, and at every command we will be ready.' The irony in speaking the ritual phrase on behalf of his reduced company did not appear to have struck the centurion.

'Is this it, Antoninus?'

'Afraid so, *Dominus*. I have sent five others off to try and rouse more of the boys.'

'It is as the gods will. As soon as you have a few more, I want you to lead them down to the tower on the south wall that is nearest the desert wall.'

'We will do what is ordered, and at every command we will be ready.'

Ballista started to turn his horse.

'*Dux*, wait.' Out of the darkness from the north came Acilius Glabrio. The young patrician was riding a fine horse and wearing gilded armour. There was a sword on his hip. Ballista felt a jet of pure anger rising in himself, but before he could speak, demand to know how the young bastard dare break his house arrest, dare disobey another command and arm himself, Acilius Glabrio slid from his mount. The horse was well trained; it stood stock still. Acilius Glabrio walked up to Ballista, then knelt in the dust, arms up in the gesture of supplication.

'*Dux Ripae*, I have disobeyed your commands. But I would not have you think that I am a coward. If the Sassanids are within the defences you will need every man. I ask your permission to accompany you as a private soldier.'

Ballista did not like and did not trust the perfumed aristocrat at his feet, but he had never doubted that the loathsome young man was a fine soldier. 'Get on your horse and come with us.'

Ballista wheeled his mount and set off south. There was no gate in the wall that separated the *campus martius* from the civilian part of the town, so they had to backtrack. After three blocks they struck the main street which ran across town from the Palmyrene Gate to the Porta Aquaria. There were more people here, soldiers and civilians, but too many of the latter and not enough of the former. Ballista turned right and reined in outside the great caravanserai. Throwing his leg over the gelding's neck, he jumped down and ran inside. In the light of guttering torches, the scene was much the same as on the *campus martius*. In the middle of the courtyard, bareheaded and exasperated, was Antoninus Prior. The centurion, since the disgrace of Acilius Glabrio the temporary commander of all the legionaries in Arete, was yelling at his men. Again there were only about ten of them. Again several looked the worse for wear. Ballista snapped out the same orders as before and ran back to his horse.

This was all taking time. No one knew what was happening.

There was as yet no sound of fighting. But all this was taking time.

They rode towards the Palmyrene Gate for a block then left down the street that would bring them out near the tower where Calgacus had seen the blue warning lantern. There was a great deal of noise but still nothing that spoke unambiguously of fighting. It could be a false alarm. But Calgacus was not given to fancies. In all the years he had known him, Ballista had never seen the Caledonian give way to panic. The lantern could have been lit by mistake. Allfather, let that be the case. But if it was, why had no messenger come from the tower to explain and offer profuse apologies? Ballista kicked on, pushing his horse into something near a gallop.

Apart from a drunken soldier who stepped out into their path then went reeling back, they reached the end of the street without incident. Ballista held up his right hand and reined in. The tower was about fifty yards away, just off to their right, across open ground.

The tower was in darkness. Ballista thought he could see men up on the fighting platform. He sat, playing with the horse's ears, thinking. A bend in the wall prevented him seeing the next tower to his left but, to his right, all looked normal on the southernmost tower on the desert wall. Torches burnt there, unlike on the tower in front of him.

He indicated that they should move forward. Walking their horses on to the open ground, they fanned out into line. Maximus was on Ballista's right, Pudens on his left. It seemed very quiet, the background noises very far away. The only sounds that Ballista could hear close to were the hooves of their horses on the hard-packed ground, the hiss of the breeze blowing through the jaws of the *draco* above his head and his own harsh breathing.

Halfway across the open space Ballista called a halt. The horses stood in line, shifting their feet. It was very quiet. The inner wall of the tower was about twenty paces away. The door was shut. Ballista sucked air into his lungs to hail the tower.

He heard the twang of the bows' release, the wisp, wisp sound of the fletchings in the air. He caught just a glimpse of the arrow. He jerked his head to the left and took a jarring blow as the arrow ricocheted off the right shoulder of his mail coat, sparks flying. The bay gelding reared up. Already off balance, Ballista was thrown. He lost his shield as he landed heavily. He rolled to get clear of the gelding's stamping hooves. The next horse was plunging, its hooves cracking down on the hard ground inches away. Ballista curled into a tight ball, his arms up covering his head.

A strong grip under his armpit hauled him to his feet. 'Run,' said Maximus. Ballista ran.

They ran towards the desert wall, arrows skittering off the ground around them. They veered right to put a fallen horse, its legs flailing, between them and the bowmen on the tower. Head down Ballista ran.

They reached the earth bank inside the desert wall. Running, scrambling on hands and knees, they reached the top. His back against the wall, Ballista crouched in the angle where the southern and desert walls met. Maximus covered both of them with his shield but no one was shooting at them now. Ballista looked around him. Acilius Glabrio and two of the *equites singulares* were still with him. There was no sign of Castricius, Pudens or the other guardsmen. He looked back the way they had come. A column of Sassanid warriors was pouring across the open ground. They seemed to erupt from the very ground beneath the wall on the near side of the tower.

'Fuck, there was another mine,' said Maximus.

Ballista raised himself up and peered over the wall. Outside in the starlight a long column of Persian warriors snaked up the side of the southern ravine. Lights flared on the Sassanid-held tower. Torches were waved to signal. In the sudden light Ballista saw a familiar figure on top of the tower. 'No, they are coming up through the Christian tombs cut in the wall of the ravine,' he said.

Bald head catching the torchlight, bushy beard thrust out, Theodotus, councillor of Arete and Christian priest, stood motionless on the tower amid the mayhem.

'Never did trust the fuckers,' said one of the guardsmen.

The Persian column was streaming north into the town, up the street that, moments before, Ballista and his party had ridden down.

There was a commotion on the wall walk to the north. Ballista drew his sword and, with the others, turned to the left to face the new threat. '*Roma, Roma*': the newcomers shouted the night's password. Turpio and half a dozen troopers of Cohors XX ran into view. '*Salus, Salus*,' Ballista and his group shouted back.

'More bad news,' said Turpio. 'Another group of Christians has overpowered the sentries on the Palmyrene Gate. They are letting down ropes for the Sassanids to climb. There are not enough sober men on the wall walks to dislodge them.' Turpio smiled. 'Who would have thought they had it in them?' His manner suggested that he was merely making a light, throwaway comment on the social foibles of a group; who would have thought that they of all people would be so devoted to the baths or the circus? Nothing about him betrayed the fact that he had just announced the death sentence for the town of Arete and almost certainly for most of his listeners.

Everyone was looking at Ballista. He ignored them, withdrawing into himself. His eyes, unseeing, gazed out over the dark ravine. They were trapped in the south-west corner of the town. Calgacus and the horses were waiting in the palace in the north-east of the town. The direct route, the streets just below them, were filling with Sassanid warriors. If they went north along the desert wall they would run into the Persians coming in over the Palmyrene Gate. The route along the southern wall walk was blocked by the enemy on the tower where Theodotus stood. Whichever way Ballista chose, they would have to cut their way out. He thought of Bathshiba. She should be in her father's house. Iarhai's mansion lay near the Porta Aquaria in the south-east corner of the town. Ballista made up his mind.

'There.' Ballista pointed at the glinting bald pate of Theodotus up on the tower to the east. 'There is the traitor. We will have our revenge.' In the near-darkness there was a low growl of approval from the men. 'Form up quietly, boys.'

The wall walk was wide enough for four men abreast. Ballista took the position on the right, next to the parapet. Maximus fell in beside him, Acilius Glabrio beyond him, Turpio next. Ballista ordered Turpio to the rear. It would be senseless to commit all the senior officers to the front rank. A trooper from Cohors XX, unknown to Ballista, took the place vacated by Turpio. Ballista looked round at the tiny phalanx. It contained just twelve men all told: four wide and three ranks deep. Maximus told one of the troopers in the rear to hand his shield to the *Dux*. The man reluctantly complied.

'All ready?' Ballista asked. 'Then let us go – quietly: we may yet give them a surprise.'

They set off at a jog along the wall walk. The tower was not above fifty paces away. There was a group of a dozen or so Persians by the open door which led from the wall walk to the interior of the tower. They were looking into the town, pointing and laughing. The Roman phalanx was almost on them before they realized. The Persians may not have been expecting a counterattack, but they stood up to it.

Ballista accelerated over the last few paces into an all-out run. The Sassanid facing him raised his long sword to bring it down on Ballista's head. Ballista ducked down and, with all his momentum behind it, smashed his shield into the man's body. The Sassanid went flying backwards. He crashed into the warrior behind him. Both fell back on to the wall walk. As the first Persian tried to get to his feet, momentarily his left leg was not covered by his shield. Ballista brought his sword down, cutting savagely into the man's knee. The Sassanid howled. All thought of defending himself overcome by the pain, he clutched his shattered kneecap. Ballista drove the point of his sword into the man's crotch. He was of no further account.

The second Sassanid had got to his feet. Ballista jumped at him over the man whimpering on the floor. The Sassanid brought his sword down in a fierce cut. Ballista took it on his shield; splinters flew from it. Quick as a flash, from Ballista's left, Maximus's short sword thrust into the Persian's armpit. The man crumpled and fell against the parapet.

With about half their number down, the Persians turned and fled.

'After them,' bellowed Ballista. 'Do not let them shut the door.'

The Roman soldiers burst into the tower on the heels of the fleeing Sassanids. The pursued hurled themselves down the stairs to find safety in the numbers pouring into the town from the Christian necropolis. Ballista went for the stairs up to the roof. He took them two at a time.

As Ballista emerged on to the fighting platform, he saw two Persians with torches, their backs to him. They were signalling to those outside still ascending the ravine. A backhand cut to the head dealt with the one on Ballista's right. A forehand cut caught the other at the left elbow as he turned. He looked bemused, at the blood fountaining out of the stump of his arm until Ballista drove the point of his sword into his mouth. For a second the blade snagged. Then Ballista pulled it free, fragments of teeth and blood coming away with it.

'Come!' A voice like thunder echoed round the tower. 'And I saw, and behold, a pale horse, and its rider's name was death, and Hades followed him.'

Theodotus was pointing at Ballista. Between the two men was a line of men fighting. Ballista could clearly see the tall Christian priest over the crouched, ducking figures of the combatants. Theodotus's face was shining. He was shouting, his voice carrying over the clash of weapons.

'The sixth angel poured his bowl on the great river Euphrates and its water was dried up, to prepare the way for the kings from the east.'

The words made no sense to Ballista.

'Why, Theodotus? Why betray your townsmen?'

Theodotus laughed, his great bushy beard bobbing. 'The number of the troops of cavalry was twice ten thousand times ten thousand; I heard their number . . . the riders wore breastplates the colour of fire and of sapphire and of sulphur.'

'You fool,' Ballista yelled. 'They will kill us all. They will not spare the Christians. They will not spare anyone.'

'I saw a beast,' Theodotus continued to rant, 'with ten horns and seven heads, with ten diadems upon its horns and a blasphemous name upon its heads . . . let him who has understanding reckon the number of the beast, for it is a human number, its number is six hundred and sixty-six.'

'Why?' Ballista roared. 'Why let the Sassanids massacre the people of this town? For pity's sake, man, why?'

Theodotus stopped chanting. He looked keenly at Ballista. 'These Sassanids are reptiles. I do not do it for them. They are no better than you. They are merely God's instrument. I do it for pity – pity for the sins of the people. The Sassanids are the punishment that God has ordained in his infinite mercy for the sins of the people of Arete. Christians and pagans, we are all sinners.'

Outnumbered, the Sassanids on the fighting platform were falling. A trooper broke through their line and made for Theodotus.

'If anyone worships the beast . . . he shall be tormented with fire and brimstone in the presence of the holy angels and in the presence of the lamb.'

The trooper swung his sword, catching Theodotus on the leg. The Christian staggered.

'Blessed are the dead who die in the Lord.'

The trooper swung again. Theodotus fell to his hands and knees.

'Salvation . . .'

The trooper despatched him in drill-book style: one, two, three heavy cuts to the back of the head.

Persian resistance on the fighting platform had ended. Ballista numbered his remaining men: Maximus, Turpio, Acilius Glabrio, two *equites singulares*, three troopers of Cohors XX; nine men including himself.

'Are there any wounded who cannot run?'

There was a pause. Turpio came forward. 'They have been . . . dealt with.' Ballista nodded.

'This is what we will do. The Persians are coming up under the wall. They are going straight on into the town. There are no Persians on the wall.' Ballista had no idea if this last were true. He found that he was pacing, crackling with energy. 'We will head east along the wall towards the river. When it is safe we will come down from the wall. We will make our way to the house of Iarhai.

There we should find . . . should gather some more men. We will make our way up through the eastern part of the town to the palace.'

Ballista saw the blank looks. 'There are horses waiting for us there.' The men nodded. Ballista knew they had no idea what he intended they would do if they made it that far and got mounted, but any plan seemed good to the men now, at least it gave them something to work towards, provided a tiny glimmer of hope.

With Ballista in the lead again they clattered down the stairs and out of the eastern door. As they exited, there was a shout and a volley of arrows. Just behind Ballista men screamed. He ducked his helmet down to meet his shield and ran. An unlucky arrow in the leg here and it was all over.

In a short time the incoming arrows stopped. The shouts of the Sassanids fell away behind them. It was a long run to the next tower. Ballista's lungs were burning. All around him he could hear laboured breathing.

The door to the next tower was open. Ballista hurled himself inside, ready to fight. The tower was deserted. He plunged on through it and out the other side.

The next tower was not far. Again it had been abandoned by its defenders. This time Ballista led them down the stairs and to the ground-floor door into the town. Just inside the door he stopped to let them catch their breath. He looked round. Just two men were missing.

Ballista peeked around. The alley by the wall was empty. He led them out and, turning right, they ran on in the direction of the river.

By the time they crossed the open area where the soldier had been hit by the arrow intended for the traitor – *Theodotus, you bastard* – there were people about, soldiers and civilians heading the same way as Ballista and his men, down towards the Porta Aquaria and the river.

After a time Ballista turned north into the street that brought him to the mansion of Iarhai.

The main gate of the house stood open. There were six mercenaries there, their weapons drawn. They looked anxious. Ballista pulled up by them. Bent over, hands on his knees, sucking air into his lungs, it took him some time to speak.

'Iarhai . . . where is he?'

A mercenary jerked his head. 'Inside.' He spat. 'Praying.'

As Ballista stepped inside Bathshiba ran straight into his arms. He held on to her. He felt her breasts against him. We are all about to die, he thought, and I am still thinking about fucking her. A man remains a man.

'Where is your father?'

She took him by the hand and led him to the caravan protector's private quarters.

In a sparsely furnished white room Iarhai was kneeling on a rug praying.

'You bastard. You knew, didn't you?' Ballista's voice was savage. 'Answer me.'

Iarhai looked at him.

'Answer me.'

'No.' A muscle twitched in Iarhai's broken cheekbone. 'Yes, I have become a Christian. I am sickened by life, sickened by killing. Theodotus offered me redemption. But no, I had no idea he would do this.'

Ballista tried to rein in his anger. He believed Iarhai. 'I will give you a chance of redemption, in this life if not the next.' Iarhai regarded Ballista incuriously. 'If I can help it, I do not intend to die in this fly-blown dump of a town. I have horses waiting saddled in the palace. If I can reach there, I have a plan which may work. I will take your daughter with me. But we will never reach the palace unless someone holds up the Sassanids.'

'It will be as God wills,' Iarhai said in a flat monotone.

'Get up and arm yourself, you gutless bastard,' Ballista shouted.

'Thou shalt not kill,' intoned Iarhai. 'Never again will I take the life of another man.'

'If there is one thing in this world that you love it is your daughter. Will you not stir yourself even to try to save her?'

'It will be as God wills.'

Ballista looked around in fury. Bathshiba was standing near. Without warning, he grabbed her by the hair and pulled her to him. She shrieked in surprise and pain. Ballista held her in front of him, his left hand in a strong grip around her throat.

Iarhai half rose. Automatically his hand went to his left hip, seeking the sword that was not there.

'Will you let her fall into the hands of the Sassanids?' Ballista spoke quietly. 'You know what they will do to her.' Iarhai said nothing. 'They will rape her. One after another they will rape her. Ten, twenty, thirty men, a hundred. They will mutilate her. She will beg them to kill her long before they do.'

There was a look of agonized indecision on Iarhai's face.

'Is this what you want?' With his right hand, Ballista gripped the neck of Bathshiba's tunic. With a savage yank he ripped it down. Bathshiba's breasts spilt free. She screamed and tried to cover her dark-brown nipples with the palms of her hands.

'You bastard.' Iarhai was on his feet, a look of indescribable pain on his face.

'Arm yourself. You are coming with us.' Ballista let Bathshiba go. She ran from the room. Iarhai went to a chest in the corner. From it he took his sword belt and buckled it on. Ballista turned and left.

At the gate there were just the six men who had arrived with Ballista.

'The mercenaries have run,' said Maximus.

In a few minutes Iarhai appeared from the depths of the house with Bathshiba. She was wearing a new tunic. She did not look at Ballista.

'Time to go.'

At a steady jog they set off north towards the palace. There was a nightmare quality to the journey. None too far in the distance they could hear screams. Already there was a smell of burning in the air. At every street junction they had to fight their way across the streams of panic-stricken people running east to the Porta Aquaria and the river. Ballista knew that there would be scenes of almost unimaginable horror down on the riverbank at the jetties, where thousands of terrified individuals would be fighting for a place on one of the very few boats. Children separated from their mothers, trampled underfoot: it did not bear thinking about. Ballista put his head down and ran north.

They had just passed the temple of Zeus Theos, were within a block of the open ground on the other side of which was the palace, when they heard the pursuit.

'There he is. Ten pounds of gold for the man who takes the King of Kings the head of the big barbarian.' For a second Ballista thought he recognized the voice of the Persian officer he had tricked that dark night in the ravine, but he realized it was only his own tired thoughts tricking him.

The Sassanids were still a hundred paces away, but there were a lot of them and they looked fresh. Ballista and those with him were exhausted.

'Go on,' said Iarhai. 'The street is narrow. I can delay them.'

Ballista looked at Bathshiba. He expected her to scream, to cling to her father and plead with him. She did not. She looked at her father for a time, then turned and ran.

'You will not delay them alone. I will stay.' Acilius Glabrio turned to Ballista. 'You do not care for patricians. But I will show you how one of the Acilii Glabriones dies. Like Horatius, I will hold the bridge.'

Ballista nodded and, with Maximus, ran after the others.

Soon there was the sound of fighting. When he had passed the artillery magazine Ballista stopped and drew breath. There was only fifty yards to go to the palace. He looked back. The end of the street was full of Persians. He could not see Iarhai. The caravan protector had not had time to put on his armour. He could not have lasted long. But there was Acilius Glabrio, a small figure in the distance ringed by the enemy. Ballista ran on.

'You took your time.' Calgacus was beaming.

Ballista smiled weakly. He was too tired to answer. He leant against the stable wall. Compared with earlier, the stables were deserted. Ballista roused himself to ask the guardsman where the other *equites singulares* were. The man looked embarrassed.

'We . . . they . . . ah, they thought that you were not coming back. There is only Titus outside and me.'

'There were a few moments when they were nearly right.' Ballista ran his hands over his face. 'What is your name?'

'Felix, *Dominus*.'

'Then let's hope that your name is an omen.' Ballista asked Calgacus about the slaves attached to the palace and was told they had all vanished. He shut his eyes and breathed in the reassuring smells of the stables. His chest hurt. All the muscles in his legs were jumpy with fatigue. His right shoulder was raw where his sword belt had made his mail coat rub. He was tempted just to lie down in the straw. Surely he would be safe, surrounded by these homely smells, surely the Sassanids would not find him here? He just needed to sleep.

The northerner's childish fantasy was shattered by the arrival of Maximus.

'We are ready to go. Everyone is outside and mounted except us.' The Hibernian threw across a water skin. Ballista tried and failed to catch it one-handed. He juggled it with two hands until he had it secure. He unstoppered it, tipped some water into a cupped palm and washed his face, rinsing his weary eyes. He drank.

'Time to go then.'

Outside, the moon was up, nearly full. The narrow alley between the palace and the granaries was bathed in its light. Ballista tried to remember if this was the harvest or hunter's moon at home. He was too tired to remember. He walked to the mounting block. Demetrius led up Pale Horse. Ballista mounted painfully.

In the saddle he felt a little better. He looked up and down the alley at the horses and riders. Apart from himself there were fourteen riders: Maximus, Calgacus, Demetrius, Bagoas, Turpio, the two remaining members of his official staff – a scribe and a messenger, the two *equites singulares* Titus and Felix, and another four soldiers who had crossed the town with him – three troopers from Cohors XX and another guardsman. And there was Bathshiba. There were three horses loaded with supplies.

'What shall we do about the other six saddled horses in the stables?' Calgacus asked.

Ballista knew that he should order them killed or hamstrung in case they aided the pursuit. 'Cut the girths and bridles.' Calgacus swung off his horse, disappeared into the stables and was back in a few moments. When the Caledonian had remounted, Ballista gave the signal to move out.

For the second time that night Ballista led a column of riders around the temple of Jupiter Dolichenus. They came out on to the broad road heading to the *campus martius* and Ballista pushed Pale Horse into a gallop. In case he should fall, he had hurriedly told Maximus, Calgacus and Turpio his plan, such as it was. They had not looked thrilled. He had not told the others. There was no point in scaring them even more.

The military quarter through which they thundered was empty. The Romans had fled; the Persians had not yet arrived. Smoke blew across the road from the south. As he flashed by the military baths Ballista noticed that the comatose soldier had gone from the steps. So had the girl. Good luck to you, brother, he thought, and to your girl.

The cavalcade careered down the street, the sound of thundering hooves echoing back off the walls.

From a street off to the left came the sound of fighting. Ballista glimpsed one of the mercenaries backed up against the wall of the amphitheatre, his sword flashing in the torchlight as he tried to keep at bay a howling mob of Sassanid warriors. In a moment the sight and sound were cut off by the building on the next corner.

'Haddudad!' Bathshiba shouted. She reined in her horse savagely. Those following her had to swerve or pull up quickly to avoid her.

'Leave him,' Ballista shouted, 'there is no time.'

'No. We must save him.' Bathshiba turned her horse and, kicking her heels in, set off back towards the corner.

'Bugger,' muttered Ballista. As he turned Pale Horse he called to Turpio to carry on with the others, Maximus to come with him. He set off after Bathshiba. What was it with her? She had left her father to certain death with no more than a significant look, but now she was risking her life for one of his mercenaries. Was it guilt at leaving her father that was making her do this? Was it something about Haddudad? Ballista felt a stab of jealousy.

Pale Horse skidded around the corner; Maximus's mount was just a neck behind. Haddudad was still upright. There were a couple of easterners prone at his feet. The press around the mercenary had slackened off with the arrival of Bathshiba. As Ballista watched she cut down a Persian on her near side. But then the mob closed. Two men grabbed her reins. Another seized her right boot and pulled her from the saddle. A loud cheer went up.

All the Persians' attention was on the girl or the mercenary. They were completely oblivious to the approach of the two horsemen. Ballista held his sword out straight along the neck of his horse, his arm rigid. The Persian jerked his head round just before the impact. It was far too late. The sword punched through the mail coat and on between the shoulder blades. The shock pushed Ballista back in his saddle. He let his arm swing through, down then up straight out behind him as the easterner fell away, the man's own weight freeing the blade.

Ballista was out of the other side of the knot of Persian warriors. Maximus was next to him. They wheeled their horses. Kicking in their heels, they drove forward again. Out of the corner of his eye, Ballista saw Haddudad launch a fierce attack on the two Sassanids still facing him.

A Persian aimed a cut at Pale Horse's head. Ballista blocked it with his shield, then brought his sword across and down in a bone-crunching blow to the top of the man's domed iron helmet; sparks flew, a loud crack, and the blade bit down into the skull.

Again Ballista was through the mob, Maximus as ever at his side. The remaining Persians were running. There were several on the ground. Among them was Bathshiba, motionless.

Haddudad ran forward. He cradled the girl's head.

'It is all right. She is coming round.' He helped her to her feet. Her legs seemed unstable. Maximus trotted up, leading Bathshiba's horse. Haddudad helped her into the saddle. Then, with a lithe jump and complete familiarity, the mercenary jumped up behind her.

'Time to go,' said Ballista, damping down his irritation.

The horses clattered back the way they had come.

Ballista and Pale Horse plunged through the inky black shadow between the *principia* and the barracks and emerged on to the moon-washed emptiness of the *campus martius*. This time there was no chance that the figure of Acilius Glabrio would appear. Ballista pointed Pale Horse towards the temple of Bel and the north wall.

He reined in as he reached the northern postern gate. It stood open. Turpio and one of the guardsmen were climbing back into the saddle. They must have had to dismount to open the gate. Most likely its sentries had left it shut when they fled. Ballista wondered where the sentries had gone. They may have taken flight on foot east along the ledge outside the wall. They would be trying to climb down the cliff near the river, hoping to find a boat – although maybe, just maybe, they had had the same idea as himself. Without horses it could not work. Without horses they would have no chance of escape.

Ballista briskly ordered that the supplies be cut from one of the packhorses. Haddudad jumped down from behind Bathshiba and mounted in their place. Grabbing one of the smaller bags of discarded provisions, Ballista asked Bathshiba if she was all right. She simply said yes.

'Time to go again.'

Ballista walked Pale Horse through the gate and turned right. The rest followed. The ledge was wide enough for two horses abreast, but the threat of the sheer drop to their left kept them in single file. He walked his horse until he reached the big landslip he had first spotted all those months ago on the day of the lion hunt. He signalled a halt and turned to face the others. He pointed down.

Ballista had half-expected a collective gasp, a flurry of protest. None came. He looked down the great ramp formed by the landslip. It started about three foot below the ledge then pulled away at a hideously steep angle, forty-five degrees or worse. In the strong moonlight the soil looked loose and treacherous. Here and there a wicked rock stuck up. It seemed to stretch away for ever.

Ballista looked back at the others. They were very quiet. No one moved. Under their helmets, the soldiers' eyes were pools of black shadow. Ballista well understood their hesitancy. A rider edged forward. It was Bathshiba. Her horse stopped at the lip. Without a word she kicked her heels and the horse jumped forward. Ballista watched it land. Fighting to keep its balance, its quarters almost on the flat on the ground, it began to scrabble and slip downwards.

Ballista forced himself to look away. He nudged Pale Horse next to the mount of Demetrius. He took the reins from the boy's hands and led the horse to the edge. He looped the reins over one of the horns of the boy's saddle. He leant close and quietly told him to forget the reins, just lean back and cling to the saddle. The boy was bareheaded. He looked terrified. *Hold tight*. Ballista drew his sword. The boy flinched. The sword glittered as it swung in an arc through the air. Ballista brought the flat of the blade down hard across the rump of the boy's horse. It leapt forward into space.

'So are you afraid to follow where a girl and a Greek secretary dare go?' Ballista called for the leading rein of one of the packhorses. He led it to the edge. He looked down at the vertiginous drop. Allfather, to think that on the afternoon of the lion hunt I thought I would like to do this for fun. He kicked hard with his heels.

As Pale Horse dropped, Ballista was lifted up, almost out of the saddle. As the gelding's hooves found the ramp, Ballista crashed back into the saddle, the impact jarring up through his spine. The lead rein went taut, snapping his right arm back, wrenching his shoulder, the leather slipping through his fingers, burning. The packhorse followed and the pressure went.

Ballista leant as far back as he could, bracing his back against the rear horns of the saddle, wedging his thighs up under the front ones. The ramp dropped in front of him. Jagged, sharp rocks poked up. The floor of the ravine looked infinitely far away. He wondered whether to shut his eyes, remembered how the awful reality had flooded in when he had opened them again in the siege tunnel and fixed his gaze on Pale Horse's mane.

Down and down they plunged. Down and down. Then it was over. Pale Horse was gathering his legs under him, and they were running on the flat of the bed of the ravine.

Ballista circled the two horses round to where Demetrius and Bathshiba were waiting. Maximus thundered past, whooping like a madman. One after another, Calgacus, Bagoas, the messenger and the scribe arrived at the bottom. Then disaster struck.

Halfway down the ramp the mount of one of the soldiers – it was impossible to tell which – lost its footing. The horse tipped forward; its rider was half thrown. The horse landed on him. Together, in an avalanche of stones and earth, they rolled down. The following rider was almost on top of them. At the last moment the bloodied, broken tangle of horse and man toppled to their fate over the far edge of the ramp. The way was clear again.

All the rest made it to the bottom. Turpio came last, leading one of the packhorses. Brave man, thought Ballista. The more horses that had made the descent the more the surface of the ramp had been cut up, the more unstable it had become.

Ballista chivvied them into line. Felix was missing. His name had not proved prophetic. The horse of one of the other soldiers was lame. Ballista jumped down to inspect its leg. It was the near fore. It was far too lame to run. Ballista cut the baggage from one of the two remaining packhorses and told the trooper to mount. He turned the lame horse free. It stood looking disconsolate.

Waving for the others to follow, Ballista pointed Pale Horse up the ravine away from the river. At the head of the line he kept them to a steady canter.

They had not gone far when they heard the shouts. Far up above them to the left, torches flared. A trumpet shrilled. Mounted Sassanid warriors were moving along the ledge, following in their tracks. Ballista felt absurdly depressed. Somehow he had hoped to be able to sneak away unnoticed like thieves in the night. Allfather, he prayed, Deep Hood, High One, Fulfiller of Desire, let their horses refuse the dreadful drop, let the courage of their riders fail them. He had little hope that the prayer would be answered. He moved to hoping that their own horses had so dislodged the surface of the ramp that it would give way and betray the Persians to share the bloody fate of Felix.

As the sounds of the pursuing enemy swelled, Ballista mastered the urge to kick his mount into a gallop. He could feel the thoughts of all those behind him willing him to increase the pace. He ignored them. It would not do. He remembered the rough going from his chase of the onager. He forced himself to keep Pale Horse at a steady canter, letting the gelding pick his own way.

Soon the bend of the ravine hid them from their pursuers. The heat of the previous day still hung heavy in the depths. Ballista rode through clouds of gnats. They got in his eyes and mouth.

Ballista approached the fork in the ravine. Before steering Pale Horse into the narrow turning to the right-hand passage, he looked behind. Bathshiba and Calgacus were close. He could not see Maximus. He had not heard a horse fall. There had been no commotion. He was surprised but not unduly worried. He cantered on. The path was beginning to rise more sharply.

Maximus had enjoyed the descent of the ramp. He prided himself on having known from the start what Ballista intended. As soon as they had seen the landslip on the day they killed the lion, Maximus had known that one day they would try to ride down it. Admittedly, he had not thought it would be in the dead of night fleeing the sack of the town. But that just added spice to the adventure.

When he heard the sounds of pursuit Maximus twisted in his saddle and looked back down the column. Everything seemed fine. But he noticed Bagoas pull his horse to the side and let others begin to pass him. Maximus did the same. Gradually he dropped back down the column. By the time they entered the right-hand fork of the ravine, there were just three riders behind Maximus. When the passage opened up again, he pulled his horse against the rock wall and waved the guardsman Titus and Turpio past.

Maximus sat still. There was no sign of the Persian boy. Maximus wheeled his horse and, drawing his sword, set off back the way that he had come. So that is your game, you treacherous little bastard. Sit at the fork and direct them after us. Well, you will be in Hades before that happens, you little fucker. He kicked on, stones rattling out from under the hooves of his horse.

Sure enough, there at the fork Bagoas sat motionless on his horse. Maximus pushed his mount faster. The Persian boy saw

Maximus coming, saw the blade in his hand. He threw up his hands, palms forward.

'No, please no. Please do not kill me.'

Without a word Maximus came on.

'No, please, you do not understand. I am not going to betray you. I am trying to save you. I will point them down the wrong turning.'

Maximus reined in savagely, his horse almost back on its hocks. He reached across and grabbed the boy's long hair. He half pulled him out of the saddle. The Hibernian's sword flashed and found the boy's throat. The tip of the blade just broke the skin. A trickle of blood, very black in the moonlight, ran down the gleaming steel.

'And why should I believe you?' Bagoas looked into Maximus's pale-blue, terribly blank eyes. He could not speak. The noise of the pursuit echoed up the ravine. With the sounds bouncing off the rock walls, it was impossible to tell how far away the pursuers were. 'Come on, we haven't got all night.'

Bagoas swallowed hard. 'Ballista and you are not the only men who have honour. You saved my life when the legionaries attacked me. Now I will repay that debt.'

For a long, long time neither spoke. The sword remained at Bagoas's throat. The staring blue eyes gave nothing away. The sounds of the pursuit were getting louder.

The sword was gone. Maximus was carefully wiping it on a rag at his belt. He sheathed it. He smiled. 'Until the next time, boy.' Maximus spun his horse round and kicked on back the way that he had come, up the right-hand branch of the ravine after the others.

High on the hills, Ballista sat on Pale Horse and looked down at the burning city. The south wind was picking up. It pulled long streamers of fire into the night sky. Now and then dense clouds of sparks like an erupting volcano rose up as a building collapsed. The dying city was at least a mile and a half away. No sounds reached Ballista. He was glad of that.

All our efforts and it has come to this, he thought. Is it my fault? Did I concentrate so much on the Sassanid siege works that I did not pay enough attention to the possibility of treachery? If I had thought properly about the Christians, would clues have been there; would I have seen them?

Another large building fell and a whirl of sparks rose up. The undersides of the racing clouds were tinged pink. An ugly, unwanted thought rose like a big pike with a mouth full of sharp teeth to the surface of Ballista's mind: this was meant to happen. This is why I was sent, not Bonitus or Celsus. This is why I was given no additional troops. This is why the kings of Emesa and Palmyra felt able to refuse my requests for troops. There never was any hope of relief. The emperors already knew that the two field armies would be needed elsewhere this campaigning season; that one would go to the Danube with Gallienus to face the Carpi, and one with Valerian to deal with the Goths in Asia Minor. Arete was always expected to fall. The town, its garrison, its commander were expendable. We were to be sacrificed to buy time.

Ballista found that he was laughing. In a sense he had succeeded. The city had fallen, but he had bought the Roman *imperium* some time. At the cost of so much suffering, of so many lives, so many thousands of lives, he had bought the Roman *imperium* some time. The emperors should welcome him like a returning hero. Of course, that would not happen. They had wanted a dead hero, not a living witness to their heartless betrayal of the city of Arete. They had wanted their expendable barbarian *Dux Ripae* dead sword in hand in the smoke-blackened ruins of the town, not staggering back into the imperial court reeking of failure and treachery. Ballista would be an embarrassment. He would be blamed, made the scapegoat, his reputation left in tatters.

One day, he vowed, this *imperium* will regret all the things it has done.

The city was still burning. Ballista had seen all he wanted to see.

Turning in the saddle, Ballista looked back down the line. All those he cared about were there: Calgacus, Maximus, Demetrius. And there was Bathshiba. Other thoughts came into his mind – the hooded figure of the big man, Mamurra entombed in the dark beneath the walls. He pushed them away. He looked back beyond the column. There was no sign of any pursuit. He gave the signal to move on.

At the rear of the line the last remaining *frumentarius* looked at the burning city of Arete. He wondered what report he would write to the emperors about all this. He took a last look at the fire in the east and kicked his horse to follow the others. He sneezed. And he wondered how this new journey would end.

Appendix

Historical Afterword

Fire in the East is a novel, but I have taken care over the historical background. The following notes aim both to show where history has been 'played with' to fit the fiction and to provide further reading for those who would like to try to create their own interpretation of the reality.

When I told my colleague Bert Smith, the Lincoln Professor of Classical Archaeology and Art at the University of Oxford, that I was writing a series of novels set in the second half of the third century AD, he congratulated me on picking a period about which so little is known for sure that no one could prove me wrong.

'The Third-Century Crisis'

The period between the murder of the emperor Alexander Severus (AD235) and the accession of Diocletian (AD284) is traditionally known as 'the third-century crisis' of the Roman empire. It is a time for which we have very few and poor ancient literary sources. Undoubtedly it was a time of relative instability both in high-level politics (too many emperors in too few years) and in military operations (increases in the numbers of civil wars and in barbarian victories over Rome: for the first time, Roman emperors were killed and captured in battle by barbarian armies). Yet scholarly estimates vary widely on how far beyond this the crisis spread. At one extreme, G. Alföldy, 'The Crisis of the Third Century as Seen by

Contemporaries' (*Greek, Roman and Byzantine Studies* 15 (1974), 89–111), holds that the empire suffered a 'total crisis' in all areas of life; social, economic and ideological, as well as political and military. At the other, H. Sidebottom, 'Herodian's Historical Methods and Understanding of History' (*Aufstieg und Niedergang der Römischen Welt* II.34.4 (1998), 2775–2836), argues that, outside the political and military, the 'crisis' is largely an illusion created by various modern preconceptions playing upon the paucity of our ancient sources.

The standard modern attempt at a narrative of the years AD235–84 is that of J. Drinkwater in *The Cambridge Ancient History* (eds. P. Garnsey and A. Cameron, vol. XII, 2nd edn, Cambridge, 2005, 28–66). More accessible (i.e., in paperback) is D. S. Potter, *The Roman Empire at Bay AD180–395* (London and New York, 2004, 167–72; 217–80).

For the history behind this novel, M. H. Dodgeon, and N. C. Lieu, *The Roman Eastern Frontier and the Persian Wars AD226–363: A Documentary History* (London, 1991) is an extremely useful collection of sources translated into English with commentaries.

An indispensable tool for all research into the classical world is *The Oxford Classical Dictionary* (3rd edn, Oxford, 1996, eds. S. Hornblower and A. Spawforth).

People

Ballista

There was a Roman officer called Ballista (or Callistus) active in the east in this period. Ironically, the very brief ancient biography of him which survives is itself largely a work of fiction (*Scriptores Historiae Augustae* [now more commonly referred to as the *Historia Augusta* or *Augustan History*], *Tyranni Triginta 18*). What little we think we may know about him features in the third novel in this series, *Lion of the Sun*. For reasons that will emerge later I have given him the *praenomen* and *nomen* Marcus Clodius. It is extremely unlikely that the historical Ballista was an Anglo-Saxon nobleman. However, in the fourth century AD many German warriors rose to high command in the Roman army. The Ballista of these novels should be seen as a forerunner of this historical phenomenon.

Places

Delos

An enjoyable way to learn about the island of Delos, and much else in classical culture, is the magnificently illustrated, but very hard to find, volume by P. J. Hadjidakis, *Delos* (Athens, 2003). A very short, offbeat introduction to the island can be found in J. Davidson, *One Mykonos* (London, 1999). In this novel I have made the island flourish rather more after the sack of 69BC than archaeology suggests was the case.

Paphos

F. G. Maier and V. Karageorghis, *Paphos: History and Archaeology* (Nicosia, 1984), with a wealth of pictures, plans and an accessible text, is the standard work. The 'House of Theseus' is illustrated and discussed in W. A. Daszewski and D. Michaelides, *Guide to the Paphos Mosaics* (Nicosia, 1988, 52–63).

Antioch

Discussion and reading for this city will be given in *King of Kings*.

Emesa

The modern city of Homs has obliterated virtually all archaeological traces of the classical city of Emesa. The first century AD funeral monument of Caius Julius Sampsigeramus, almost certainly a member of the ruling dynasty, was pulled down to make way for the railway station. Modern certainties about the site of the great temple seem misplaced. As so often, the best way into the archaeology and its literature is the now somewhat elderly *Princeton Encyclopedia of Classical Sites* (eds. R. Stillwell et al., Princeton, 1976), *see under* Emesa [Homs].

The description of the temple of Elagabalus draws on images on coins. Some of these are nicely reproduced in R. Turcan, *Héliogabale et le Sacre du Soleil* (Paris, 1985, *see* esp. plates 1–7), although my interpretations are slightly different.

For the rituals, the main inspiration (somewhat altered) is book five of Herodian's *History* (translated by C. R. Whittaker in two volumes in the Loeb series (Harvard, 1969/1970).

Fergus Millar, *The Roman Near East 31BC–AD337* (Cambridge, Mass. and London, 1993, 302–4), has doubted that the elite Emesene family which produced the Roman emperors Caracalla, Geta, Elagabalus and Alexander Severus in the third century AD was descended from the royal house of Emesa of the first century AD. However, it should be noted that some of the former carried close variants of the names of the latter (Sohaemias/Sohaemus; Alexianos/Alexio); above all, both families had the *nomen* Iulius. It suggests that at the very least the third-century family wished to be seen as the descendants of the old royal house. Similarly, the pretender Uranius Antoninus carried the name Iulius and, like Elagabalus, was a priest of the god of Emesa. So again, *pace* Millar (308–9), it is likely that either he was or wished to be thought of as a member of the same family. The priest-king Sampsigeramus of this novel is a fictional member of this family.

Palmyra

A popular (but not always totally accurate) introduction to this great caravan city is R. Stoneman, *Palmyra and Its Empire: Zenobia's Revolt against Rome* (Ann Arbor, 1994). The best place to discover the unusual world of the caravan-protecting leading men of the city is J. F. Matthews, 'The Tax Law of Palmyra: Evidence for Economic History in a City of the Roman East' (*Journal of Roman Studies* 74 [1984], 157–80). Further reading will be given in *Lion of the Sun*.

Arete (Dura-Europos)

The town of Arete is of course modelled on the town of Dura-Europos on the Euphrates, which was besieged by the Sassanid Persians probably in AD256. (Actually, Dura was one ancient name for the town, used by locals, Europos another, used by its original settlers; the combination is modern). For the benefit of the plot I have played around with the topography of Dura and the siege works, mainly simplifying them, and have imported the political/social structure of neighbouring Palmyra. A good introduction to the place is an account of its excavation by one of the directors of the dig, C. Hopkins, *The Discovery of Dura-Europos* (New Haven and London, 1979). The essential study of all military aspects of the town is now S. James, *Excavations at Dura-Europos 1929–1937. Final Report VII: The Arms and Armour and Other Military Equipment* (London, 2004), which is both wider ranging and more interesting than its title suggests. For the atmosphere of the place, it is still well worth looking at the boxed set of pictures published by F. Cumont, *Fouilles de Doura-Europos (1922–1923), Atlas* (Paris, 1926). Possibly the most accessible introduction to Dura-Europos in the Roman period currently available in English is in N. Pollard, *Soldiers, Cities and Civilians in Roman Syria* (Ann Arbor, 2000).

The speeches made by Callinicus and Ballista on the arrival of the new *Dux* at Arete are drawn from the roughly contemporary treatise on rhetoric ascribed to Menander Rhetor, specifically the section on making a speech of arrival (translation by D. A. Russell and N. G. Wilson, Oxford, 1981, 95–115).

Warfare

Naval

H. Sidebottom, *Ancient Warfare: A Very Short Introduction* (Oxford, 2004, 95–9; 147), provides an introduction to ancient Mediterranean naval war. R. Gardiner and J. Morrison (eds.), *The Age of the Galley: Mediterranean Oared Vessels since Pre-Classical Times* (London, 1995) is a superbly illustrated guide. Any idea of what it was like to sail a *trireme* must be based on the sea trials of the reconstructed Athenian *trireme* the *Olympias*: J. S. Morrison, J. E. Coates and N. B. Rankov, *The Athenian Trireme: The History and Reconstruction of an Ancient Greek Warship* (Cambridge, 2000, esp. 231–75). Yet, for very understandable reasons, the *Olympias* never goes out in a storm (it is no part of the project to see how quickly and nastily a crew of some two hundred can drown!). However, Tim Severin's far less scientific reconstruction of a galley was caught in a gale: T. Severin, *The Jason Voyage: The Quest for the Golden Fleece* (London, 1985, 175–82).

Siege

A brief overview of siege warfare in the classical period is given in H. Sidebottom, *Ancient Warfare: A Very Short Introduction* (Oxford, 2004, 92–4; 146). Other scholarly introductions are P. B. Kern, *Ancient Siege Warfare* (Bloomington, Indiana, and London, 1999), which covers from earliest times to AD70; C. M. Gilliver, *The Roman Art of War* (Stroud, 1999, 63–88; 127–60), which looks at Roman siege warfare down to the fourth century AD; and P. Southern and K. R. Dixon, *The Late Roman Army* (London, 1996, 127–67), which considers the late empire to the sixth century AD. A nicely illustrated popular introduction is D. B. Campbell, *Besieged: Siege Warfare in the Ancient World* (Oxford, 2006).

Sassanid Persians

Introductions to the history of the Sassanid (or Sasanid, or Sassanian, or Sasanian) dynasty can be found in E. Yarshater (ed.), *The Cambridge History of Iran, volume 3 (1): The Seleucid, Parthian and Sasanian Periods* (Cambridge, 1983, 116–77), R. N. Frye, *The History of Ancient Iran* (München, 1984, 287–339); and P. Garnsey and A. Cameron (eds.), *The Cambridge Ancient History*, vol. XII (2nd edn 2005, 461–80, by R. N. Frye).

For an overview of the military practices of the Sassanids, see Michael Whitby, 'The Persian King at War', in E. Dabrowa (ed.), *The Roman and Byzantine Army in the East* (Cracow, 1994), 227–63. D. Nicolle, *Sassanian Armies: The Iranian Empire: Early 3rd to Mid-7th Centuries AD* (Stockport, 1996) is a splendidly illustrated guide designed for a non-specialized readership. Some of Nicolle's attributions of images are corrected by St. J. Simpson in a review in *Antiquity* 71 (1997, 242–5).

Religions

Classical Paganism

Two well-written and enjoyable ways into Roman paganism are R. MacMullen, *Paganism in the Roman Empire* (New Haven and London, 1981) and R. Lane Fox, *Pagans and Christians* (Harmondsworth, 1986, 7–261).

Norse

We have no literary sources to tell us the religious views of an Anglo-Saxon nobleman in the mid-third century AD, so I have drawn material from earlier – Tacitus's *Germania*, written in AD98 – and later – using both *Beowulf*, composed some time between c. AD680 and 800, and the even later Norse Sagas. For the latter two my guides have been Kevin Crossley-Holland's wonderful books *The Anglo-Saxon World* (Woodbridge, 1982) and *The Penguin Book of Norse Myths: Gods of the Vikings* (London, 1993). M. P. Speidel's provocative *Ancient Germanic Warriors: Warrior Styles from Trajan's Column to Icelandic Sagas* (London and New York, 2004) suggests that such a 'long view' has some scholarly credibility.

Christianity

As with paganism, the two most enjoyable works that I know to begin the study of early Christianity are written by Ramsay MacMullen (*Christianizing the Roman Empire (AD100–400)*, New Haven, 1984) and Robin Lane Fox (*Pagans and Christians*, Harmondsworth, 1986, 7–231; 263–681).

Zoroastrianism

A very brief introduction to Zoroastrianism under the Sassanids is given by R. N. Frye in *The Cambridge Ancient History* (eds. P. Garnsey and A. Cameron, vol. XII 2nd edn, Cambridge, 2005, 474–9). A rather more detailed introduction is J. Duchesne-Guillemin, 'Zoroastrian Religion', in E. Yarshater (ed.), *The Cambridge History of Iran: volume 3(2): The Seleucid, Parthian and Sasanian Periods* (Cambridge, 1983, 866–908).

While Zoroastrianism seems to have been rather more tolerant under Shapur I than is suggested here, the alert reader will have noted that the main characters' impressions of the religion are totally derived from the views of just one Persian, Bagoas, and Ballista comes to suspect that Bagoas is something of a fanatic.

The Roman Day

Based on profound knowledge of the classical sources, J. P. V. D. Balsdon, *Life and Leisure in Ancient Rome* (London, 1969, 17–81), is a superb guide to the ways the Romans thought about time and passed their days. There is no better introduction to Roman social life in general.

Linguistic Problems

Unlike English, Greek and Latin were inflected languages (i.e. the endings of words changed with their case or tense). After some thought and discussion I decided that to mirror this in this novel (e.g. *Dominus* changing to *Domine*, *Dominum*, etc., depending on its role in a sentence) would be a scholarly affectation which would irritate many English-speaking readers. The only exception to this is the plural (thus a siege engine, a *ballista*, becomes *ballistae* when there is more than one).

Previous Historical Novels

Any historical novelist who claims to have used only contemporary sources and modern scholarship is lying. All historical novelists read other historical novelists. In each novel in this series it is a joy to include homages to a few of those novelists whose work has greatly influenced me and given me a lot of pleasure.

The late Mary Renault should need no introduction. Bagoas is named after the hero of her novel *The Persian Boy* (London, 1972).

Mystifyingly, Cecelia Holland seems little read on this side of the Atlantic. Maximus's original name, Muirtagh of the Long Road, is a combination of two of her heroes, Muirtagh from *The Kings in Winter* (London, 1967) and Laeghaire of the Long Road from *The Firedrake* (London, 1965)..

Various Quotes

The Anglo-Saxon poetry from his youth that comes into the mind of Ballista, of course, is *Beowulf*. The translation used here is that of Kevin Crossley-Holland, *The Anglo-Saxon World* (Woodbridge, 1982, 139).

The 'Persian poems' sung by Bagoas are (gloriously anachronistic) quatrains from Edward FitzGerald, *The Rubaiyat of Omar Khayyam* (1st edn, 1859).

When Acilius Glabrio and Demetrius quote sections of Ovid, *The Art of Love*, the translation is that of Peter Green in the Penguin Classics *Ovid: The Erotic Poems* (Harmondsworth, 1982).

The translation of the *Iliad* of Homer is that of Robert Fagles in the Penguin Classics (New York, 1990).

Thanks

As with all first novels, the list of people whom I have to thank is long. First, my family. My wife, Lisa, for looking after our sons, Tom and Jack, and keeping some normalcy and contemporary fun in our lives when I have been living so much in an imaginary version of the third century AD. My mother, Frances, and my aunt, Terry, for their wonderful faith in the idea and for taking on the roles of tireless unpaid publicity agents. Then, colleagues and friends: Maria Stamatopoulou at Lincoln College, Oxford, and John Eidinow at Greyfriars Hall and St Benets Hall, Oxford, for helping me find the time away from teaching to write the novel. All my students at Oxford – especially Vicky Buckley, Ed Maclennan and Mohan Rao, who managed to take excellent degrees, despite their tutorials often turning into extended discussions of historical fiction. Simon Swain of the University of Warwick for checking the Historical Afterword and the Glossary for any really awful mistakes. Anne Marie Drummond, Senior Tutor at Lincoln College, Oxford, and Michael Farley of Woodstock Marketing, for providing me with two ideal refuges in which to write the thing. All my friends in Woodstock for their encouragement – especially Jeremy Tinton. Last, but crucial, Jim Gill, my agent at United Agents, and Alex Clarke, my editor at Penguin – I could not hope to have a better team around me.

Harry Sidebottom
Woodstock

Glossary

The definitions given here are geared to *Fire in the East*. If a word has several meanings only that or those relevant to this novel tend to be given.

Accensus: The secretary of a Roman governor or official.

Adventus: An arrival; the formal ceremony of welcome of a Roman emperor or high official.

Agger: Latin term for a siege ramp.

Agora: Greek term for a marketplace and civic centre.

Agrimensores: Roman land surveyors.

Ahriman: In Zoroastrianism, the evil one, a demon, the lie, the devil.

Alamanni: A confederation of German tribes.

Angles: A north German tribe, living in the area of modern Denmark.

Antoninianus, plural *antoniniani*: A Roman silver coin.

Apodyterium: Changing room of a Roman bath.

Archon: A magistrate in a Greek city; in the fictional city of Arete the annual chief magistrate.

Auxiliary: A Roman regular soldier serving in a unit other than a legion.

Bahram fires: The sacred fires of Zoroastrian religion.

Ballista, plural *ballistae*: A torsion-powered artillery piece; some shot bolts, others stones.

Ballistarius, plural *ballistarii*: A Roman artilleryman.

Barbalissos: A town on the Euphrates, scene of a defeat of the Roman army in Syria by Shapur I, probably in AD252.

Barbaricum: Latin term for where the barbarians live, i.e., outside the Roman empire; in some ways seen as the opposite of the world of *humanitas*, civilization.

Barritus: German war-cry, adopted by the Roman army.

Borani: A German tribe, one of the tribes that made up the confederation of the Goths, notorious for their piratical raids into the Aegean.

Boukolos: A Greek official supervising the entry and exit into a town of herds of animals.

Boule: The council of a Greek city, in the Roman period made up of the local men of wealth and influence.

Bouleuterion: The council house in a Greek city.

Bucinator: A Roman military musician.

Caestus: Roman boxing glove, sometimes with metal spikes.

Caldarium: The hot room of a Roman bath.

Caledonia: Modern Scotland.

Campus martius: Literally Field of Mars, a Roman parade ground.

Cantabrian circle: A Roman cavalry manœuvre.

Caracallus: A northern hooded cloak.

Carpi: A barbarian tribe on the Danube.

Centuriation: Roman system of marking out land in squares or rectangles.

Clibanarius, plural *clibanarii*: heavily armed cavalryman; possibly derived from 'baking oven'.

Cingulum: A Roman military belt, one of the symbols that marked out a soldier.

Coele Syria: Literally 'Hollow Syria', a Roman province.

Cohors: A unit of Roman soldiers, usually about 500 men strong.

Cohors XX Palmyrenorum Milliaria Equitata: A double-strength Roman auxiliary unit, consisting of about 1,000 men, part mounted, part infantry; historically part of the garrison of Dura-Europos; in *Fire in the East* part of the garrison of the city of Arete.

Commilitiones: Latin term for '*fellow soldiers*', often used by commanders wishing to emphasize their closeness to their troops.

Concordia: Latin term of harmony, concord; in *Fire in the East* the name of a Roman warship.

Conditum: Spiced wine, sometimes served warm before dinner.

Consilium: A council, or body of advisors, of a Roman emperor, official or elite private person.

Conticinium: The still time of the day, when the cocks have stopped crowing but men are usually still asleep.

Contubernium: A group of ten soldiers who share a tent; by extension 'comradeship'.

Curule: A chair adorned with ivory, the 'throne' that was one of the symbols of high Roman office.

Cursus publicus: The imperial Roman posting service, whereby those with official passes, *diplomata*, would be given remounts.

Denarius: A Roman silver coin.

Dignitas: Important Roman concept which covers our idea of dignity but goes much further; famously, Julius Caesar claimed that his *dignitas* meant more to him than life itself.

Diplomata: Official passes which allowed the bearer access to the *cursus publicus*.

Disciplina: Discipline; Romans considered that they had this quality and others lacked it.

Dominus: Lord, Master, Sir; a title of respect (Latin).

Draco: Literally a snake or dragon; name given to a windsock-style military standard shaped like a dragon.

Dracontarius: A Roman standard-bearer who carried a *draco*.

Drafsh-i-Kavyan: The battle standard of the Sassanid royal house.

Dromedarii: Roman soldiers mounted on camels.

Dux Ripae: The Commander, or Duke, of the Riverbanks; a Roman military officer in charge of the defences along the Euphrates river in the third century AD; historically based at Dura-Europos, in this novel based at Arete.

Elagabalus: Patron god of the town of Emesa in Syria, a sun god, also name often given to one of his priests who became the Roman emperor formally known as Marcus Aurelius Antoninus (AD218–222).

Epotis: The 'ear timber' of a *trireme* projecting out from the side of the vessel just behind the ram.

Equestrian: The second rank down in the Roman social pyramid, the elite order just below the Senators.

Equites singulares: Cavalry bodyguards; in Rome one of the permanent units protecting the emperors; in the provinces ad hoc units set up by military commanders.

Eupatrids: From the Greek, meaning the 'well-born', aristocrats.

Exactor: The accountant in a Roman military unit.

Familia: Latin term for family, and by extension the entire household including slaves.

Franks: A confederation of German tribes.

Frigidarium: Cold room of a Roman bath.

Frumentarius, plural *frumentarii*: They were a military unit based on the Caelian Hill in Rome; the emperors' secret police; messengers, spies and assassins.

Germania: The lands where the German tribes lived.

Gladius: A Roman military short sword; generally superseded by the *spatha* by the mid-third century AD; also slang for 'penis'.

Goths: A confederation of Germanic tribes.

Harii: A German tribe, renowned night fighters.

Haruspex, plural *haruspices*: A priest who divines the will of the gods; one would be part of the official staff of a Roman governor.

Hibernia: Modern Ireland.

Hyperboreans: Legendary race of men who lived in the far north, beyond the north wind.

Hypozomata: A rope forming the undergirdle of a trireme; there were usually two of them.

Ides: the thirteenth day of the month in short months, the fifteenth in long months.

Immortals: A Sassanid guard unit of (possibly) 1,000 men.

Imperium: The power to issue orders and exact obedience; official military command.

Imperium romanum: The power of the Romans, i.e., the Roman empire.

Jan-avasper: Those who sacrifice themselves, a Sassanid guard unit.

Kalends: The first day of the month.

Kyrios: Lord, Master, Sir; a title of respect (Greek).

Lanista: A trainer of gladiators.

Legio IIII Scythica: A Roman legion from the second half of the first century AD based at Zeugma in Syria; in *Fire in the East* a detachment, *vexillatio*, of this legion forms part of the garrison of the city of Arete.

Legion: A unit of heavy infantry, usually about 5,000 men strong; from mythical times the backbone of the Roman army; the numbers in a legion and the legion's dominance in the army declined during the third century AD as more and more detachments, *vexillationes*, served away from the parent unit and became more or less independent units.

Libertas: Latin for liberty or freedom, its meaning was contingent on when it was said and who by.

Librarius: The bookkeeper or scribe of a Roman military unit.

Liburnian: A name given in the time of the Roman empire to a small warship, possibly rowed by about fifty men on two levels.

Limes imperii: Latin for the limits of empire, the borders of the Roman *imperium*.

Magi: Name given by Greeks and Romans to Persian priests, often thought of as sorcerers.

Mandata: Instructions issued by the emperors to their governors and officials.

Margazan: Persian term for one who commits a sin, like cowardice in battle, and deserves death.

Mazda: (Also Ahuramazda) 'The Wise Lord', the supreme god of Zoroastrianism.

Mentula: Latin obscenity for penis, i.e., 'prick'.

Meridiatio: Siesta time.

Meshike: The site of a battle fought some time between 13 January and 14 March AD244 in which Shapur I claimed to have defeated Gordian III. Greek and Roman sources do not mention this battle. Renamed Peroz-Shapur, the 'Victory of Shapur', by the Sassanid king, it became known as Pirisabora to the Romans.

Miles, plural *milites*: Soldier.

Mobads: Persian name for class of priests.

Murmillo: A type of heavily armed gladiator with a helmet crest in the shape of a fish.

Nones: The ninth day of a month before the *ides*, i.e., the fifth day of a short month, the seventh of a long month.

Numerus, plural *numeri*: Latin name given to a Roman army unit, especially to ad hoc units outside the regular army structure, often units raised from semi- or non-Romanized peoples which retained their indigenous fighting techniques; thus in *Fire in the East* the titles of the units formed from mercenaries and local levies and commanded by the caravan protectors.

Oneiromanteia: Greek term for telling the future by the interpretation of dreams.

Oneiroskopos: A 'dream-scout', one of the Greek names given to an interpreter of dreams.

Optio: Junior officer in the Roman army, ranked below a centurion.

Paideia: Culture; Greeks considered it marked them off from the rest of the world, and the Greek elite considered it marked them off from the rest of the Greeks.

Parexeiresia: The outrigger of a *trireme* which allowed the upper level of oarsmen to row.

Parthians: Rulers of the eastern empire centred on modern Iraq and Iran overthrown by the Sassanid Persians in the 220s AD.

Paedagogus: Schoolmaster.

Pepaideumenos, plural *pepaideumenoi*: Greek term for one of the highly educated or cultured.

Peroz: Victory (Persian).

Pilus Prior: The senior centurion in a Roman army unit.

Porta Aquaria: The Water Gate; in this novel the eastern gate of the city of Arete.

Praefectus: 'Prefect', a flexible Latin title for many officials and officers, typically the commander of an auxiliary unit.

Praefectus fabrum: A Roman army officer, a general's Chief of Engineers.

Praepositus: Latin term for a commander; in this novel the title given to the caravan protectors as commanders of *numeri*.

Praetorian prefect: The commander of the Praetorian Guard, an equestrian.

Princeps peregrinorum: The commander of the *frumentarii*, a senior centurion.

Principatus: (In English, the 'principate') Rule of the *Princeps*, the rule of the Roman *imperium* by the emperors.

Principia: The headquarters building of a Roman army camp.

Procurator: A Latin title for a range of officials, under the principate typically a financial officer of the emperors operating in the provinces.

Provocator: A type of gladiator.

Pugio: A Roman military dagger, one of the symbols which marked out a soldier.

Retiarius: A type of lightly equipped gladiator armed with a trident and net.

Sassanids: The Persian dynasty that overthrew the Parthians in the 220s AD and were Rome's great eastern rivals until the seventh century AD.

Senate: The council of Rome, under the emperors composed of about 600 men, the vast majority ex-magistrates, with some imperial favourites. The senatorial order was the richest and most prestigious group in the empire, but suspicious emperors were beginning to exclude them from military commands in the mid-third century AD.

Spatha: A long Roman sword, the normal type of sword carried by all troops by the mid-third century AD.

Speculator: A scout in the Roman army.

Strategos: General (Greek).

Strigil: A scraper used by bathers for scraping oil and dirt off their skin.

Subura: The district of Rome between the Esquiline and Viminal hills, a notorious slum.

Synodiarch: Greek term for a 'caravan protector', the unusual group of rich and powerful men historically known in Palmyra and in this novel in the city of Arete.

Tadmor: The name for the city of Palmyra used by the locals.

Telones: Customs official (Greek).

Tepidarium: Warm room of a Roman bath.

Testudo: Literally, tortoise (Latin), by analogy both a Roman infantry formation with overlapping shields, similar to a northern 'shieldburg', and a mobile shed protecting a siege engine.

Touloutegon: A Roman cavalry manœuvre.

Tribunus laticlavius: A young Roman of senatorial family doing military service as an officer in a legion; there was one per legion.

Trierarch: The commander of a *trireme*, in the Roman forces equivalent in rank to a centurion.

Trireme: An ancient warship, a galley rowed by about 200 men on three levels.

Turma, plural, *turmae*: A small sub unit of Roman cavalry, usually about 30 men strong.

Venationes: Beast hunts in the Roman arena.

Vexillatio: A sub unit of Roman troops detached from its parent unit.

Vinae: Literally Latin for vine trellises; name given to mobile covered siege shelters because of their shape.

Vir egregius: Knight of Rome, a man of the equestrian order.

Xynema: A Roman cavalry manœuvre.

List of Emperors in the First Half of the Third Century AD

AD 193–211	Septimius Severus
AD 198–217	Caracalla
AD 210–211	Geta
AD 217–218	Macrinus
AD 218–222	Elagabalus
AD 222–235	Alexander Severus
AD 235–238	Maximinus Thrax
AD 238	Gordian I
AD 238	Gordian II
AD 238	Pupienus
AD 238	Balbinus
AD 238–244	Gordian III
AD 244–249	Philip the Arab
AD 249–251	Decius
AD 251–253	Trebonianus Gallus
AD 253	Aemilianus
AD 253–	Valerian
AD 253–	Gallienus

List of Characters

To avoid giving away any of the plot, characters usually are only described as first encountered in *Fire in the East*.

Acilius Glabrio: Marcus Acilius Glabrio, *Tribunus Laticlavius* of Legio IIII, commander of the detachment of the legion in Arete; a young patrician.
Alexander: A nondescript councillor of Arete.
Anamu: A *synodiarch* (caravan protector) and councillor of Arete.
Antigonus: A trooper in Cohors XX, selected to serve in the *equites singulares* of Ballista.
Antoninus Prior: Pilus Prior, First Centurion, of Cohors I of Legio IIII.
Antoninus Posterior: Centurion of Cohors II of Legio IIII.
Ardashir: King of Adiabene, son and vassal of Shapur.
Bagoas: The 'Persian Boy', a slave purchased by Ballista on the island of Delos; he claims his name before enslavement was Hormizd.
Ballista: Marcus Clodius Ballista, originally named Dernhelm, son of Isangrim the *Dux*, warleader, of the Angles; a diplomatic hostage in the Roman empire, he has been granted Roman citizenship and equestrian status, having served in the Roman army in Africa, the far west and on the Danube. When the novel starts he has just been appointed *Dux Ripae*.
Bathshiba: Daughter of Iarhai.
Bonitus: A famous Roman siege engineer.
Calgacus: A Caledonian slave originally owned by Isangrim sent by him to serve as a body servant to his son Ballista in the Roman empire.

Callinicus of Petra: A Greek sophist.

Castricius: A legionary in Legio IIII.

Celsus: A famous Roman siege engineer.

Cocceius: Titus Cocceius Malchiana, a *decurion* in command of the first *turma* of cavalry in Cohors XX.

Demetrius: The 'Greek Boy', a slave purchased by Julia to serve as her husband Ballista's secretary.

Dinak: Queen of Mesene, a daughter of Shapur.

Felix (1): A centurion in Cohors XX.

Felix (2): An unlucky trooper in the *equites singulares* of Ballista.

Gallienus: Publius Licinius Egnatius Gallienus, declared joint Roman emperor by his father, the emperor Valerian, in AD253.

Haddudad: A mercenary captain serving Iarhai.

Hamazasp: King of Georgia, a vassal of Shapur.

Hannibal: A nickname given to a *frumentarius* from North Africa serving as a scribe on the staff of Ballista.

Iarhai: A *synodiarch* (caravan protector) and councillor of Arete.

Ingenuus: A Roman general on the Danube.

Iotapianus: A pretender to the Roman throne in AD248–249, from Emesa.

Isangrim: *Dux*, warleader, of the Angles, father of Dernhelm/Ballista.

Josephus: A Christian mistaken for a philosopher.

Julia: Wife of Ballista.

Karen: A Parthian nobleman, the head of the house of Karen, a vassal of Shapur.

Lucius Fabius: Centurion of Cohors I of Legio IIII, stationed at the Porta Aquaria.

Mamurra: Praefectus Fabrum (chief of engineers) to Ballista.

Mariades: A member of the elite of Antioch who turned bandit before going over to the Sassanids.

Maximinus Thrax: Gaius Iulius Verus Maximinus, Roman emperor AD235–238, known as 'Thrax' ('The Thracian') because of his lowly origins.

Maximus: Bodyguard to Ballista; originally a Hibernian warrior known as Muirtagh of the Long Road, sold to slave traders and trained as a boxer, then gladiator, before being purchased by Ballista.

Odenaethus: Septimius Odenaethus, Lord of Palmyra/Tadmor, a client ruler of the Roman empire.

Ogelos: A *synodiarch* (caravan protector) and councillor of Arete.

Otes: A councillor of Arete, a eunuch.

Philip the Arab: Marcus Iulius Philippus, Praetorian Prefect under Gordian III, became Roman Emperor AD244–249.

Priscus (1): *Optio*, second-in-command, of the *trireme Concordia*.

Priscus (2): Gaius Iulius Priscus, brother of Philip the Arab.

Prosper: Gaius Licinius Prosper, a young *optio* serving in Legio IIII.

Pudens (1): Centurion of Cohors II of Legio IIII.

Pudens (2): A lumpen Macedonian soldier who ends up as standard-bearer to Ballista.

Romulus: A trooper of Cohors XX appointed standard-bearer to Ballista.

Sampsigeramus: King of the Roman client kingdom of Emesa and high priest of Elagabalus.

Sasan: Prince, 'the hunter', a son of Shapur.

Scribonius Mucianus: Gaius Scribonius Mucianus, Tribune commanding Cohors XX.

Seleucus: Pilus Prior, First Centurion, of Cohors II of Legio IIII.

Sertorius: Nickname given to a *frumentarius* from the Iberian peninsular, serving as a scribe on the staff of Ballista.

Shapur I: (or Sapor) Second Sassanid King of Kings, son of Ardashir I.

Suren: A Parthian nobleman, the head of the house of Suren, vassal of Shapur.

Theodotus: A councillor of Arete, a Christian priest.

Turpio: Titus Flavius Turpio, Pilus Prior, First Centurion, of Cohors XX.

Uranius Antoninus: Lucius Iulius Aurelius Uranius Antoninus, from Emesa, pretender to the Roman throne AD253–254.

Valash: Prince, 'the joy of Shapur', a son of Shapur.

Valerian (1): Publius Licinius Valerianus, an elderly Italian senator elevated to Roman emperor in AD253.

Valerian (2): Publius Cornelius Licinius Valerianus, eldest son of Gallienus, grandson of Valerian, made Caesar in AD256.

Vardan: A captain serving under the Lord Suren.

Verodes: Chief minister to Odenaethus.

Vindex: A trooper in the *equites singulares* of Ballista, a Gaul.

Zenobia: Wife of Odenaethus of Palmyra.